Dancing on Glass

Pamela Binnings Ewen

Dancing on Glass

B&H
PUBLISHING GROUP
www.BHPublishingGroup.com

ISBN: 978-0-8054-6430-6

Published by B&H Publishing Group,
Nashville, Tennessee

www.BHPublishingGroup.com
www.pamelaewen.com

Dewey Decimal Classification: F
Subject Heading: ROMANTIC SUSPENSE NOVELS \
WIFE ABUSE—FICTION \ LAWYERS—FICTION

1 2 3 4 5 6 7 8 • 14 13 12 11

For my beloved husband,
James Craft Lott

Prologue

———————⚮———————

The images have no color. There are only shades of gray, like ash, and each one flashes through her mind and disappears before the next one takes its place. There is a raw, harsh scream, but as she struggles through the mist, the thoughts and sounds slip away. Won't stick. What was the question, anyway?

"Where is Phillip, Amalise?"

Through heavy lidded slits she can see a man in white bending over her. A doctor. His grave eyes focus on hers. "Are you cold? You're shivering." The voice is deep and low and soothing. He reaches across the bed, and she can feel him tucking something warm around her, binding her arms against her sides, wrapping her in a cocoon. The cocoon feels safe and warm.

"Where is your husband?" he asks again. "Think of Phillip. Can you remember?"

His face wavers before her. She cannot part her lips—cannot speak.

"Try to remember. It's important. Think of the cottage on the lake and of Phillip and try to remember."

She shuts her eyes and the room disappears. In a split second a hand grips her shoulder. "Wake up, Amalise."

The dark is soft, but the images emerge again and sharpen—shards of Phillip's face—the flat smile, those high, angular cheekbones, brown eyes, protruding brow—moving, bending, twisting like reflections in a fun-house mirror that slip away before you pin them down. Around her there is sand and water.

Her heart begins to pound. The blanket constricts, no longer a cocoon. She shoves the blanket away, twisting, pushing at it with her elbows as she fights to loosen the grip. Pain knifes through her head, and surprised, her eyes fly open and she cries out.

"Careful!" The doctor's voice is strident, loud. "You've had an accident."

The pain lingers, but she stops struggling and listens.

"It's a fracture—just here, on the side."

She feels the pressure of a touch on the side of her head. The voice turns milky now, soothing.

"That's it. Stay with me. There's nothing to worry about, but you must try to stay awake for awhile, Amalise." Two beats. "Can you hear me?"

Something frightens her. *Don't say a word.*

"Where is Phillip? We need your help." Someone else's voice. Hard. Hostile.

"Phillip," she repeats. As the stranger bends forward, she can feel his breath on her cheek. Images emerge from the dark and recede, one after the other. A lake. A pier. A beach. White bird. And Phillip.

"Phillip," she whispers. "The beach . . . white bird."

"And? Go on, Amalise."

Footprints. She sees footprints on sand, but they disappear into the black, and she is sleepy, so sleepy.

The doctor interrupts, loud, urgent—Leave her alone—and that other one, harsh, impatient—doc, doc, there's not much time.

"Don't push. Not now. She's fragile."

"She's dreaming, doc. There's no beach out there. Outside that clearing we got water, we got woods, we got swamp."

Shuffling footsteps moving away. A door opens. The harsh voice says, "I got men out there in the rain, and there's not much time. It's almost dark." A sharp laugh follows. "Guess we'll have to follow that bird, huh?"

A door closes.

Dad's voice comes—"Wake up, Amalise!"

And Mama's voice, from somewhere far away—"Don't go to sleep . . . concussion . . . please don't sleep!"

Images explode. Phillip's eyes, hard with sudden recognition, lips twisting, contorting. Comes again the white coat's milky voice . . . don't sleep, don't sleep, don't sleep. . . . She fights to stay awake, and there's an electric hum around her now. . . . Judge, we're losing her. . . . Amalise, wake up . . . and then that harsh raw scream intrudes—that silent fateful scream that shatters thoughts—and voices in the room are fading, and Phillip now is pleading, pleading.

She moans, fighting the memories, willing darkness to veil the terror. The white bird soars in the light, a pulsing light inside of her . . . sheets of stark and angry light that blind . . .

Phillip loved her, loved her, always loved her. . . . Ama, Ama, Ama. You are mine.

But the voice is filled with something fierce, something she cannot name. And then the voice shatters into glassy, glittering points of light, like stars, and at last the stars wink off one by one so that the merciful black haze, called upon, descends.

Echoes from the past, present, future, pulse and disappear.

"Amalise, wake up!"

"She's slipping away."

But the voices fade. Here is peace—here is silence, refuge. Nothing exists. There is no space, no boundary, no time.

THEY'VE PUSHED US OUT of the room, me and William. We're her parents, what can they be thinking?

Hands splayed, Maraine Catoir pressed them against the cold glass window that separated her from her daughter, pressing, pressing against the glass to find her child's life spirit. *My girl, ma 'tite fille . . . ahhh . . . she's so still, Lord, and they won't let me come to her now, won't let me hold her here with me.*

She leaned forward, touching her forehead to the glass, eyes riveted to the bits and pieces she could see of Amalise lying on that bed surrounded by doctors, nurses, technicians. Watching, she held her breath as tears washed her cheeks. *If I could just hold her.*

And then . . . slowly, as if in a trance, she took one step back from the window, pulled in a long, deep breath, closed her eyes, and arched her hands so that only the smooth tips of her fingers remained on the glass, touching it lightly as you would piano keys.

After a moment she felt it, the uncertainty, the shimmering stir of her daughter's earthly life ebbing and flowing in the ether, like the vibration of music not yet heard, as a musician feels in that split second just before touching the keys.

Amalise, don't leave us!

Chapter One

Not a stir of air on the streets of New Orleans on that September day in 1974 when a small black cloud shuttled in on winds aloft and exploded over the Vieux Carré like a child's tantrum. Amalise ducked into Porter Gallery on Royal to avoid the deluge instead of continuing on to work. And her life changed forever.

At first she stood near the door in front of the plateglass windows watching water pool in gutters and people scramble for shelter. When the rain had emptied the sidewalks and streets and there was no sign of it letting up, she secured the book bag onto her shoulder, turned, and with an exasperated mutter, ambled toward a display of artwork to her left.

Glancing up, she stopped and caught her breath. Before her, hanging on the wall, was a series of pictures painted in shining black and bold colors that diminished all other work in the gallery. Slashing strokes of the thick black paint in each one sketched women in various poses, striking, even pretty, in an offbeat way, but looking lost, bored, defeated. These were women drained of light—flattened for a moment in time by the contrasting movement and bright reds, blues, yellows, and spectrum of colors in between that the artist had used in the surroundings. Books were tossed on tables, fluted curtains pooling on floors, dresses, skirts, stockings, shoes thrown carelessly around the room, beds and tumbled pillows, sheets and blankets, and always in the background, glass windowpanes closed against the living, vibrant world outside.

Despite a vague feeling of malevolence, there was also something oddly whimsical about the pictures. The models were lifeless, yet each painting as a whole was brilliant and provoking. Amalise stepped close to the first one. Here was a nude woman sitting in a blue room. She was hunched on the edge of a single unmade bed, weight on her hands, elbows bent, fingers curled with a small vestige of defiance into the mattress. Her spinal column twisted unnaturally as she gazed over her right shoulder with dull eyes. The woman's pale flesh was stark against the wild streaks of violet, lavender, and blue around her. Amalise stared, feeling the malaise. A tag posted at the side gave the artist's name, the price, and the title of the picture: *The Blue Hour.*

Someone brushed against her and she started, stepping aside. Ignoring her, a man reached down and rubbed his thumb over a spot at the bottom right-hand corner of the canvas. An initial flash of irritation faded into curiosity as Amalise watched him stoop to rest on his heels while he pressed his thumb against the canvas, working a dense spot of paint with a small circular motion.

There was something familiar about the man, she realized, when he stood. He moved back away from the picture, studying it with concentration as he wiped the residue of paint on his jeans. She examined him from the corners of her eyes.

The bone structure would stick in your mind, the sharp protruding brow and cheekbones, the angles and shadows. His head was thrown back as he looked up at the picture; his hair was slicked off his face in a careless manner.

"Are you the artist?"

"Yes." He did not look at her as he spoke.

He wasn't that tall, but he seemed to loom over her. Amalise moved on, skipping the next picture. She was surprised when he followed. He stood close, almost touching, boxing her in.

"What do you think?"

She looked at him, up at the painting, and stepped to one side. "They're good."

The corners of his mouth turned down, and she couldn't tell whether this was the hint of a smile or contempt.

"Come." He touched her elbow with just the tips of electric fingers as he guided her to the next picture. When they reached it, he dropped his hand and looked down at her. His eyes appeared gray at first, and then black, as a slight dip of his forehead cast them into shadows. His brows were thick and unruly, drawn together. "What about this one?"

She looked at the picture but her mind refused to focus. Something about this man was intriguing. *He's intense,* she decided, pretending to study the picture. *An artist. And he cares what I think about his work.* A French film she'd seen a few months ago came to mind. A chance encounter in the rain at the coffeehouse door . . . a red umbrella rolled and dripping in the corner, a small table by the window. The room bathed in yellow light was warm against the storm outside. They sat, smiled, and talked—and he reached across the table for her hand.

The man beside her shifted his weight from one leg to the other with a small sigh, and she shook off the daydream, feeling foolish. He was waiting for an answer to his question.

She should leave. She'd be late for work. But she didn't move. "I like this one, too." She tilted her head.

"No other thoughts?"

His tone was insulting, not what she'd expected. She bristled. "Yes." She turned away and the words slipped out. "They're powerful, but I wouldn't want to own one." With a quick sideways glance: "Sorry. I don't mean to offend you."

He laughed—a low, tight chuckle—and followed her to the next picture. "Why should you care?" He touched her arm. Startled, she looked down at the long fingers, and he released her.

The flesh tingled where he'd touched her. She turned back toward the picture, flustered. The picture. Here a woman wearing a bored expression sat in front of a mirror as she applied lipstick. She wore a slip with one ribboned strap dangling loose, off shoulder. Again the slashing black outline. Again the flat perspective of the faded model against the lively bright strokes of paint around her. A frisson ran through Amalise, a sense that she was viewing something beautiful and dangerous. Later, much later, she'd remember the prescient nudge.

He bent and spoke in a stage whisper. "And what thoughts on this one?"

Chills rose as his breath brushed the back of her neck. She ducked her head and moved away from him, clasping the book bag.

"Why wouldn't you want to own it?"

Intruder. But if he wanted her thoughts, she would give them to him. She turned and looked, unable to contain the small jerk of her chin. Still, he stared back without smiling, waiting while she struggled for an honest answer, conscious that he wouldn't like it. "Your work is disturbing," she said at last. But it wasn't in her nature to hurt, so at once she softened the truth with a half-smile. "I suppose it's because the women in these pictures seem more like objects than people. There's such life and color around them. But the women appear . . . lost."

"You'd have to understand the technique." He pursed his mouth into a silent shrug. She had offended him, she saw, averting her eyes. She glanced past him at the door and the street outside.

"Don't leave yet," he said in a tone that pulled her eyes back to him. "Besides, it's still raining."

This isn't a French film. With a slight lift of one shoulder, she moved to turn away. "I'm late for work."

"Don't go." When she looked at him, he smiled. This time his eyes were wide and shining as if he'd read her thoughts. "I'm not offended. My work's unusual. It's something new; it takes time to understand. But most people aren't honest." He looked deep into her eyes.

She nodded, feeling a strange, almost magnetic pull between them.

The bell over the front door chimed and a voice called out, disrupting the spell. "Darling."

He looked up and Amalise turned to follow his gaze. A woman wearing a raincoat and a blue beret tipped to the side stepped in, closed her umbrella, and hurried in their direction. The rain had almost stopped, now no more than a drizzle. Amalise stared, recognizing the woman in that painting, *The Blue Hour.* The hat was the color of blue in the painting.

The woman's eyes flicked over Amalise. As she drew near, Amalise could see the thick patch of makeup that covered dark circles underneath her eyes. Unlike the painting, deep lines ridged her mouth, the corners of her eyes, her forehead. He'd made her more beautiful than she was.

"Sorry I'm late." She stretched out her hand to the stranger, and he turned with a frown. As the woman reached his side, she linked her arm through his. Ignoring Amalise, she whispered something into his ear. His back stiffened and he pulled his arm free. Amalise watched as they walked toward the door without a word or a backward glance.

She'd meant to leave when the rain stopped and knew that she'd be late for work, but resolved not to trail them from the gallery, Amalise turned back to the picture instead. It was the mirror in this one that was strange.

There was no reflection of the woman in the mirror.

JUDE SAT ON A stool in his usual place at the bar watching the news and waiting for Amalise. She was late. The mahogany bar ran the length of the old Café Pontalba, from the front door beside Jude to the back wall that separated customers from the kitchen. A long mirror framed in chipped gilt hung on the wall behind the bar. The café was crowded and noisy on this rainy night; every table behind him was filled. Overhead fans did their best, but still a haze of smoke hung dream-like over the room.

To Jude's left beyond the door to the café was St. Peter Street, and just across St. Peter was Jackson Square Park. Facing the park, at the corner of Pirate's Alley and Chartres Street was the old St. Louis Cathedral, already bathed in light, flanked on the side nearest the cafe by the Cabildo and on the other by the Presbytere. Despite the rain, the café's long shutter doors were opened to the sidewalk. Light from black iron street lamps in the square glowed silver in the rising fog. Near the spiked fence around the park, Jude could see a few artists still huddled near their easels under umbrellas, waiting, smoking, sketching.

His eyes roamed back to the television set over the bar. Henry Kissinger was still going on about the peace treaty signed last year— supposed to free us from the grip of Vietnam. And more covertly, from Cambodia. And yet the troops were still there, at least in Vietnam.

He grimaced. Politicians! The story switched to the new dome stadium near completion down on Poydras and then to that seven-hundred tons of waste Mayor Moon Landrieu was shipping out daily to New Orleans East for landfill.

Just then the door beside him creaked open, and Jude felt a cool, damp draft. He looked up as a pair of small hands pressed down upon his shoulders and Amalise's reflection appeared in the mirror.

"Welcome back." She grinned, squeezing him. "I've missed you."

"I just got in. Where've you been?" Smiling, he patted her hand with his free one. She slid onto the stool beside him.

"The rain held me up." She swiveled to face him. "This rain! You could set a clock by it in the summertime." Leaning on her elbow, her eyes swept the café behind him, probably looking for Gina, her boss. "Have you been waiting long?"

"No. You working late tonight?"

"Yes. Twelve or there bouts."

He nodded.

"You don't have to come back for me. I'll be all right."

He stifled a sigh. Amalise could be unreasonable. She lived four blocks away. He didn't like her walking home at night alone through the dark streets of the French Quarter. He'd promised the judge he'd look out for her when he was in the city, which he was glad to do even though he was only in town part of the time. Her father was a hard man, but he trusted Jude.

Well, he would try talking some sense into her again.

He leaned on his forearms and turned his head, looking at her instead of her reflection. "It's not safe to walk alone late at night, Amalise. You should move uptown. Get a job in a library or something."

"We've had this conversation before."

"Tourists are gone by midnight in this area. Streets are deserted." He traced an imaginary line on the countertop.

"Parish judges like Dad don't make much money, Jude. You know that. And law school isn't cheap. I'm in classes all the day. And I make more in tips one night here than a week's salary at any library."

"Your dad worries."

"My parents pay the tuition. I pay for everything else."

He pushed his tongue against his cheek, and, watching her in the mirror again, he caught a glimpse of that same determined little face glaring up at him from the water years ago, flushed and furious after rolling the pirogue into the brown bayou back behind her house in Marianus. The memory brought a short laugh. She hadn't changed a bit.

"What's funny?"

"Nothing." He smiled inside, remembering. She was in the pirogue, a delicate little thing, struggling to paddle the unpredictable canoe; he was behind her in the skiff, making sure she didn't drown. She'd refused his help. Said she could do it by herself. The thing flipped fifteen times, but she kept at it, kept climbing right back in. She'd figured it out, though. He'd say that for Amalise: once she got the hang of that pirogue, she could cut through the marsh as quick and cagey as a catfish.

"Jude?"

Her voice was demanding, familiar. He gave her a sideways look. "I was thinking how stubborn you can be." He snapped to and swung around to face the room, planting his elbows on the bar behind him and leaning back, letting his eyes wander over the interior of the café. Customers were settled in on this night. Overhead the futile fans beat slowly, but despite the smoky air he caught the lingering scent of rain through the open shutters.

She spun around, too, and braced the heels of her hands on the seat near her hips, sitting straight-armed and upright—ready for takeoff, he supposed. "Are we finished?"

Her words were terse, but from the corner of his eyes he saw her smiling. "Yes."

It was hopeless. She would cling to this job and her cracker-box apartment down on Dumaine Street, and she would continue riding the streetcar everyday to the university campus uptown because she'd fallen in love with this eclectic village within the city, bounded on three sides by Canal Street, Rampart, and Esplanade Avenue, and on the fourth by the Mississippi River. The Vieux Carré—the French Quarter. Personally, Jude condemned the old buildings down here collapsing from subsidence and disrepair, but he kept it to himself. He'd been poor—he saw the faded colors and peeling paint, the cons, the lost, the unrepentant, and the ring of danger slowly encroaching from the outside, smoldering around the edges of history.

He shook his head. He'd tried to explain the dangers to Amalise many times, but she strolled right on through the narrow village streets following her own trombone, second-lining the ghosts. Amalise loved life here, didn't take anything for granted. She loved the pink crumbling old brick of the low buildings and the boxy Creole cottages right on the street with their cool, shaded courtyards secreted inside, and she loved the cafes, like Napoleon House, where the decrepit phonograph played whatever record one picked out—the changer slamming them down on the turntable one at a time with a clunk and a bang—and how Pete Impestato in his snowy white shirt would always stop at your table to ask how you were doing that day.

"The music of the Quarter gets inside you," she'd once said. *"The wind chimes, foghorns, soul music, blues, jazz, the honky-tonk that fills the air, and when you breathe it in, it becomes a part of you, like oxygen."*

Jude worried, just like the judge. Amalise was the little sister he'd never had. She held practical views most of the time, but there was the dreamer, too—the girl whose judgment sometimes weighed on the sentimental side. That made her vulnerable. And she could be stubborn. He shook his head just thinking of it. Once she'd made up her mind about a thing, there was nothing you could do.

He glanced at her now, threw up his hands, and laughed. "I give up."

He stood, brushed a kiss on her cheek, and jammed his hands into his pockets. She rubbed his back when he passed by, heading for the door. He'd been isolated in Pilottown at the mouth of the river for two weeks. He'd go see what was up at Cosmo's while Amalise finished work, and then he'd come back to walk her home.

AFTER JUDE LEFT, AMALISE headed for the kitchen. She tied an apron over her jeans and returned to the dining room, grabbed two menus, and went to work taking orders, ferrying drinks, balancing trays while dodging customers entering and leaving. An hour later during a brief cessation in business, she drifted to the end of the bar. Dropping onto a stool, her eyes swept the room and lit on a couple sitting at a sidewalk table just inside the open shutter doors. Her heart drummed an extra beat. The man was the artist who'd spoken to her in the gallery. The woman still wore that odd blue hat.

The couple sat across from each other in silence. The woman, somewhat older than the man, stared past her companion while he looked off into the distance. They were married, she decided. Still he seemed familiar, and she wished that she could remember where she'd seen him before today. Gina walked up and stood beside her.

"Table three needs even more of your undivided attention, honey."

Amalise swiveled to Gina. Together they looked at the couple she'd been watching. Suddenly it came to her. She'd seen the man around the university. He was a professor, she thought, frowning. "That's not my table."

Gina raised her brows. "It is now." The owner of the café, she spoke in a no-nonsense tone. Her voice was low and hoarse from years of breathing smoke. "Cynthia's not around, and they need more drinks, or else you got to take an order. They can't just sit there using space." She wiped her hands on a limp white towel and prodded Amalise with a little push. "Go on now. They're at a window table. Get that cash register ringing or move them on."

Amalise sighed and, pushing her hair back behind one ear, grabbed two menus from the bar. Clutching the menus to her chest, she wove her way through customers to the table near the window.

"Are you ready to order?"

The man glanced up with a frown, looked away, and his eyes shifted back to her. "Didn't we just meet in Porter's?" He tilted back his head and studied her under half-closed lids.

"Yes." She nodded and held out a menu.

His wife set her wine glass down on the table with a careful movement and inspected it, turning the base with the tips of her fingers. "No menus." Her fingertips traced the stem to the globe, touching the curve. "I'd like to go, Phillip." A frosty demand.

He waved away the menu, raised his eyebrows, and leaned back in the chair. "Have we met before . . . I mean, before today?"

His wife gave the glass a little shove, plucked a small purse from her lap, set it down on the table, and giving it all of her attention, snapped it open.

"I don't think so." Amalise tucked the menus under her arm and reached for his glass. He straightened, drank the last of the drink, and handed it over, brushing her fingers as she took it from him. "But I've seen you around the Tulane campus, professor."

"Ah." He folded his arms, and his eyes roved over her. "Let me guess. English literature."

She shook her head, amused. "I'm in law school."

His wife held up a mirror and ran a tube of red lipstick over her mouth with a furious swipe.

He tilted back the chair without moving his eyes from Amalise. "Is that so? What class?" His look held hers, and she felt that strange pull toward him that she'd noticed earlier at the gallery, like the tug of an undercurrent hidden in still water.

She blinked and stepped back. "I'm in my second year; one more to go." She turned away. To the wife: "Can I get you something else?"

"No." The woman dropped the mirror and lipstick back into her purse and snapped it shut. "Phillip. I'd like to go." She struggled to slip her arms into a raincoat.

His chair dropped back into place. "Looks like we're leaving. Just bring us the check, please."

"Yes, sir." She reached for the woman's glass.

"Please," he said with a wry smile. "Don't call me sir. You'll make me feel old."

The wife's battle with her coat increased. Amalise crossed the room to retrieve their check from the cashier, and when she returned, the woman held out her hand.

"What's your name," he asked, while the wife ran her eyes down the computation.

"Amalise Catoir."

The woman poked into her purse and grabbed a handful of dollar bills. He reached across the table and took them from her.

"Here, Amalise Catoir." He pressed the money into the palm of her hand. "I'm Phillip Sharp. Keep the change." His fingers stroked her flesh before he curled her hand around the money and pulled away. His wife turned cold eyes toward Amalise, scanned her quickly from head to toe as she shoved back her chair, and stood. The man stood as well.

"Thanks. Have a nice evening." Amalise turned, conscious of his gaze on her as she walked away. *He's married. Forget him.*

At eleven forty-five the café was empty of customers. Shutters were closed, and Amalise and Gina had set up tables for the morning. The kitchen was dark. The new bartender held up a bottle of beer, lifting his brows and tilting it toward her. Henry was the name, she remembered. When she shook her head and sat down to wait for Jude, he picked up a clean white cloth and began polishing a row of glasses, placing them one by one on shelves under the mirror.

"Your friend's a river pilot?" he asked.

"A bar pilot. Guiding ships in and out of the Gulf through those sandbars and passes at the mouth of the river where nothing's ever certain. Freighters, tankers, cruise ships. The channels and currents there are tricky." Elbow on the bar, she rested her chin on her knuckles. She was tired tonight. "Once they're in the river, the Crescent River Pilots take the helm the rest of the way up from Pilottown to New Orleans."

Henry put the last glass on the shelf and turned back to her. "Pilottown?"

"It's an island about one mile long at the mouth of the river, just before you reach the Gulf. The pilots bunk in station houses down there."

"I haven't seen him in here before."

"You'll get to know him. He works two weeks on and two weeks off. He has a house here in town for when he's off duty."

"Nice job. I wouldn't mind."

"The river's hard work. He's on watch twenty-four hours a day when he's down there, holidays too."

Henry leaned back against the counter, crossed his arms and looked at the lights inside the café reflected on the glass door. "You known him long?"

"Since we were kids. Jude's my oldest, dearest friend. We grew up together in Marianus." Glancing at the clock over the kitchen door, she saw that it was almost midnight. She stifled a yawn, slipped off the stool, linked her hands, and stretched her arms toward the ceiling. Jude would be here any minute to walk her home. And she still had hours of work ahead tonight to prepare for tomorrow's classes, but she hoped he'd come in for a cup of coffee like he sometimes did. She couldn't imagine life without Jude, but then she really didn't have to worry.

Jude would always be around.

Chapter Two

Crossing the university campus from St. Charles Avenue the next morning, Amalise was conscious of a slight coolness in the air, the first sign of a break from the lingering summer heat. The rain last night seemed to be ushering in an early fall. Squinting through the clear yellow light, she saw Phillip Sharp coming toward her. She tightened her arm around the canvas bag stuffed with books, notebooks, wallet, lunch, and other odds and ends. He spotted her and halted, waiting just in front of the law school building. When she reached him, he planted both hands on her shoulders and held her before him at arm's length, scrutinizing her.

"Amalise, isn't it?"

"You have a good memory." She smiled at him. He was a man you would look at twice—slim, with that angular face.

His brows flattened. "I tend to remember my critics." Looking past her, his eyes widened and he yanked her off the sidewalk, encircling her with his arms as a bicycle flew past, just missing them. Over his shoulder she saw the rider weaving on, scattering a group of students congregated at the bottom of the steps.

"Sorry." He looked down at her, and his grip seemed to tighten for an instant before he released her.

"No . . . that's all right." She caught her breath. "Thanks." She stepped back, clasping the book bag. "He came out of nowhere and—"

"I have something to celebrate. Come have a cup of coffee with me." Before she could answer, he took her elbow and began steering her down the sidewalk, away from the law school building.

"But I can't." She pulled away with a glance at the now deserted steps in front of the building. "I have class in a few minutes."

His eyes clouded, and he dropped his hand to his side. "Some other time then."

"All right." It would never happen. She shifted the book bag into both arms so that it stood between them.

He seemed to be studying her, weighing something.

"What's the good news?"

He shrugged. "The gallery's extending my exhibition. They called this morning."

"That's wonderful."

Without saying anything, he reached out and touched her chin. She started, then stood motionless as he braced his knuckles under her jaw to tilt up her face. Looking back at him, suspended, she waited in silence.

With a sudden nod, he stepped back. "I'd like to paint you. That pale skin, dark hair. You're beautiful." She wasn't, she thought; she was ordinary. He cocked his head to the side. "I'll see you later."

She stood watching as he turned and walked away. He wanted to paint her picture. Was that what he'd just said? He did not look back. With a slow, self-confident stride down the sidewalk, he reached into a pocket of his jeans to pull something out. There were streaks of paint on the back of his jeans.

She started up the steps into the building, imagining him in his studio working at an easel or lecturing in a classroom.

Pushing open the heavy glass door, she hurried down the hallway, forcing images of the professor from her mind. He was off limits. Past the student lounge she reached the bank of student lockers and halted before her own. She pulled open a metal door and dropped the heavy book bag on the floor beside her feet, then stooped and reached into the bag.

"Who's your friend?"

She glanced up to find her friend, Rebecca Downer, beside her. Amalise tossed some books into the locker. "He's a professor. I think he's in the art school." She stood, picked up the bag, and slammed the door.

Rebecca nodded. "The art school. I've seen him around." She yanked open her locker, and two books tumbled out onto the floor. She squatted on her heels, picked one up, dropped it back in, and held onto the other. "Are you dating?"

"He's married." Amalise shook her head and leaned against the wall to wait. On the television set in the student lounge, President Ford urged Congress to fund an orderly U.S. evacuation from Vietnam. She tilted back her head, only half listening.

"Married? Well, that's too bad." Rebecca rummaged through her locker and pulled out another book. "Hah." She rocked back on her heels, holding up the casebook. "I ransacked my apartment for this last night."

She pushed up, glancing at Amalise while she shuffled the books and a notebook into the crook of her arm. "I'm not prepared for this class," she said, closing the locker. Amalise envied the long red curls Rebecca pushed back from her face as they started down the hall. "If I'm called on, I'm doomed."

"We still have twenty minutes." Amalise glanced at her watch. "Let's stop at the library, and you can take notes from my outline."

There was an empty table on the main floor of the law library, and, telling herself to forget the professor from the art school, Amalise slid her notebook over to Rebecca and opened her own book bag. While Rebecca scribbled beside her, Amalise reviewed case summaries, focusing on the issues, the decisions, and rationale of the courts—and not on Phillip Sharp. Only once did she let her thoughts wander—she wondered if it was merely coincidence, their running into each other that way this morning.

Focus, Amalise. Focus.

"IT'S RIGHT UP HERE, Jude." Amalise stopped and turned, waiting.

"What's your hurry?" When he caught up, he slung his arm over her shoulder and tugged her back toward him. She'd been walking ten steps ahead since they'd crossed Canal Street and entered the Quarter, but he wasn't in any rush to see these pictures she was so eager to show him before she went on to work. He could think of better things to do with his time off. A pretty woman wearing tight bell-bottom jeans and a low-cut peasant blouse gave him a slow smile as she brushed past Amalise. The sun was going down. The Quarter was waking up, stretching out, ready to rock and roll.

Amalise's arm slid around his waist. At the next corner they stopped before crossing to watch two old men sitting on three-legged stools, hunched over drums and a steel guitar. They wore identical red flannel shirts and baggy blue cotton pants. Their dark faces contorted with the music as they played.

Jude dropped fifty cents into the torn straw hat on the sidewalk. Amalise smiled. He rolled his eyes and smiled, too, when she halted before a shop window full of colorful silk scarves, mismatched brass candlesticks, lace towels, china teacups, and a set of shining silver boxes. "You can shop when you finish law school." Jude nudged her on. "Let's get this over with. Who is this guy anyway? This painter."

Two small barefoot boys shoved past, jumping the curb into the street, dodging slow-moving cars as they ran with whooping cries. He shook his head, looking after them.

"I told you"—Amalise gave him a sideways glance—"his name is Phillip Sharp and he's a professor." The children swerved back onto the sidewalk ahead, burst through a group of businessmen, and disappeared. "I haven't seen anything like his work before. Want to see what you think."

He turned his attention back to her. "Why? Are you going to buy it?"

"Of course not." She halted. "Here we are. Porter Gallery."

Jude followed as she pushed open the door. A bell tinkled overhead, and a young man behind a desk in the back looked up. "May I help you?"

"We're just browsing," Amalise said. The clerk nodded and returned to his paperwork. Jude trailed Amalise to a display of paintings on the wall to their left. "These are the ones," she said, stopping before them.

Jude scrutinized the pictures and frowned. Painted in bright, flat colors with crisp dark outlines, they looked like cartoons. Was this modern art? Moving along behind Amalise, he observed the models dressing, sitting listless before empty mirrors, lounging against doorframes, sprawled over beds or couches, splayed flat and dull and unsmiling in stark contrast to the vivid scenes around them.

He shifted his eyes to Amalise. She stood before the last picture, arms folded across her chest, studying it. "You say this artist's a professor?" Her concentration struck him.

"I met him a few days ago."

"Where does he teach?"

"Newcomb Art School. At Tulane." She seemed to have to drag her eyes from the picture to look at him, eyebrows lifted. "So, what do you think?"

Jude glanced at the one beside her. The scene dampened his mood, but he worked for a casual tone. "It's certainly unusual . . . The artist has a different take on things."

Amalise turned to the picture again. He stuck his hands in his pockets, nudged her, and jerked his head toward the door. As they walked toward the entrance, Jude was silent.

"I think he's talented." She sounded disappointed.

Jude frowned and a shadow slipped through his mind. She was certainly interested in this guy. "I didn't say he wasn't." He held the door open as Amalise passed through and halted at the curb. "You go on to work. I'll be there later."

"You don't have to come back. I have an early shift and some studying to finish after so that tomorrow will be free."

"You sure? It's Saturday night. Walter Wolfman's playing uptown. You like his music. Good blues."

"I can't."

"All right. See you tomorrow? Nine o'clock Mass?"

"Yep. It's my turn this time. St. Louis."

He nodded. The time shared between them on Sunday mornings was a special bond created when they were children. They took turns when he was in town, alternating between Holy Name on St. Charles Avenue near his house and the St. Louis Cathedral, near Amalise. She always kept track.

He watched her progress down Royal, struggling to dismiss nagging images of the paintings she'd dragged him to see. She turned onto St. Peter and was soon out of sight, but still he stood ruminating, rooted to the spot, looking off and trying to reassure himself. It was the models that disturbed him most, he realized—the deliberate degradation of the women.

What sort of man thought of women like that?

The thought of Amalise in the sphere of that kind of darkness . . . he didn't like it. She was an unusual mixture of worldly and innocent. Once, when she was about ten, he'd seen her walking alone on the riverbank, lips moving, smiling, pointing. "Who were you talking too?" he'd asked her later on in the day.

"My Abba," she'd said. "I was asking Him why so many things are round. Apples, the sun and moon, our earth, turtle shells, and acorns." Abba—her father in heaven. Her name for God. She'd called Him that since she'd heard the ancient word in Sunday school when she was very young. "He needs a name," she'd said when Jude asked why. She talked to Him all the time, so He needed a name.

A tug horn sounded out over the river, breaking into his thoughts. With an unusual helpless feeling, Jude slowly walked on down the street. He knew the river and the feel of a shift in the wind and currents and how a ship rolls. What did he know about art—or more to the point, the psychology of art?

He turned left and crossed Bourbon Street walking farther on into the Quarter. A clarinet. A sax. The rattle of drums. The bluesmen were ready, and as he picked up his pace, he shrugged his worries off. Music always lifted his spirits. One week left before returning to Pilottown and work. He'd meet some of his friends at Cosmos and then maybe go on over to Frenchman Street in the Marigny district across Esplanade. Good sounds there, and it wasn't far.

Lights winked on around him, giving the streets a warm glow; and, as always, this made him think of Pilottown, where chill wet winds would soon blow off the Gulf, seeping between cracks in the cypress boards of the station house, and he'd be sitting there waiting for those deep-draft vessels with his name on them. The contrast cheered him. But as he turned the corner onto Burgundy, those pictures from the gallery intruded into his thoughts and he frowned.

That professor certainly held a strange view of life and women.

Chapter Three

Maraine Catoir lay in bed, her husband asleep beside her. The window was open, and the night was cooled by the breeze from the attic fan. She folded her hands over her chest, looking out through the trees at the full moon hanging over Marianus. Remembering . . .

It was a hard time, Lord, letting Amalise go, taking her side against William when she announced she was going off to the city to work and go to law school. It was the most difficult thing a mother had to do—letting go of a child. *I know You're looking out for her, but still, there's that freewill problem from all the way back to Adam and Eve.*

As much as Maraine hated to admit it, one never really knew what one's children would do, the decisions they'd make, until they were out there on their own. *All we can do is hope, and pray.*

She sighed and turned her eyes to the ceiling. She was excited for Amalise. Her daughter was a good girl, and now she had the chance to be a lawyer like her dad. And to travel, live in her own place, earn her own way . . . just as her little girl always dreamed. And as Maraine had always dreamed for her.

She glanced at William from the corner of her eye. He was deep in sleep, arms flung around his pillow. *I always encouraged that independent spirit in my girl. I never talked about it much with William. But I recognized her longing. Didn't want her to live her whole life out here in Marianus without trying other things first so she can choose what she really wants. But now . . . here I lie worrying about that very thing—those very choices.*

The back of her hand rested on her forehead as she yawned and her eyes began to close. Muscles relaxed into the mattress. An owl hooted in the backyard.

Help her stay on the right path, Father. I'm excited for her and afraid at the same time. But the thing that makes it bearable is I know her faith is strong. And I know You're there with her. And knowing that . . .

She let out a long, slow breath. *I can be at peace.*

Chapter Four

Amalise had stopped thinking about the professor by Monday night when the café closed. Jude said he had business to take care of so he couldn't be there to walk her home, and despite the bravura she'd held up for him, the streets were dark, and the walk home when he was out of town did frighten her a bit, so she was happy to see the last customers drift out a little early.

Henry closed up the bar. Amalise helped Gina wipe down the tables and set them up with knives and forks wrapped in crisp, white napkins, and they placed clean glasses beside each napkin for the breakfast crowd. Together they pulled the long wooden shutter doors together, latching them from the inside. When they'd finished, Amalise waited for Gina to check the kitchen and secure the back door of the café before leaving her there, reconciling the cash at the register in a dim circle of light at the end of the bar.

She left the café and stepped out onto the pavestone sidewalk, automatically scanning the area across the street in front of the cathedral as she swung off as if this were the middle of the afternoon. But as she neared the corner, a shadow emerged from the evening fog and slipped a hand under her elbow. She yelped, jumped, and whirled.

The shadow threw up his hands and stepped back while her heart drummed. As the face came into focus, she took a long deep breath.

"Sorry." Phillip Sharp's eyes were round.

"You frightened me, professor."

"Professor's too formal. Call me Phillip." He dropped his arms to his sides. "I'm sorry. I was just leaving the theater and saw you come out."

She nodded, still breathing hard, and glanced across the street at the theater, La Petite. It was dark.

"The play's just finished."

"Oh," she said, with a short, relieved laugh. "Yes."

He touched her shoulder. "Let's try again. Come with me for coffee." He nodded in the direction of Café du Monde. The café, nestled against the levee at the far corner of Jackson Square, still blazed with light.

"It's late." And he was married.

"It's just a cup of coffee. And it's not polite to reject me twice." When she hesitated, he took her arm and steered her down the sidewalk in the direction of the river. "We'll have beignets and coffee and relax for a few minutes."

She stole a glance at him. "All right, but I can't stay long."

"Fifteen minutes."

They started toward Decatur in the direction of the river. Across the street she glimpsed a shadow moving near the fence surrounding the park. She halted and Phillip's hand slid from her arm.

"You're working late tonight, Mouse." She watched the small man pull his sketches down from a line strung between fence posts.

He turned, peered into the darkness, and waved. A picture fluttered from his hands, and he stooped, chasing after it.

"A friend of yours?" Phillip asked as they walked on.

She nodded. "Did you see his pictures?"

He snorted. She drew back.

"I didn't mean that the way it sounded." He dropped his eyes to the sidewalk. "I'm sure he's talented. It's just that . . . I worry about my students. It's difficult to earn a living as an artist. I feel sorry for anyone who tries it." He picked up his pace as he strode on, and she found herself hurrying to keep up with him.

"Occasionally students will come by after graduating, and there's always an excuse, some reason why they're bartending right now, or waiting tables, or"—he swept his hand out over the park—"struggling to make ends meet in places like this."

Beside him she nodded, thinking of the run-down empty duplex near Esplanade on Bourbon Street that Mouse shared with an ever-changing group of wanderers he barely knew. No furniture. No lights, no heat, other than from the open gas jets in the walls.

"You can see it in their eyes, the resignation."

She glanced at him. "They must think a lot of you. You're a good example."

"I try. I've been lucky." With that he fell silent.

A carriage clattered past on the wrong side of the street. The driver snapped the reins against the tired mule's flanks, and Amalise flinched. The mule spurted into a quick step . . . one, two, three, four . . . slowed again and dropped its head.

"Poor animal."

"What?" He seemed to start and followed her eyes. "Oh." He gave a careless laugh. "Well, they're used to it. Mules are worthless creatures. Neuters—nature's mistake."

She frowned. "They're smarter than you think and gentle when they're treated right. God doesn't make mistakes; people do." She glanced at him as they strolled along. "They're outsiders, hybrids of horses and donkeys, so maybe that makes them work harder."

Just then a long blue note from a saxophone drifted from the direction of the river. Amalise halted, turning toward the sound, and he stopped beside her. A musician sat on a makeshift bench at the top of the levee, a shadow against the moonlit sky.

"That's nice."

"Yes." Phillip moved close behind her. He rested his hands on her shoulders.

This isn't right. She took a step forward, and he dropped his hands. For a moment she stood still, listening to the musician's riff and watching a ship just visible over the top of the levee gliding down the river. Fingers of fog drifted toward them. Back home in Marianus lights were off this time of night and the only sounds you'd hear were the songs of frogs and crickets and night birds. She took a deep breath, loving this city and wanting to hold on to the scene and make it last. But instead she turned, and they walked on.

Ahead the slice of yellow moon hung high over the farmer's market. "'Hey diddle diddle, the cat and the fiddle, the cow jumped over the moon,'" she murmured in a singsong cadence.

"What was that?"

With a quick look at him, she laughed, feeling foolish. "It's a nursery rhyme. Do you remember?" He shook his head. "'The little dog laughed to see such fun . . . and the dish ran away with the spoon.'" Her voice trailed off. She ducked her head and swept her hair behind her ear. They stepped down from the curb and began crossing the street toward the café.

"Little girls." Phillip shook his head as they crossed Decatur. He looked down at her. "I bet you're a dreamer." They crossed against the light, but he didn't seem to notice. Amalise peered in both directions.

He chose a table near the sidewalk and pulled out a chair. "Am I right?"

"Sometimes I'm a dreamer, I suppose."

"Why law school?" He sat down across from her. "You don't see many women lawyers around."

"That's changing."

He offered an almost imperceptible shrug. "I just don't know why you'd choose that profession. It'll grind a nice girl like you into little pieces." Glancing around, he signaled the waiter. "It doesn't fit."

She leaned back smothering a sigh and dropped her hands into her lap. This was close to Dad's line. "That's absurd." If Dad could have his way, he'd have her married with two babies by now. And living in Marianus.

The waiter appeared and Phillip ordered coffee and beignets.

"Sorry," he said after the interruption. "The few lawyers I know are men, and they're aggressive . . . ah . . . oh, never mind." He grinned. "Now you, on the other hand . . ." He shook his head. "I have a hard time with mutually exclusive concepts."

"I wouldn't know that from your work."

His eyes widened, and he hunched forward, forearms flat and angled on the table. "Why did you say that? Tell me what you mean by that." He thumped his hand as he spoke, looking deep into her eyes and emphasizing each word.

His tone had turned hard, insistent, and his presence seemed to expand around her, pulling her into his space. Unnerved by the somewhat extreme reaction, she dropped her hands to her sides, thinking of the sharp angles and edges in his pictures, the abrupt contrast between the vibrant colorful scenes surrounding the disengaged models. She hid her discomfort even as she forced herself to hold his steady gaze. After all, he was a professor.

But truth was always best. So she'd give her opinion. "The paintings are . . . unsettling." He frowned, so she added, "That's not a criticism." He was silent, still watching her intently as if every word she uttered mattered. As if she had suddenly become an expert on art. His focus was so intense that, without thinking, she scooted her chair an inch back from the table.

"Go on."

She sensed that strong criticism from her could crush him. And what did she know about art? Choosing her words carefully, she went on. "Your women subjects are interesting, but they almost seem to disappear in the lively surroundings." She looked past him, as if envisioning the pictures. "No. That's not right. They don't disappear. They're a strong part of the picture, central really. That's what's so provocative I suppose." She looked back at him.

One corner of his mouth curled up . . . the beginning of a smile?

"Provocative." He repeated her word in a flat tone. "Yes. Well, of course they are. But I paint what I see."

He pressed both hands down on the table before him, flat, splayed, and held her eyes so that she could not look away. His tone turned challenging. "But you think the women are . . . what, flat? Lifeless?" He arched one brow.

Heat rose to her face. He was pushing, testing. She gave a slight lift of her chin. "Something like that. There's no joy, as if they've been drained of it."

"Joy." He looked off with a little shrug. "In art that would be uninteresting. Anyhow"—his eyes returned to her—"flaws spice things up. Besides, what's joy without suffering?" He went on before she could reply. "But why did you go back to the gallery if you don't like my work?"

She shook her head. "You misunderstood. I do." At least the lively parts. And the colors.

At that he smiled and seemed to exhale. She watched as he fished a pack of cigarettes and a lighter from his jacket pocket and held out the pack. She shook her head.

Tamping the package on the edge of the table, he plucked out a cigarette and stuck it in the corner of his mouth. A minute passed as he hunched to light it, straightened, and tilted back his head, blowing smoke at the ceiling.

Thankfully the waiter returned with two cups of coffee and the plate of beignets. He turned his attention to the coffee—spooned in some sugar, stirred, picked up the cup, and sipped.

Two elderly men entered the café, and she watched as they worked their way through the empty tables until they found one that suited them. A boat on the river broke the silence with a sultry moan. She glanced toward the sound and the levee and saw that the saxophone player had gone.

"Let's see . . ." he looked up, the slight smile still present, and set down the coffee cup. "Porter's has . . . *The Blue Hour, Lady and Mirror,* and *Repose* . . . Oh . . ." He seemed to brush off the thought and shook his head. "I can't remember all of them . . . which gallery has which ones."

"You must be successful." She cradled the warm coffee cup in her hands. "Are there many galleries showing your work?"

He nodded. "But Porter is the best." Suddenly he ground out the cigarette in a small glass ashtray. Hunching, he clasped his hands and rested his chin on his knuckles. "They know their stuff. The woman you met at the café is the manager."

The words escaped before she caught them: "But I thought she was your wife."

A frown flicked across his face and disappeared. "No." He glanced at her left hand. "And you?"

"Am I married?" She dropped her eyes and sipped the coffee. "No."

"I know that. I meant is there anyone special?"

She hesitated, realizing that she hadn't had a real date in over a year. There wasn't time in her schedule. Jude didn't count. "Not right now."

He smiled, and this time the smile reached his eyes, softening the lines on his face. "Good." He leaned forward and touched her fingers with his. "You interest me. I meant what I said before; I'd like to paint your picture sometime."

"Why?"

"Because I want to. Isn't that a reason?" His look closed the space between them. He moved his chair around the table, closer to her, and boundaries wavered. As in the gallery he seemed unconscious of spatial constraints. "Will you sit for me?"

The untouched beignets sat on a plate between them growing cold. Her arm brushed his as she reached for one, broke off a piece, and popped it into her mouth. What if he was teasing and she said yes. She'd be humiliated.

"I'd like you to make time if you can." He stroked her forearm with one fingertip.

When she turned her head to look at him, his eyes shone with a dark light. She was the only person in the world that interested him in this moment, she realized. She was fascinating, beautiful to him.

He was unlike any man she'd ever met. And he was not married.

Excitement cloaked the spark of danger. She smiled. "I can do that." She imagined him behind an easel in his studio painting her picture, glancing up with that same intent look.

"Good." He lifted the coffee cup to his lips and drank without taking his eyes from her.

Enough of this scrutiny. "It's late." She reached down for the book bag. "I should go. I still have to study."

He set down the cup. "Don't go yet. I want to know more about you." She hesitated. "Before we leave"—he grinned as his hand slid onto her shoulder—"tell me one important thing about yourself." His tone was light now, teasing, so different from before that, again, she felt off balance. "Where did you grow up?"

"Marianus, about one hundred miles west of here, past Baton Rouge, a few miles on the other side of the river there. It's bayou country, a small town. Not much going on."

"And college?"

"A state university in Lafayette. After that I moved here and worked for a year, saving money for law school."

"Did you work at the café then?"

She nodded.

"What kind of music do you like? What books—what do you read? Fiction?"

"Fiction. Yes. Hmm." She tilted her head and looked up. "Well, the classics are my favorites, I guess. Wharton, James, Fitzgerald. I'm not a big lover of Hemingway . . . but Virginia Wolfe, Forrester. And I like poetry, especially."

"What movies?"

"Movies?"

"Do you have a pet?"

"What?" Her thoughts reeled as he jumped from one subject to the next. She dropped the book bag into her lap.

He laughed. "A pet. You know . . ." He formed vague shapes with his hands. "A cat, a dog, a bird."

A dog. A cord still tightened in her throat when she remembered Sally. Just a little stray, but how she'd loved that dog. "Mama's allergic. Wouldn't allow animals in the house. And she hated the mess. But she made an exception once when I was in the second grade. A puppy, the only pet I was ever allowed to keep. Even slept with me at night."

"What kind?"

Amalise looked off. "Oh. She was a mutt."

"How'd you find it?"

"Her."

"Tell me."

"She was starved when I found her, all wet and huddled on the sidewalk. I was coming home from school and four or five older boys . . . they had her trapped in a circle, pelting her with chinaberries and laughing."

Even all these years later it hurt to remember that cruel laughter and Sally's helpless yelps. She could feel those hard little berries stinging as she barged through the wall of boys with a strength she hadn't known she possessed and snatched up the puppy. They'd crowded closer then, pelting her while she bent over the puppy—and then Jude came along, and there was a fight, and she'd scooped Sally up and run.

She looked up and saw a flicker of something in his eyes, as if she'd revealed an important secret. He understood.

His brows drew together, and the corners of his eyes pulled down. "What was its . . . her . . . name?"

"Sally." Her voice broke, and she cleared it, emitting a short laugh. She looked away, shrugging. "Just Sally."

"And your mother let you keep her?"

"Yes. She knew the minute I came home that day that she was stuck with this one."

Phillip grinned, watching her under his lashes as he let smoke steam from his mouth. "Little girls and puppies usually get what they want."

Amalise shrugged, cupped her hands around the warm coffee, and sipped. "Mama loved me. So she loved Sally, too, because of me. Call it a touch of grace." She smiled. "Sally was redeemed through Mama's love for me."

"Redeemed. That's a strange word to use." Seconds passed before he spoke again. "I had a dog once, too." He spoke in a new, quiet tone. "A yellow lab named Banjo." His lips tightened, and he pushed back his chair. "I know how you must have felt to lose Sally. Banjo was hit by a car." Phillip's eyes shone with moisture. He dipped his chin. "I saw it happen. Had to pick him up and carry him home in my arms." He looked at her. "It was like losing my best friend."

"Yes. Yes, that's exactly what it's like." She leaned toward him. "Animals are so trusting. We're the caretakers. They count on you, and when they suffer, you know you're letting them down."

He blinked, brushed the corner of one eye with a finger, and stood. "Well, there goes the mood." He offered a strained smile. "I apologize for asking the wrong question. Thinking of Banjo . . . well. His death always gets me down." He pulled a wallet from his coat and looked around. "I'll find the waiter. They're never around when you want them."

She watched as he crossed the empty terrace and went inside. He was sensitive. She liked that about him. Through the window she saw him handing the waiter a few bills, slapping the man's shoulders and saying something that made him laugh.

Her apartment was just a few blocks away.

"I'll walk you home. I'd drive you home, but I don't have a car. Took the streetcar tonight." He glanced at his watch. She said that wasn't necessary, but he slipped the book bag from her shoulder and slung it onto his without a word.

"Thanks."

He slanted his eyes at her and smiled. "This thing's too heavy for an imp like you. Now. Here's what I know so far about Amalise Catoir."

She was startled. He'd remembered her last name and pronounced it right.

"You may or may not be a paradox . . ." He gave her a sly look. "Admit it, sharkie—you were a softie for that mule." She laughed.

"You like rhymes and poems and full moons and dogs. You love to read. And movies, I'll bet. You didn't answer that one. Am I right?"

She nodded, smiling.

"And you went back to the gallery. So even though you might not want to own it, my work struck a chord." She began to protest, but he interrupted, taking her hand in his. "You're a small-town girl in a big city, unattached at the present time, and someday I suppose you'll be a rich lawyer."

"That's pretty good."

His fingers curled around hers and squeezed. "It's a start."

Her heart seemed to skip a beat at these words. "Here's what I know about you"—Amalise stole a look at him—"you're a professor and an artist. You loved your dog, Banjo. Where's home?"

"New York. Manhattan. But I'd rather talk about you."

As they strolled down Decatur, he asked her about Marianus, and Mama and Dad. When he found out that Dad was a parish judge, he nodded. "So that explains it then." He smiled down at her. "A daddy's girl, too. Are you going to follow in his footsteps? Somehow I still don't see you in a courtroom." He threw up his hands and stepped aside. "Sorry."

She smiled. "I'm leaning toward corporate law."

He looked up at the moon and asked her to recite the nursery rhyme again, and then repeated what he remembered, line for line, picking up each slight nuance of her tone, the cadence, her inflections.

She laughed, delighted. "You're a good mimic." When they arrived at the building where she lived, he stopped and scanned the brick walls, the heavy wrought iron door, the shining brass handles and keyhole plate.

"Nice." He handed her the book bag.

"It is. It's a little drafty at times, but I love it." She dug the key out of the book bag, opened the gate, and turned back to him.

He didn't ask to come in. He just tipped up her chin, brushed her hair back from her forehead, and gave her a hard look. "I *will* paint your picture. I want to hold on to you, Amalise Catoir."

Inside the apartment she leaned back against the door, smiled, and hugged herself. Phillip Sharp was not married after all.

Chapter Five

⸻

A t the end of her shift on Saturday afternoon, Amalise lounged with Jude at a café table just outside the shutter doors, a place where the sun slanted across the sidewalk and warmed them. It was mid-afternoon and early fall. Business was slow right now, but the area in front of the park and cathedral was thronged with automobiles, bicycles, tourists, artists, musicians, shoppers, mothers pushing strollers, children playing, spinning tops, darting birds, bouncing balls.

Jude sprawled beside her, legs stretched and feet propped up on a nearby chair. A worn brown canvas duffel bag lay on the ground beside him. He crossed his ankles and lifted a glass of iced tea.

"Back to work this afternoon," he said, taking a swallow. Pilottown was located at the mouth of the Mississippi.

Amalise nodded. They didn't call Pilottown the end of the world for nothing. "Don't you get lonely down there?"

The island hamlet, rising out of the marsh wetlands on the east side of the Mississippi River as it empties into the Gulf about eighty-five miles south of New Orleans, could be reached only by water. Originally built by French settlers in the eighteenth century as a seamark—La Balize—and ravaged over the years by hurricanes straight off the Gulf, it was isolated. A few hardy residents lived there year-round, along with the pilots—commercial fishermen, boatmen, mess men. There was a post office where mail arrived by boat, and a zip code, the small Board of Trade building manned by an elderly couple on twelve-hour shifts, a one-room schoolhouse and a house for the teacher next door, and a row of stilt houses built along the boardwalk.

There were separate station houses for the river pilots and bar pilots to live in, too, with dormitories and good cooks, and not much else. No grocery store, although there was a small place that sold some alcohol. There was electricity in Pilottown, and the intermittent telephone service was through microwave. There were rabbit-ear television sets with poor reception but good fishing and good trapping and hunting.

"I'm used to it." Jude shrugged and glanced at her. "But you wouldn't like it, chère. It makes Marianus look like a big city."

"I wouldn't like it then."

"The Regal Theater made you into a city girl. All those Saturdays dreaming."

"Tickets were cheap. Sixty cents for a dream."

"Thirty-five with a Blue-Plate mayonnaise label."

Amalise watched two teenagers walking past, feeling that old rush of excitement. The Regal Theater in Marianus had teased her with possibilities since she was a child—dreams of the time when she was grown and could go down to the city to law school. *The City.* That's what Mama always called New Orleans. Even now sitting here with Jude, she could see those lights blazing up there on the theater screen, calling her, city lights that stayed on all night in glittering glass towers—two stories was a tall building in Marianus.

She looked around at the café—the busy, colorful corner of Jackson Square—and smiled. Finally, she was here. *Abba, such a beautiful day and so much to explore.* A flush of guilt washed through her as she thought of Mama and Dad back home. *It's not that I didn't like Marianus. It was a nice place to grow up. But . . . thank You for this.*

They sat in the sun for a few minutes, then Jude yawned and stretched. Pushing back from the table, he stood, leaned down, and kissed her forehead. "Got to go or I'll miss the bus." Hefting the duffel onto his shoulder, he waved across the room to Henry behind the bar. "Take care of my girl for me."

Henry glanced his way and nodded.

Jude took off in the direction of the Greyhound station where the watch crew would be waiting for the ride down to Venice, on the Gulf and eight miles from Pilottown. The pilot boat would meet them in Venice and take them on to the station.

Amalise wandered toward Chartres in the direction of her apartment. She would study this afternoon, but her feet dragged, and before reaching the entrance to Jackson Square, she found Mouse parked in front of his easel near the fence in the shade of a magnolia tree.

"Sit a minute." He gestured to an empty canvas chair he kept for customers.

"I don't have time." But the sun felt good today, seemed to soak into her skin. She halted beside him and looked over his shoulder as a picture of the café, lit for the evening crowds, formed on a sketchpad he'd placed on his easel. "How's business?"

"Slow."

Mouse's eyes moved back and forth between the paper and the street and Gina's café as he sketched the bright interior shining against a night's darkness outside. Across the street he sketched in the corner of the Cabildo. "Who was that guy with you the other night?" He leaned forward and ran the edge of his thumb over the sketch, softening the lines.

"Jude?"

"No." He shot her a look over his shoulder. "Not him. The man that waited outside the café for you last Monday night while you were working." Details of the shutter doors appeared as the chalk in his hand brought the picture to life.

"Oh." Amalise frowned. "He'd just come from La Petite. Happened to see me leaving."

"Theater's not open on Monday nights," Mouse said, without looking up.

She stared at the back of his head, thinking about that. "He's a professor at Newcomb Art, Tulane."

"Umm." Mouse set the chalk down and picked up another piece. He sketched in the outline of a man hunched against a post in shadows at the edge of the Cabildo. "He waited over there." He nodded toward the corner. "Must have been about twenty, thirty minutes he waited in the dark, watching you inside."

Amalise tore her eyes from the picture, folded her arms, and looked at the old building across from La Petite Theater. "You must be wrong."

Mouse glanced up. "No. There's something strange about him. I worried he was a stalker until I saw you with him."

Heat flushed her face at that.

A man and woman stopped to look at Mouse's sketch. Amalise stepped aside. Mouse set down the chalk and turned to them.

"Would you like a portrait of your lady, sir?" The woman shuffled her feet and watched her husband.

The man looked down at his wife. "How about it, Emma?"

"He's good," Amalise said.

"I don't know." The wife lowered her eyes and stepped closer to her husband. "How long would it take?"

"How long would it take?" The husband channeled the question to Mouse in a brusque, business-like tone.

Mouse studied the woman's face for an instant, and she giggled, turning her eyes to Amalise, who gave her an encouraging smile.

Mouse nodded. "Good color." He looked back at her husband. "No more than a half hour, I'd guess."

Before they could object, Mouse moved into action, gesturing the woman toward the chair. "Sit here." He stood and pulled an empty canvas from a stack that he kept nearby on the sidewalk.

The woman hesitated.

"Let's do it, Emma," the man said. "It will be a nice remembrance."

"All right." She sat down in the chair, shifted her weight, and looked up at her husband. "All right."

Amalise saw the look that passed between husband and wife— years of memories shared, children raised, a house, a garden. The portrait would hang on their wall at home to remind them of this lazy, sunny day when time hadn't seemed to matter.

Melancholy rose within her. Would she ever have that life? She wanted her career in law, but she wanted love, a family . . . she wanted all of that too.

Mouse returned with the clean canvas, and, removing the sketchbook, propped it on the easel.

"How much?" the man asked.

Amalise glanced up at the clock on the cathedral and sucked in her breath. Time did matter to her. As she turned to slip away, Mouse stopped her. He ripped the sketch from the pad, swiveled, and handed it to her. "This is for you."

LATER THAT AFTERNOON, SITTING at the kitchen table in her apartment surrounded by books, notebooks, pencils—she preferred them to pens, easier to correct mistakes—and two empty bottles of soft drinks, a half glass of warm milk, and the remains of a sandwich on a napkin, she stared at the picture Mouse had drawn. He had made it clear: Phillip lied about bumping into her on Monday night.

She shivered a little and looked around the small bright kitchen, thinking of him watching in the darkness, waiting outside the café while she'd closed up with Gina. There was an edge to the professor that she didn't understand. At first she'd thought his pictures were somewhat misogynistic, until he'd explained the artistic technique. But then she supposed artists are given license for things like that.

Picking up a pencil, she tapped the eraser against her bottom lip, mulling over their conversation at Café du Monde. Phillip was unlike anyone she'd ever known. She pressed the pencil against her lip. Despite the hard—sometimes rough—exterior he'd exhibited at first, he'd softened over the course of the evening. He'd been so interested in her, in everything she had to say. Walking her home—he hadn't had to—he'd carried her book bag. She smiled, remembering how he'd struggled to memorize the nursery rhyme, how he'd laughed at himself for that. And when they'd reached her apartment, he hadn't asked to come inside. He'd been a perfect gentleman.

She gazed down at the sketch that Mouse had made. So what if Phillip had told a little lie in order to see her . . . a small fabrication. Perhaps he was shy. After all, he'd tracked her down because she'd criticized his work, and maybe . . . perhaps she really did interest him. A small thrill shot through her, and she rolled the pencil between her thumb and fingers, suddenly realizing how much trouble he'd taken to see her. Riding the streetcar down to the Quarter at night from the university area. He didn't own a car.

The pencil flipped from her hand and fell to the floor. Rousing herself, she picked up Mouse's sketch, crushed it into a ball, tossed it into a trash can nearby, and dragged the Evidence casebook across the kitchen table. Mouse was reading too much into what he'd seen. Besides, she couldn't afford distractions right now. She needed to concentrate and study. Dad and Mama were scraping together money for tuition; she couldn't let them down. With Dad already uneasy with this whole idea—poor grades would make things worse. Why couldn't she return to Marianus after college and work in his office, he grumbled at every chance. What about marriage? What about children . . . his grandchildren?

Even so, he'd sold the bass boat last year. He was tired of the old clunker, he'd said, but she knew better.

It was Mama who'd lit the spark, put the idea of becoming a lawyer into her head. It was the summer she turned nine. Dad took her to the courthouse with him often on those hot bright days when the air was heavy with the scent of dry grass and simmering algae along the banks of the bayou, and there was nothing else to do unless Jude came around. She'd sit beside Dad on a tall stool behind his raised desk, looking out over the courtroom. Most of the time she knew everyone there, and the bailiff and the court reporter would say "your Honor" to Dad and then "Mornin', Miss Amalise."

A railing separated spectators from two long tables, and there were two rows of chairs for the members of the jury. Each person who came inside the rails would sit at a table and wait, shuffling papers and whispering. Sometimes they'd just tell their story to Dad, and sometimes a jury would come in to listen too. The stories were mostly ho-hum—a neighbor building a fence over the line, a cow that strayed onto the road and got hit by a car, or someone like Kat Murphy would get caught driving down the wrong side of the street again late at night, and that's when Amalise would look off through the windows and wish that she was outside with Jude.

But one day a woman was shot coming out of a grocery store over near Livonia. It happened in the springtime when Amalise was ten, and at recess in the schoolyard the story spread like spider eggs on grass. The dead woman was Mrs. Guillard, and lots of people saw it happen. It happened right out in the open, in daylight, at three in the afternoon. The killer wore a Batman mask, shot her in the face, and drove off in an old blue truck. Shot her three times . . . five . . . seven the kids had said, and there was a knife, too.

The mask was found in a cane field. Someone saw the husband driving around near that field in a blue banged-up truck past its days, but Mr. Guillard said he didn't even own a truck—said he didn't ever need to ride in an old beat-up truck.

The gun was never found, but Mr. Guillard was arrested in March. His case was set for trial in Dad's court in May, and when it was moved to the end of June instead and school was out, Amalise was ecstatic.

Did he do it, Abba?

He wouldn't tell.

The murder was all everyone talked about in town for months. On the day the trial began, Amalise planted herself on the courtroom stool beside Dad.

The district attorney had come up from Baton Rouge. He wore a seersucker suit, a white shirt, and shiny shoes. A younger man sat with him at the table inside the railing, pulling papers out of cardboard boxes and running in and out of the courtroom.

Mr. Guillard, the defendant, made his entrance with three lawyers from Baton Rouge. The minute she saw him, she knew he hadn't killed his wife. She could see the truth in the way he carried himself, the way he strode down the aisle and pushed through that railing as if he owned the place, the way he smiled, so unconcerned. She could see it in the faces of the jury as they watched him all that first day.

She was wrong.

Day by day Amalise sat riveted as each piece of information was presented, and one after another, parts of the story she'd believed to be true right up to that moment were proven false, just flipped upside down because of new evidence. Fascinated, she'd watched the truth unfold, studying Mr. Guillard's smile as it faded, disappearing somewhere around the Fourth of July when his girlfriend took the stand. She owned an old blue beat-up truck, she admitted.

After that, Mr. Guillard missed the Fourth-of-July picnic.

Dad wouldn't talk much about the trial. She guessed she wasn't a very good judge of people, she told Mama after it was over and they were in the laundry shed. She never would have thought it was Mr. Guillard who murdered his wife. It wasn't so much the trial that fascinated her, though. It was watching the facts unfold, like putting together the pieces of a puzzle.

"Sometimes the truth is hidden." Mama wiped her hands on her apron. "But Dad knows how to find it." She hesitated, then took a quick breath that made Amalise look up. "How about you, Amalise? Will you be a lawyer like Dad when you grow up?"

Amalise had stared, unscrambling her thoughts. Jude was taking her fishing after the laundry was done. She'd been restless, wondering if he was already waiting on the pier. But Mama's question interested her. "Can girls do that, too?"

"Certainly." Mama softened her snappish tone. "A woman needs to get out in the world. Go to school, get a job, hold money." The old washer rattled to a stop, and Mama reached down to lift a soaked towel from the tub. Twisting it, she fed the towel through the wringer above, cranking the handle so that water streamed down into the tub, and the cloth rolled out, pressed flat and stiff. "Get me that basket, please."

Amalise dragged the large woven basket across the cement floor, and Mama shook the towel out and handed it to Amalise. "You know, it's strange"—she turned her head, looking off, hiding her expression—"when I graduated high school, no one ever mentioned college."

Amalise dropped the towel into the basket as Mama reached into the washer for another one.

"I would have liked that, I think." Mama's voice came out low enough that Amalise had to strain to hear. "Having an education. Going to college."

"Why didn't you, Mama?"

With all of her attention, Mama wrung the towel and fed it through the wringer. Her voice turned brisk, as if Amalise had asked a foolish question. "Well, I married Dad instead, and I'm glad I did."

Amalise took the next towel from her without saying anything.

Mama went on—bending over the washtub, straightening to reach the wringer, handing off pressed towels to Amalise while she mused out loud. "Still, sometimes I think what it might have been like to have my own place, pay for things with earned money . . . just for a little while." She turned and looked around the shed, as if visualizing something all her own. Amalise held up her hand for the next towel, but Mama pressed it to her chest with both hands.

She turned her eyes to Amalise. "But you can do it, chère. When you're a woman."

Amalise stared at Mama, listening. She'd never thought of things such a long way off into the future before.

"Times have changed, chère. Girls . . . women . . . have choices now." She pronounced each word with emphasis, dropping the towel back into the washtub. "If you work hard, you can do anything you want."

"I guess I could do that." She'd wanted to please Mama.

Mama lifted the basket, hiked it onto her hip, and they walked out of the cool shed through the drying yard to the clothesline. When Mama didn't say anything more, she added: "I'll be a lawyer, too, when I grow up."

Mama nodded, smiling down at her. "You'll go to college. And then to law school." Mama's tone turned Amalise's words into a promise, and a promise was a bond.

So this became The Plan. After that day Mama talked of it all the time—the dream, The Plan, until it became ingrained and Amalise understood that she held not just her own dreams in trust but Mama's dreams too.

Now, sitting in the kitchen, she could almost smell the scent of laundry soap in the shed and the hint of fresh air in the sheets at night. Pushing all thoughts of Phillip Sharp aside, she told herself to get on with The Plan. She picked up another pencil and began to read again with heightened focus, underlining the facts, the issues, the rationale of the court.

JUDE HITCHED THE DUFFEL bag over his shoulder and climbed into the chartered bus where the rest of the crew already waited. At the end of the highway at Venice, the pilot boat waited to discharge the go-home crew and take those on watch back to the island. As they cut through the waves, Jude squinted into the sunshine, feeling the Gulf breeze, and letting the calm settle over him as it always did when he was on the water. Here—in the push and pull of the waves, the shifting wind and currents, in the marshes teeming with fragile life—he saw and felt God's power.

Near the Southwest pass, the station house came into view. Long, two-storied, the white building with a front porch was surrounded by marshland. The Crescent River pilot station of West Indian architecture was nearby, and there was the pier and slip for small boats.

The crew boat pulled alongside the pier, and the pilots disembarked. Luggage carts were ready for those who'd brought more than Jude. He glanced back, walking down the pier toward the station house. The sun was sinking into the marsh, and gulls lifted off the pilings near the pier at his approach, sailing out over the rushing brown river, calling back through the damp wind blowing from the southwest.

In the distance he could see a man on a bicycle appearing to glide through air over the watery marsh as he rode the one raised walkway that ran the length of the island for about a mile. The strip of concrete built high above the wetland was the only connection between the pilot stations and the rest of the hamlet. When Jude reached the porch, he stopped and turned, inhaling the fresh salt air and watched a pelican dive at a ninety-degree angle into the middle of the river.

Jude opened the screen door, walked through the main room and back to his locker where he stored his bag. He was hungry, so he would unpack later. He checked the blackboard that tracked vessel arrivals and departures—his work schedule. Couches and the overstuffed chairs in the main room began to fill with sprawling pilots, just arrived, smoking, opening magazines, or just gazing at the board. Some trudged on upstairs to the dormitory to catch up on sleep before the watchman called and their ships arrived. In the corner the *bourree* group formed around a table. They called to Jude, but he was tired and hungry and waved them off.

The chef wasn't around when he entered the kitchen, so he located a roast chicken in the refrigerator, cut off a leg, rewrapped the rest, and stuck it back inside. Chewing on the drumstick, he wandered back through the front room, checked the board once more, and headed upstairs to bed. He had about four hours to sleep before his first down-bound ship.

He'd already forgotten Phillip Sharp.

Chapter Six

Over a week since she'd last seen Phillip, but it seemed longer. She'd thought he would call earlier, or show up at the café one night, or at least that she might run into him around the campus. But, of course, she reflected later, it would happen when she'd given up and least expected to see him.

And so it did, after a long day of classes. She grabbed her books from the locker, stuffed them into her shoulder bag, and hurried down the hallway past the lockers and the student lounge, waving off Rebecca and calculating in her mind how much time it would take her to get to the café. Twenty minutes to cross the campus to St. Charles Avenue, where the streetcar ran. Another forty-five to get downtown at this time of day, a half-hour at best to walk through the Quarter. But, as she pushed through the double doors at the entrance to the law school, six o'clock bells tolled from the church across campus.

She was already running late.

Still, she halted for an instant at the top of the stairs, relishing the crisp autumn air that always reminded her of the first months of the school year when she was a child. For an instant she was that little girl again, just home from school—second grade—wearing the new plaid dress sewed by Mama, and she could smell the burning leaves from down the road, and wood smoke. She could see Jude waiting down at the bayou with the pirogue. He smiles as she runs toward him, picks her up, and swings her into the little boat and slides in, too, tucking her between his knees on the seat. She feels his strong hands over hers on the paddle as they glide across the bayou into the swampy water-forest of thick rushes, and pine, oak, tupelo, and gum trees, and cypress hung with Spanish moss.

She pulled herself from the memory, then looked around the campus. This was the same time of day, when the air was cool and in the shadowed swamp the fading light turned the cypress trees to gold. In a dreamlike state she hurried down the stairs and almost collided with Phillip.

He lounged against a low cement wall near the sidewalk, smoking. When she heard him call out her name, she spun around and stumbled.

"Whoa!" Without moving from the place he'd staked out, he reached over and grabbed her waist, catching her before she tripped. She laughed as he steadied her. When she'd caught her breath, he let her go, tossed away the cigarette, and pushed off the wall. He stood close, looking down at her with a frown. "Are you all right?"

Still smiling, she stepped back, hugging the book bag. "Yes. Thanks. Hello." She struggled to hide the surge of pleasure washing over her. Fingering the strap on the bag, she was conscious that she'd be late for work if she didn't hurry, but she wanted to linger.

"I've been waiting for you." He ran his eyes over her. "Come." He stretched out his hand for hers, and when she didn't move, he beckoned, as if this meeting had been prearranged.

She stood motionless, still smiling, but staring without comprehension, and he dropped his arm to his side with a sigh. "Come with me." He gave a jerk of his head in the direction of the art school building.

"Where?" She took in his rumpled, faded clothes. He wore sandals, even though the air today was brisk, and his hair was still raked back from his forehead in that careless style.

"I'm going to paint your portrait. I want you to sit for me, Amalise." He gave her an exultant look and reached out his hand again. "Come on, let's go. The light's just right."

Had she forgotten something? She glanced around and caught

herself, feeling foolish. Reluctantly, she shook her head. "I'm on my way to work."

His smile died and then hers. She stole a glance at her watch. Gina would be furious.

His eyes narrowed and his brows drew together. He folded his arms over his chest, cocked his head to one side, and spoke in a studied, patient tone. "You don't understand. I've rearranged my entire schedule today for you." He glanced at the sky, frowned, and looked back to her, holding her eyes. "I cancelled a class so we could get started. We're wasting time."

Her thoughts spun as she stared back. He'd cancelled a class because of her? What was he talking about? "I'm sorry." An edge of irritation whispered through her. "But I can't come with you now. I'm late for work."

Something in her voice caused him to blink. His arms dropped to his sides, and in a split second his expression transformed. His mouth softened and curled into a half smile. Fine lines sprayed from the outer corners of his eyes. His shoulders seemed to swallow his neck as he dipped his chin, looked at her under hooded lids, and slowly shook his head. "I'm sorry if I sometimes seem abrupt."

Her tense muscles eased, and she allowed a small smile. Had she embarrassed him? She hoped not. "Maybe *intense* is the word." Amalise reached out and touched his arm. "You love your work." As she spoke, his eyes held hers, seeming to probe for something more. She pulled her hand back, hugging the book bag again.

"Yes. I've been thinking of your picture and how it will be. It's time to get to it now." He straightened, cupped the side of her face with the palm of his hand, and gave a short, self-deprecating laugh. "I think I'm obsessed. I want to capture you." He paused, then a sly grin eased across his features. "On canvas, of course."

She listened, speechless, as his hand slipped down the curve of her neck and he described the scene he'd set for the work of painting, how the light would catch one side of her face, leaving the other in shadows. How her dark hair would gleam against her skin. As he went on, she stood transfixed by the hypnotic cadence of his voice, like listening to metered poetry and rhyme.

When at last he released her, she flinched. "Will you let me paint you?" He took her hand and circled the tender underside of her wrist with his thumb as he waited for her answer.

No man had looked at her and spoken to her in this way before, eyes and words leaden with tension, as if she were the very focus of his life, his passion. Suddenly she was no longer that girl who was never unprepared for class, who outlined every case herself and hustled through nights at the café and scheduled her time right down to every second of every day and night, working toward The Plan.

In this instant she was a woman on the brink of something completely new, uncharted.

His eyes probed hers as if he'd searched for and finally found her, as if she were unique, a beauty to be immortalized by his talent. But she wasn't beautiful, she reminded herself. Skin-deep, she was ordinary.

And yet . . .

Phillip held her hand and looked at her in that way . . . and slowly she let the dreamer emerge—the romancer, the seeker of love up on the silver screen at the Regal Theater. She let herself envision the studio where she would pose. The observer of life in her mind— the little interior voice that spoke to her at times, that described and interpreted, argued and egged on—that observer conjured up details of the scene for her.

Phillip would paint a portrait that would hang in Porter Gallery, but her picture would be different from the others. In hers the woman would be smiling—bright instead of dull, content instead of searching, happy with her place in God's creation.

Besides, the ghostly observer whispered, *there might be something special between you and Phillip Sharp, and you don't want to let go the chance, now, do you?*

Footsteps pounded down the law school steps, and the reverie vanished. "See you tomorrow, Amalise." It was Rebecca, flying past. Phillip's hand dropped to his side. Amalise looked up and stepped back.

"Will you let me paint your picture?" His voice was tight, urgent.

"Yes." She struggled to shake off the fog. She wanted to go with him right now, this moment, but the sun was rapidly descending and reality intruded. Gina was waiting for her at the café. "I will." She would. "But not today."

"When then?"

"Tomorrow? In the afternoon?"

He hesitated. "All right." Frowning, he took the book bag from her and slung it over his shoulders. "Let's plan on tomorrow." He took her hand and started down the steps.

"What time tomorrow?" What *was* her class schedule for the next day?

He glanced at her and shrugged, pressing his hand on the small of her back while they walked, and she felt that electric jolt of connection again. "We'll just have to see how it works out . . . about the light."

His casual tone took her by surprise, but his hand was warm through her blouse. She did not want the romantic dream to disappear. Class schedule or not, she blurted a time in the late afternoon—four o'clock tomorrow—and he nodded.

"How will I find you?" They'd reached the crossing light at Freret Street.

He halted, dropping his hand as he turned to her. "You know where the art school is, don't you?" He flashed a grin, but for a fraction of a second she imagined a flicker of impatience crossed his face.

"Sure."

He smiled at her then, and she dismissed that little worry as he glanced over his shoulder in the direction of the art school. "Just come to the main entrance, first floor, and take a left at the end of the hall." He slipped the book bag from his shoulder and gently onto hers. "I'll be waiting."

Before she could say another word, he kissed her on the cheek, wheeled around, and strode off, arms swinging at his sides.

She looked after him, but he did not look back, and as she turned around to wait for the traffic light to turn green, the observer repeated in her mind, word for word, the things that Phillip had said only minutes ago as they'd stood together on the steps, and described the way Phillip had looked at her. For an instant as she crossed Freret Street and walked on, Phillip's fleeting but transforming moods over the past few minutes touched off Mouse's warning.

But the gloomy note was subsumed in the fading light of dusk, the fragrance of new-cut grass on the quadrangle between the old stone buildings, the sound of the school band practicing in the Willow Street stadium, the church bells pealing again—all filling her with a sense of excitement, of something new about to happen. Suddenly she picked up her pace until she was almost running, wanting to drop the book bag instead and throw out her arms and spin.

Professor Phillip Sharp had singled her out and wanted to *capture* her on his canvas!

Is he the one, Abba?

Chapter Seven

If each city could be identified with a particular fragrance, Amalise thought, New Orleans's would be the pungent scent of sweet olive blooming in the fall and spring. Here it was, already October, and the season had finally turned. The air was unusually fresh and cool. Amalise took deep breaths as she walked across campus to the art school building the next afternoon. She'd never deliberately skipped a class before. But she'd never been asked to pose for a painting before either.

Leaves and acorns cracked beneath her boots as she walked. Acorns. The thought slipped in—potentially entire oak trees crushed under her new boots! The boots were new, expensive, a splurge to celebrate . . . what? Phillip? Something. She'd stopped to buy them on the way to school this morning, and that had made her late. But she loved the swish of her long skirt over the soft leather, and she loved how free she felt right now, and with no one around to see or hear, she began to hum.

This morning, standing in front of the mirror, she'd noticed for the first time that her short hair shone in the electric light and that it did fall like dark silk against her pale complexion. And she'd experimented today with a new crimson lipstick and decided the color was good with her hair and skin—it brightened her up a bit. She smoothed her hair. Perhaps she'd let it grow.

The two-storied brick building tucked into a corner of the campus that housed the art school looked old and sacred. Giant elephant ears, ginger and banana plants, and thick lacy fern grew up against the building and around the front steps, giving the garden a wild, disorderly, and tropical look. The brick was worn, the red color softened by the years. A crumbling sidewalk curved toward the front entrance through a cluster of mature live oak trees. In places gnarled roots pushed up through the cracked cement.

A tremor of anxiety gripped her as she approached the entrance between spiky rows of monkey grass. What if Phillip didn't remember that he'd asked her here today? Or what if he had changed his mind? What if she'd misunderstood? Her heart raced as the new boots slipped on slick algae and wet moss on the stone stairs that led to the entrance of the building. She grabbed a banister and held on, saw water glistening on the dark green elephant ears below.

The cool dim hallway had the musty smell of all old buildings in a perpetually damp climate. The ceilings were high, and the sound of her boots on the wooden floors echoed as she walked. She followed Phillip's perfunctory directions, wandering past the frosted-glass-paneled admissions office, dean's office, and a restroom, until she came to another hallway at the back. Turning left, she passed two heavy wooden doors bearing brass plaques with names of professors on them, but none bore Phillip's name.

When she reached the end of the hallway and turned back, she stopped for an instant before a pair of double doors that she'd not noticed before. The doors were paneled with the same thick glass of the admissions office but were bare of identification. One was slightly ajar, and after a moment's hesitation she gave it a push. It swung open and she peeked in.

Phillip sat before an easel in the middle of the large room. He was engrossed in painting, oblivious to her arrival. She watched for a moment as he brushed paint across a canvas with sweeping strokes, glancing back and forth between the canvas and an overstuffed, sagging couch set at an angle in front of him. The studio was spacious. Phillip must be held in high regard to rate such a large place of his own. The ceiling was two stories high, with rough wooden beams, and light streamed through rows of mullioned windows across the back, providing an open, airy look. She stepped inside. The room was redolent of paint and turpentine, and it was chilly, too.

Phillip glanced up. "Good." He set the brush down into a small tray at the bottom of the easel, then stood. "I was beginning to think you'd forgotten."

"No." She suppressed a sigh of relief. *Thank you.* She looked about and saw canvases strewn around the room, some piled neatly in stacks, some just tossed into corners, several upright against the walls. Some pictures, not all, were similar to the ones she'd seen in Porter's Gallery. And there were three other easels standing empty.

Phillip bent and measured liquid into a small cup on the table beside him. He dipped a brush into the fluid, stirred it, picked up a dirty rag and wiped it clean. As he continued, absorbed in cleaning brushes, she walked over to a series of canvasses nearby and stood examining them, conscious of the prolonged silence. "Are they yours?" She waved her hand over the scene.

"Yes." He answered without looking at her.

Feeling a damp chill, she crossed her arms and hugged herself. Turning, she ambled over to a rough-hewn table beneath the windows on which rows of miniature figures were carefully displayed. There was a dancer carved from a light-colored, smooth wood, wearing leotard, tights, and ballet slippers with delicate ribbons crossed over her ankles. There was a young girl in a blue dress, painted in muted, antique colors, with rosy flesh and pink lips and cheeks. Her eyes and hair were brown, and leaning close, Amalise could see flecks of gold in her hair. There was a soldier, his cap and uniform washed in sheer stains of navy, gray, and ancient gold. And there was a plump robin, a plain bird as yet unpainted, and a ball cut from dark wood with intricate, swirling designs. She touched the ball with the tip of her finger, imagining the skill this required.

Next to the carvings were several knives of different sizes and shapes, other instruments that she couldn't name, and a small, rectangular stone.

"You like them?"

She swiveled. He stood beside her, almost touching, looking down at the carvings on the table. "They're beautiful." She dropped her arms to her sides. "Did you make them?"

He nodded, stepped around her, and picked up the figure of the dancer. "I've worked on these on and off over the past year. It takes time. I don't carve with a design in mind. It comes from inside."

"Inside yourself?"

"And from inside the wood." He set the dancer down and touched one of the knives. "Best hardwood carving knife made." He slid his thumb over the handle. "Birchwood, laminated steel blade, professionally honed—sharp as a razor. Always ready."

Setting it down again, he picked up a pocketknife with a distinctive handle made of rich, grainy wood. When he opened it, the edge of the blade glinted in the light. "This one's a pocket carver. The blade's longer than most, high-carbon stainless steel. Look how sharp this is."

Her eyes grew wide as he sliced the knife across his forearm with a quick stroke and a thin line of crimson rose. "Don't!" She reached for the knife without thinking.

He looked amused and drew back, away from her. Setting the knife down on the table, he walked to a sink in the corner, turned on the water, and let it stream over the cut.

"Doesn't it hurt?"

He grabbed a paper towel and pressing it down on the cut, walked back to her. "No." He stood directly in front of her, too close, and looked down into her eyes. "Do you care?"

"Of course," she said, stepping back. "Why did you do that?"

He shrugged and smiled, watching her. "To show how sharp the knife is." When she frowned, he picked up the carver, cleaned the blade with the paper towel, and handed it to her, handle first.

Despite an uneasy feeling, she liked the feel of the smooth, curved handle that fit into the palm of her hand. The wood had a sensuous feel. *Sensuous but dangerous*, the observer whispered. She handed it back to him. "How long have you been doing this?"

"Carving? Forever. Cavemen carved. I started when I was little, alone much of the time . . . just whittling sticks at first." He turned the knife in his hand, looking at it. "It's an art to take a small piece of wood and turn it into something else." Shrugging, he set the knife on the table. "We're wasting time." He glanced at the windows. "Over here."

He put his hand on her shoulder and turned her away from the worktable, steering her around the easel until she stood behind it, facing the couch. A black cloth bearing an intricate design covered the couch; the pattern was woven in rich colors—burgundy, gold, blue, black, and cream—and the cloth fell in folds to the floor. "This is where you'll pose. The strong colors will suit you."

She felt his eyes on her as she looked over the easel at the setting he'd planned. "All right."

He stepped aside and swept his arm in the direction of the couch. "Let's get started."

She walked to the couch, dropped her book bag on the floor near one end, and perched on the edge of the cushion, facing him. He stepped back and stood behind the easel, arms crossed, studying the scene, eyes darting over Amalise, the patterned cloth, the couch. Frowning, he turned to the windows behind him. Without a word he moved the easel and chair closer to Amalise, positioning it a few feet to the left.

Her eyes roamed past him while she waited. In the far corner of the room, near the door she'd just entered, was a high makeshift shelf of rough, unpainted planks resting on metal wall braces. The boards sagged under the weight of papers and notebooks and boxes shoved onto it in a haphazard way. Underneath was a half-sized old refrigerator with rounded edges. The white paint was chipped and peeling. Next to that was an old, deep sink with exposed pipes.

"Ama!" His voice echoed through the room. When she looked back, she saw that he was smiling. "Stretch out"—he gestured over the length of the couch—"get comfortable. Lean back against that pillow behind you, and put your legs up."

She did as he asked while he sat and turned his attention to an assortment of paint-smeared tubes on a table beside the easel. Some were squeezed flat, she saw, and ribbons of color swirled from their tops onto a wooden pallet. Some looked as though they'd never been used.

When he glanced up at her again, he stopped what he was doing. "Not like that." He pushed back from the easel. "Take off those boots."

She bent and removed them, placing them on the floor beside her purse. When she'd finished, she tucked the skirt around her legs and resumed the rigid pose.

Suddenly he laughed and shook his head. "You look terrified." He moved toward her. She laughed too, feeling foolish. She told herself to relax as he bent and lifted her left arm, placing it over the back of the couch. He straightened and looked down at her. "Now. Isn't that better?"

She nodded. "Much better; more comfortable."

"Good." His voice was soft, patient. "Just let go." Bending over her again, he gently pressed her shoulders into the cushion behind her. "Lounge against the pillow. You've had a hard day. It shouldn't be too difficult to get comfortable on those cushions. I brought them here for you."

She exhaled and did as he said. He stepped back and rubbed his chin, still studying her. "Bend the back leg up just a bit." She did this, and he bent and reached out, yanking the skirt from under her so that it fell loose around her thighs before returning to his place behind the easel.

"Better. Look off. Over there." He nodded his head to the right. "Now empty your mind of serious thoughts. Think of that laughing dog and the dish running away with the spoon."

Her eyebrows lifted. He'd remembered the nursery rhyme.

"I want you light and dreamy," he went on, sitting down behind the easel and picking up the paintbrush. "Forget law. I'm painting you, Ama. A happy, pretty girl, not a lawyer."

"Amalise, not Ama. It was my grandmother's name."

"I prefer Ama. With me you're Ama."

She opened her mouth to object, but he set down the brush and began to rub his forehead, making small circles between his eyebrows with his thumb. "You're distracted and too tense. I'll put on some music, and you can think of that."

He went to a record player on a small table near the door. The light in the studio had grown dim. She glanced at her watch, surprised to see that forty-five minutes had already flown by. "How long will this take?" she asked as he stooped to sort through a stack of record albums. "I'll have to leave soon."

He stopped what he was doing and twisted around to look at her. "Are you serious? We haven't even begun."

She shrank back into the pillow at his harsh tone, her cheeks heating. Seconds passed, and suddenly he tossed the record album onto the floor and rose. Turning, he raked her with his eyes, then dropped his head, fingers pressing into his forehead once again.

"I'm sorry. . . . I've never done this before."

"We've wasted an afternoon." His voice was tight, controlled.

Stunned, she sat up straight and dropped her feet onto the floor. She'd been a fool to come here, to skip a class. What was she doing? Still confused, she made up her mind. "I have to leave." She reached down for her book bag.

He crossed the room and stood before her, looking down. "Don't leave. Not yet."

Her hand, reaching for the book bag, halted midair.

"Give us just a few more minutes, Ama."

She straightened, hesitating. Us. He'd used that word, *us;* and the illusive dream reemerged.

He smiled and spread his hands. "Please."

"All right"—she relaxed, leaning back on the couch—"a few minutes more."

She watched as he went to the refrigerator and pulled out a partially full bottle of white wine, held it up, and turned it in the light. He held it up to her and raised his brows. She shook her head.

With a tip of his head and a quirky smile, he returned the bottle to the refrigerator, pushed himself up, and walked back to the couch.

"I'm sorry about the time." She shifted to make room for him. He heaved a sigh and sat down beside her. "This takes longer than . . . umm . . . I'd thought." She gave a short laugh and turned to look at him. "I don't know much about this sort of thing."

He threw his arm over her shoulder and leaned back. "I didn't explain, but this picture is important." He stared at the back of the easel. "It will take at least two, maybe three weeks to finish." He pronounced the words slowly, carefully, as if to make her understand.

She stared at him as the words sank in. She'd thought a couple of hours here and there would do it. School, work, commuting back and forth, and studying didn't leave much time to invest in modeling for a picture. Even so, as she gazed around the studio bathed in the medieval light of early fall, she knew she would do it. She wanted this to last.

He's special, Abba. This feels right.

"You wouldn't have to sit every day," Phillip was saying when she looked back at him. He turned to her, and she saw the worry lines had smoothed. He touched her cheekbone as if memorizing with his fingers. "I can do some of it without you once I've blocked in a preliminary sketch."

He dropped his hand. She could manage somehow. She could make time for classes and work and posing if it only took three weeks. "All right."

He didn't seem to hear. "Of course"—he shrugged, looking off into the distance—"if you can't manage, I'll understand. But you'll have to tell me now."

She could make this work. But before she could say anything, he lifted his arm from her shoulders and stood. "Oh well"—he gave a dismissive wave—"it was just a thought."

Suddenly things had turned about. He'd drawn her into this fancy— this will–o'–the–wisp idea—and now he'd changed, lost interest.

What had she done wrong? How could she make it right? It wasn't just the idea of having him paint her picture that she was losing, she realized, looking around the room golden with last light. There was more to this. Surely he felt something for her, too.

She reached out, touched his arm. "I was going to say—"

"Don't worry about it." He moved so that her hand slipped away. He walked over to the easel, and she watched as he picked up a tube of paint from the table and replaced the cap, working it on with a twist. She thought . . . she wasn't certain . . . perhaps he was watching her from underneath his lids. But seconds passed, and he remained absorbed in those tubes of paint, and she felt invisible. Stunned, her throat grew thick and tight. Then with a sigh and a deep sense that she'd lost a unique opportunity, she reached down for her boots.

Pulling them on, she covertly watched Phillip gather up the tubes of paint and brushes, walk across the room, and store them on a shelf. He picked up a folded cloth and returning to the easel, placed the cloth over the canvas. During all of this time she imprinted everything on her mind so that she could remember: the amber light filtering through the windows, the canvases and easels and paints, and Phillip himself, standing next to the easel, infused with the aura of his talent and the world of art, so different and apart from her own regimented world of law and rules and shuffling food in the café.

When Phillip moved toward the door, Amalise rose. Feeling as though she'd been dismissed from class, she clutched her book bag, and the long bleak walk across campus to the streetcar loomed in her mind. She thought of the noisy café where Gina would be waiting and angry, and struggled against the comparison between her ordinary life and the now shimmering scenes with Phillip that she'd envisioned.

"Think about it some."

She gave him a quick look. Did he still want her to sit for him?

"Let me know if you change your mind."

She *would* make this work. She could not let this end. "I'll rearrange things." He halted at the door and turned, lifting his brows. "Can you do that? Rearrange your schedule?"

She shouldn't. "Yes, of course."

"Ah. Well, that's different." A smile lit his face, changing everything in that instant. He walked back to where she stood and cupped her face in his hands. "I'm so glad, Ama," he said in a husky voice. He bent to kiss her, and his lips were silk as they moved over hers. As suddenly as it started, the kiss ended.

"All right!" He stepped back and pressed his hands together. "That's it, then. You're mine for a few weeks, Ama, my girl."

The world spun backward, the dream beckoned again. Once, when she was eight, Jude had taken her to the parish fair and she'd felt like this. At the top of the Ferris wheel, she'd looked down over the scene spread before her like a picture on a page: the tents with flags on top beating in the breeze, the flashing colored lights on the midway, the milling crowds, the game stalls and barkers and stages. She had seen it all at once in that instant before the wheel continued its turn, the full untarnished glamour of the carnival without the dirt and shoving people, gravity, or any other earthly limitation, all hers to enjoy for that one day—and she'd let out such a joyful whoop that she'd startled Jude.

Swallowing that excitement now, Amalise looked at Phillip and scanned the studio. "When do we start?"

"How about tomorrow?"

She nodded, still anchoring her thoughts as he glanced over his shoulder at the windows.

"We'll begin at the same time, about four o'clock when the light's right, just before the sun goes down." He curved his arm around her shoulders and leaned close. "It's the blue hour. I'm always lonely at this time of day, aren't you?"

AFTER WORK ON THE portrait began, Gina was irritable. Amalise had been late for work three times already, and so tonight she'd doubled her efforts to make amends, urging Gina to leave early and let her close the café.

At midnight, as the last customers were leaving, Jude walked in. Amalise hurried over and threw her arms around his neck.

He grinned. "How's life?" When she let him go, he slipped an arm around her waist. "If you're finished up here, let's go find some music, someplace where we can let go. I just got in."

"Can't," she said, disappearing into the kitchen. When she reappeared with the book bag, she crossed the room and, with a gentle shove, pushed him through the door. Turning out the lights, she pulled it closed behind her and locked it. "I'm tired. Walk home with me, and I'll make you a cup of coffee."

"Oh, come on. I've been in Pilottown for two weeks." He took the book bag from her.

She hesitated and he nudged her. She couldn't help it; she smiled. "Just for a little while." Studies could wait one hour.

Walking toward the river, turning right on Decatur, she told him about Phillip and the portrait he was painting.

He mugged a face. "Is this the professor who did the cartoons at Porter's?"

"They're not cartoons," she snapped, and he laughed.

LaCasa's was a raucous bar located directly opposite the darkened and recently abandoned Jax Brewery, consisting of three adjoining rooms frequented mostly by seamen just off the ships, women who roamed the docks, locals with a taste for loud Latin music, and occasional university students out on a binge.

Amalise and Jude entered through the door at the corner. They squeezed their way through the crowd milling around the long bar in the first room and into the empty middle room. Here the floor was slick with beer and cheap wine and other questionable liquids, and dank odors permeated this room. But it was dimly lit and a little less noisy. The band this night had settled in the third room. Latin music, heavy on the drums but with a good beat, blared through the wide-open doorway.

Jude found a table in a corner, deposited Amalise, and signaled that he'd be right back. A Tab with ice for her, she called out. He'd order ginger ale himself. His father was a drunk, and Jude had learned the lesson early on. She rested her chin on her knuckles to wait.

Five minutes later Jude returned with the drinks. Taking a seat beside Amalise, he poured the Tab over ice for her, picked up his bottle, and settled back.

"Now tell me more about the portrait this guy is painting. The professor. Where is this event taking place?"

The drums in the next room reached a new level. She raised her voice. "At the university. His studio's in the art school."

Jude straightened. He followed her eyes to the activity in the third room. "Didn't you say that he was married?"

Jude's voice held a touch of steel that made her look off and fix her eyes upon the band. "Yes. I'd thought he was at first. But he's not."

"Not what?"

"Married!"

Jude nodded. "Well, I'd like to meet him."

"I want you to, Jude." She sipped her drink. "You'll like him, I think." Jude would understand a man like Phillip, so absorbed in his art, his teaching, his students. Jude poured all of his energy into everything he did. Over time she was certain she'd discover that same quality in Phillip, the quiet strength that Jude had.

"How are you managing the time? With your job and school and studying?"

She stole a look at him. There it was. That's what was bothering him. A flutter of anxiety ran through her as she thought of the classes she was missing to pose for this picture. The sleepless nights, playing catch-up on her studies, Gina's constant irritation as she appeared later and later for work during the dinner rush at the café.

A headache squeezed the back of her neck. Maybe Jude was right to worry. What was she doing arranging her time around Phillip Sharp instead of classes? She'd thought she could manage at first, squeezing in the time for posing here and there. But it was all out of control now and she didn't know how to pull things back together. The painting just went on and on and she didn't know how to end it. Because, to be honest, she didn't *want* to end it. She didn't want to lose Phillip, but she wouldn't derail her career either.

She wanted them both. And she could handle that.

She met Jude's gaze. "I'm managing." When he studied her features, she set her jaw and looked away. One thing about Jude: he wouldn't press.

She didn't want to think about Phillip and class schedules and time right now, so she put on a bright smile and turned back to him. "Tell me what's been going on downriver, Jude."

He shrugged. "Things ran pretty much on a steady course." He lifted the bottle and took a drink. "Had a dead ship to tow one day. Engine failure. Took six tugs—one ahead, two each side, and a tail tug on the stern."

"You had to coordinate?"

"That's my job. When we reached the jetties, one of the port side tugs called, worried about rough seas. Wanted us to throw the lines off and cut him loose."

"And then what?"

"He was in a key position, needed to stay alongside. I talked him into holding course. Told him any time he felt in danger to let me know." He turned his eyes to her. "Just let me know. I'd be there."

Amalise lowered her eyes, picked up the glass, and took a sip.

Jude tapped his fingers on the table to the beat of the music in the other room. Amalise smiled and he smiled back.

But later, walking home, Jude grew quiet. She tucked her arm in his, and they strolled along without saying anything. Perhaps he was disappointed in her spending so much time with Phillip. But once the two men got to know each other, Jude would understand, she was certain. That certainty vanished when they arrived at the apartment and Jude refused to come inside as usual for coffee. He merely planted a cool kiss on her forehead. Said he'd see her later.

"When?"

He didn't know. "How's your schedule this week? I may have trouble getting down here in the next few days."

Better that way. Her schedule was erratic right now, to say the least. "It's not necessary. Gina's letting me out early for the next few nights. Business is slow." That was true. Gina had found her sound asleep, head on her arms, at the table in the back of the café kitchen earlier this evening.

He nodded. There were things to be done, he said. A meeting tomorrow night with a contractor about work on the duplex he owned on State Street uptown. Errands to run, people to see.

With a heavy heart Amalise watched Jude hurry away down the street. She wanted to call him back, to tell him how thrilling it was to have an artist like Phillip, a professor at the university, interested in painting her picture, and more, interested in her. She wanted to tell Jude how unusual Phillip was, what passion he had for his art, including woodcarving.

Suddenly she saw again the cut on his arm. And though she couldn't explain why, she shivered.

Chapter Eight

Something's different about Amalise, Father. I can't decide if she's excited and happy or if she's worried. I can hear it in her voice when she calls home—a tension that tightens her throat, jumps the sound up a notch too high, fragile, like the sound you get when you tap a crystal glass with a spoon. She says everything's just fine and I'm trying not to worry. But even so . . . a mother worries.

Ahhh . . .

Kneeling in the garden, Mama reached for the trowel and shoved it into the ground with both hands, uprooting the tough vines one at a time. She had to dig around and pull. Lifting her eyes, she looked at the stubborn brown vines, remembering how they'd looked years ago ruffled with sweet peas, fragrant delicate curls of pink and red and blue and white. Amalise loved those flowers. They'd run wild in the past few years when she'd abandoned the dry yard after William purchased the washing machine and dryer and turned the laundry shed into storage.

She sat back on her heels and swiped her forehead, suddenly feeling tired and a little sad. But she'd felt the need to work hard today to take her mind off her fears for Amalise, and this needed doing. These vines were out of control. She gave one a hard yank.

Look out for her, Lord. The things we read in the newspapers and see on the television at night about what's happening in the city!

Any city is like that I guess, and I suppose I wasn't paying so much attention to the news before we let her go. But Lord! Murders . . . other things I can't bring myself to think about. Please keep her safe, Father. Watch out for our little girl. I'm beginning to think that maybe Amalise is keeping something from us. Some problem that she doesn't want to talk about just yet.

But a mother knows.

Chapter Nine

A malise lay stretched across the couch in the silent studio. She'd been frozen in this position for over an hour, was bored, restless . . . when Phillip asked her to remove her clothes. He made this request casually, without looking up. When she stared, he went on.

"Because I've almost finished the picture," he said, dabbing the brush on the canvas.

Amalise wasn't sure she'd heard right.

"It's called figure modeling," he said when she didn't answer. He glanced up for a half second, then went on painting as if he'd just said that today was Wednesday.

She looked at him without moving.

His eyes met hers over the easel. "Are you really worried about this, Ama?" His voice carried a hint of amusement. "Would you hesitate to undress for your doctor if that were necessary?"

"Of course not."

"Would your mother worry if you did?"

"This isn't the same."

"But it is." He set the paintbrush down and stepped back from the picture. "Nudity is necessary to art." He folded his arms and raised his eyes to the ceiling. "It's essential. Do I have to take you through the art museum to prove my point?"

"Your other work isn't—"

"My work evolves. If I kept painting the same thing over and over again . . . well"—he shook his head and threw up his hands—"I could find a Xerox machine and accomplish that sort of repetition with much less work. But it wouldn't be art." He dropped his arms to his sides, came to her, and knelt, taking her hands in his.

"Ama." He tilted his head back and looked up at her. His voice gentled, touching her deep inside. "I want to paint you as you were created. The female form is a glorious work of art. Don't hide. Trust me."

Though she'd lived through the sixties, she was not a child of the sixties. She looked at Phillip, and his look was understanding but layered with disappointment. His hands were warm. His eyes were so sincere. He was an artist.

She faltered.

"God doesn't make mistakes. Isn't that what you said? We were born naked . . . so isn't that a natural state?" His eyes didn't move from hers. "I'd say if there's any sin in what I'm asking of you, it's in the eye of the beholder."

Her heart stirred. "Do you believe? In God?"

"I'd like to." He pressed her hands between his. "Maybe you can help me with that." He brushed her cheek gently with the back of his hand. "But I'm asking you right now to open your mind and understand that we . . . you and I together . . . we're creating beauty on this canvas. This *is* natural."

For a split-second she hesitated. It was *before* sin that Eve went unclothed, not after. But she knew that she was only rationalizing.

When she still didn't answer, he let go of her hands and stood. His brows drew together as he gazed at her. "Do this for me?" His voice was low, soothing. "If you don't trust me, then all the effort we've put into making this picture will be for nothing. Wasted."

She looked up at him and swallowed. She didn't want to lose him. And yet . . . "I'm sorry, Phillip." Ahhh . . . would she lose him now? "I can't."

He pressed his hand across his forehead. Seconds passed as he studied her, his expression sheer frustration. Then he turned on his heels and walked back to the easel. Eyes focused on the table holding brushes, paints, oil, and a dirty cloth, he sat, chose a brush, held it up, and looked at her.

"It's all right, Ama." She heard his sigh from across the room. "Go ahead and get back into position." With a glance at the widows to his right: "Hurry. The light will soon change."

TODAY PHILLIP WANTED TO talk before they began work.

Amalise glanced at the windows. "What about the light?"

"This is more important." Phillip lounged on one end of the couch; Amalise sat at the other, facing him. "I want you to understand why I asked you to trust me yesterday."

Her heart sank.

"Don't worry. I've just been thinking about . . . how little you really know me."

She nodded. "You haven't told me much about yourself."

"There's a reason." He pulled a pack of cigarettes and a lighter from his pocket and looked at her. "The first day we started working on the picture. Remember? You asked about those wood carvings." He nodded toward the table where the miniature figures were displayed.

"Yes."

He gave her a long look, seeming to gather courage, then he exhaled the next words. "I'm going to tell you something I've never told anyone else." His eyes flicked to the wood carvings as he went on. "I . . . care about you, Ama. And I haven't cared about anyone in a long time."

She held her breath.

"I trust you. So . . . I want you to understand why my art is so important to me. Why . . . I believe . . . that sometimes it takes precedence over old protocols, rules . . . old ways."

Slowly she released her breath and nodded.

He sucked on the cigarette. Watched the smoke curl toward the ceiling. When he looked back at her, his eyes gleamed. Were those tears?

"I started carving when I was a boy, maybe five, six." His voice grew thick. With another puff, he dropped his lids. "I was so lonely.

Carving was a way to let myself know that I was still there." He gave her a quick glance and dropped his eyes again. "That I was alive."

With a self-deprecating little laugh, he shrugged. "You see, carving was real. I could take little pieces of wood, and hold them in my hands, and turn them into something else. I'd created something. It meant that I was real, too." He pushed up from the couch, found an ashtray on the table near the easel, and crushing the cigarette out, returned with the ashtray to the couch.

She fought to keep the frown from her expression. What was he saying? She straightened, sitting with her back straight and legs crossed, watching him. "Where were your parents?"

"Mostly they traveled. But I seldom saw them even when they were home." Stretching out, he crooked one arm behind his head and looked at the ceiling. "They were gone most of the time. Him on business. Her?" His tone turned bitter. "She'd follow him anywhere he went." He snorted and glanced at Amalise. "I guess she just couldn't live without him. She existed for him. He existed for work. In fact, I'm surprised either of them ever remember my name."

Seconds passed as she absorbed his words. "I'm sorry, Phillip."

A broken sound came from deep inside of him. A smothered sob? She couldn't tell. She sat very still, waiting.

"I was always alone." His tone was flat now, devoid of emotion. "Raised by nannies. One after the other came, those interchangeable women." He shook his head. "There were too many to remember their names so I called them all Nanny."

A shadow dulled the usual amber light in the room. He pulled out another cigarette and lit it in the gloom, looking down, balancing the ashtray on his chest. She was quiet as he went on, smoke drifting around him while he talked, avoiding her eyes.

"The nannies raised me." A red flush mottled his neck and rose to his cheeks. "Not Mother. Not Robert, my father. Mother and Robert couldn't remember the nannies' names either." At that he fell silent and tucked his chin under.

She formed her words with care. "You were never alone, Phillip. God understands our prayers, even when we don't speak them. Even when the thought is deep inside, hidden even from us. He knows what's in our hearts."

His lips curled. He studied the burning ash of the cigarette between his fingers. When he answered, his voice was low and strained. "Maybe so." He glanced at her from the corners of his eyes. "Maybe someday I'll understand."

Filled with pity, she heard the shudder in his deep sigh, like a small child does after weeping.

"By the time I was five, I'd figured it out. Before that . . . they'd leave, and I'd wait for days in my bedroom, expecting them to return any minute." When he looked at her, his eyes held the pain of memories that jolted. "Waiting for them to come home . . . and the nannies." He stabbed the cigarette into the ashtray on his chest. "I hated those old women. Turned out the lights so they'd go away. That usually worked."

"How terrible." What would it do to a child to know he wasn't loved? She took a deep breath. "How long did that go on?"

"Until I was old enough not to care anymore." He paused. "I got used to it. That's when I began carving. It passed the time and . . . you can carve alone." With a small shrug he flipped his hand as if swatting a fly. "There were shelves and shelves of woodcarvings in my room."

She twisted to look at the ones in the studio. "Are these some of them?"

"No. I threw those away."

Her brows drew together. "Why?"

With a shrug: "Why not? I was leaving."

She felt him watching as she sank back against the cushion, filling in the blanks—imagining him alone year after year carving those miniature wooden figures, enduring those nameless nannies, women paid to care for him. She thought of the cut he'd made across his arm with the carving knife.

Understanding bloomed, filled her. Phillip needed her. He trusted her.

His eyes moved to the table of carvings. Heaving a sigh, he picked up the ashtray on his chest, straightened, and swung his legs off the couch. His feet hit the floor. "Enough of my story. Let's get to work."

THE NEXT AFTERNOON WHEN she arrived, a package wrapped in white tissue paper lay on the couch. Phillip stood by the easel, eyes twinkling, as she picked it up and turned to him. "What's this?"

He shrugged, smiling. "Open it up."

She sank onto the couch and pulled off the wrapping. No ribbon or tape, so it was easy. With an exclamation, she held the dress up by the slender embroidered straps. It was lovely—satin in the palest shade of gold. The embroidery, small flowers almost invisible against the cloth, flowed from the straps across the heart-cut décolletage. The material was soft and supple, shining, simple, with a flare of needle-thin pleats of sheerest lace at the bottom.

"Do you like it?"

She'd never seen a dress so beautiful. "Of course." She folded it up and set it down on the wrapping paper. "But I can't keep this, Phillip."

He laughed. "Nonsense. It's for posing. I'm accepting your rules, Ama." He shoved back the chair, rounded the easel, and strode to her. Setting his hands lightly upon her shoulders, he looked down into her eyes. "I bought it for you. It's perfect for the picture."

"But . . ."

He picked up the dress and handed it to her. "Look at the color and texture, perfect for the portrait." Releasing her, he returned to the easel. His voice was casual, confident. "I found it in a shop in the Quarter. Just wear it for the picture, even if you don't want to keep it." Sitting in the chair, he picked up the brush.

She looked down at the dress. "All right."

He nodded toward the door. "There's a restroom right down the hall where you can change."

Holding the dress, she stood.

"And barefoot. No shoes," he added.

He busied himself at the easel while Amalise stood there, holding the dress draped across her arms. He had never let her see the picture. Wanted her to be surprised when it was finished. Kept it covered when they weren't working. Turning, she studied the couch with the patterned cloth Phillip had draped over it—because the colors would be wonderful for her, he'd said—and she visualized the gold dress against this background.

Yes. She understood.

When she returned, barefoot, clothed in satin, yet covered, Phillip looked up from the easel.

"It's a little big," she said, feeling shy as she smoothed the fabric.

"That won't show in the picture." He smiled and gestured to the couch. "You look beautiful." His head bent as he went back to work with the brush.

She walked to the couch and, smiling, resumed the pose he'd set from the first day. The dress felt wonderful,

Phillip studied her over the top of the easel, set down the brush, and walked to the couch. Bending over her, he rearranged the patterned cloth behind her, letting it fall in loose folds in places. His knuckles brushed her bare shoulders as he did this and chills rose, but he straightened when he finished, inspected her again, and returned to his place behind the easel.

Raising the paintbrush, he gave her a thumbs-up.

She smiled to herself as he painted. He'd managed to solve the problem with consideration and finesse. It was almost as if he'd passed a test.

FOR THE NEXT FEW days Amalise hurried from the law school building to the art school, from classes to Phillip's studio, and afterward, on to the café for work. Then home to study, and afterward three or four hours of sleep. Her lids grew heavy in the classroom. Half-moon shadows formed under her eyes. Guilt surged as she skipped some classes to meet Phillip's schedule, according to the time of the light.

Sometimes Phillip was in a quiet mood. And on those days, in the silence of the large studio, she would fall asleep. If it didn't interfere with that day's work on the painting, he wouldn't wake her until quitting time.

Occasionally Phillip felt like talking. On those days he told her more about his lonely years. She wondered again and again how such things could happen. She wasn't a foolish child who didn't understand the nature of evil in the world. Many times she'd talked that question over with Jude, and with Abba, but usually on the level of grand scales of misery in remote places, where poverty and hopelessness and disease ravaged thousands, like the war in Vietnam, and you feel so overwhelmed and helpless and guilty in your own comfort, watching all of this on the screen at the Regal Theater or on TV news.

No one had ever seen details of war, moment by moment, played out on television screens in their living rooms before. Never. It was shocking to sit in comfort inside four walls and watch the savage cruelty before your eyes—innocents, like children, injured, orphaned, starving. She knew to pray, of course. And she believed in the power of prayer with all her heart. But what else exactly could you do to help those children in Vietnam or Cambodia. Or to help even one child, now grown, like Phillip?

What exactly could . . . should . . . she do?

What you do for the least of them, you do for Abba.

She struggled not to weep when Phillip talked about his childhood, and her sympathy seemed to cause him to open up, to confide more and more each day, as if she were the valve that opened a spigot from which burst his stored up pain.

Abba. Abba?

Phillip's trust, his growing comfort with her, became her gift to him. Slowly she began to believe that this was why they'd met. *She was* the answer to the question, for Phillip. She could show him that he was not alone. He needed her.

"I'M COLD."

Phillip looked up from behind the easel. "Not much longer, Ama. Have patience. We're creating something beautiful together that will last."

His words recalled the miniatures he'd told her about, the ones he'd carved when he was a boy and had thrown away. Those were gone, but she was here now. She was special to him, she knew. Warmth flooded her at the thought and a nudge of soft emotion, a stirred-up feeling that she couldn't name.

Time passed and his detached manner calmed her thoughts. The room had grown chilled again and damp. She watched him dip the brush, first into one pot of paint and then another, mixing them on the pallet. A half hour more stiffened her muscles. Bones began to ache. She shifted her weight, but in a monotone he told her to stop moving around. Sometimes he would lean back from the easel and study the picture of her in the pale golden dress from one angle, then another, and that soft-cotton feeling inside would rise again.

"I'm tired," she said after awhile.

"Have patience." He stepped back to examine his work. "I've almost got it." He dipped the brush into paint and stroked the canvas in a loving way.

Amalise stifled a sigh. If a fence artist like Mouse took this long on his portraits, he'd starve to death. The thought of Mouse, who seemed to think of Phillip as some dark force, made her cringe. Her arm was numb and she flexed it.

At the easel his hand stilled. He looked up and frowned, waiting, holding the paintbrush midair. Her arm dropped back into the position, and he resumed work.

With growing boredom she watched him dip the brush, first into one swirl of paint and then another. Her muscles and bones ached now. She shifted her weight, but without looking up he told her to stop moving around. Sometimes he would lean back from the easel and gaze at the picture in the way that she wanted him to look at her.

Amalise sighed. The pillows now seemed to absorb her, soft, cradling, taking on the curve of her back. In the chilly room they took on her body heat. "May I close my eyes?"

"Yes."

She let her eyelids close and imagined herself floating, bathed in a warm yellow light. Slowly the room and Phillip disappeared, and she dreamed of lights and shadows moving around her, of fishing with Jude while paint colors swirled through the air. After a while Jude became Phillip, and he was standing close, tickling her with a feather, and she was in a foreign place, cloudy and gray, everything vague, as if veiled in mist.

The feather drifted down her neck as the gray dream dissolved. Under half-closed lids she saw the blur of Phillip standing over her in the waning light as his finger traced the line of her neck. Her heart began to race.

"No."

But he lowered himself to the couch, slowly pulled her to him, and their lips met. She could feel the heat from his skin, the intangible connection growing between them in the kiss, something she'd never felt with any man before.

Oh . . . no, no . . . no . . . Hands against his chest, she pushed, resisting, but he bent his head so that his lips brushed her ear, and she could feel his breath, and the hair rose on her neck, on her arms, as he whispered over and over the words of love—Ama, Ama, you belong to me. I love you. I need you. You're mine—extinguishing the candle in her mind.

Dream and reality flowed together, illusion, dissolving her mind's calibration of what was real, what was right. *This was where dreams can take you,* the observer whispered, *to the moment you'd imagined, just as it was on the screen of the Regal Theater.*

PHILLIP SLEPT.

Light in the studio had faded. Amalise stood by the couch wearing her regular clothes. The golden dream dress was carefully folded and placed on the arm roll at the other end of the couch. A strange revulsion that she recognized as guilt warred with an overwhelming emotion that seemed to bind her to Phillip. Like heavy water his need pressed around her, a new weight that she'd not felt before—a nurturing as strong as any she imagined she'd ever have for her child, a fierce resolve to protect him, to help him. He trusted her.

The conflicting emotions shook her. Was this love?

Maybe. Yes . . . she didn't know. Whatever it was she felt for Phillip was a powerful, wrenching emotion. Even so, watching Phillip sleep, his chest rising and falling with even breath, she was conscious that she'd crossed a line she hadn't meant to cross, and in that instant she wished more than anything that she was still that little girl in Marianus and that Jude would come, and they would sit together on the swing on the back porch and everything would be as it was before she'd crossed the line, just as before, just as the sun rose and set over the bayou back behind the house in Marianus in the same way every day.

The cry in her heart came unbidden: *Abba, Abba, what have I done?*

Hugging herself, she turned and gazed about, at the easels and the paints and the row of mullioned windows glazed with a thin layer of dirt that she'd not noticed before.

Her eyes stopped on the easel with the picture that had brought them together, she and Phillip. Still, she wanted this to last. She wanted this dream to last!

Abba. I know I've asked for many things before. But I think I'm in love with this man . . . . Is this love? He needs me so. Is this love? She squeezed her eyes closed. *Please understand . . . You've said we should lead the lost sheep to the fold. Well, I will do that. I will bring him to You.*

But even as she prayed, she knew what she was doing. Only Abraham could get away with this kind of negotiation. Whipsawed by emotions, she walked to the end of the couch where she'd been sitting and retrieved her book bag. She had to leave . . .

And then she would lose him.

"Perhaps you're the answer to my unspoken prayers when I was a boy, Ama."

She started. He was awake. How had he known what she was thinking? Remembering, blushing, she stepped back, distancing herself.

"Let's go find something to eat," he said.

Yes. Yes. The words were there. All she had to do was speak them, and she wouldn't lose Phillip Sharp. *We'll go somewhere quiet. There will be a small table with candles, and we can talk.*

But instead she hugged the book bag and glanced at the door. "I have to get to the cafe. Gina will be waiting."

Phillip made a sound in the back of his throat as he rose, and she saw the tightening of his lips before he smiled. "Well, I'm hungry, and I'm flat out of cash, babe." He reached out for her, putting his hands on her shoulders and gazing down into her eyes. "Can you loan me a few dollars before you go? I left my wallet at home."

"Sure." She wanted the moment to last. She wanted his hands to stay on her shoulders, right where they were. She wanted him to continue looking at her in that way.

But she braced herself. Principles, beliefs, aren't things that you just shove aside like old clothes that no longer fit. She didn't need Mama or Dad, or even Jude, to remind her of that.

Ah, but this was difficult. So hard.

He stood aside while she dug into her purse, struggling to hold back the tears. If she let go, she might not have the strength to leave. As she pulled the money from her wallet and handed it to him, she stepped back, away from him. Turning, she walked toward the door.

"Ama!" His voice ratcheted up the scale. "Wait!"

She halted. "I can't come back here again." She looked at him over her shoulder.

His brows arched, his eyes widened, and he moved toward her, arms spread wide. "But we have to finish the picture at least!"

"No." Shaking her head, she turned to face him, clinging to the book bag. Her throat was thick, tight. She was walking away, a complete rejection in Phillip's mind. Another rejection. And if this feeling inside of wanting to be with him, of wanting to take care of him and make him happy . . . if this was love, she was giving it up.

For an instant he froze, seeming not to understand. Then his jaw tightened, he lowered his brows, and drew back. Shoulders hiked up around his neck. He stuck his hands in his pockets and tilted his head.

"You're mine, Ama. This connection between us is a power." His voice shook. "I felt it the moment I saw you standing in the gallery looking at my pictures. I knew right away that you were mine."

Careful, Amalise.

"I'm not."

Leave now and don't look back. Don't think. Just go.

The click of her boots seemed to echo around her as she pushed through the double doors and, like a shadow of herself, hurried on down the hallway. *I want him, Abba.* She answered herself with an internal sigh.

I know. I know. But not like this.

Chapter Ten

J ude saw it right away. Amalise's face was drawn. Her smile was flat, and her eyes had lost that sparkle. He was sitting at the café bar waiting for her. It was two o'clock on a Saturday afternoon, and her shift was ending. As she moved among the customers wearing that lost expression, he knew.

Something was terribly wrong.

He glanced at his watch—his two-week break was up. But instead of taking the bus down to Pilottown, he'd gotten the promise of a lift on a crew boat headed out to the rigs. That would give him a few more hours in town. When he caught her eye, he patted the seat on the stool next to him. She nodded and walked into the kitchen, untying the apron. Frowning, he squared his elbows on the bar and gazed at the mirrored reflection of the room behind him.

"She's a hard worker; tougher than she looks." Henry leaned back against the counter. He picked up a bar towel and idly stretched it between his hands.

Jude looked up. "Amalise?"

He nodded.

After a beat Jude said, "I've always looked out for her. She was six when we met. I found her getting pounded by chinaberries. She was huddled over this little mutt she'd found, surrounded by a group of older boys. The brats had them penned in and wouldn't let her pass." He linked his hands together and cracked his knuckles. "She was trying to shelter the puppy. Ever been hit by one of those chinaberries?"

Henry shook his head.

Hands dropped to the bar. "Her arms were bruised for days. Little round bruises." He traced an invisible circle on the counter in front of him with one finger. "She wouldn't give up that mutt to those kids, though." He smiled. "I got her out of there, the dog too."

"Fight?"

"One of them." He chuckled. "Hung that one up on a picket fence by his belt."

Henry laughed. Twirled the bar towel into a twist.

"Last I saw of him, he was two feet off the ground and kicking." Jude smiled again at the memory. "We were broke. The judge, her dad, made work for me after that cutting grass, cleaning boats." He paused. "Kid stuff, you know. But I needed the money. The judge and Maraine . . . eh, her mother, they helped out like that."

"Good people." Henry shook out the bar towel and dropped it on the edge of the sink. His eyes roved over the café. "Good country people."

Jude nodded. "Yeah. My mother passed when I was ten. My old man . . ."

Forget it. The only worthwhile thing Pop ever did was marry Mom. Home was Amalise and the judge and Maraine.

Jude's fingers rapped the counter. He had few memories of his mother before the cancer struck. In the end she was tired and thin as a dry twig, skin turning gray, hair disappearing day by day. Sometimes in bed at night he could hear her crying while Pop shouted, arguing, she and Pop, sick as she was. Pop never explained when she died. Just grew even more sour after she was gone, crusty and silent. Only got worse as he got older, coming and going, sometimes gone for days and staggering home, mean and drunk.

Amalise walked over. She sat on the stool beside him, and Henry drifted off.

In the mirror he looked at her reflection. "Is something wrong?"

"No." She shook her head, fingers rapping on the counter. "I've just been busy."

"Umm. How's the picture coming along?"

He saw the spasm, a small defensive jerk of her chin. "It's finished." She swung around to face the room. "It's good." She braced her elbows on the bar behind her.

He spun around too. He hated the thought of Amalise painted flat, cartoonish on that canvas, he realized. Surprised at the force of his thoughts, he leaned back against the bar and gazed over the room. "You say this guy's a professor?"

She nodded.

"Where's he from?"

"New York." Jude cut his eyes at her, but she just shrugged. "I'll be right back."

He watched as she walked over to Gina, said something, and went into the kitchen.

IN THE KITCHEN AMALISE wound her way around the busy cook and his helper to a nook on the other side of the room that was hidden from view by the large storage freezer. There she pulled a chair from under a small plastic table piled with receipts and account books and sat, dropping her face into her hands. The heat and noise in the kitchen were giving her a headache. The odor of fried food wafted toward her, hot grease and fish and hamburger meat.

A bright light overhead annoyed her. She squeezed her eyes shut and reminded herself that Jude was waiting for her right this minute. Jude, not some stranger, and she had to get control over her emotions. She hadn't seen Phillip in three days, since she'd left the studio in such a rush. She supposed he'd finished the picture without her. The thought caused her to slump forward, arms on the table to cushion her face. Pain ripped through her midsection, squeezing.

Would she ever see him again? She'd made the right choice, but it brought her nothing but misery. Perhaps she'd see him someday again, and they could start over. He'd said he loved her, hadn't he? He'd said that he needed her, that she belonged to him, hadn't he?

Her throat tightened and she fought back tears. What was happening to her life?

Get hold of yourself, Amalise!

She sat up. Rubbed her eyes. She should think of school; there was make-up work to do this afternoon. And Jude was waiting on the other side of the kitchen wall; he was leaving today, and she wanted to spend a little time with him before he left. At least Jude was always Jude. You knew where you were with him. Raking her fingers through her hair, she pushed back the chair, hesitated, and inhaled.

All right, Amalise. One step at a time. Stand up. Smile. And go on back to Jude.

Jude's feet hit the floor in front of his stool when she approached. He reached down for his duffel bag and swung it up and over his shoulder. "Let's go down to Seven Seas and play some Ping-Pong."

Amalise glanced at her watch. She should study, but it was Saturday, and she needed to relax, just for a little while, then she'd crack the books when Jude was gone and really be able to focus. "Good idea." Did Phillip like the game? She thrust thoughts of Phillip away.

"Let's do that." With a wave to Gina, she followed Jude out onto the sidewalk.

They stopped to talk to Mouse before starting across the square where a tour guide at the entrance to Pirate's Alley held up a fringed purple-and-gold Mardi Gras second-line umbrella, twirling it, gathering his flock around him for a lecture. The umbrella glittered in the sunlight. As they walked along and Jude told her how he was changing the house he'd bought uptown, the thought trained through her mind: *Phillip loves me. He said he needs me.*

So, listening with half her mind, she said "ummm" and "that's nice" when Jude paused and focused her eyes on the Mardi Gras umbrella dancing ahead in the yellow sunshine. When the umbrella disappeared into the cathedral, she switched her thoughts to final exams coming up after Thanksgiving. But remembering how much time she'd spent with Phillip over the last few weeks instead of studying, her stomach plummeted, and she envisioned herself in the classroom looking down at the exam booklet—unprepared.

Black clouds of pigeons rose as they approached the entrance to the park, and hordes of small children inside the fence shrieked and chased the birds when they descended. Ice cream cart bells rang, and street musicians strummed beat-up old guitars and sang in raw, whiskey voices, hoping for coins. An organ grinder's monkey wore a green-and-yellow-striped jacket and a straw hat. His owner sat on the curb in front of the cathedral, squeezing an accordion while the monkey danced. As they strolled along, slowly her spirits lifted.

A clown with a yellow straw wig and a painted smile juggled colored balls and called out to Amalise as they passed by. She laughed when he lifted one hand to wave and the spinning balls came down, bouncing one after the other onto the wide pavestones. The clown grimaced and tore after the balls, dodging around children who had stopped to watch. Beside her, Jude shook his head, but as they turned to walk on, a car screeched to a halt before the children, the horn sounded, and a red-and-white Lucky Dog cart rolled to a stop in the middle of the swarm of people. The driver yelled at the clown and shook his fist. Customers at the Chart House across the street hung over the upstairs balcony to watch.

Amalise glanced over her shoulder at the melee, squinting through the bright haze of sunshine at the driver of the car flinging open his door and lurching from the front seat. It was then, as the crowd gave way and parted, that Phillip's face emerged from the others, and for one instant their eyes met. She could see, even from the distance, his eyes were fierce. She blinked, halted, turned, and stared. The crowd closed and Phillip disappeared.

Jude stopped, following her gaze past the infuriated driver and hot dog vendor and on to the clown still chasing the tumbling balls. "He'd better keep running," he said in a laconic tone as the yellow wig disappeared behind the milling crowd, the car, and the hot dog cart.

Amalise shaded her eyes with her hand, searching the faces for Phillip.

"Come on." Jude pulled her along with him. "Let's get out of here. I only have a couple of hours before the crew boat leaves."

With a backward glance, Amalise followed. Was it really Phillip she'd seen? And, if so, why had he disappeared? Was he hiding? Playing some kind of game? Or watching? Had he come down here to find her and spotted her with Jude? She tensed, hearing Phillip's voice in her mind.

Ama, Ama, you are mine.

By the time they reached the sidewalk shaded by overhead balconies on the other side of the square, she could feel Phillip's eyes following her. She was certain he was there. Once she glanced back, but the driver and hot dog vendor were arguing, gesturing, and shouting, and the crowd had thinned. Phillip was nowhere in sight. A cloud drifted past the sun, casting shadows.

Don't be foolish. But a vise gripped her neck, and confusing emotions welled up inside. Jude gave her a questioning glance, and she forced a smile.

At Seven Seas they stopped first at the bar in the dark front room for ginger ale and Tab, then carried the bottles to the courtyard in back. There was a Ping-Pong table in the courtyard and a game was in progress, and there was a rise of wooden bleachers for spectators. They stood watching the game for a few minutes before climbing up the bleachers to wait their turn to play.

Phillip would not like this place, Amalise reflected as she lowered herself beside Jude and rested her feet on the lower bench. She brushed ice chips from the bottleneck and sipped, watching the small white ball bounce back and forth between the player.

Thwack!

Phillip, classes, work missed . . .

Thwack, thwack!

The plan . . . her dream, and Mama's . . .

Thwack!

. . . back to Phillip, always back to Phillip.

The shade was cool, but heat shimmered on the pavement around the Ping-Pong table. After a moment she leaned back against the bench behind her and rubbed the cold bottle against her cheek.

Closing her eyes, she imagined Phillip the way she liked best to think of him, working behind his easel in the studio with the pale autumn light filtering through the windows high above. For an instant it occurred to her that these memories, luminous in her mind, might be enhanced by time, imagination, and her mood, but the idea didn't linger. A sudden strong desire struck—to be alone so she could cry. She wanted someone to talk to. She wanted to talk to Jude, but he wouldn't understand.

Nor, if he knew the whole truth, would he approve.

"What's wrong?" Jude lifted the bottle to his lips. She opened her eyes and looked at him. "Are you worried I'll beat you again?" He grinned and looked at the Ping-Pong table.

Amalise lifted her Tab and took a swallow. Tears rose and she fought them back. The words exploded before she could stop them. "Jude. I think I'm in love."

Jude stared. Seconds passed. "With that painter?" When she didn't answer, he shook his head. "You hardly know him."

"I think I'll go on home." Amalise tried to steady her faltering voice. "I need to study. I need to be alone." She longed to get her life under control. She stood without looking at him, gave his shoulder a gentle shove—*it's not you, Jude, it's me*—and climbed down the bleachers. "See you when you get back."

JUDE SLUMPED ON THE bench, dangling the bottle between his knees as he watched Amalise disappear through the door. She'd just met this man. How could she know enough about him to be in love? With a rising wave of unfocused anger, he took a gulp of the drink and stared after her. His gut hurt as if she'd punched him. And why should he care? She was a grown woman, smart, making her own decisions.

But images of those strange paintings Amalise had taken him to see rose in his mind. He'd hated them—the deliberate degradation of the women, the desolation he'd seen in their faces, in their bodies. Amalise was not like them. She'd always been sparkling, happy, loving—innocent of such things.

Eyeing the ball bouncing across the table below, he tried to order his thoughts, tried to imagine Amalise with the man who'd painted those pictures.

Bile rose in the back of his throat.

He frowned as another worry reared its head: Amalise would be an easy mark for a man without a conscience. She'd lived all her life in Marianus, population twenty-five hundred give or take a few, where her father was the parish judge and she was the judge's only child. He could see her now at seven or eight . . . after Mass on Sundays with

Maraine and the judge and him, wearing white gloves and that funny little hat with ribbons, smiling up at him as she smoothed her skirt and waited for his sweet talk.

She'd always been different. She had a few good friends at school but went her own way most of the time and seemed content to spend her time with books and with him when he was around. Except for him, she hung around mostly with adults—the bailiffs at the courthouse; Sheriff Conkle and his sister, Leanne, whom he deputized during lunch each day; old Tom down at the bait shop—ninety if he was a day, but Amalise loved his stories. Dr. Bernie Gilbert, an old family friend, and Mrs. A. P. Prieur at the drugstore—that's what Amalise had always called her, Mrs. A. P. Prieur. They all doted on Amalise. So Amalise trusted. She had no reason not to.

She wouldn't recognize a double-dealer if he showed her the marked cards.

Jude had been her tutor, her best friend, her protector. He saw himself huddled beside her at night at Maraine's old desk, explaining algebra to someone who always wanted to know the *why* of things. He was good at mathematics. She wasn't, but she was a perfectionist and driven. He almost laughed now, thinking how she'd wear an eraser down to the nub so that no trace of a mistake was left when she made corrections. She always saw the bright side of things, the daughter who could do no wrong so far as the judge and Maraine were concerned. Smart as the judge. Ambitious, determined, and stoic like her mother.

A Ping-Pong ball bounced off the rough bleachers in front of him, and Jude snapped out of the spell. He glanced at his watch. An hour left before losing his ride to Pilottown. He picked up his bag and climbed down the bleachers, then went into the cool dark front room to finish off the drink. Setting the bottle down on the end of the bar, he headed for the door.

The day had turned steamy and hot. His shirt was streaked with perspiration by the time he reached LaCasa's. In daylight, without the band, LaCasa's lost its charm, but it was near the levee and the pier where the crew boat docked. It was almost empty when he entered. Someone called his name, and he saw the overweight, red-faced man waving him over.

"How's business, Mac?" Jude slid onto an empty stool and signaled the bartender. "A tall glass of water, with ice, please." The bartender nodded.

Mac gave him a look. "Not so good. I'm taking the day off. Fish ain't cooperatin'. Hookin' nothing but look-downers and hardheads in that water." He coughed. Smacked the top of the bar with the flat of his hand. "To tell the truth, it's a lucky day if I reel up a crab." His round eyes bulged at Jude in the mirror over the bar.

"Take a couple off. Luck changes."

Mac shook his head. Swigged the beer. "Can't afford to, but when I get some saved up, think I'm gonna take me a vacation. Gonna treat my kids to a cruise."

Jude leaned on the counter. "That's great! Where you going?"

Mac gave him a sly look. "The islands." He lifted his beer and drank. "The Chandeleur Islands."

Jude smiled at the thought of those desolate, uninhabited sandbars off the coast. "I'm on my way downriver. I'll give the tour guide your regards." The bartender slid the glass over to him.

"That would be the alligator." Mac finished his beer and ordered another.

Jude took a long drink of the cool water and set the glass down on the bar, turning it in circles, tracing his fingers through the cool condensation. "You know anyone that does detective work?"

"What for? You want somebody followed?"

"I need information. Background on someone." Jude pushed aside a flicker of conscience. Amalise would be furious if she knew.

Mac nodded. "My cousin's got an office in Commerce Tower." The bartender set down a beer, and Mac picked it up, took a swallow. "He ain't cheap, but he's good."

"You got a number where I could reach him?"

Mac leaned over the bar and roared, "Hey, Mitchell. Mitchell!"

"What!" From the open cash register, Mitchell glared down the length of the bar at Mac.

"Gimme a dry napkin, something to write on. And a pen. You got a pen?"

Mitchell went on counting change, separating coins and bills, and dropping them into the register one at a time without looking up. Mac sat back, slumped, and lifted the bottle. When Mitchell had finished business, he rummaged in a drawer and handed a pen and a napkin to Mac.

Mac scrawled a name and phone number on the napkin. "Here you go." He folded the napkin into squares and handed it to Jude.

"Thanks."

"I'll let him know you might be calling, that you're on the up and up. Like that."

"I appreciate it." Jude drained the glass and chewed on a piece of ice, struggling to forget the catch he'd heard in Amalise's throat. LaCasa's front doors were open, and the breeze had shifted. A ship horn sounded out on the river, reminding him of the time. Reaching down for his duffel, he tapped Mac's arm and nodded.

He'd catch the crew boat and think about whether he should call that detective.

Chapter Eleven

Mama stood at the sink washing the dish and looking through the window over the backyard and down to the bayou. William had just motored up. She stuck the dish under the faucet for three seconds, then set it carefully in the drain, looking past William to the line of trees at the edge of the swamp on the other side as she picked up another dish to be washed.

Amalise hadn't telephoned in five days. She usually called three or four times a week. Lately Mama found herself staring at the phone, willing it to ring. Of course, Amalise had a difficult schedule, what with school and work and studying late at night. She was so hard to get hold of. Mama had called several times but no luck.

She sighed. *I could leave a message for her at the café where she works, Lord, but that might seem strange. Or I could write her a letter, I suppose.*

Amalise was such a dreamer. Mama could still see her as a teenager, coming home from the Regal Theater with stars in her eyes. And the books she read. Books where everyone was a hero, and people who tried hard enough, worked hard enough, overcame any problem.

Mama shook suds from her hands. *She does have self-confidence, Father. I'm proud of that. But, Lord . . . if you're never exposed to evil, how do you recognize it when it comes? How do you know to ask for help?*

With both hands in the warm, soapy water, she closed her eyes. She had to stop this worrying before it drove her crazy. *Father, let her faith ground her. Let me be just a mother worrying about nothing. Keep her safe. Give her wisdom, Father, and let her hear and understand.*

Well. Time to leave her worries in God's hands. Amalise would call when she could. And in the meantime . . . *Lord, keep a special eye on her.*

Setting down the dishrag, Mama turned off the faucet, ran her hands through her hair, and smiled at the sight of William down on the pier untangling fishing lines. *Please, let Amalise meet and fall in love with a man as good as her father.*

She felt the frown ease from her features and smooth her forehead. William worried, too. He wanted Amalise with them in Marianus. He wanted her to marry someone she loved and live in a little house nearby. And he wanted grandchildren. Lots of them. *Give her time, I say. Amalise wants to see what her own future holds.* Things had changed so in the last few years. Nowadays a woman could run a big company or be a lawyer. Or become president of the United States if she wanted it bad enough. Mama was certain Amalise could do all of that and have a family too.

But what do I know? Maybe she'll come back here to us after all. Either way, Father, Thy will be done.

Chapter Twelve

Two days later on Monday night, through the open doors of the café, Amalise spotted Phillip standing at the corner of Chartres and St. Peter streets, watching her. For an instant she froze. She'd sensed his eyes on her several times in the past few days, since the day she was with Jude, and each time had told herself that she was crazy to think such a thing. So when she saw him actually standing there under the streetlight outside the cafe, it was a moment before the fact sank in.

He didn't move. She stood beside a table near the sidewalk, and as her heartbeat gradually calmed and she began handing menus to the customers, she studied him from underneath her lashes.

Please, let him come inside.

And then what—they lived their lives by different rules.

She forced herself to turn her attention to the customers, two businessmen wearing suits and ties. She wrote down their orders and gave them a rundown on the menu—what was best today, favorites and such. Another covert glance told her that he was still there, and she brightened, moving with a lighter step. Uneasy but still filled with new hope.

Perhaps they'd get together again. Perhaps he understood her limitations now.

When the café finally emptied and Amalise glanced again across the street, Phillip had disappeared. With a sinking heart she turned back into the room, and there he was, sitting on a stool at the bar talking to Gina. Gina's head was bent, listening as if entranced. Weaving toward them through the tables, she came up behind Phillip and tapped him on the shoulder. Gina looked up, eyes shining.

Phillip swiveled and reached for her. "Here's my girl."

"Your friend's been telling me about his show at Porter," Gina said as she vacated the stool. "That's something."

"I've been waiting for you." Phillip slipped one arm around her waist and pulled her against him. Gina disappeared.

Amalise smiled. "I saw you earlier." She was conscious of a flutter of relief that he hadn't lied again . . . well, *pretended*, she corrected. Or—the thought came unwanted—stalked, as Mouse had charged.

Phillip's eyebrows lowered and he gave her a long look. "It's been a hard weekend without you, Ama."

The words radiated through her like a secret smile. "Wait here." She touched his chin with the tips of her fingers. "I'll help Gina close. It won't take long."

He nodded, folded his arms, and leaned back against the bar.

"Will you let me lock up tonight?"

"Sure." Gina arched her eyebrows. "Why didn't you tell me about him?" She lowered her voice as she bent to slip the heavy metal bolt across the double doors. "He's a charmer."

Amalise moved ahead, closing the next set of shutters. "Yes. I would have told you soon." She glanced over her shoulder at Phillip. He was deep in thought. "He's a professor at Tulane, in the art school."

"Oh. Even better. He just said he was a painter." She reached across Amalise and pulled the bolt. "The register's done, but be sure the back wall lights are on when you leave." She straightened and looked at Amalise. "Will you remember?"

Amalise nodded. "Sure." She cast another glance at Phillip, and he smiled from across the room. "Thanks." Amalise trailed Gina to the kitchen, where Gina pulled her coat from a hook on the wall and slipped it on, adding while she struggled with the sleeves, "I'll buy you both dinner, too."

"Great." Gina must like Phillip.

Gina nodded toward the back of the kitchen. "Help yourself. Fix whatever you like." She gave Amalise a long look. "A professor, hmm? He's a good catch, I think."

Amalise gave her a sideways look. "You think?"

"Yes." Gina patted her arm, and when she'd gone, Amalise flipped off the overhead lights and fans, leaving on only the dim back wall lights and the fan over the bar before returning to Phillip.

He pulled her to him and in the emptied room kissed her. "I've missed you."

"How about something to eat?"

He sat up straight, releasing her. "Don't bother with food. Maybe a beer."

In the kitchen the depression she'd felt all weekend lifted. Phillip was busy—working at the peak of his profession. Pulling a Tab and a beer out of the refrigerator, she picked up clean glasses from the counter and turned. For a moment she stood in the doorway and pictured Phillip standing behind the easel in his studio again, so confident, intent on his work. Through the sepia light he gazed back at her . . .

She smiled to herself and pushed through the door.

He'd moved to a table near the bar. She set the bottles and glasses down and pulled out a chair across from him. He reached over and touched her hands when she sat. "I had to work all weekend."

A chill ran through her, and she withdrew her hands from his. Working? But she saw him in the crowd on Saturday afternoon when she and Jude were walking to the Seven Seas. *Please, please. Don't let this be another lie.*

"I thought I saw you down here on Saturday afternoon." She lifted her head, looked at him, and nodded toward the cathedral. "Over there."

He held her eyes with no change in his expression. "I just said that I was working." He spoke in a firm but pleasant tone.

She picked up the glass, poured in some cola and watched it fizz, then sipped. What, exactly, did she see on Saturday afternoon? Had she really seen Phillip's face in the crowd? She was no longer certain.

Perhaps she didn't even want to know.

He fished in his pocket and pulled out a knife, a small piece of wood—partially carved—a pack of cigarettes, and a blue plastic lighter. Setting aside the knife and the wood, he lit a cigarette, sucked on it, and stuck the knife and wood back into his pocket, leaving the lighter on the table beside him. He looked at her. Blew smoke off to the side.

He'd been hauling pictures to a new gallery, he said after a minute, somewhere uptown. He told her about the gallery, about having to deal with the difficult owner when he'd wanted to be with her. Head tilted, he paused, waiting, until she nodded, wanting to believe him, struggling to shake off doubt. His eyes shone as he went on, fixing on hers as he described the pictures chosen for the show, shaping his hands to indicate the composition of each one, the poses of the models, the colors and textures and medium—oil or watercolor or acrylic. His smooth, calm manner of speaking, the numerous details, gradually overcame her suspicion. As she listened to Phillip, she cringed inside, remembering the mood she'd exposed to Jude at the Seven Seas.

He was telling the truth. Of course he was. How could she have doubted him? She smiled and he grew animated. She attempted to envision each picture as he described it. His voice took on a lecturing tone, and she leaned forward, braced on her forearms, feeling his excitement, drawn by his need for a listener like an object pulled toward a void. When he mentioned a slighting remark the proprietor had made, she tightened her mouth. Who did the woman think she was to say such a thing to him?

Phillip noticed and reached across the table. "She's just in it for the money, Ama." He threaded his fingers through hers. "It's all right." His eyes widened and his brows drew together—her vulnerable boy was back. "She doesn't have to like me. But she knows good art."

"It must be difficult to have to deal with someone like that."

"We worked it out in the end." He withdrew his hand. "She wanted all of my work for the show."

"My picture as well?" Ama couldn't conceal her excitement.

"Of course. It's finished." A smile lit his face. "I can't wait to show you. It's the first one I offered her."

She would call Mama and Dad and Jude, invite them to the show. They'd meet Phillip. . . . Professor Sharp, she'd say, introducing them. Mama and Dad would love him instantly.

Jude . . . ? A nudge in the back of her mind reminded her that wasn't quite as certain.

She watched Phillip light another cigarette, cupping his hands around it. He leaned forward, toward her, smoke streaming from the corner of his mouth as he talked. "Art openings are fun. You'll come with me to this one, and I imagine the critics from *The Times Picayune* and *New Orleans Magazine* will be there too." She fanned smoke as his eyes wandered past her. "They'll want photos."

"When is it?"

"What?"

"The show. When is it?"

He looked off and inhaled. "I don't know yet." He gave an irritable flip of his wrist, waving away the question. "I have to work out some other things first. Come on." He stood and held out his hands. "Where's that book bag you lug around? Let's go. I'll walk you home."

She let him pull her up and then freed her hands to pick up the bottles. When she returned from the kitchen, he was waiting by the door. He carried the book bag.

Jackson Square was dark. Artists, including Mouse, had packed up and gone home. The cathedral bells tolled eleven o'clock as they left the café behind. Phillip glanced up at the bell tower, took her hand, and asked if that's where she went to church.

She nodded. "Would you like to come with me sometime?"

"You're Catholic?"

She smiled. "Are you in South Louisiana?"

He dropped her hand and lit a cigarette. "Sure, I'll come along with you sometime. I'd like that." He pulled on the cigarette as they walked on.

When they reached the apartment building, he took the key ring from her hand, and she stood aside as he unlocked the heavy iron gate. "Nice." He took in the courtyard that extended beyond the entrance foyer.

"This area was a carriageway 150 years ago." Would he kiss her now, before he left? Ah, how she wanted his kiss. Should she offer coffee before he left?

"Can you show me around?" He looked down at her and smiled. "I'd like to see where you live." She nodded as he unlocked the apartment door. Just then he turned and cradled her face in his hands. "Thank you, Ama."

"For what?"

"Your company tonight." Releasing her, he wheeled around. "Today's my birthday." He spoke in a casual tone, strolling through the living room into the other rooms—the kitchen, the bedroom, the bathroom. "I never tell anyone. You're the only one that knows."

Amalise blinked. Not even his parents remembered?

He ran his hands over the exposed brick walls as he toured the rooms, touching the worn edges of the bricks. "This is good old stuff. You don't see much of this uptown." When he'd seen everything, he turned to her and smiled. "Mind if I have a beer?"

"I don't have any." She trailed him into the kitchen, then sat down at the table piled high with books as he crossed to the refrigerator door. Tugging open the door, he stood looking in. "It's mighty empty, Ama."

"I know." She offered an apologetic grimace. "I usually eat at the café. There's some cereal and milk. And bread. Peanut butter. Jelly."

"Don't worry about me." His tone was jovial. She looked up and he shuffled a little two-step as he came toward her. "Happy birthday, Phillip!"

"I wish I'd known. We could have planned a celebration."

"I don't celebrate. Never have." Reaching out, he pulled her up from the chair and whirled her around. She laughed. "I'll use *your* birthday, babe. We'll celebrate them both when yours comes around."

Kitchen lights sparkled while they spun. Suddenly he stopped, standing close. Her heart raced as he lowered his eyes to hers. His glistened, and she realized that all evening he'd been covering up his loneliness.

As he took her in his arms, her skin tingled, and she closed her eyes and saw him in the amber glow of the studio, and she remembered how he'd cried that he needed her, and how he'd whispered that he loved her, loved her, loved her.

Abba!

Opening her eyes she braced her hands against Phillip's shoulders and with a gentle push, arched back, away. But his eyes held hers, and in that instant she saw the longing, the fear.

He cupped his hand behind the nape of her neck and pressed her head to his chest so that she could hear his heart beating, beating. His plea was a whisper. "My life is empty without you. All around me is darkness, and I'll admit that I'm . . . I'm lost." He stroked her hair. She was precious, fine, and delicate and treasured.

The observer editing, urging, sang to her the siren song: *You can change him.* Unbound, she listened to the call. *You can change him.*

Yes. She could change Phillip Sharp. She could love him. Justify him.

The sirens continued their song.

She could light his way and transform his life with love and trust. Again she heard the cathedral bells tolling as they'd sounded when she'd left the café earlier with Phillip.

Phillip tipped up her chin and kissed her. Then, when her senses sparked and emotions churned like seas in a violent storm and she could no longer think, all of her defenses crumbled.

Chapter Thirteen

Jude stood at the helm as the pilot boat raced through the mouth of the river at the Head of Passes and then through the Southwest Pass and into the Gulf where a freighter waited outside the channel at the twenty-two-mile buoy. To the east the sun was rising, casting a golden net over the blue water. Geese and duck shot from rushes in the wetlands behind them. The air was cool and fresh out here; he took a long breath and exhaled, feeling good.

Adrenaline coursed through his veins. Muscles tightened as the small boat slapped over the waves toward the rusty old freighter, *Ariana,* out of Marseille, looming ahead. There was a strong breeze; he watched the ship pitch and roll in the waves, studying its position. The gangway was down, and the rope ladder swung over the side as the pilot boat approached. Thoughts of Amalise and her strange new friend intruded, as they'd done since he'd returned to Pilottown, and now he struggled to thrust them off and concentrate on work.

Their speed slowed. Jude stood ready port side as the engine idled and the pilot boat, *The Delta,* maneuvered close to the ship's hull, near the dangling ladder. Jacob's ladder, pilots called it, and some had died falling. *Holy Father, protect us.*

When the ladder was within arm's reach, Jude caught both sides of it and swung out over the water, catching a rung with his foot, then bracing both feet firmly upon the ladder as it whipsawed back against the rolling ship. But the ladder was fast and he hung on, steadying himself as he climbed. He could hear the slap of water below as he climbed, voices calling to him from above. *The Delta* sheared off from the hull and headed back to the station, the sound of the engine lost to Jude in the grinding interior noises of the ship, the slap of water below, voices calling to him from above.

The mate on deck gave him a hand up, and Jude headed for the bridge. There he greeted the captain, the mate on watch, and the helmsman at the wheel. The captain's face lit when Jude pulled a newspaper out of his backpack, his pilot bag, and handed it to him. "It's been a long time since I've gotten news," the captain said, slapping Jude's shoulder.

Jude glanced at the rudder indicator on the bulkhead just above the forward window as he walked over to stand in front of the helmsman. "Starboard ten and bring her back to ahead one-third."

The helmsman nodded, repeating the command aloud.

As they approached the pass, fog lingered from last night. With his eyes constantly shifting to the rudder and speed indicators and the depth log, Jude guided the ship over the bar and through the deceptive water with the master's skills honed in a year at sea and seven years apprenticeship before licensing and commission. He knew the ship's draft, had studied the latest soundings. He knew the shoals and currents and river bottom as if he were a part of it all—and so he guided the old freighter into the Mississippi despite the vessel's outdated radar, using the whistle when the fog grew thick.

Jude disembarked at Pilottown, scrambling down the ladder to the *Crescent River* pilot boat and exchanged information with the river pilot. When the *Crescent River* pilot climbed on board the *Ariana* to guide it on up to the port of New Orleans, the crew boat returned Jude to the dock.

The sun was at ten o'clock, and he strolled down the pier toward the station, released from duty for a few hours. With work behind him now, the expression on Amalise's face last week haunted him again. He flicked his hand over a stand of fluffy cattails growing along the steps as he climbed up to the screened porch of the station house and sank into a rocking chair.

Who was Phillip Sharp? Jude knew nothing of painting, but even he could see the violence, the anger reflected in Sharp's so-called art. A heron screeched out over the marshes, a doomed craggy sound. Jude huffed his exasperation. Why should he worry? But immediately he answered his own question: because God had put Amalise in his care when she was six years old and he'd been looking after her ever since. And because he cared about her.

She needs an angel this time, Lord.

His arms rested on the arms of the wooden chair, and he rocked back and forth; couldn't seem to let it go. Phillip Sharp—even the name put him off. And Amalise seemed to know almost nothing about him except that he was a professor at Tulane. That thought shut him down for a moment. Out on the wetlands seagulls called as they soared on the wind. Watching the birds but seeing instead those dark, strange pictures of Phillip's at Porter Gallery, he debated calling the detective Mac had suggested. Hesitating. After all, the man was a professor. And Amalise would be furious if she found out; he pictured the look that information would put in her eyes and grimaced.

But the idea took hold and wouldn't let go.

He would think about it. If he called that detective, he'd ask for no more than a background check on the professor. That way, if he was wrong about the guy, Amalise would never know. But if he was right, he'd better approach her with some facts. It would take more than his opinion to deflect her, driven as she was. Once Amalise made up her mind about a thing, she never looked back; she'd just keep moving forward like a loose tire rolling down a hill. She'd always been that way.

Like that time with the wild hog. He shook his head, remembering how dangerous her determination sometimes could be. She was ten to his fourteen. They'd gone fishing in the marshland near the Marianus Swamp. She paddled the skiff while he sorted gear and directed her to the spot he'd found. Suddenly the boat rocked and weeds thrashed around them. They almost capsized as a wild hog, grunting and terrified, burst from the marsh grass.

Jude shuddered, thinking of what might have been. He'd reached for the paddle, but she wouldn't give it up! The skiff rocked and skimmed in the draft of the panicked animal. "I can do it. I can do it!" She'd jammed the paddle over and over into the mud, fighting to halt the forward movement of the little boat. That tiny girl with not enough weight on her to stop a rubber ball fighting the way she did. It would have made him laugh if it hadn't been so serious.

Finally he'd yanked the paddle, twisting it loose from her grip and punching it down into the mud with all his strength. But the skiff skimmed on toward the slough where the hog was thrashing, grunting, fighting something underfoot. As the frantic animal loomed close enough for them to count bristles and smell the sodden hog scent of terror, the hull of the boat struck a sandbank. Jude pushed up, rocking the boat as he reached over Amalise and jammed the paddle into that sandy mud, this time at an angle, knowing this was the last chance. Praying, he used every ounce of strength to push against that paddle, holding, straining—and at last the boat slowed its forward speed. When the skiff lurched to a halt, they were only fifteen feet from the bucking, furious hog. Jude could see the quicksand below, sucking and pulling the beast under.

Even now years later, the memory tightened his jaw, the muscles at the back of his neck. She'd almost got them killed holding onto that paddle. They'd had to wait there a while, and he'd sent up a stream of silent prayers. It had been too dangerous to move while the desperate animal struggled against the swirling quicksand. Amalise had sat motionless for a long time, silent, eyes wide, until at last the hog was well and truly caught.

When they were safe, Jude pushed them off in the opposite direction from the sandbar. Only the snout was still visible.

"Will he die?"

It was the kind of question you had to answer with the truth. "Yes." He'd lifted her with both hands onto the opposite seat and turned her so that she faced him instead of the hog. He navigated the skiff back through the weeds, around logs and cypress knees, through trees, and down the river toward the judge's pier, trembling as he thought of that last sandbar that saved their lives. *Thank You, Lord. I thought we were goners for a minute there.* Through it all she sat limp and despondent, fishing forgotten.

"How long will it take?"

"To die?" He turned his eyes to her. "Not long. Not long at all. But you can't fight quicksand. It's deceptive. Looks solid on the surface, but it's liquid underneath, from underground streams and pools. You have to stay calm and float on top to survive."

"Let's go back," she'd begged. "Maybe we can save him."

That was another thing about Amalise. She didn't think like other people. She'd given him a piteous look, like maybe that would make him turn the boat around, go back, and try to drag that hog right out of the muck with his bare hands.

"It's no use. Sometimes you just have to admit defeat, Amalise. He'll put up a fight, but it's the fight that'll kill him. Struggling creates a vacuum under the quicksand, a suction. That's what pulls him under."

She'd thrown him an angry look, but he'd seen the shine of tears before she glanced away.

The memory shook him. The rocking chair slowed to a stop as he gazed, unseeing, over the river. If he was right about Phillip Sharp . . .

Amalise might really be in trouble.

Something stirred in the center of his chest. A man like Sharp—confident, smooth on the surface, but if his paintings were any indicator, churning anger underneath—could pull Amalise into an emotional maelstrom before she had time to think.

With a new sense of urgency and a flying prayer, Jude pushed up from the chair, turned and entered the station house, heading straight for the telephone in the hallway. This was the only phone, and he was glad to see that it was free.

He'd ask the detective to check out the professor—make sure he wasn't married, had no arrest records. He'd dig up what he could without raising Cain with Amalise. In the end he'd probably come up dry. The professor would turn out to be an ordinary crank, and Amalise would be just fine.

At least, that was his prayer.

OLD BELLS TOLLED FROM the cathedrals nearby, St. Louis and St. Mary, calling. Behind her, Phillip slept.

Amalise stood at the window gazing at the tree in the courtyard, trying to remember the exact moment she'd realized that Phillip had moved into the apartment. At first he'd begun meeting her at the café every night at closing time and walking her home, carrying the heavy book bag, and each time he stayed on through the night. He had even bought groceries, and there was actually food in the refrigerator.

He'd had an argument with his landlord, he said. This would just be temporary.

But temporary had never been in her plan. For the hundredth time she fought the impossible internal war. This was wrong, but how could she ask Phillip to leave? *I'd lose him, Abba. And You know he'd be lost without me. That's why You brought us together. So I could help heal the wounds he's suffered.*

Staring blindly over the courtyard, she waited for a sense of peace. The assurance she was right.

Nothing.

Phillip loved her with a fury, like a fire burning out of control. It frightened her sometimes. Memories stirred—the day he'd cut his arm, the times he'd cried that she couldn't leave him . . . that she was his. She'd come to believe this.

A need like that binds you to him as tight as any chains.

She closed her eyes against the troubling thought, shutting out the world, her own uncertainty. It was too late to go back to the way things were before . . . before that day at the studio. And it was too soon to think of marriage.

She opened her eyes. The problem was . . . she faced the fact . . . somehow she'd already made the choice.

I will lead him to You, Abba. You know the beginning and the end. He's a lost sheep . . . been that way since he was a child and it isn't his fault. But even now he's searching for the fold.

She swallowed. Surely she was right.

She had to be.

She dressed quietly and quickly, so as not to wake Phillip. She was late for church. She tiptoed through the living room into the kitchen to make coffee for him before she left. But rummaging through cabinets, she found none. Phillip couldn't wake up without coffee. She'd pick up some on her way back. She scribbled a note to that effect and put it on the kitchen table, grabbed her purse, opened the door and shut it behind her quietly so that he wouldn't wake.

Her old blue bicycle was in the entryway where she always left it. Phillip didn't have one, and he'd claimed not to know how to ride. She couldn't imagine such a thing. She unchained the bike and wheeled it through the gate. The morning air was brisk. As she sailed down the street, she lifted her hands from the handlebars, arms spread, balancing and humming, feeling the breeze.

She chained the bike to a light post near the cathedral. Pulling a small round black lace veil from her purse, she placed it atop her head and entered the church. Inside was dark and cool. Light filtered through the stained-glass windows, throwing rich-colored patterns across the altar. Jude was in Pilottown, but she glanced around anyway, hoping to see him on the off chance. Sometimes he surprised her.

While the congregation murmured along with the priest, Amalise knelt, bowed her head, and prayed. As always, an otherworldly feeling that she experienced nowhere else came over her. *It's me, Abba. Amalise.*

With that she began to cry. *Forgive me, Abba. Forgive me! I'll make things right. I can do it. Forgive me. I can fix this.*

He already knew what was in her heart, and there was nothing more she could say. So she talked to Him of the beautiful day instead, and listened to the choir, and lost herself in the words of the prayer book. But she could not make herself go up to the altar for Communion, although she longed to. She gave thanks for Mama and Dad, and Jude, and for everything the future held, avoiding any further mention of Phillip.

She knew what Jude would say about that particular dodge—*The bed's too short and the blanket's too narrow for cover, Amalise.* But she didn't yet know the prayers to pray when it came to Phillip.

Emerging into the bright daylight when the service was over, Amalise folded the veil, slipped it back into her purse, and squinted in the glare. Mouse was across the street, near the Jackson Square fence, she saw. Amalise unchained the bike and rolled it over to him.

Mouse looked up and grinned. "Hey! Where've you been?" He pulled a rag from the corner of the easel and wiped paint from his hands. "Haven't seen you in a while. I've been worried."

She shrugged. "Just the usual frantic race."

"Good. The usual race is okay." He gestured to the chair sitting in front of the easel. "Sit awhile. It's a nice day. I'll sketch you while we talk."

Amalise looked off. "I can't right now. I've got company." She fixed her eyes on the Pontalba Café on the corner, just past Mouse's post. The place was busy today; it always was on Sunday morning after Mass. Every table was filled.

"Who's visiting?"

She hesitated a beat too long.

"Aw, Amalise." Mouse drew out the words as he turned to look at her, studying her face. "Not that professor?"

She straddled the bicycle, planting one foot on the pedal. "I don't know what you have against him, Mouse." Looking at him, she shook her head. "You don't even know him. How can you judge someone you've never met?"

"There's something wrong with the man." His tone was flat, and she caught his quick glance toward the corner of the Cabildo where Phillip had been waiting for her in the dark on that first night . . . according to Mouse. Stalking, Mouse had said.

"Don't say another word about him, Mouse." She lifted her chin. "We're in love."

His eyes narrowed. "I thought you were smarter than that. Artists are quick—and good—judges of character. We study people, their expressions, how they stand, who they really are. That's how we make a living." He shook his head. "And I have a bad feeling . . ."

"Phillip is a kind . . ."

"Your professor was hiding in the dark that night. Standing right over there and hiding." He swept his hand in the direction of the Cabildo. "Hiding and watching. And he lied to you about being at the theater across the street. Just look at the facts. The guy's off somehow." He hesitated for a beat. "Love blooms in light, Amalise."

He wouldn't take his eyes from hers, and she grew angry. Her hands tightened around the rubber bicycle grips and the heat rose in her face. "That's absurd."

He broke the connection, picked up a paintbrush, and frowned. "There *is* evil in this world, little girl. He's picked you out for a reason, and he's dangerous."

With a hard look at Mouse, Amalise shoved her foot down on the pedal and rode off without another word, dodging people still emerging from the cathedral doors. Poor Phillip. And how dare Mouse condescend to her like that!

She rode on around the square and down Decatur to the grocery store across from the farmer's market, still angry. The old man who ran the small store was out front when she arrived, wearing his butcher's apron and hosing down the sidewalk. The scent of wet stone and cement rose as she stopped in a spot he'd finished cleaning.

"That old bike's got some miles on it, Amalise," he grunted, flapping the hose up and down across the sidewalk.

A smile cleared her thoughts. "When it goes, we'll have a funeral, Mr. Butts." Feeling better, she tapped the kickstand down with her foot and turned the wheel to balance the bike. "I'm here for coffee."

He didn't even look up. "Don't have any. Try Morning Call."

"A bag of Community, not a cup."

He heaved a sigh, turned off the water, and followed her into the store with heavy steps.

She purchased the coffee and stashed the red-and-white bag in the basket. Phillip was awake when she returned, sitting at the kitchen table, carving. "It's a beautiful day," she said, closing the door behind her. She crossed the living room and walked into the kitchen holding up the bag of coffee, then planted a kiss on top of his head before heading for the coffeepot. He ducked and gave her a cold look.

She set the coffee bag on the counter and opened it. "Is something wrong?"

"Where've you been?"

Setting the pot down on the burner, she glanced over her shoulders. "Didn't you get my note?"

"Yes." He set down the wood and the carving knife, and his voice was low. "You were gone so long I thought you'd left me. Thought you'd changed your mind about us."

She frowned. What was he talking about? To hide her confusion, she began filling the coffeepot with water from the tap. His chair scraped on the floor behind her. "I went to Mass."

"You left me for church?"

"And then I stopped at the store around the corner to buy the coffee. And I stopped for a minute to say hello to Mouse."

She turned to face him, backing up to the counter as he rose from the table still wearing that grim look. He walked over to her and stood close—too close—dipping his forehead so that it touched hers, and resting his hands on her shoulders. "It's your day off, babe. We've got better things to do than spend time with some fence artist."

"Mouse is my friend."

He smoothed her hair, pushing it back behind her ears, and as his hand dropped, she saw the smear of dark blood on his inner forearm.

"What's this?" She grabbed his wrist, staring.

He pulled his arm back. "It's nothing." Such a strange tone of voice, almost like a child left sitting on the school bench after the baseball team's been picked, pretending he doesn't care.

An unfamiliar sense of gloom descended as she watched him wet a paper napkin under the faucet and clean off the crusted blood. "The knife slipped, that's all." He balled up the napkin and tossed it into the basket before turning back to her.

"What have you done?"

He shrugged and took her hands in his. "I was careless, worried. I don't want to lose you, Amalise."

She frowned, glancing again at the cut on his arm.

He moved closer. "I want you to myself." He kissed the knuckles on her hands as he watched her from under lowered lids. "Sunday should be *our* day. And forget Mouse. He's no friend. I don't want you around him."

Amalise shook her head, but he tugged her toward the kitchen door. "Let's start the day over. We'll have breakfast here, then go down to the studio. You like to watch me paint—bring your books and you can study too."

She glanced at the sun shining through the kitchen window. She'd already mapped out the day. Just as every other Sunday morning, just as she had this morning, she'd start off early when the shopkeepers were still hosing down the sidewalks and that good, musky damp smell permeated the Quarter and the whole place was filled with possibilities.

First she always went to church and, when Jude was in town, he met her there. Then to the farmer's market to buy something for dinner that night, the only night she cooked. She'd take her time, choosing carefully from heaping stalls of redfish, speckled trout, bass and drum, and shrimp right off the boats. There were live chickens and turkeys, but she'd pass them up. In the season she'd purchase satsumas and blood oranges, Ponchatoula strawberries and Meyer lemons, and sometimes there would be sweet cherries, and she'd pick out the firmest, darkest ones.

And after she brought those things home and stored them away— she loved that part, storing them away in her own cabinets in her own kitchen—then she'd take a book or *The Vieux Carré Courier* to Jackson Square and plant herself on a bench under a tree in the shade until it was time to go study, glancing up from the pages now and then to take in the razzle-dazzle, the whole pastiche, the greens and blues, the shades of yellow and thin transparent orange—the colors of the Quarter on a sunny Sunday morning—sunshine and daisies and clover, the brightly striped umbrellas, bobbing balloons.

It had never occurred to her that Phillip might have different plans, that Sunday did not mean the same to him. But his look was expectant, smiling.

"Come, Ama. I need you with me."

Love . . . relationships . . . are commitments, she reminded herself, looking through the kitchen window at the sunlight, the tree leaves moving in the breeze, the sparkling fountain. Phillip was demanding more and more of her time—all of it, really, when she wasn't at school or working or studying. This was the way it was supposed to be, he said. They were sharing their lives. She missed seeing Mouse and Jude and having time free for herself. But this was all new; she'd fix the problem soon.

And so she followed along, struggling against an unwelcome sense that walls were closing around her.

Chapter Fourteen

L ate on a Saturday afternoon one week later, Amalise sat with Phillip in the courtyard. Phillip was drinking bourbon, a new habit he'd acquired. Or perhaps she'd just not noticed it before. After her shift at work, they wandered over to Port of Call on Esplanade for hamburgers—good time spent together, he said, to make up for the hours they were apart.

Her chair sat at an angle to his, and she lounged with her feet resting in his lap. The sun was going down. Water from the small fountain in the center of the courtyard splashed on the elephant ears she'd planted in pots last spring. She looked around thinking what a piece of luck it was that she'd gotten the ground-floor apartment. None of the other tenants in the building used the courtyard much, although over the years different people had left pieces of unmatched furniture behind—a black iron bench, three chairs, and a small table made from part of a varnished ship's hatch cover that Jude had bought for her in a store around the corner on Decatur Street.

Thanksgiving was a week and a half away. She was going home for the holiday, and Jude would be there; and, though she hadn't asked him yet, Phillip would come with her too. He could meet her family and her best friend at one time. Dad would like Phillip. They both took control of situations, knew how to handle themselves. She smiled. She didn't need someone to take care of her, but Dad thought she did. So he'd take to Phillip, she was certain. Even though . . .

She swallowed hard. She wasn't looking forward to explaining her new living arrangement to her parents, but she was an adult, and she'd have to make them understand. For now, at least. Having Phillip beside her would make this easier. She thought of Mouse's warning based on an instant's judgment and frowned.

Yes. Better to have Phillip with her so they'd really get to know him.

She'd given some thought to how she would phrase this invitation to Phillip. He'd grown up in Manhattan. What would he think of country life in Marianus? On the other hand, he loved her, and he was curious about her past, quizzing her constantly about the town, her parents, what interested her when she was young, and what she'd thought about various people, especially friends. Especially Jude.

What he'd confided to her about his past strengthened her determination to introduce him to her family. They would welcome him, love him because she loved him. All she knew about Phillip's years before they'd met was the revelation about his lonely childhood. He never talked about the later years. It wasn't that he was evasive exactly. But questions about that part of his life in New York and his family always seemed to be flipped around. He was more interested in her, he said.

Phillip seemed preoccupied right now, and she took the quiet time to form the right words. A breeze fanned wind chimes in the tree, and she turned to look at them. Her eyes lit on the small white birdhouse hanging on a branch nearby. He'd made it, he said, and the bluebirds he'd painted in the squares on each side represented the two of them, Amalise and Phillip. This gave her the courage she needed.

"Phillip?"

"I hear a question in your voice and the answer's probably no."

She laughed. "Listen. I want you to come home with me to Marianus for Thanksgiving. I want Mama and Dad to meet you, and Jude will be there, too. You'll like them all, especially Dad."

"I was right. The answer's no."

What? She turned to him. "Don't you want to meet my family?"

His tone had been sharp, but his face when he looked back at her was wan. "I'm sorry, babe. Didn't mean to be abrupt. But I can't come with you, not this time. Duty calls."

"What do you mean?" It had never occurred to her that he'd have other plans.

"Perhaps I should rephrase that." His expression hardened as he shook ice cubes against the glass. "Mother calls." He lifted the glass and sipped the drink.

Disappointment fell over her, a dense cloak that darkened her mood. She'd looked forward to showing him off in Marianus. Avant-garde Phillip. Sophisticated Phillip, as if he'd stepped right off the screen at the Regal Theater, an artist, a city man who knew his way around, different from everyone in town.

She watched a blackbird hopping on a branch of the tree, but all she could think to say out loud was: "How am I to explain to my parents that I'm living with a man they've never met?"

He flipped his hand. "Easy. Don't tell them."

She'd never considered that. The ground seemed to shift beneath her. She'd never kept secrets from Mama and Dad. Not even from Jude. Inhale. Exhale. She would have to think this through, take it step by step before making a decision.

At last, with a resigned sigh, she said in as mellow a tone as she could manage, "I suppose your parents would be disappointed if you don't go home."

He snorted. "Banjo will be disappointed but not my parents."

She looked at him. Banjo was dead—wasn't that what he'd said?

"With them it's a question of money. If I don't show up once in a while, they'll forget I'm alive."

"Well, your parents must be proud of you now." She held onto his hand and rested her head on the back of the chair, watching clouds drift by. She squeezed his fingers. "You're a university professor. Galleries show your work, and"—remembering what he'd said on the night that he'd moved in, she added—"and you'll be famous soon. Written up in the newspapers. When is that show, by the way, professor?" She closed her eyes as the sun warmed her face.

He jerked his hand from hers, startling her. "What show? I don't know what you're talking about."

Eyes wide, she rolled her head toward him. Why this new tone in his voice today? She steadied her own. "The one you mentioned a few weeks ago. You said my picture would be in the show. And *The Times Picayune.*"

"I don't know what you're talking about."

She stilled.

His eyes went flat. "And quit calling me *Professor.* I'm tired of that joke."

Her voice locked in her throat as she struggled to process what she'd heard. He looked off while his words bounced through her mind like that clown's colored balls. As she caught one, the others slipped away. She couldn't make sense of it. Surely she'd misunderstood. She settled back, forced a smile, and shook her head.

Please, please, please.

"You are a fine professor," she said in a firm tone. "A fine professor at the university, Phillip Sharp. You should be proud of what you've accomplished." She clasped her hands over her stomach and watched him from the corners of her eyes.

No response. Seconds passed as he tucked his chin onto his chest again, picked up the glass and lifted it to his lips. Sensing the abyss looming deep and close, she worked to summon a cheerful tone. "Quit playing around, professor. I spent weeks sitting for the picture in your studio."

Slowly he turned to face her. "I am a teaching assistant." He spat out each word. "A mere graduate student. Otherwise known as a TA." With a quick, dry laugh, he raised the glass and turned it, inspecting the melting ice and dregs of bourbon, as if fascinated.

Seconds passed and still she couldn't find any words. There was an immense difference between a professor and a teaching assistant.

Phillip broke the silence. "What difference does it make? I'm still good old Phillip Sharp." He paused, finished off the drink, and turned his eyes to her. His voice dropped a key. "What's your game, Ama?"

She straightened in the chair, dizzy, lightheaded—what, exactly, did he say when they first met? What had convinced her he was a professor at the university? Nothing fit. Could she have been mistaken?

Again?

She thought of his studio at the art school and the missing nameplate on the door. Suddenly she realized what she should have seen before: the studio was too large for one person, and there were those unused easels—three or four of them—things she'd not registered at the time. Breathless, she gulped for air. How could she have been so wrong?

"It was all a lie?"

"It was our private joke." A short laugh. "You promoted me."

"You lied." She closed her eyes, unable to comprehend. She could hear him set the glass carefully down on the table, then moving, rising from the chair. She could hear cars driving by on Dumaine Street, a horn honking down on Decatur, the entrance gate opening. And closing. Footsteps going up the iron interior stairs.

When she opened her eyes and looked up, Phillip stood near the fountain, hands planted on his hips, arms akimbo, head thrown back as he gazed into the sky. Even in turmoil she was struck by how different he was from other men she'd known. After a moment he seemed to snap to. He slapped his thighs, pulled up—straightening—and clasped his hands behind his neck as he began turning in a slow circle, elbows winged, inspecting the overhanging roof, the tree, the rows of windows in the apartments, until at last his eyes reached hers. She braced herself for his words.

His mouth was set in a grim tight line; his eyes tugged down at the corners. "I didn't realize that you'd . . . misunderstood." She heard pain. Slowly he shook his head.

He seemed far away, as if she were standing at one end of a tunnel and he at the other. His voice rolled toward her through the long hollow. "Does it matter so much, Ama?"

She shook herself. *This is Phillip,* the observer reminded. Rising anger and disbelief warred with deep, powerful sympathy. Painful, wrenching compassion. *He has no one else but you. No family love. No friends.*

Stumbling, he moved toward her, knelt, and clutched her thighs. "I love you . . . need you, babe. Look at me."

She closed her eyes.

His grip tightened. "It's only for one more year. Look at me!"

She obeyed.

"I have a small salary. It's not much, but things will be settled soon, and I'll have my masters' degree, and there'll be an offer to join the faculty." His voice turned fierce. "They *owe* it to me."

A breeze rustled across the patio, and the wind chimes sent out a harmonious crescendo. As the chimes faded, Phillip dropped his head onto her knees and quietly wept. She stroked the back of his head, and the lonely child's face rose before her. She saw the closed door in his darkened room. She could hear the boy's heart beating in his chest, could hear him whispering through the years . . .

Mama, Mama . . . Ama, Ama . . . don't leave me, Ama.

The full horror of Phillip's childhood swept her, and suddenly she understood his constant fear that she, too, would abandon him. He needed her. He needed her. But perhaps, standing by him, she could still lead him from this darkness. Her strength would be his.

We who are strong ought to bear with the failings of the weak. You told us that, Abba. How, then, can this be wrong? She looked down at his bowed head. She could help Phillip, protect him, give his life new direction. She would be his refuge.

"Nothing's changed," she said gently. "We'll be fine."

"I'll have a good salary when I'm on the faculty."

"Money's not the problem."

He looked at her, swiped his eyes dry, and nodded. "Money is my problem, Ama. But you . . ." His gaze rested on her, and something glittered in the depths. Something she didn't recognize. Didn't understand any more than his pleased tone when he went on.

"You'll make plenty after you graduate."

Chapter Fifteen

———❦———

I n Marianus for the Thanksgiving holidays, she skated on the surface of things the first day, struggling with the problem of Phillip,
of how to tell Mama and Dad, and, of course, Jude, when he arrived.
Putting off the telling from one hour to the next. But Mama seemed
to sense shadows underneath and watched her for clues.

Dad, on the other hand, was easy, and this added to her feeling
of guilt. Once she opened her mouth to tell him, just to let it out and
face their disappointment, but eyes shining with pride, he peppered
her with questions about her life in the city . . . seeing it in his mind
before she could even answer.

So instead she regaled both of them, Mama and Dad, updating
the old, ongoing stories of school and the Quarter and characters that
frequented the café. Dad had gone to Tulane too, and he nodded while
she talked about certain classes and professors, as if he saw himself
thirty-five years ago.

When dinner was finished, she rehearsed in her mind what she
would say. Now was the time. They were sitting in the living room,
having coffee. But Dad got up and switched on the television set.

On channel 6, the news anchor was joking about that hijacker,
D. B. Cooper, parachuting out of the Northwest Orient passenger jet
midflight three years ago on Thanksgiving Eve in 1971. The Cooper
caper, he drawled. "That crazy jumper." Dad laughed at the story like

112

he always did, even while admitting he shouldn't; and then they all joined in because he said this every year when the story was repeated. And then the scene on the television set flicked to a flat open field somewhere in Southeast Asia.

That was the problem with the news, Amalise's smile faded as whimsy morphed to misery with a click of the switch. On the screen children gathered in a field were looking up, scouring the clouds, the sky. Waiting.

"What are they doing?"

Dad looked at Mama and sank down in his chair. "They're in Cambodia. Haven't you seen it before?" Mama shook her head. "It happens almost every day now. The children are waiting for food."

"But they're babies!"

"We're flying in food from Vietnam or Thailand."

"Who's *we?*"

"I think it's USAID or CARE, maybe." Amalise had seen this story before, and it always dragged her down. "Look . . . here they come."

She could hear the droning engines in the distance as they all watched on the television set in Marianus, nine thousand miles away. Vietnam and the spillover into Cambodia—the first intimate war, minute by minute, real-time suffering brought into living rooms on the other side of the globe. It gave life a different frame of reference. And she could not look away.

The mass of children stirred. Craning thin necks, they pointed as the aircraft emerged from cloud cover, banked, and began circling the field. In that instant a jeep rolled into camera range, swerving to a stop in a cloud of dust. Behind the jeep a small rusty corrugated metal building simmered in the sun. The children, energized, began waving and shouting as three men wearing helmets and flak jackets burst from the Jeep.

"Food for Phnom Penh has been cut off by communist guerillas, the Khmer Rouge. They're starving." Dad shook his head. "It's the same every day."

One aid worker ran toward a narrow dirt landing strip, signaling the plane on its final approach. On the other side of the world, Amalise watched as the others took positions in front of the children, arms spread wide, holding them back. The aircraft headed in, nose down, taxied toward the news camera, and at the last moment, in a flare of dust, swerved half-circle to a stop with the engines running, facing the airstrip for a quick getaway. When dust settled, she could see *Air-America* was painted on the fuselage.

Food packets were quickly unloaded from the cargo hold. There was always danger of rocket attacks, the reporter explained in a hushed tone.

"They're ravaging the country, the Khmer guerillas," Dad said. "Look how thin those children are."

"I wish we could do something." Amalise envisioned the food that would be on Thanksgiving tables around the country tomorrow.

Mama pulled a handkerchief from her pocket, ducked her head, and dabbed the corner of her eye. "Ahhh . . . let His face shine upon them and give them peace."

On the set the scene switched to a holiday sale at D. H. Holmes department store on Canal Street in New Orleans. The sudden change was jolting.

"Well," Dad exhaled. "Let's talk about something else. He looked at Amalise. "Is Thompson still teaching?"

"Yes." Those children still hovered ghostlike before Amalise. It was the old question again: *Why, Abba?* The problem was so daunting, so big, so far away. She forced her attention back to Dad.

What had he asked? Oh yes . . . his favorite old professor, Thompson. "I had a class with him this semester."

"Does he still do that first-day thing?" Dad asked in a cheery voice.

Amalise roused herself. "Yep," she managed a smile, "every time. Professor Thompson comes in shaking his head and says we look like a roomful of mean Joe Greens." Dad chuckled. Mama smiled, too. She enjoyed these stories as much as Dad.

At nine o'clock she went off to her old bedroom to study for semester exams. She would tell them about Phillip tomorrow. But the inner conflict rose again, her own war, to tell or keep Phillip a secret for a little longer. She knew what ought to be done but shoved the worries back, back, deep into the recesses of her mind, just for the moment so she could tackle the books instead. Spreading casebooks and notebooks across the bed, she propped pillows up behind her back and forced herself to think of class outlines and notes, not Phillip.

Jude showed up the day before Thanksgiving, a ray of sunshine peeking through dark clouds. She threw her arms around him, squeezing.

"I've got Wednesday 'til Sunday off." He was staying with his father.

She and Jude sat together on the swing on the back porch, rocking back and forth and talking about Pilottown and law school, Christmas—just around the corner—a new car Jude was thinking of buying. A flock of Canadian geese honked into the bayou, skidding over the water down near the pier. When Jude stopped talking to watch the geese, she stole a look at him, hoping that he'd forgotten her mood at the Seven Seas. How pitiful she must have sounded!

He turned his head, caught her look, and smiled. "I wish they'd stay, don't you?" He nodded at the geese.

"Yes, they're safe from hunters here."

"Not necessarily,"

"Jude!" She pinched his arm and he laughed.

She loved seeing Jude again, loved hearing his laugh. Looking out over the bayou, relief flooded her as she decided that she shouldn't tell them about Phillip moving in with her just yet. Not yet. Not before the Thanksgiving feast. The news would spoil the day.

DINNER ON THANKSGIVING DAY was just the four of them: Mama, Dad, herself, and Jude. Jude's father declined, as he always did. They joined hands and Dad said grace, giving thanks and adding a special prayer for those children mixed up in the war. Afterward, while everyone chattered, Amalise envisioned Phillip eating the traditional dinner with his parents. They'd be dressed up in New York, she was sure. Not like here. The table would be a long one, with a white lace cloth, silver, china, candles. Perhaps there'd be a serving maid. She wondered if he'd mention her to his parents.

Jude nudged her and asked her to pass the merlitons. Dad was exclaiming over the turkey, and Amalise said something about how pretty the table looked, how hungry she was. Would Phillip's friends be there, too? She frowned, recalling the antisocial family Phillip had described.

"Excuse me." Jude reached across her plate, picked up the casserole dish, and handed it to Dad.

"Thanks, Jude." Dad gave Amalise an amused look.

She raised her eyebrows, realizing she'd missed a beat. Dad laughed, and Jude said something about daydreaming.

Mama shot her a worried glance, so Amalise stretched a smile across her face as she tucked into the turkey. She talked a lot, consuming a large store of energy on describing examinations beginning in a few weeks, and she rambled on about stories of Rebecca, Henry, Gina, and Mouse—and once in a while she'd mention Phillip, as if he were just a friend.

She mentioned him once too often. "Who's Phillip?"

Mama's fork stopped halfway between the plate and her mouth as she looked at Amalise. "Is he nice?"

Jude shifted in his chair and made a low noise in the back of his throat. Amalise ignored him, nodding to Mama and shoving the guilt way back in her mind behind a clutter of diversions as she said, "He . . . ah . . . teaches at the university." The turkey she was chewing turned dry. "And he's a painter."

Seconds passed as Mama's fork was still. "*Mais, pensez donc! Think of that!*" With that she resumed eating.

"How about a little fishing this afternoon, Amalise?" Jude asked when they'd finished and cleared the table. They all stood in the kitchen surrounded by dirty pots and plates and knives and forks and glasses.

"Oh go on, chère." Mama gave her a little push. "Dad and I'll clean up. You go with Jude."

The turkey platter sat on the counter. Dad and Jude pushed the bones around until they'd gathered up some with shreds of meat still hanging on—a neck bone, a backbone, some others. "What's that for?" Mama asked, tying on her apron.

"An old alligator gar." Jude winked at Dad.

"It's not." Mama pushed them aside. "I'm not having that fish in this house." She gave Jude a grim look. "Won't cook it. And sure won't eat it."

Amalise left them in the kitchen bantering over the garfish while she changed into an old pair of blue jeans and a sweater and wrapped a cotton scarf around her head, tying it in back. As the screened door slammed behind her, she could see Jude waiting at the landing. They took Dad's flatboat this afternoon. The air was cool and sharp. Turned leaves fluttered from trees like tarnished gilt.

At Old Tom's landing a quarter mile upstream, Jude bought some minnows and dumped them into the live bait box in the bottom of the boat. He moved aside while Amalise started the outboard again, and they took off in a spray in the direction of the Marianus Swamp. While she navigated the winding bayou, Jude sat in the bow stringing a trotline with markers, weights, and heavy hooks. As they entered the swamp, the light dimmed, shimmering down through the green canopy.

Amalise eyed the brown paper bag in the bottom of the boat near Jude's foot. It was moist from turkey parts. "You actually brought that with you?"

He nodded without looking up from his work "I *am* after a gar. He's a big one; lives in a new spot I found. He'll clean it out if I don't get him first. We'll set a line if he's still around."

She slowed the speed as they wove through clusters of cypress knees and rushes, tree stumps and roots and bushes according to his directions. He threaded the hooks with turkey bones dripping with meat. "This'll get him," he muttered, with a half-smile.

The spot was a small half-moon pool of deeper water almost hidden under trees laced with Spanish moss. She stopped the engine, and they cast out, sitting in silence while minutes passed.

"What was your pop like before your mama died?" Like Phillip, Jude had a hard childhood, she knew. But he didn't talk about it much.

"He was tough."

"How do you mean? I only met him once."

"He isn't around much. He's an alcoholic, a mean drunk."

She sucked in her breath. "Even after your mama died?"

"Worse." He glanced her way. "Why?"

She ducked her head, gave all her attention to the line. "Just wondering. I didn't know it was that bad."

Amalise watched ripples on the water expanding. "That must have been hard. Do you think about it much, Jude?"

"Not anymore." He bobbled his line, tugged, reeled it in, and threw it out again. "You make your way through the bad times the best you can. The Lord shows us the way, and we just get through 'em. I don't think about those days unless Pop's around, which isn't often." She caught his glance. "You have to know when to give it up."

The image of Phillip kneeling before her on the patio, weeping, struck her. And then she thought of Jude and his father, and all the years he'd apprenticed on the river making peanuts for wages before he was made and commissioned, and she knew that couldn't have been easy either.

"How's that friend of yours? The professor?" Jude watched his line. She flinched.

"He's fine." *Professor.* She fell silent. It was an automatic response yet a lie of omission not to tell Jude about her discovery. She'd never lied to him before, and this kindled an unpleasant discomfort, a feeling that she was caught between the loyalty of long friendship and disloyalty to Phillip. Still . . . she had yet to adjust to the fact that Phillip was not really a professor. She shouldn't talk about it until she'd absorbed the information herself.

Jude glanced up. "Amalise." When he hesitated, she gave him a sideways look, and he arched one eyebrow. "Are you really in love with him?"

She meant to say certainly, but that sense of the walls closing around her suddenly returned so that she almost couldn't breathe. "I . . ." Her throat closed. Jude studied her. "Yes, I think so." She lifted her chin. "Yes, of course I love him."

His mouth pressed tight, and his eyes turned back to the water.

So she was relieved when Jude broke the silence, pointing. "There he is," he hissed, as the garfish surfaced.

The fish turned, rolling in the water, and as the foaming ripples spread and disappeared, Amalise could see it gliding just beneath the surface. "It must be four feet long." She watched it dive and disappear in the murky water.

"Yep." Jude reeled in his line. "He's already cleaned us out. We won't catch a thing until that old boy's out of here."

Reluctantly Amalise reeled her line in too. It was peaceful in this shaded spot; she wouldn't mind staying all afternoon. But Jude seemed determined and somewhat out of sorts, so she handed him her rod, and he lay them down together in the stern. She paddled the boat while Jude secured the trotline between two trees so that the markers floated on top of the water and the weights and baited hooks hung underneath. When they'd finished, Jude wiped his hands on his jeans and gazed at the trap with a satisfied expression.

"He'll love your Mama's cooking, Amalise." He chuckled.

They switched places, and Jude steered the skiff out of the inlet, through the swampy forest, and back into the bayou, still chuckling. Amalise untied the scarf, crossed her arms behind her head to form a pillow, and leaned back to watch the tops of trees sailing by under the clouds. Knowing Jude was close and breathing in the pine scented air, she felt every muscle in her body relax. Such a contrast after the turmoil she'd lived with for the past few weeks in the city.

Her cheeks were rosy, touched with sun, and the breeze blew her hair back from her face as the boat picked up speed. Deliberately she shook off thoughts of the garfish breaking through the water to catch the warmth of the sun, rolling, gliding, diving back down into the cool dark, never suspecting the three large hooks on the trotline baited with Thanksgiving turkey were waiting for him . . . Thanksgiving turkey, of all things. How long would he fight before he'd give it up, exhausted?

"While you're at it, chère"—Jude's murmur broke into her thoughts—"there're some wicked teeth in that old gar's mouth."

"How'd you know what I was thinking?" She looked up, watching the clouds. From under her lashes she could see his smile.

Chapter Sixteen

Mama and William put Amalise on the bus back to the city early in the morning, and the house seemed empty without her. But there were things to do, and she hummed as she opened the front door and closed it behind her. William had walked down to the courthouse, but he'd be home for lunch, he'd said.

Amalise is fine, just fine. She picked up yesterday's newspaper from the table in the living room where William had left it and carried it with her into the kitchen. *She's fine, Father.* When she first arrived, Mama had still been afraid Amalise might be hiding something from them. *You know how I felt, Lord. . . . It's the fear that grabs your chest and squeezes tight.*

And sure enough, instead of being comforted by seeing her daughter, the unease had persisted. Something was wrong. Mama could see it in the way Amalise seemed to lose track of her thoughts when William and she would ask their daughter about school and classes and work and friends. And then suddenly she'd snap to and give the kind of answer someone gave when they'd been only halfway listening, when one's mind is really somewhere else.

In the kitchen Mama switched on the lights against the gloom outside and put the newspaper into the trash can. *But I was wrong. She was just winding down. It took a few days . . . getting used to being home again. And then Jude arrived, and after Thanksgiving dinner they went off in the boat for the afternoon and had a fine time. Did you see the change in her? When they returned, the lines between her eyes had smoothed. She was laughing, joking with Jude and William and me, and the glow had returned to her face. Maybe it was the sunshine and fresh air. Maybe it was the peace and quiet of the swamp. I don't know. Maybe it was home.*

Or maybe . . . it was Jude?

When the thought struck, she halted in her tracks. *Lord. Father! Is it possible?*

She stood still in the middle of the living room, hand over her heart, and looked at the wall visualizing the possibilities, giving the thought free rein. She could see the two of them together in the years ahead. Why hadn't she thought of this before? She could feel her heart beating underneath her hand. Turning, flesh tingling, she set both hands down flat on the counter and looked out over the bayou.

Why not? Please make it true. What would be more natural, after all? For deep friendship to become something more. She smiled and lifted her face to heaven. *Well, I'm not going to let myself think of that—Thy will be done.*

Her daughter was in the best hands possible.

Chapter Seventeen

Amalise took the bus back to New Orleans on Monday morning after Thanksgiving. Leaning back, head turned to the window, she watched the gray November landscape rolling by. The bare branches and gray sky reflected her mood right now. The bus was damp and cold, and she huddled, hugging herself, wanting to cry. The lies of omission to Mama and Dad and Jude weighed heavy, and she knew that in the last few days her life had irrevocably changed. By not telling the truth, she'd accepted Phillip's lies. And why had that occurred?

Because if she had done what she should, she'd have been forced to take actions, make decisions that she dreaded.

But somehow she had to make things right. During Mass on Sunday morning with Mama and Dad and Jude, she had closed her eyes against the thought of losing Phillip, a thought that sent her spiraling into a dark place for reasons she didn't understand.

I know I've taken a turn from the path, Abba. But I'm not real clear on what's right and what's wrong now. There's a bond between us—Phillip and me—like a steel cord that draws me to him, makes me want to create a home for him, protect him, be the family he's never had.

Was what she felt for Phillip really love? Was she ready to make a lifetime vow, to marry a man she hardly knew? She didn't know. And yet he needed her so; he trusted her. She could help him. She could *fix* him. And what would he do without her? *He's lost, Abba. Did You send him to me for that?*

Silence.

Abba?

But the answers she sought had eluded her. Or, now, sitting in the bus and looking back, she wondered if perhaps she hadn't really listened. The truth slowly rose: as she'd knelt in the old church in Marianus, she'd had a one-sided conversation with God. Did He listen to prayers like that—when one of His flock, though loving Him, still strayed? Knowingly?

She thought about that. Yes. Even then. He was still her Abba. His love was constant. That's one thing she knew she could count on.

These worries clashing, raging inside, pummeled her as the bus rambled up, up the steep climb of the Mississippi River Bridge and over the brown water below, on through Baton Rouge toward New Orleans and Phillip. As they rolled along, her eyes closed. She longed to sleep. Right now she longed for nothing more than to blot out the world and just dream.

SHE FOUND PHILLIP AT home and stretched out on the couch watching TV. He'd arrived last night, he'd mumbled without getting up. She sat on the edge of the couch and asked how things had gone in New York. All right, he said vaguely, running fingers up and down her forearm. He didn't ask, but while she unpacked, she told him how things were in Marianus, about Thanksgiving and fishing with Jude. He watched her from a cocoon of cushions under sleepy lids and didn't say much, as if the trip home had sapped his strength. He was asleep when she left for class.

The café was busy that evening; tables were all filled. So when the woman barged through the line at the doorway and seemed to be headed in her direction, Amalise sighed and walked over, holding a stack of menus in the crook of her arm.

"I'm sorry, we're full." She had to work to hide her annoyance. Didn't the woman have eyes? There wasn't one empty table in the place. "If you'd like to wait, the line's back there." She nodded toward the bar, where customers milled around with drinks. "It will be about half an hour."

When the woman pushed a package toward Amalise, she stepped back. What on earth? The bundle was bulky, wrapped in slick brown paper and tied together with a dirty string. "You're Amalise Catoir, aren't you?"

"Yes." The woman's face was familiar, but she couldn't place her.

"Good. Here you go." She shoved the package into Amalise's arms, slapping it on top of the menus. "These are Phillip's."

Amalise flinched, and the package tumbled to the floor along with the menus. Customers at tables around them glanced over as Amalise stooped, scrambling to pick up everything. When she'd gathered the menus, she rose, holding the package by the string, looping it over her fingers. The woman stood watching her.

Gina walked up. "What's going on?"

She hissed the question at Amalise as she took the menus from her. Frowning at the package, the woman, and Amalise, she curled her mouth into a glittering smile as she nudged Amalise away from the tables. "Let's move. We're causing a disturbance."

The woman raised her brows and turned to leave, and that's when it all fell into place. Amalise saw her in the blue hat at Porter's Gallery and later sitting with Phillip at the window table on that rainy night. Joanna was her name. Amalise glanced at the window table and back to Joanna.

Confirmation dawned in the woman's eyes.

"Oh yes," she said with a small, tight smile. "These are his." She tilted her head. "It's Phillip's laundry, my dear. And my gold dress is in there too. I thought you might want to keep it." She pressed a finger against her lip. "I certainly won't wear it again. He left in a hurry, but it's all yours now, along with the rest of his problems." Her voice was mocking. "And you can tell him, by the way, that the money he borrowed . . ." She lifted her chin and twisted her mouth, "He still owes me."

The gold dress Phillip had brought to her to wear for the portrait? The room spun, and Amalise reached out, bracing against the back of a chair. Perhaps if she stood very still, Joanna would go away.

But the woman's eyes traveled down Amalise and back up again.

"That shouldn't be a problem, should it? You're young and strong. Looks like he's found a brand-new meal ticket." Her lips curled up. "But then Phillip's good at that."

Before Amalise could say a word, Joanna wheeled around and stalked to the door without a backward glance. Amalise gripped the package to her chest, staring at the woman's rigid, retreating back. Gina turned her toward the kitchen. Amalise's face grew hot as customers gaped while Gina steered her through the tables.

In the kitchen Amalise tossed the package onto a table and gave it a fierce look, blinking back tears. Ignoring the stares of the cook and workers, she pushed through the kitchen door, back into the dining area. Bright lights burned her eyes as she worked, taking orders, refusing to think of what had just transpired. The second time she got an order wrong, Gina sent her home. With the book bag hanging from her shoulder and the hateful package in her arms, she walked through the dark streets faced with reality and dreading what was coming.

Phillip's eyes darkened, seemed to sink into his head when she entered the kitchen with the package hugged to her chest. "This is from Joanna. It's your laundry and that gold dress." She forced back tears and lifted her chin. Whatever happened, he wouldn't see her cry.

That mottled flush crept up his neck as he yanked the package from her hands and slammed it down onto the kitchen table. His jutting forehead, sunken eyes, and angular cheekbones gave him an ominous, almost simian look in the harsh overhead light. She stepped back.

"I'll kill her."

"You said she was just a friend. Just the manager of the gallery."

He walked over to the counter and grabbed a half-empty bottle of bourbon. She watched in silence as he filled the glass, added a splash of water and a few ice cubes. With his back to her, he took a deep drink.

"What did she mean to you?"

His shoulders tensed and rose. He set the glass down with care and turned to face her.

"Were you living with Joanna?" Her heart raced as she spoke. Had he lied again? Was he married after all?

All he offered was a careless shrug. "What do you want me to say?"

"She said you owed her money."

Tendons on his neck tightened and swelled. He leaned back against the counter, folded his arms, and gave her a hard look. "I don't like being interrogated, so I'll only say this once, Ama." His voice was a low, steady monotone. "Joanna is crazy about my work and put me up for a few months. That's it." He shook his head. "She owns Porter, the gallery. It was a business arrangement in my mind."

"Did you love her?"

"No." He smiled but his eyes were cold. So cold. "Does that satisfy your curiosity?"

The revelation, Phillip's misleading description of his past relationship with Joanna the night they'd had coffee at Café du Monde, dropped through her like a stone. The tears threatened despite her resolve. She shielded her face with her hand and sank into a chair at the kitchen table. So many lies. Had he ever told her the truth? Who *was* Phillip, this man she thought she loved?

He sat in a chair across from her and gave her a studied, incredulous look. "Why are you so upset, babe?" He jutted out his chin and dropped his arms to his sides. "I walked out on her. I had to get away. She was like a python, smothering me." Lowering his chin, he rested his forearms on the table and looked at her from under his brows. "And I fell in love with you."

Amalise closed her eyes, concentrated on stars sparkling in the darkness behind her lids.

"Men don't always confess old relationships, Ama. What's so strange about that?"

She opened her eyes and looked at him, tamping down the anger. She spread her hands before her. "I was humiliated in the café. And in front of all those people!"

"Joanna means nothing to me. Never did." He rose, came around the table, and stood behind her, pressing his hands upon her shoulders. His voice turned soft, soothing. "I didn't tell the whole story at first because I didn't want to lose you."

"Was she in love with you?"

"Probably. What does that matter?"

Why did she have to know all this? Why couldn't things just have stayed as they were?

"Being around Mother and Robert at Thanksgiving opened the old wounds." He stroked her hair, and after a minute she leaned back against him. "Let's pretend Joanna doesn't exist. You and I are family now. We belong together."

Images of Joanna faded as he pulled her up from the chair and encircled her with his arms. His lips pressed her forehead. She spread her hands on his chest and felt his heartbeat. The lonely, unloved little boy surfaced and dropped his head to rest in the crook of her neck. "Ama, Ama."

She was his world. He needed her. Without her he was alone. Her arms slipped around him, and she rubbed her hands over his back in big circles with the strongest desire to soothe and protect him, to let him know he could trust her. Joanna was forgotten.

"We should get married." Phillip's arms encircled her waist.

"You haven't even met my parents."

"You're mine, Ama. Mine."

A chill crept through her, knowing there was something more she did not quite understand.

Something dark and intense.

But she'd had everything growing up that Phillip had missed—Mama and Dad's unconditional love, the strength of her faith, Jude's friendship, her relationship with Abba. Still, as she held him, the slashing lines of thick black paint in Phillip's pictures seemed to surround her, encasing her as if she, like those other women, was separated from everything in the world but the artist.

Something that Phillip had said when he'd first asked her to sit for the portrait came back to her: *"I want to capture you . . . on canvas, of course."*

She shoved the thought aside. That comparison was foolish.

Chapter Eighteen

Jude leaned across the front seat and handed the taxi driver two dollars before sliding out of the car.

"Thanks man," the guy mumbled as he drove off. Jude hefted the duffel onto his shoulder and opened the wrought-iron gate to his side of the duplex he'd bought on State Street, such a contrast to the station he'd just left in Pilottown. Each entrance to the house had a small square front yard inside the fence. On his side an oak tree grew, towering over the roof. Just outside his bedroom on the second floor was a screened-in porch with an old lounge chair and two cane chairs. The shaded porch was the main reason he'd bought the house. He spent a lot of time out there, thinking, reading, even napping.

The frame house was built on brick pilings that rose three feet from the ground, keeping it cool in the summer and safe from occasional flooding that occurred in New Orleans even here on the high ground near the river. On Jude's side a narrow alley ran to the backyard, which was gated and fenced with rows of high-weathered cedar planking. Except for the small area he'd cleared for a porch, the backyard was overgrown with ginger, iron plants, banana plants.

Mrs. Landry's front door opened. "Jude! Is that you?"

Jude halted on the top step. As always it took his elderly tenant almost a full minute to negotiate her way out onto the front porch to greet him. He'd timed it once. Her gray head emerged from the screen door, face beaming over rounded shoulders.

She held up her hand, as if stopping traffic. "You're back just in time."

He smiled, dropped the duffel on the porch by his feet. "Good morning, Mrs. Landry."

"I've got a bill for you." She beckoned and turned back into the house. "Wait one minute."

When she reappeared, he hopped over the half-wall that partitioned the porches and took the invoice from her, while she told of the plumber she'd had to call for the sink. He said he'd pay and she looked relieved. Slipping his hand under her elbow, he helped her back into the living room. With a swift kiss on her cheek, he deposited her near a tall wingback chair that she could hold onto for balance.

Closing Mrs. Landry's door behind him, he climbed back over the partition and picked up the duffel bag. In his own living room he tossed the duffel bag onto the couch, took a deep breath, and looked around, glad to be home. The place was old but spacious, with wooden floors he'd finished himself and high ceilings. There were fireplaces in every room. None worked yet, but he'd fix them soon.

He walked through the living and dining rooms identical to Mrs. Landry's on the other side of the wall, through the hallway and into the kitchen. Palmetto bugs ruled in here at night, scurrying in from the outside as they did everywhere in New Orleans, but in daylight the kitchen was a free zone. He strode to the refrigerator, pulled out a ginger ale, and drank it while gazing through the window over the sink at the riot of foliage in the backyard. Amalise had said she'd help him make a garden, and when the porch was finished, she'd wanted him to hang a swing out there like the one at home in Marianus.

But all of that would have to wait awhile. Besides, she'd been distracted at Thanksgiving, and he hadn't seen her since. Unwanted, a vision of Phillip's pictures in the gallery rose. He frowned and gulped the sweet, cold drink. Amalise thought she was in love with that professor; at least that's what she'd claimed at first. An intense foreboding flooded him. He set the bottle down on the counter and walked back to the living room and the telephone. Something was wrong. He'd felt the undercurrent of tension in her glib conversation during Thanksgiving dinner and again when he'd brought up Phillip while they fished.

Standing over the telephone table, he pulled his wallet out and fingered through the crumpled folds of paper until he found the phone number. Mac's scribble was difficult to read, the napkin was worn— might have gone through the wash a time or two since he'd called the detective from Pilottown. He had to squint to read the numbers. He hesitated. Amalise wouldn't like him butting in, but on the other hand, he'd already made the first call. He dialed the number, he'd see what the guy had found. If there was nothing there, well, he could quit worrying.

The phone rang four times, and someone answered, a woman's voice. "He's not in," she told Jude. But he'd be in tomorrow morning— about ten or so. Would he like to come down to the office tomorrow, around midmorning?

She penciled him in for ten.

ROMAR LEBORDE SAT BEHIND his desk in front of glass window-panes so thick with layers of dirt on the outside that the brick building ten feet away was only a shadow limned in haze. Electric lights on the desk and a table and a fluorescent light on the ceiling gave the room an almost iridescent glow.

"Coffee?"

"No thanks." Jude pushed back in the uncomfortable wooden armchair. "Have you come up with anything on Phillip Sharp?"

"Yes and no." Romar slid his hand over a manila folder on top of the desk in front of him. He pursed his lips as if thinking how best to summarize, then flipped open the folder and ran his eyes down two pages of handwritten notes.

Two pages, Jude noted. Not good. He couldn't have found much.

"In the first place"—Romar looked up at Jude—"he's who he says he is. Phillip Ramsey Sharp. Ramsey's the mother's name. His father's vice president of design engineering at Craig Corporation. Lives in New York City, like you said. Well off, not rich but pretty comfortable." He turned the folder around and slid it across the desk to Jude. "The address is in the report—upper east side. Phone number. Birth dates, clubs . . . like that."

He leaned back. "His mom and dad have college degrees. Dad's got a master's in business from someplace in the Midwest." He flipped his hand toward the folder. "It's all in there."

"Forget them. What about the professor?" Jude stretched his legs and spread out in the chair. "Has he had other teaching jobs before this one? Anything strange in his past? Ever been married?"

Romar swiveled and gazed at the window. "That's the second part. The guy's not a professor."

Jude stared at the detective's back.

"He graduated from Tulane, undergraduate, last spring. Majored in art. Now he's taking two graduate courses and teaches a freshman class for the Newcomb art school. He's a teaching assistant of some sort. Part-time."

Jude bent forward. "Are you sure of that?" His stomach tightened. There was a world of difference between a part-time TA and a professor.

Romar nodded, swinging back to face Jude. "I took a ride over to the school the other day. Walked all over that building looking for his name on a door. Finally asked for Professor Sharp at the front office. The girl laughed, said isn't that just like Phillip?"

Jude frowned.

Romar curled his lower lip and nodded. "Your instinct was right. We know he's a liar if nothing else." He looked down, shining his fingernails with his thumb. "This office girl, she and I got friendly. She says they're letting him take his time about leaving. He teaches that one class and uses one of the large classroom studios off-hours. She says he's a pretty good artist but temperamental." He gave Jude a wry look. "I think they're all a little off, those artists."

"Anything else?"

"Not much. He doesn't own property of record. No telephone number. No arrest records, here or New York, except one bad check misdemeanor a few years ago in Manhattan. Dad probably cleared that up, but it's still on the record. The front-desk girl says she thinks he lives with someone, but she wasn't sure. I can dig further if you want." He paused. "It's up to you. Depends on how much you want to spend."

"Maybe. Let me think about it."

"The rest of it's in the report." He flipped the manila folder closed. "I'll have Peggy type it up for you. My handwriting's hard to read." He hesitated, watching Jude. "He's a drifter if you ask me. After he finished high school . . . good grades, but no sports or clubs in the yearbooks, not much of anything during that time. No roots after that. There's about five or six years where he seems to have moved from one low-paying job to another."

Jude's eyebrows drew together. "Before he entered Tulane."

"Yeah." Romar twisted his neck from side to side until Jude heard a cracking sound. "College kept him out of Nam, I suppose. That and flat feet, maybe. Before college, I figure him for something like door-to-door sales, bartender, working a counter. Never made much money but never got in real trouble . . . no record of trouble anyway."

"Where'd he live?"

Romar shrugged. "Here and there. It's hard to tell after high school. Appears to have stayed in New York City until he came down here. Lived at home some of the time according to the doorman at the parents' place—I have a friend up there did a favor. Might have lived with girlfriends too, but there's nothing to prove it. No electricity bills in his name, no credit cards."

"Wonder how he paid for school? Tulane's not cheap."

"Neither is New York." Romar shook his head. "His parents have money. I suppose they paid, although I'd bet a buck they're tired of him by now."

"If you've seen his paintings"—Jude shook his head—"they're grotesque."

Romar spread his hands flat on the desk before him. "He's older than the average undergraduate. Wasted those earlier years. It's in the report. Lived in the dorm when he first got here. After that?" He shook his head and pushed up from the chair. "He either found someone else to pay the bills, or he's robbing banks, or his parents are still on the hook. I don't see a source of income."

Jude stood. "No divorce record?"

"Nothing." Romar walked around the desk and clapped his hand on Jude's shoulder, steering him toward the door. "Legally he's clean. I'd say he's just a loser. Want me to look further?"

Jude shook his head. "Not right now." He'd heard enough. How on God's green earth was he going to tell Amalise that the guy wasn't a professor, as she believed? What else had he left out?

Romar slapped him on the shoulder as he left.

Jude stabbed the elevator call button with his forefinger. He had to tell her. No way around it. But one thing he knew for certain: she'd want to kill the messenger.

JUDE DROPPED HIS HAND as the door opened. He found himself staring into the face of a stranger. It was Sunday morning, and he should have called first, but Amalise hadn't met him at church like she usually did when he was in town. He was worried. "Uh." He hesitated and took a step back. "Is Amalise here?"

The stranger smiled and opened the door wider. "I'll call her. You must be Jude. Come on in." Without waiting for an answer, he turned and yelled over his shoulder. "Ama, you have company."

Ama? Jude fought to form a polite smile and failed. So this was Phillip. But where was Amalise?

Then her voice came from the bedroom. "Just a moment."

Phillip stuck out his hand. "Phillip Sharp."

He shook. "Jude Perret."

Phillip moved aside and motioned Jude into the small living room. "Jude!"

He turned to see Amalise standing in the doorway, barefoot and wearing a short, flowered bathrobe. Her eyes were wide, stricken. Her mouth rounded. "Oh. Hello, Jude." Her hands clung to a towel wrapped around wet hair.

"Didn't mean to interrupt." He raked his fingers through his hair. He glanced over at Phillip and back at Amalise. "I should have called. But . . . ah . . . I thought I'd see you at church this morning. I came down to the cathedral."

"Sunday is our day," Phillip said, moving toward Amalise.

Amalise flushed. "We're glad you're here."

Phillip halted.

"I've wanted Phillip to meet you," she went on, looking first at Phillip, then at Jude. Jude nodded. Turning back toward the bedroom, she called over her shoulder, "Phillip, can you get Jude some coffee while I change clothes?"

"Coffee?" Phillip walked over to the television set. He flipped it off and walked past Jude, into the kitchen. "Ice tea? Beer?"

"Coffee's fine." Jude sat at the kitchen table while Phillip poured out two cups of coffee and set them down on the table with two spoons. We, Amalise had said. We are glad you're here. He watched as Phillip retrieved a carton of milk from the refrigerator, brought the sugar bowl Jude recognized as one of Maraine's, and sat.

Phillip poured a few drops of milk into his coffee cup and slid the carton over to Jude.

"No thanks, I take it black." He sipped the coffee and looked at Phillip. A wave of dislike swept him again, but Phillip seemed unperturbed.

"Glad to finally meet you." Phillip spoke in a staccato burst, stirring his coffee. "You're a river pilot, I hear."

Jude nodded. Bar pilot, river pilot—Phillip wouldn't know the difference. He put the coffee cup down on the table.

Phillip leaned on his elbows and cradled the cup in his hands midair. "How'd you get into that?"

Jude turned the cup round and round on the table, staring into the coffee. "By way of my Uncle Oren, Pop's brother. He was a bar pilot and taught me, took me with him on the river when I was young, passed on his skills, his knowledge." He thought of the pictures of all the men in the family going back for hundreds of years on the wall in Uncle Oren's house, associated branch pilots all, except Pop. For as long as Jude could remember, Pop was deep in the bottle. But that was none of this guy's business.

"Take them from the Gulf into the river, right? Back and forth, those ships?"

"Yes."

"To Pilottown," Phillip droned on in a flat tone as if reciting something he'd been forced to memorize. "Now that sounds like an interesting place. You live down there?" Without waiting for an answer, he tipped his coffee cup to Jude, took a swallow, and set it down. "Fine place for a man, right? Good fishing and hunting down there, Ama says."

What was with that name he called her? "Uh, yeah. There's some trapping and fishing, when you've got time," Jude said, in a dry tone. How was he going break the news to Amalise that Phillip was a fraud with the man sitting right here? He certainly couldn't tell her now that he'd hired a detective to spy on the man she thought she loved. His heart sank. He looked at the kitchen door, wondering when Amalise would appear. Pressing his fingertips on the table, he pushed back. He shouldn't have come. But here he was, sitting across the table from Phillip Sharp.

"Has she told you about me?"

"Not much." Jude didn't try to hide the chill in his voice. "She showed me some of your paintings, the ones at Porter Gallery."

Phillip looked pleased.

Jude drummed his fingers silently on the table in front of him. "She mentioned you're a professor. At Tulane, isn't it?"

"Not yet." Jude looked up at the smooth correction. Phillip's smile was smug. "I'm a teaching assistant at the moment. They've made an offer for a faculty position, though, and I'm thinking it over." He took a drink.

Jude frowned, picked up his coffee and drank, watching him. "I was certain Amalise said you're a professor."

"Ama gets her facts mixed up." He chuckled.

Amalise came into the room and stood behind Phillip, hands braced on his shoulders as she looked at Jude. "I misunderstood."

Jude stared at her, seeing the truth in her eyes. She was covering for this man. So much for the money he'd spent on the detective. He broke the connection, looked away as his heart thumped an erratic beat. Amalise wore jeans and a white cotton shirt that she'd tied tight around her waist. He'd never noticed those curves before.

Phillip reached up and covered her hands with his. "Well, well. Here we are. Three old friends—I trust you don't mind thinking of me that way?" There was an edge to his tone. Jude said nothing.

Amalise freed herself and sat down between them. "Phillip's staying here for a while." She picked up Phillip's coffee and drank, seeming to scrutinize the inside of the cup.

Jude looked at her, struggling to clear his thoughts. Staying there? As in . . . *living* there? With her?

She avoided his eyes.

The full implication hit him. She was *living* with the guy. Living with Phillip Sharp!

Once when he was at sea, on a tanker out of Portland loaded with grain, they'd come upon four men in a lifeboat and three out in the water. A small ship had gone down in rough seas. The tanker rolled in swells so large that when the ship rolled, freezing water swamped the deck and men on board. He'd never been so cold.

The sailors were Chinese. They'd managed to rescue every man but one, and he would never forget the look on the drowning man's face as he'd flailed time and again for the rope, battered by the wind and waves. Standing alongside an AB, an able-bodied seaman, they'd fought to get that line out to the terrified, floundering swimmer, swinging the rope out over and over and over again until every one of his muscles ached and trembled from the effort.

He was just an ordinary seaman. When the man was lost to sight, he'd stood watch all night with a spotlight, praying as he swung the light out over the endless dark water. When the tanker at last moved on, he'd worked without stopping until they'd reached port, purging the images from his mind with a deep heavy sorrow, and a sense of loss, of having failed. He'd never felt that way before.

Until now.

Amalise asked him about Pilottown and the weather down there, and still shaken, he drank coffee and answered her questions. And she asked about the painting on his house on State Street—how was it coming along? And about progress on the back porch, and he answered those questions too, all the while sifting in his mind through details of Romar's report. The man sitting across from him was a drifter, a parasite.

A sudden silence reminded Jude that he was the intruder here, not Phillip. He saw a look pass between them, and he pushed the coffee cup away, preparing to rise.

"Did you catch that garfish?"

He scooted back the chair. "Yep. He was a big one."

"Mama was afraid you'd bring it around."

"Not likely." Jude turned his eyes to Phillip. "I'd like to talk to Amalise alone for a minute."

Phillip's face turned expressionless. With an exaggerated shrug, he turned his head toward the kitchen door and the living room. "This is a small place."

"Amalise?" Jude gazed at her.

She hesitated, then pushed back the chair and stood. "Sure." She touched Phillip's shoulder. "I'll be right back." To Jude: "We can talk outside."

Phillip said nothing as Amalise trailed Jude to the front door. He grasped the doorknob, feeling the smooth, solid surface of the metal in the palm of his hand. Somehow that was comforting.

Outside, with the door closed behind Amalise, he leaned against the iron gate and gave her a long look. "What's going on?" His voice was hard; his words clipped and sharp, for probing. "How long has he been here?"

Amalise leaned against the brick wall of her own apartment, arms crossed, one foot up, braced flat against the wall behind her. "Since before Thanksgiving."

He gave her an incredulous look. "Slipped your mind when we were in Marianus?"

At least she had the grace to blush. He saw her fingers tighten on her arms, twisting at the flesh underneath. "It happened suddenly, Jude. When you were out of town. He . . . I love him."

"That's interesting. You weren't so sure of that the last time we spoke."

"Don't be rude."

Two steps forward and he grasped her, holding her by the shoulders. Wanting to shake her. "Everything about this is wrong, against everything you believe." His voice was low. Urgent. "Get rid of him, Amalise. Before it's too late."

"Too late for what?"

"You're making bad choices and there will be consequences." When she stared at him, mute, he released her. He turned toward the gate, then hesitated.

"Jude." Her voice came from behind him. "You don't understand. I'm going to fix this."

Ama, Phillip had called her. She'd always insisted on her full name. *Amalise.* He let the name drift in his mind for a moment, remembering. "There's only one way to fix this, Amalise. Tell him to leave." When she said nothing more, he pulled the gate open, walked through, and let it slam shut behind him.

Walking in the direction of Canal Street and the streetcar, he thought with fervor that he didn't understand that it was time to make some changes in his life. Maybe he'd get that car. Fix up the house some more. Find a girl he could count on when he was in town.

But swinging through the Quarter, he saw Amalise's face as she'd looked lounging in the skiff last time they'd been together, skin glowing, hair lifting in the breeze, eyes half closed, and the image kindled a new emotion that didn't quite rise to the surface for examination. It was a feeling he'd never before connected with Amalise, and so he left it alone to simmer, focusing instead on his dislike for Phillip Sharp.

By the time he reached Canal Street where the streetcars ran, Jude struggled to console himself with the thought that surely, and soon, Amalise would return to her senses. *God, Lord. Please make that so.*

SHE'D THOUGHT THIS THROUGH since Jude's visit. She *was* in love with Phillip Sharp.

She was.

Classes, the café, the streetcar ride between the university and the Quarter, routine things like shopping for groceries, buying flowers for the kitchen table, listening to Phillip breathing beside her in their bed—everything took on a new sheen with Phillip in her life. The observer inside tallied the credits: Phillip rearranged his schedule whenever possible to walk home with her from work late at night. When he was able. He was often needed late at the studio uptown, so sometimes getting back to the café on time was quite a sacrifice. His students were demanding.

He'd gone to church with her a few times. She couldn't tell how engaged he was because the service was all so new to him. But it was a start. Not every Sunday. Last week he'd begged off, not feeling well, and had insisted that she stay with him that morning.

Well she didn't need the four walls of a church to talk with Abba.

Phillip was unique. Unlike other men she knew—Jude, for instance. Her relationship with Phillip was intense. *You're mine, Ama,* he'd say. He could be demanding, almost consuming, she admitted to herself. Sometimes it seemed he tried to control every facet of her life. She set boundaries where school, work, and studying were involved. But, still, Phillip's domineering personality was sometimes overwhelming.

That was because he loved her so, he explained, when she'd once confessed that sometimes she felt smothered. He was an artist, he said, guided by a different set of rules. An arrogant statement, but over the past months she had come to a deeper understanding of this complex, somewhat difficult man, and understanding his painting helped. *Edgy* was the word he liked to use to describe his work.

He took her down to his studio to see the painting he'd done of her one day. He'd finished it alone. She'd prepared herself for the gold dress, but it wasn't the dress that struck her like a cold, punishing wave when she finally looked at the portrait. It was the expression on her face. The pale girl lounging on the colorful couch seemed disconnected, lifeless, like all the other women in his pictures, gazing at something just out of reach.

That wasn't her. That wasn't Amalise!

They'd been sitting on the couch together. His arm encircled her, and she'd looked at the picture for a minute and then slumped against him. "Why is it that the women in your pictures never smile?" she'd murmured without thinking. He'd been twirling a lock of her hair around his fingers, winding and unwinding it when she spoke.

With a sharp little jerk that pulled her scalp, he'd released her hair. "Ah, my little critic's returned." As she'd rubbed the spot, he'd risen from the couch, walked over to the easel, lifted the canvas, carried it across the room, and set it face in against the wall. She hadn't seen it since.

Phillip wasn't always an easy man to please.

But she could be difficult, too, she knew. For instance there was the television set he'd brought to her apartment. That was still a nuisance, a problem they were working to resolve. It was difficult to focus on studies when the thing was on—one of those differences that couples work through, she supposed. But sometimes when the news came on and she saw those children again, standing in the blazing sun outside Phnom Penh waiting for food—at those times Phillip's television set was more than a distraction. At those times she couldn't focus on her work, couldn't read. She just could not dismiss those sad little faces from her mind. She was used to fixing problems, but this recurring one was too big, too far away.

But she couldn't just do *nothing*! And one small step was better than doing nothing at all. So she broke the problem down to a level she could handle, and after Thanksgiving she'd begun saving a portion of her café tips to send to those children. Maybe the money would feed one or two for a few days. It had taken a month, then she'd sent the money off directly to the U.S. Embassy in Cambodia—cash because she didn't know what a check would be worth over there. And really, how would you know if the money even arrived, or if it had, whether it got to the children, or ended up in someone's pocket?

But she couldn't just do nothing.

Still, the constant strum of news in her home was driving her crazy. Three days ago she'd stormed into the living room and told Phillip that she couldn't stand listening to the news any more, not one more minute. Phillip said she was obsessing over something she couldn't control, but he turned the volume down and kept it down since. So he was trying in his own way.

In turn, she resolved she would be his rock. She would guard the secrets of his childhood wounds. She was certain those years he'd suffered explained his shifting moods—the occasional fabrications, his need to know exactly where she was at all times, and with whom. All of her free time was spent with Phillip these days, and sometimes, she had to admit, she found this a bit crushing.

Crushing. Well, that was a harsh word she'd not meant to use.

When Christmas rolled around, Phillip refused to come with her to Marianus. He wasn't going to New York, and he thought that she should spend the holidays with him. He'd begged her not to leave him alone. But she had weighed Mama and Dad's disappointment and told him no. Phillip had been angry again, called this her rebellion. Like it was a test.

So she compromised. She went home for just two days, Christmas Eve and Christmas Day.

When she returned, Phillip was quiet and irritable, and she found herself apologizing—it was the easiest thing to do. She shouldn't have left him alone, she finally said to quiet him down, even as she hated speaking those words.

"Was Jude there?"

"No." And, if she were honest, she'd admit she'd been disappointed. Worried, too. Jude always came for Christmas. He'd always before managed somehow to get the day off, but not this year. And it hadn't been the same without him. But then, since the visit, Jude had made himself scarce.

But after a few hours Phillip's anger over her trip home dissipated. He lifted her up in his arms and swung her around and told her how precious she was to him. That evening they celebrated at La Boucherie down on Chartres, at a corner table decorated with candles and Christmas holly. She sang her own prayer of thanksgiving inside. He was a different person when they were alone together.

"Just the two of us," he said. "I don't want to share you."

As the months progressed, she realized the bond between them had strengthened. That nurturing feeling took root in her heart. She sensed an *otherness* about Philip that made her ache for him. Amalise was the only person he would trust, he said, and she believed him.

She had changed her life for him, but this was only temporary she told herself. When Mama and Dad met Phillip, they'd love him. Perhaps Jude would come around and get to know the real Phillip, the vulnerable man underneath, the talented artist she knew. And then they would get married. Perhaps. Perhaps. Perhaps.

"When you're not with me, I'm not alive," Phillip often said. "I don't exist without you. You're mine, Ama."

She would nod, not really understanding but wanting to show that she'd heard. And that's what seemed to matter to Phillip.

Being heard.

Chapter Nineteen

M arch is a deceiver. There's always one last cold, wet spell strag-
gling along when you think it's spring." Henry looked through
the door at the damp haze hiding Jackson Square. He leaned back
against the counter behind the bar, his expression glum. The last
customers had left an hour ago.

Amalise followed his eyes to the door. "Yep." She rested her chin
on the palm of her hand, waiting for Phillip. She wore a coat, but it
wasn't a raincoat, so she hoped he'd have an umbrella. It was after
midnight, cold, and still drizzling outside. Even with the shutters
closed, even with her coat already on, she could feel the damp chill
in the air.

She could hear Gina closing things up in the kitchen. Phillip was
late. She could have left fifteen minutes ago, but here she sat, still
waiting.

Henry gave her a sideways glance. He swiped the counter around
her with a damp cloth. "You planning to spend the night here?"

Amalise shook her head. Gina came through the kitchen door
wearing her coat, and Amalise spun around on the stool as she turned
off the lights, except for the back wall lights. Hitching her collar up
around her neck, she walked toward Amalise and Henry.

"You two ready to go?"

Henry shook out the dishrag, folded it, and hung it on the sink.

Reaching under the counter, he grabbed a jacket, which he put on and zipped up in one smooth motion. Amalise retrieved her book bag from the stool beside her, stood, and glanced at her watch. It was twelve twenty. Spring term projects must have held him up again. Students racing the clock, needing help. It happened two or three times last week. It might be this way from now until the end of the semester. She sighed.

Gina stopped before her. "Don't you have an umbrella?"

"No. The rain's light. I'll just run for it."

Gina narrowed her eyes at Amalise and held the door. When Amalise and Henry followed, she closed and locked it behind them. Shivering, Amalise waved and headed across the silent square in front of the cathedral. She avoided looking at the church—hadn't gotten there in more than a month now. Phillip had become forceful about her leaving him alone. He said he was willing to go with her, but he needed time. Hunching over the book bag, she kept her eyes on the pavestones as she hurried past.

Abba. Amalise here. Do You understand?

Artists and tourists and locals were long gone on this weeknight. Street lamps glowed through the mist, casting shadows as she walked past the fenced park toward the darker area, telling herself there was no reason to be afraid. Before Phillip came along, she'd made this walk alone every night, unless Jude was in town. Nevertheless, she made herself small, scouring doorways and the alleys as she passed them.

Leaving the square behind, the balconies of the Pontalba apartment building sheltered her from the rain. As she drew close to Dumaine, she saw lights still on in Harry's Bar. Despite the weather the windows were open, and an old man slumped over the sill like a rag doll. She turned the corner and headed toward her building.

The telephone was ringing as she inserted the key into the front door. She rushed to pick it up.

"Hi, babe." She grimaced as she heard the apology coming. "Sorry I couldn't make it again. I'm at the studio, finishing up."

There was music in the background. He had the record player going as usual. "No matter," she said, dropping the wet book bag onto the kitchen table. "I just got home."

"You sound breathless."

"Do I?" Brushing damp hair back from her forehead, she closed her eyes, tired and conscious of time. She still had work to do for tomorrow's classes. "I'm fine. When will you be home?"

"I don't know. Soon."

It was two thirty in the morning when she closed the books she'd spread across the kitchen table, turned out the light, and went into the bedroom. The rain was falling harder now and she could hear the wind chimes moving in the wind as she undressed for bed. If only Phillip were here so that she could curl up beside him.

AS PHILLIP TALKED ON the phone, Jude watched him from under lowered lids. Jude was sitting with his date at a table in the Hound & Hare, a popular spot near the university. The Hound & Hare had the best jukebox in the city.

It was past midnight. Since that day at Amalise's apartment, he'd resolved to keep in touch with her only when Phillip wasn't around, but he wasn't finding that easy. Phillip always answered the phone, and Amalise was never "available" right then. He wondered if Phillip ever told her he'd called.

But why was Phillip here at this time of night?

Jude frowned and glanced at his watch. Amalise would be walking home from the café alone, and here was Phillip. Something wasn't right. Last time he'd seen her, she'd seemed so tired, tense.

Was Phillip talking to Amalise? If so, what was she thinking right now on the other end of that line? How did he explain the background noise? Phillip's face contorted as he hunched away from the loud music, covering the receiver with his hand. Then he turned to the wall, as if he'd heard Jude's thoughts.

"Jude?" Angela shouted over the jukebox.

He tore his eyes from Phillip. Angela cupped her hand behind her ear and pointed toward the area of the restrooms. Jude nodded.

She slipped away, and he continued watching as Phillip hung up the phone and turned to survey the room. His eyes skimmed past Jude and stopped on two women sitting at the bar. Girls. They were girls. Seventeen or eighteen at most, laughing, preening, glancing sideways over their shoulders each time the front door opened. When the record changed, one of them tossed her blonde hair, thrust out her arms, and shimmied.

Phillip walked up behind them, slung his arms over their shoulders and ducked between them. They drew back and looked at him for a second, forming an empty *V* space. He said something that made them laugh, and the space closed around him.

Jude could hear Phillip's voice as he shouted over the music: "What are you drinking?"

He didn't catch the answer, but Phillip slid onto a barstool beside them and motioned to the bartender, circling his fingers overhead for drinks all around. Jude hooked his arm over the back of his chair, watching. Neon lights—hot pink, yellow, green, purple—flashed from the jukebox.

Phillip pulled out his wallet, reached inside, and threw money on the bar. According to that detective, a teaching assistant's salary was almost nothing. Amalise was probably supporting him. A vise tightened around Jude's chest at the thought.

Angela returned. She followed his gaze as she slid into the chair beside him. "Someone you know?"

"I've met him. He's at Tulane."

The bartender picked up the money—Amalise's tip money, likely—and Phillip said something that made the girls laugh. The bartender gave him thumbs-up.

Jude averted his eyes, fighting to quell a surge of rage. "Ready?" Angela nodded and he stood, holding her coat. The place was almost empty now. Crossing the room, he halted as they reached the door. "Wait here for a moment," he murmured, touching Angela's arm as he walked past her over to the group at the bar.

He put his hand on Phillip's shoulder.

Phillip was curled toward the women. He turned, and a beat passed before his eyes registered recognition. Straightening abruptly, he swung around on the barstool. Jude stepped back.

"Jude, isn't it?" Phillip spoke in a jovial tone, stretching a smile across his face and holding out his hand.

Jude nodded but made no move to take the proffered hand. The vise had spread, leaving his chest taut and heavy, as if something underneath would burst through, splintering his ribs. Phillip's smile turned brittle as he lowered his hand. The two girls had turned their heads to watch. Phillip folded his arms over his chest and gave the girls a look and a shrug before turning back to Jude.

Jamming his hands into his pockets, Jude leaned in close, within inches of Phillip's face, close enough to smell the alcohol and smoke on his breath. Phillip drew back. The jukebox lights reflected in Phillip's eyes.

Jude's voice was harsh, low, and fierce. "If you hurt Amalise, I'll come after you and you'll wish we'd never met." He straightened, still glaring. "Tell her I'm in town." Without waiting for an answer, Jude turned and walked quickly to the door where Angela waited. "Let's go."

Behind him, he heard the girls' muffled laughter.

His right hand curled into a fist by his thigh. *I want just five minutes alone with him.* He opened the door and ushered Angela out. He flexed his hands, feeling the corded tendons swell through his arms into his neck. Angela shivered and pulled her coat tight around her. He said that it was cold and she agreed, hurrying toward the new car he'd finally bought.

As he opened the door for Angela, he looked back over his shoulder. He was on watch in two days, but maybe he'd try to have a talk with Amalise before he left for Pilottown. Who else would tell her?

"SAW YOUR BUDDY LAST night," Phillip said as she was getting dressed for school. He slid up from between the sheets to give her a look and dropped his head back onto the pile of pillows, watching her pack the book bag.

"Who's that?" She didn't really care. She had no idea what time he'd come home, and this morning her bones ached with fatigue, and all she could think of was crawling back into that bed and forgetting about classes and work and studies.

"That ship pilot . . . what's his name, Jude?"

Amalise looked up. "He's in town?"

Phillip's eyes held hers, as if monitoring her thoughts. When he nodded, the corners of his mouth twitched into the ghost of a smile.

"I stopped at a bar near campus for a quick beer on my way home. He was with a knockout—couldn't keep his hands off her."

Her stomach tightened at his words, and she lowered her eyes to the book bag. What was this strange feeling . . . this betrayal? She shifted a large book to the side in the canvas bag to make room for two smaller ones and her notebooks and forced a smile. "He always was a ladies' man." She closed the bag, snapped it shut, and lifted it onto her shoulder.

"Certainly was last night." He slid back down between the sheets and closed his eyes. "She was a looker."

She dropped her eyes and turned away, putting a lilt into her voice. "That doesn't surprise me."

"I gave him the high sign and he laughed. Didn't ask about you though, so that's good. He was having a fine time when I left. I'm surprised you're so fond of him though. I never did think much of him."

Grasping the strap of the book bag on her shoulder, she headed for the door. "He is my oldest, dearest friend." She closed the door behind her quickly, to shut out Phillip's laughter.

Chapter Twenty

As she reached Freret Street later that afternoon, crossing the campus from the law school building, a horn honked and Amalise looked up. There was Jude sitting in a shining black car. He whistled and waved her over. She hesitated. She hadn't seen or heard from him since the day he'd dropped by her apartment when Phillip was there. He hadn't cared enough to ask about her when he'd seen Phillip last night either. Too busy with that girlfriend of his.

But this is Jude.

She walked over to the car. He gestured and she opened the door and leaned in.

"I've been waiting for you. Gonna drive you downtown to work, chère."

She slid into the front seat, dropped the book bag on the floor by her feet, and looked around. "It's beautiful." She twisted around to inspect everything. "What kind of car is this?"

"Pontiac Grand Prix." He started up the engine. "Bought it a few weeks ago."

She ran her hands over the leather seats, the smooth-grained dashboard.

"Only six thousand miles on her."

"It's cool." The anger dissipated like smoke when she saw the smile he tried to hide. Jude may have grown up poor, but he was doing well now. That pleased him . . . and her.

"Good mileage."

"Good thing."

"Yeah. Sixty cents per gallon. Those gas lines are something else. I waited almost an hour at the station on Magazine Street yesterday." Jude reached over and switched on the radio. "Hi-fi. Listen to that bass. That's Aaron Neville singing." He glanced her way. "Do you have time for a detour?"

"A little one."

They entered Audubon Park from St. Charles Avenue and swung around the half circle to the right toward the back. He tuned the radio to a soft-rock station and lowered the volume. They passed the swan boat in the lagoon, then crossed Magazine and passed the huge swimming pool and the old zoo, and when they reached Monkey Hill near the river—the highest point in New Orleans, locals said—he parked. Children ran up the hill through deep dirt ruts to a flat rock on top and rolled back down in the grass. Two mothers sat in swings in the shade nearby, watching.

Jude leaned forward and turned the engine off.

"I don't have much time, Jude." Amalise shifted, leaning against the passenger door so that she could look at him.

A fine line formed between his eyes as he turned to her. "I have to talk to you, Amalise. It won't take long."

"Is something wrong with Mama. Or Dad?" She drew in her breath, waiting.

"No." He gazed to his left at the children. "It's about Phillip."

A wall seemed to rise around her. Exhale, Amalise told herself. Breathe slowly, carefully. This is Jude. This is Jude.

She sat wide-eyed and said nothing while he talked to her. He told her he'd gone to a private detective, someone called Romar. The man had done a report. On Phillip. He listed what was in the report, then told her he'd seen Phillip two nights ago. At a bar. With two young girls.

"I'm worried, chère. This man . . . I know you think you love him, but something's not right. I . . . I'm afraid he's not the man you think he is."

Each word struck as a blow, and that same fear spread through Amalise—followed by a wave of anguish—as his words penetrated and her thoughts spun.

And then she remembered everything Phillip told to her this morning. Jude was in no position to criticize. What was going on?

He reached for her hand, and she pulled back as if he'd burned her. "How *dare* you interfere, Jude?" Her voice rose, and the tears she'd fought as he talked now spilled. That he'd hired a detective roused a feeling of betrayal that swamped all other thoughts in her immediate fury. Clasping her hands together, she gasped for breath and stared at him. "How dare you hire a detective to spy on Phillip!"

"I didn't spy."

"How dare you say that I don't understand him." She pressed herself against the door, away from him. "He loves me! He *needs* me."

"Love and need are two very different things. A real man puts the woman he loves first in his life. He should cherish you above his own needs, protect you, rejoice when you succeed." His voice was low and controlled, but suddenly he slapped his hand on the steering wheel and she jumped. "Remember the words, Amalise? 'Love is patient, love is kind.'"

She could not answer.

"Love isn't just feeding a man's need. It's a two-way street."

"You don't know anything about our relationship."

Jude's expression hardened as he turned, leaning back against his car door, facing her with one arm thrown over the steering wheel and the other over the back of the seat. "Well now, let's see . . ." An angry white line began to trace his upper lip. His eyes were riveted on her. "Let's just examine who you're in love with here, Amalise."

His voice was low and caustic as he ticked off each point by thumping the leather upholstery with the flat of his hand. "We've got a professor who's not a professor. We've got an artist who's not an artist. An artist who, in fact, paints like a sadistic madman. If nothing else, we've got a soul on the dark side because we know he lives on lies."

Amalise narrowed her eyes.

He cocked an eyebrow in response and continued. "This person has moved in with you and yet seems to have no visible means of support. He doesn't appear to be honest or faithful or to worship any god but himself. We know what he's not, Amalise! But how much do we know about what or who he is?"

"*We?*"

"Correction noted." His arm dropped from the seatback, and he turned toward the steering wheel, looking off through the windshield. This was a side of Jude she'd never seen before.

Through the window she watched the children running up and down the hill. In the distance sea lions barked. It was feeding time.

Jude gripped the top of the steering wheel with his fist. "You're going down the wrong path, Amalise, and if you do that, you'll walk alone. God gave us brains for a reason. Think!" She could see his knuckles turning white as he looked out over the park. "I've said this before and you didn't listen. But I'll say it again. You're making bad choices with consequences you won't be able to control."

She clenched her teeth against the denial. Why lie when they both knew he was right. But oh! How she hated him for saying it.

Suffused with rage, she leaned forward, jutting out her jaw. "Who are you to criticize me or Phillip?" Whatever Jude had seen or heard, he'd misunderstood. He had no idea of Phillip's childhood, of what he'd suffered, of the depth of his need for her. And no understanding of Phillip's work.

"He's broken, Amalise. You can't fix him. Only God can heal Phillip Sharp."

She didn't want to hear these things, didn't want to think of them. She wanted to lash out, to diminish and hurt Jude. Her voice shifted to a higher, urgent key. "Who are you to decide that, *Jude Perret* from Marianus? You . . . you know how to fish and hunt, and you know about boats, but you don't know a thing about Phillip, or art . . . or . . . or . . . or Phillip's *suffering.*" She coughed, choked, flailed her arms, and doubled.

Jude lurched forward and grabbed her shoulders, pulling her to him while she struggled, sobbing.

"I don't believe a word you've said, Jude! You're wrong." She turned her face away, but she let him hold her while she cried. When at last the tears subsided, she sagged against him, hiding her face in his chest . . . just for a moment . . . just to get her bearings.

This is Jude.

Yes. And he had hurt her. Inside the battle between her friendship with Jude and loyalty to Phillip took a new and confusing turn. Phillip drew such compassion from her, and, yes—she was certain now—love. Jude's hands moved across her back, comforting as she nested against him, thoughts roiling.

Jude would never understand a man like Phillip.

"I'm so sorry, Amalise."

Still leaning against him, she nodded, shuddering. Would she lose Jude's friendship now? "Take me to work, please. I'm late."

His hands slipped from her and they both moved. He turned, fixed his eyes on the dashboard for an instant, then started the engine. Amalise sat upright, hands folded together in her lap, looking to the right through the passenger window as they drove down Tchoupitoulas Street. They passed the Hanson's Sno-Blitz red-and-white store, and she longed for a wild-cherry snow cone that Jude always joked tasted like cough syrup, even though she knew he liked it. But she wouldn't ask him to stop. Refused to ask him to stop.

"Have you said anything to Mama or Dad?"

"No."

"All right."

It was a long drive. When he stopped at the corner of Chartres and St. Peter outside the café, she opened the door, picked up the book bag, slid out, and slammed the door behind her. As the car began to pull away, she turned, shouted his name and ran back to the window. Jude slowed, braked, and rolled down the glass.

She peered at him without smiling. "He told me he wasn't a professor, you know. I misunderstood."

"Sure."

"And I don't believe what that detective told you."

He nodded.

She watched as he drove off.

Later, when she told Phillip of the confrontation, he said he only stopped for a beer after work that night. Amalise watched carefully for a change in expression that would give him away, then chided herself. Didn't she love him? Didn't she trust him? Whom did she want to believe?

His eyes narrowed, grew cold. "What's Jude trying to do, telling you these things? I don't trust him, Ama. You're going to have to choose. I love you too much to share. I'd rather die."

As he took her in his arms, Amalise pushed aside thoughts of Jude. "It's you I love."

"Yes. You are my whole world, my family. Let's get married."

She tucked her head under his chin and sighed. She had to make the choice, one way or the other. "All right." Why not agree. The wedding would be a long way off, and she could think about it all later.

"When?"

"Soon."

"But when?"

"You'll have to meet my parents first."

Phillip's lips slid along her throat, tingling. "You're mine, Ama."

Chapter Twenty-One

Who said April was the cruelest month? Amalise couldn't remember, but she figured it was right. One early April day she couldn't help herself and sat down next to Phillip on the couch in the living room, staring at the television set unblinking as the announcer in Saigon picked up a piece of twisted metal and held it up for the camera. Behind the announcer, spread over the blackened airfield outside Saigon, was scattered wreckage of a plane. Air America. A C-5A Galaxy, the announcer said.

She had to watch. Operation Babylift, they called it. The flights had been running day and night, pulling homeless children out of Saigon ahead of the Vietcong invasion that was coming. The Americans were finally leaving.

One of the Operation Babylift planes had crashed on takeoff. The plane was smoldering scrap metal now. On the screen was fire, blood. Tiny bundles covered with blankets and tarps, some left still uncovered—fragile little things, those bodies—twisted, bent, thrown about like broken dolls. And spread across the burned field were rescue workers in rickshaws and oxcarts, bicycles, cars, army Jeeps, ambulances.

Smoke began to veil the carnage—she could almost smell the smoke. Fire. Sirens. Police. Soldiers. Men, women, and children, all weeping, all turning to the camera with vacant eyes when the microphone was shoved into their faces—what has happened, how could this have happened, who would think . . . Doctors, nurses, medics . . . running, calling, shouting—out of the way!

Over there. There. No, over here!

One hundred thirty-eight presumed dead, the announcer rasped, choking on the words. Most of them were children going to America. Plucked from hot, malignant, mosquito-infested orphanages, bound for homes made of solid brick and stone and wood in the States, where new mothers and fathers and sisters and brothers were waiting. Two thousand orphans were to be whisked away like magic from the horror of war in Operation Babylift.

But these children didn't make it. Amalise stared at the scene, struggling to absorb the horror. Her eyes filled with tears. How could such a good idea have gone so wrong?

Phillip, sprawled on the couch beside her, lit a cigarette, took a puff, and exhaled. He patted her knee and said, "I thought you weren't going to watch this stuff anymore."

"I can't just ignore it."

"Why not? What do you think you can do about it?" He lifted his hand from her knee with an abrupt laugh. "It's sad, I know. But, honestly, Ama, how do we know any of this is real?" He flipped his hand, cigarette clamped between his fingers, toward the screen. "Ever wonder if these kids you worry about all the time are really orphans? Those people are different from us. They'd give up their kids in a snap. Ever think of that?"

She tightened her lips. Watched from the corner of her eyes as he pinched a grain of tobacco from the edge of his lower lip.

"Who'd ever know?" he went on, flicking the tobacco off. "Taxpayers foot the bill."

Amalise's head snapped around, and she gave him a fierce look. "Phillip!"

He started. "Well, I didn't mean that the way it sounded, babe." His eyebrows knitted together. "You just need to calm down."

Eyes riveted against her will to the screen, she wondered if Jude was watching this too. Jude would care.

She shut out the room and Phillip and prayed for the children who'd died that day and for those little ones who still lived in the dark corners of the world, the shadow children. She prayed that Abba would provide food and shelter for them, as He would do for any little sparrow, and that He would lead the children to families who'd love them. "What a tragedy."

"I agree, babe. But it's not our problem. And you shouldn't watch. It makes you depressed." He clicked off the set. "There. Gone. What's for dinner?"

THE FOLLOWING FRIDAY, ON payday at the Pontalba Café, Amalise took her share of tips from the cashbox and added them to her savings. Eighty-five dollars. She'd decided not to mention this to Phillip—money was tight these days. Next week she'd add some more and send it all off to the embassy in Phnom Penh again. Cambodian children weren't included in the Babylift rescue flights, and today she'd learned that Congress had cut off funding for the children's food runs.

It was probably a futile gesture, but still she needed to do something. She had so much—those children had so little. Walking home from the café when the shift was over, she thought of those children again, and she thought of the home where she'd grown up in Marianus, sprawling at the edge of the bayou, well lit, safe, and Mama's cooking and her loving advice, the look in her eyes when she bandaged a knee or cleaned a cut for Amalise—as if the injury were hers. And she thought of Dad, their talks sitting together out on the pier in the evenings when the birds fed and fish jumped and squirrels put on their shows. And Jude, always there for her.

Swinging along now, she smiled. Such a happy, safe childhood, she'd had. And then, just when her mood had lifted, came again those images of the small thin children waiting on the airstrip in Phnom Penh for food, the babies spread across that tarmac in Saigon.

Why the difference, Abba? Why?

Turning the corner on Dumaine, she slowed as she approached the apartment, wondering if Phillip would be home. He hadn't called to say he'd not be there to walk her home tonight. He'd been moody lately, irritable. But it was the end of the semester—classes were winding up, and he was busy these days. Poor Phillip. She thought of his childhood too.

Why did bad things happen in God's world?

She pulled the keys out of her purse and unlocked the gate. She and Jude had suffered through this conversation many times over the years.

They'd never understand it, really, Jude believed. Once he'd tried to explain. They were sitting on a branch of the oak tree just outside her bedroom window, and he'd been chewing on a piece of sugarcane. He stuck the cane in the corner of his mouth. "The best we can know is that it's us—you and me and every human being on this earth—not God, who causes pain and sorrow in the world. And that's because God gave us free will."

"What's that?"

"It's our right to choose our own paths through life ourselves, to choose between right and wrong. But along with each choice comes consequences and responsibility. And that's the rub."

"Why?"

He'd frowned. She'd figured he might be winging it here, and she had more questions, but she'd kept quiet because she wanted him to go on. And Jude . . . well, Jude was smart.

"Look at it this way"—he shaped his hands into a ball—"take a bad choice you might make. A lie to your dad or something. Your lie is like a snowball, rolling down a hill, getting bigger and bigger each time you repeat it, or cover it up, or add to it. It doesn't only hurt you but also the judge and Maraine and probably me. And then finally, when you're caught and have to pay the price, it's much worse than if you'd just come clean in the first place."

"Yes."

"So, if you think of this on a grand scale,"—he'd leaned over and spat to the ground—"of all the bad choices made by other people with power and money and the people around them, then you've got those snowballs rolling on through centuries. Added all together, they create an avalanche of trouble." He shrugged. "So we end up with people like Hitler, or Stalin . . . and wars, genocide, famine."

"But why doesn't God just tell us what to do?"

He'd chewed on the cane for a minute. And then he said something she'd never forgotten. "He doesn't want to pull the strings. I think He wants our love. Think about it, chère. *Of faith, hope, and love . . . the greatest of these is love.* Love's the only thing we have to give to Him. He created everything else. But He wants us to give our love freely. To *choose* Him, because otherwise we're just mindless puppets."

He'd pulled the cane from his mouth and spat again, then looked over at her. "So we have been given the right to choose." He shrugged and looked off. "Or not. Anyway, that's the best I can do."

She remembered the conversation like it had happened this morning. She'd sat beside Jude for a while trying to remember a moment when she hadn't loved her Abba and couldn't. She just loved Him.

But maybe just loving Him wasn't enough.

Closing the gate behind her now, she hesitated for a moment before inserting the key into the apartment door while that last thought burrowed down deep in her mind, unnoticed, and took seed.

Chapter Twenty-Two

Mama stared down at the laundry. *Father, the call last night from Amalise . . . what does it mean?*

Amalise had called last night to say she was bringing home a fellow she liked. Some man named Phillip Sharp. Who in the world was Phillip Sharp?

She shook her head. She and William hadn't known what to say. Was this what she'd been sensing, what Amalise was keeping from them? Lately when they'd talked, Amalise sounded like a record playing on high speed. *I pray she's following the path You've set while she handles whatever it is she's doing in that city.*

But she was bringing home Phillip Sharp, not Jude.

Not Jude.

Mama bundled up the clothes she was carrying to the washer and lowered herself into the soft armchair William had bought for her years ago. Placing the bundle in her lap, she folded her hands on top and looked off. Fingered the collar on one of William's shirts.

I pray I've taught her right. Her faith's never been tested, Father. Her throat grew thick. *At least not that I know. Her faith is still . . . childlike. She's too trusting, William says. This man, this Phillip Sharp . . . he's an artist, Amalise says. And he teaches at the university, but I couldn't quite understand what she was saying about that part.*

Maybe this man was just a friend. Mama held up William's shirt, folded it in half, then half again. Laid it back down on her lap.

I wonder what Jude thinks of this man. I'd trust his judgment any day. Jude is a rock.

Amalise and Jude. How well she remembered the day they met.

A smile played around the corners of her mouth. Amalise's first week of school, and she was still shy, uncertain about things. But after that first day she insisted on walking home by herself. It wasn't far, and the whole town was her neighborhood. So Mama said all right, and every afternoon she'd watch for Amalise to make the turn onto their street down by the stand of trees near the Marsh house. Mama made sure to wait behind the screened door so her daughter couldn't tell she was watching.

A little laugh escaped. *And when I'd see her coming safe and sound, I'd go back into the kitchen and pretend to be doing something . . . making cookies or something when she arrived.*

And then, one day, Amalise came running down the sidewalk instead of walking, and even far away Mama could see she was crying. Her heart almost stopped. Amalise had a scraggly wet puppy in her arms as she tore down toward the house. Mama couldn't help it—she flew out that door for her. *Oh my, the commotion. My heart did a real flip that day, You remember, Father?*

Hmmm. We ended up with the dog. Amalise never could walk past anything hurt—people, animals. She'll stop to turn a doodlebug right side up! Oh well. You know how I feel about dogs in my house, but that puppy was really pitiful, and as Amalise says, You've made us the caretakers. Plus, I know You've got Your reasons, Lord. And sure enough, a few minutes later here comes little Jude, a ragtag little blessing, fists pumping, headed for our house.

Mama never got the story straight what with the puppy and Amalise wailing and Jude on the scene, breathless, covered with bruises and cuts and dirt—and the only thing he'd wanted to know was if Amalise was all right. *It was what tipped Your hand, Lord.* And if ever there was a child that needed some family love, it was Jude. Mama had seen him around town once in a while with his dad, the town drunk. His mother died of cancer. *I pray she's with You, Lord. And please tell her how we love her son, me and William and Amalise. Thank You for sending Jude.*

She picked up the bundle of clothes and stood. *But who is Phillip Sharp?*

Chapter Twenty-Three

In the beginning of May, Amalise and Rebecca were both offered summer jobs with Mangen & Morris, a large law firm downtown. They were the first women ever to be hired as law clerks by the firm. Second-year clerkships with a firm like Mangen & Morris were prestigious, difficult to obtain. And the pay was high. If all went well, Amalise knew the job could lead to a permanent offer upon graduation. This was the beginning of her career! She'd have to quit her job at the café for the summer, although Gina said it would be waiting for her in the fall when the clerkship was over.

She and Phillip took a short trip on the Greyhound bus to Marianus in June before she was scheduled to start work at the firm. There were seven stops along the way, including a long one in Baton Rouge before they crossed the river and turned north into the shaded bayou country. Tunnels of trees along the route sprouted new leaves, wildflowers, banana plants, and palms. Elephant ears crowded the banks between the road and the bayous. But the roads were bad, crumbling from spring rain.

Phillip stared out of the window and refused to say a word to Amalise throughout the trip. He'd never ridden a bus before, he said when they got on and the stench of bodies and food and dank upholstered seats first hit, and didn't think he ever would again. There were civilized taxicabs in New York, private car services, and decent trains.

So he was in a fury by the time they arrived in Marianus four hours later, wiping perspiration from the inside of his collar with exaggerated swipes as they stepped down from the bus. Phillip was behind her muttering under his breath.

As she looked up, she caught sight of Mama and Dad waiting in the shade under the overhang just outside the bus station, and she waved, a big arc of a wave. Dad wore his good straw hat with a dark blue band around it and his seersucker suit . . . all dressed up to meet Phillip. Mama, too, wore a hat, a black straw hat with the net pushed up over the brim, a blue skirt, and a soft white blouse with a bow at the neckline. When they saw her, they beamed and Mama rushed forward.

"We thought you'd never get here." Mama was breathless as she hugged Amalise and turned to Phillip. Dad, beside her now, slung his arm across Amalise's shoulder and said, "How's my girl?" like he always did.

"This is Phillip." Amalise smiled as she rested her hand on his arm and looked from Phillip to Dad and Mama.

Dad cleared his throat, stepped one foot forward, leaned toward Phillip, and stuck out his hand. "Glad to have you visit, son. We've heard some about you from Amalise, so we're glad to have you here."

Mama stepped between Amalise and Phillip and spread her arms around them. "Amalise has never brought a beau home from school before. We're pleased to have you."

"Mama!"

Phillip laughed and pecked Mama on the cheek. "I've been looking forward to this trip. It's good to get out in the country, away from the bedlam in the city. I'm a city boy, myself, from New York. So I'm anxious to have a look around." Mama released them both, and as they started toward the car, Amalise walking beside Mama, and Phillip with Dad, Amalise heard him say how he wanted to learn to fish the way her dad did. He'd never fished. Never had the chance in New York.

Mama was her cheerful self as they drove home, but Amalise, watching from the backseat where she sat with Mama, thought Dad was very quiet, as if he sensed something offbeat. Phillip was talking fast, as if he wanted to get all the words out in one big rush. From time to time Dad glanced at Phillip with a slightly puzzled look. For a moment she worried that Jude might have spilled the beans about her living arrangement with Phillip, but she didn't worry long because Dad wouldn't have kept silent if he had. When it came to the judge's daughter, he'd speak right up if that were the case. Dad had never been shy about the pecking order in the family.

Amalise had extracted a promise from Phillip—no talk of marriage yet. It was too soon. Of course Mama put them in separate bedrooms and that put him in a temper too. Dad took Phillip fishing on Saturday, showed him how to bait a hook, how to cast out, reel in, wait. He came back in a good mood, carrying the ice chest and rods and reels up from the pier for Dad, and he'd hugged her when they'd reached the house.

"If this is what it takes," he whispered, eyes sparkling, "I'll do it."

That evening dinner was outside on the picnic table down near the pier. Mama had fried the catfish and bass caught that afternoon, and they ate corn on the cob cooked in crab boil, spiced just right, turnip greens, a plain salad with Creole tomatoes, and crunchy, hot French bread. The sun was going down by the time they finished, and they sat around talking while it slid down into the forest across the lagoon, lighting the trees, glazing the water around them.

Phillip leaned back, lounging, and looked at the sky. "Mighty pretty."

Amalise glanced at him, surprised at the tone and cadence of his words. He sounded much like Dad. Was he imitating him?

Dad didn't seem to notice. "Mama and I built this house right before Amalise was born." He folded his hands over his stomach and gazed at the scene. "The minute we saw this spot we knew this was where we wanted to raise our little girl."

"Amalise says you teach at Tulane?" Mama's voice, soft, shy.

"Yes. Newcomb Art School at Tulane. And I show my work at galleries."

"At galleries." Mama looked at Amalise and back at Phillip. "Well, *pensez donc*! I imagine that's a good feeling, seeing your work hung up on those walls."

"Is that what you did in New York, too? Before you came down here?" Dad's voice now, curious, probing. He picked up his glass and sipped the iced tea.

"Yes, sir." Phillip straightened in the chair, looking at Dad. "But I have to say I like the slower pace down south. Like that fishing trip you took me on today, just winding our way through the swamp, taking our time. No rush. No hustle."

He'd turned the conversation around, Amalise realized. "In fact," he reached over and patted her knee," let's go fishing together in the morning."

Dad's eyes followed Phillip's hands and their retreat.

"The bus leaves at ten thirty."

Mama looked at her. "We'll go to early Mass then."

"That's fine, Mama. Eight o'clock?"

Mama nodded and turned to Phillip. "Phillip, will you come with us?"

Amalise saw the slight movement at the corners of his eyes, but then he smiled. "Go on without me." His tone was breezy, unconcerned. "I'm not Catholic. And I didn't bring along the clothes for church."

"I can lend you—" Dad broke in.

Phillip waved the words away. "No need. I'll catch the service when we get back in town. Tomorrow."

Amalise fixed her eyes on the skiff tied to the wharf. The night was still, the little boat barely bobbed at the mooring.

Mama smiled, said something about the nice weather, and rose, and Phillip and Amalise pushed back their chairs and followed suit. "We'll get the dishes, Mama," Amalise said, and Phillip said they surely would, and the meal was wonderful, and she was not to worry about a thing, that they'd clean up.

Dad rose without saying anything. Amalise watched as he stuck his hands in his pockets and walked slowly down to the end of the pier, where he stood looking out over the bayou into the swampy forest on the other side.

By the time they left on Sunday morning, Phillip was on an even keel. Mama was happy—she thought Phillip was charming—and Dad? Well, Dad seemed at least to reserve judgment, which didn't surprise Amalise a bit. If Dad could have his way, Jude would be here with her instead. On the bus the thought of Jude made her close her eyes and pretend to sleep all the way back to New Orleans. She was too wrought up to make sense of the conflicting emotions that arose when she thought of Jude.

THE OFFICE THE FIRM assigned to her for the months of June, July, and August was a small box on the fourteenth floor, but she loved it anyway. There was a large desk, a comfortable chair behind the desk, and another placed in front of it for visitors. The furniture was dark, shining mahogany, and the floor was carpeted. There was a filing cabinet in the corner, and a row of built-in bookcases facing the desk on the far wall. The bookcase shelves were bowed under the weight of heavy leather-bound books with gold lettering on the spines. They were "deal books," Josephine Boudreaux, the secretary assigned to her for the summer had said—bound copies of all of the agreements negotiated in various business transactions. Amalise liked the sound of that. Deal books.

The Merchant Bank Building on the corner of Common and Baronne Streets was an imposing structure eighteen stories tall, high for New Orleans. There was one window in her office covered with thin black blinds. She walked over, pulled the blinds up, and peered through the glass. Below on the narrow street, toy cars negotiated their way between the towers.

Just across the street, rows of windows faced hers through airspace. She strained to see what was inside, but the copper-colored reflection from the morning sun prevented that. Would the sun prevent someone in those windows from looking back at her right now? Probably not. She lowered the blinds halfway, shook off the thought, and returned to the chair behind the desk.

Josephine had said that one of the partners would come by to welcome her this morning. She wanted to look busy when this person arrived, but she had nothing yet to do. Keeping her ear tuned for the sound of approaching footsteps and feeling like a racehorse waiting for the starting gun, Amalise swiveled the chair from side to side and picked up the telephone, listening to the dial tone, imagining herself on a conference call with clients. She pulled out a slim drawer on the right-hand side of the desk and found some new, sharpened pencils, pens, paper clips, and a stack of clean tablets of yellow paper to write on. Not bad, she thought, wondering why the paper was yellow, wishing that the phone would ring so she'd have something real to do.

She scanned the room once more, wanting to memorize all of this to tell Phillip. The framed diplomas from Princeton and Harvard Law School on the walls bore one name: Marshall Eugene Poche. His name was on the spine of the deal books too. Who was Marshall Eugene Poche?

She examined the photos hung in groups around the diplomas. They must be family members, she decided. Most of the pictures included elderly people and small children. One picture she especially liked was of a pretty woman standing alone in front of a colorful fruit stand somewhere in Europe. She wore a summer dress and she was laughing, reaching down and touching the fruit when the photo was snapped. Mrs. Marshall Eugene Poche, perhaps?

A series of taps on the door frame caught her attention. A slim, well-dressed man stood in the doorway. "Hi, there, Amalise." He walked in with an outstretched hand. She rose and grasped it.

"Doug Bastion," he said, releasing her. "Just Doug." His tone was jovial, smooth, and confident. "Welcome to the firm." He looked around. "How do you like your office?"

She loved it. "It's fine."

Her words seemed to drift past him as he shot the sleeves of his starched white shirt and examined them, adjusted his gray suit jacket, fingered the burgundy tie, and sank into the visitor's chair on the other side of the desk. Angling the chair to face her, he stretched out his legs, propped his elbows on the arms of the chair, and sighed, steepling his hands together under his chin.

"It's better than school, wouldn't you say?"

She nodded. "I can't wait to get started." Her heart was pounding as she struggled to hide the wave of excitement that swept through her, but he looked amused.

"We try to give our summer clerks a good time." His lips curled down when he smiled. "We provide good work, too, of course."

"What sort of work will I—"

"All right," he went on in a brisk tone, seeming not to hear. He pulled a piece of paper from an inside pocket of his coat and glanced down at it, reading at a rapid pace. "Let's see. You'll have orientation this morning—ten o'clock sharp in the conference room." He glanced up. "Your girl will show you where that is. Bring something to write on. You'll have a break for lunch, but the meeting will last all day."

She nodded and he went back to the schedule.

"You'll finish up around five thirty or so. Lunch today is with Joe Antonio and Rusty Peterson. They'll stop by for you in the conference room at noon. Joe's your new best friend this summer"—he looked up at her and grinned—"your summer advisor. You'll like him."

She nodded.

He tossed the piece of paper across the desk so that it landed in front of her and having dispatched his duties, seemed to relax, leaning back now and watching her. "Any questions?"

"Who's Marshall Eugene Poche?"

He frowned. "Who?"

She pointed to the diploma and he turned. "Oh." A short laugh like a bark. "Marshall. He's in our trial section. Off on a case for a few months, Minnesota, I think." She wondered what happened to Mrs. Marshall, when her husband simply disappeared for the summer and Amalise Catoir inhabited his office.

"Okay." He slapped his hand on the arm of the chair and pushed up. "That about covers it. Oh"—he hesitated, adjusting his tie as he looked down at her—"I almost forgot. We're having a little dinner party at my house tonight. You'll come, won't you?"

"Sure, thanks."

He nodded. "It's just us. The other summer clerks, a few associates, some of my partners. Wear what you have on. Most people come straight from work, so you'll catch a ride." He waved his hand toward the schedule he'd dropped on her desk. "Starts at seven, I believe. The address and directions are there." He gave her a look. "Are you married, Amalise?"

"No."

He nodded. "All right. I wasn't sure. Wives . . . er . . . spouses are invited to most functions as well, of course."

"Oh." But from what he'd said, Phillip was not included in the invitation. Her stomach tightened. He wouldn't like that. Scanning the schedule, she tensed as she saw an event planned for each night of the week.

Doug gazed around the office. "We're happy to have you here, you and Rebecca," he said, frowning. His eyes stopped on the photographs. "We'll take those pictures down and put some others up for you. Something nicer. And you should have some plants, too. We'll get what you want. Just let us know."

"Thanks, but it's fine as is."

"I'll send someone around to take care of that."

Slapping the desktop double time, he headed toward the door. "Soon as you're settled, Joe will fill you in on your first assignment." He stopped in the doorway, turned, and asked, pronouncing each word with care, "Is there any reason . . . ah . . . that it might be difficult for you to work late when it's necessary?"

She frowned and shook her head. "No." What an odd question.

"Well, I realize it's 1975, but we haven't got much experience with girls—excuse me—women, ah, female lawyers." He shifted his weight and his eyebrows rose. "So I thought I'd better ask, just in case." He watched her as though measuring her response.

"There's no problem." She envisioned the walk home alone at night through the deserted streets downtown. The Quarter just across Canal Street was always lively, at least until you reached Jackson Square and then she had only a few blocks more to go. But the business district at night was another matter. She hadn't thought of this, and the expense of a taxi every night was out of the question.

As if reading her mind, he said, "We have a private car service when you need it."

"Oh." She stared. He turned and disappeared down the hallway.

A few minutes later Josephine dropped a prospectus and two files on her desk. "From Mr. Bastion," she said over her shoulder as she walked out. "It's background information for the meeting tomorrow morning."

Amalise glanced at her watch and realized that she'd have to hurry to make orientation on time. She looked at the prospectus—it was at least an inch thick and bound. She picked it up and flipped through it—the paper inside the cover was thin, like onionskin, and the type was small—it would take hours to read. The two files underneath were also large. Her throat grew tight as she looked at the size of the bundle and realized that with orientation lasting until five thirty and dinner beginning at seven, she'd have to read these overnight. She swallowed and picked up the phone, dialed the front office in the art school, and left a message for Phillip.

He wasn't going to be happy about any of this.

Every morning Amalise was in her office by eight thirty. Her desk was usually covered with documents that had to be proofread. Sometimes she was asked to research a question related to a particular section in a prospectus or agreement. She especially liked the broad, familiar issues like due process, questions focused on in law school. At noon each day someone appeared to take her to lunch, usually one or two partners and several associates and summer clerks. There was always a crowd because summer clerks rated the best restaurants for lunch, the firm paid, and lunch sometimes lasted for hours.

In the afternoons after the heavy meals, Amalise's eyes drooped as she worked. The type on the pages often lost meaning and blurred, and she sometimes fought to stay awake. Rebecca had the same problem and suggested that the answer was caffeine. So Amalise and Rebecca met in the firm's small lunchroom area and drank Tabs and black coffee every afternoon until the sluggish feeling was defeated, usually around five o'clock, allowing them some productive work time before the ubiquitous evening social schedule commenced.

"I'd sure like to skip some of these parties," Amalise whispered to Rebecca one late afternoon. The caffeine hadn't kicked in yet.

"Can't do that." Rebecca added cream and a spoonful of sugar to her coffee. She stirred it and looked at Amalise. "Not if we want permanent offers." Her hair swung forward, shielding her face as she leaned toward Amalise and lowered her voice. "They want to see if we know which fork to use."

She sat back and took a sip of the coffee. "They want to see if we fit in."

Amalise nodded. "I know."

Rebecca shrugged. "I have a friend at Allen & Cook. It's the same over there. But things will slow down after the first few weeks, I think."

It wasn't the work she was given that was difficult. It was balancing this new career and social schedule against Phillip's constant need for attention. Phillip was irritable these days. He hadn't been given a teaching assignment at the university this summer. He was disappointed, frustrated . . . just at the time that her career was taking off. He could still use the university studio to paint, but that wasn't the same.

She ducked her head and sipped the coffee. It wasn't just the long hours that bothered him. His exclusion from the dinners and parties at night and on weekends had taken him by surprise. But he wasn't her spouse, she'd tried to explain. And it's just for the summer, she reminded him.

"Spouse!" He'd spit out the word and gone off to bed.

She sipped the coffee and watched Rebecca. "Phillip's not happy with this schedule."

Free, unattached Rebecca set down her coffee cup and looked at Amalise. "Well, he'll just have to get used to it, won't he?" She jerked her head, flipping hair back over her shoulders, and frowned. "Long hours and socializing come with the package. And we'll be traveling once we're associates."

"Yes, I know. You're right."

Rebecca stood, stretched, and picked up her empty cup. "It's early times, Amalise, and we're competing with the men. So he'll be dealing with these issues as long as you're . . . together."

Amalise gave her a quick look and rose too. They left the empty cups in the sink where someone would clean up after them. As she returned to her office, she cut off thoughts of Phillip. Right now she resolved to focus all of her energy on the firm's expectations.

Phillip would have to understand.

JUDE HAD PLANTED HIMSELF on a slat-wood bench outside the terminal at the end of the highway to the Gulf in the town of Venice. He waited with the Go Home crew for the bus to arrive, as he did every other week. He sat, yawning, not looking forward to the next two weeks in New Orleans. Since the rupture with Amalise, he'd put off work that needed doing at the house on State Street and instead had spent his time off duty in Marianus, fixing up Pop's shack, such as it was. He didn't really know why he bothered. The old man didn't know where he was most of the time, but when something needed to be done for Pop and he could do it, that thing just nudged him and wouldn't let go until he'd gotten it done.

So now he was headed back to State Street, and all the left-behind projects in the city loomed before him. Clearing the backyard, building a new porch back there, maybe a patio, as well. The house needed painting, too. The duplex was an investment. And there'd be more. He'd buy more when he could and fix them up and rent them out, and when he and Amalise got old . . .

Amalise.

He glanced at his watch and pressed his lips together, his shrug quick, impatient. He had a date this evening, and if the bus delayed much longer, he'd be late. Marilee Bernard. Good looking, easy to talk to, laughed a lot. They had reservations at the Blue Room at the Roosevelt Hotel where Bobby Blue Bland was playing.

Amalise had collected all those old records of Bobby Blue Bland, B. B. King, and Jimmy Reed. He wondered if she still had them around. They'd both grown up to that music. He smiled to himself remembering how she'd sidle up to an invisible microphone sometimes when he was in a bad mood and sing "Cry, Cry, Cry," almost sounding like Bobby.

Leaning his head against the back of the bench, he let the sun warm his face. He didn't really care about Marilee Bernard, and he didn't really care about the Blue Room. In fact, he'd tried dating several women over the past few months, and none of them had held his attention. He flicked a pesky fly off his arm without opening his eyes.

The problem was simple: he missed Amalise. He missed talking to her about the little things, like what she'd done that day, or how school was coming along, or the latest news on the judge and Maraine. Truth be told, he'd felt like a ship anchored at sea since that day they'd argued over Phillip.

Phillip Sharp.

Just thinking that name ruffled him. If only Amalise had never met the man.

Sucking in his breath, Jude stood, wandered inside the bus terminal, and looked around for a magazine stand. Something to occupy his mind on the trip back up to New Orleans. Something to pass the time.

WITH NEW RESOLUTION WEEK after week, Amalise gave her full attention to her work at Mangen & Morris, banishing each intrusion as it arose: Phillip . . . work . . . parties, dinners, lunches . . . putting off thoughts of everything outside the office. Distractions like those news reports of children in Cambodia, Operation Babylift in Saigon, her drift away from the church. Yes, she had to admit she hadn't actually been in church in a while. Phillip always had some reason why she couldn't go. And the argument with Jude still bothered her, and the troubling fact that she hadn't seen him since that day in Audubon Park. . . . all that had to wait.

For relief, after a few weeks she began slipping away from the office once in a while in the late afternoons, leaving a jacket flung over the chair behind her desk, as if she were still somewhere in the vicinity—in the library or a meeting or the restroom. A throw-down jacket, they called it. Joe taught her this. She'd walk through the business district just to simmer down after the day's fast pace before going back to the office or on to a scheduled event.

As the sun dropped behind the buildings and shadows fell during these walks, she loved the feel of being a part of the downtown business world. She loved the cement and stones and gleaming glass, the Whitney Bank clocks, the church bells striking six from every direction, the streetcars' clangs and rumbles as they ran the tracks up Carondelet to Canal, and back down St. Charles, car horns, newspaper boys hawking on corners, and the old woman selling tangerines in front of Jesuits church, the rustling packages, laughter, the crowded narrow streets and sidewalks and surge of the purposeful rush-hour crowds, just like those she'd watched year after year on the screen of the Regal Theater in Marianus when she was young. Always her spirits lifted while she strolled downtown in the late afternoons, imagining what it would be like to be a real lawyer, an associate employed by the firm after graduation next year.

It was a dream, of course. But a dream that, as the days passed, seemed more and more possible.

Chapter Twenty-four

One evening in mid-July the stars were favorably aligned, and Amalise and Phillip found themselves together at home by eight o'clock. "It shouldn't be so hard to get together," Phillip said. She'd just arrived, and they were in the kitchen where she'd collapsed in a chair at the table. She said that she couldn't move another muscle and that she wished they could spend more time together too.

Her stomach growled. She hadn't eaten a thing since noon.

Phillip grinned at her. "Hah! You sit right there while I prepare a ham sandwich."

Her brows shot up. *He* was fixing *her* a sandwich? He'd never done this before. She watched him pull out the bread and ham, mayonnaise and mustard and tomatoes and lettuce from the refrigerator.

When he finished, he brought the sandwich and a glass of milk to the table. "You should take better care of yourself." He set them on the table, then sat down beside her.

She picked up the sandwich and ate. "I will, later on. Let's get past this summer first. I can't think of anything right now but work. Everything depends on it."

"The parties aren't work."

"They're work. Ask Rebecca."

He frowned. "I don't trust Rebecca. Watch out. She's not your friend."

Amalise stopped eating and gaped at him. "Of course she is. Why do you say that?"

He shrugged. "She's your competition."

"It's not like that, Phillip."

"You're naïve."

She saw something in his expression that made her put the sandwich down on the plate and wait.

"I love you, Ama," he began in a studied tone that she'd never heard from him before. "But . . ." His eyes dropped to the table, and he traced his finger over the woodcarving he'd been working on that day. "But you're going to have to make some decisions." He looked at her and automatically she nodded, waiting.

"I can't live like this anymore. It's absurd. You're off at dinners and parties every night with people that I've never even met." He reached for her hand. "How do you think that makes me feel? You act as though you're single."

"I guess I am single so far as the firm's concerned."

"Then we need to change that, Ama."

He stood, walked to her, and held her face between his hands, looking deep into her eyes. "Marry me now, Ama. I won't stand in your way at the firm, or school, or with your work later on, but I have to know that you're mine. I want to be a part of your life. And I want everyone to know."

Pressure, like a tight elastic band, squeezed her chest so that she almost couldn't breathe. This was the moment Jude had said would come. She had to choose her path now, and Jude was right about one thing: it was time to take responsibility for her actions. By living with Phillip, she'd already limited her options. She had to make things right and marry him or walk away.

No middle ground was left.

A flicker of impatience crossed Phillip's face. "Now. You have to choose."

Her mind was chaos as she heard the ultimatum in his voice. She'd thought she'd have the bumps in their relationship smoothed over before this moment came. He didn't share her religious views . . . although he said he would get there in time. And she could help him with that, she was certain. In fact, he needed her for that.

But there were his myriad past lies . . . all in the past, she hoped . . . no, not just hoped. This she believed. And there was his strange dislike for Mouse, Rebecca, but he seemed to love Mama and Dad. And he loved her. Jude's warning that day in the car in Audubon Park came back to her, but that was based on something he'd misunderstood, she was sure.

Her thoughts spun as Phillip held her eyes, and then his voice emerged, rising above these thoughts and swamping the obstacles as he said simply that he loved her and that for once in her life she should step outside of the box and take a chance.

"Love is not selfish—love is giving." The question was in his eyes: Did she really love him?

She looked at him. Was what she felt for Phillip strong enough for a lifetime, to nurture a family? Career, marriage, children—she wanted it all. She glimpsed girls she'd grown up with in Marianus, settled now and married, comfortable, serene and secure. Some had children, cute toddlers with features that resembled the parents— living testimonials. She wanted children, had always pictured herself with a flock of children around.

She'd hesitated too long. Phillip stepped back and brushed her lips with a kiss, releasing her. "I'm sorry. If you love me you'll make the decision. Otherwise . . ." Arms at his sides, he left the word dangling in the air between them.

Otherwise? Otherwise he couldn't trust her. Otherwise she didn't love him. Otherwise he had no one. Otherwise he would disappear from her life forever.

She walked over to the kitchen table, pulled out a chair, and dropped into it. She'd been living as if they were married for almost a year. Why was she hesitating?

Knotting her hands together in her lap, she was surprised to hear that her voice remained calm. "All right. We'll be married right away, as soon as we've completed marriage instructions. One of the pastors at the cathedral will help us with that." She looked over her shoulder at him. "We can ask Father Peltier. He's nice, easy to talk to. You'll like him."

"That will take too long. And I'm not ready for that yet. You've got to let me get there in my own way . . . in my own time. But we can be married at the courthouse in the meantime. Tomorrow."

She gave him a steady look.

Phillip threw up his hands. "Let's end this discussion. You're good at boiling things down. It's simple. We get married tomorrow or never. We'll have the marriage blessed, or whatever you call it, in church later on, when I'm more comfortable with that. But right now you have to decide because I find the position I'm in with your firm humiliating."

Her tongue rooted and she found she couldn't speak. So quickly! Phillip's face turned dark as he watched her struggle with his demand. An angry line formed between his eyes for an instant—an exclamation mark for his words. But then his face softened. His mouth trembled, tightened, and curled down. Five, six, seven seconds dragged by as they looked at each other, and then he turned toward the door, nodding.

"In that case"—his voice seemed to echo from far away— "I'll pack up and leave."

She stood, pushing back the chair, reached out and caught his arm. When he turned to her, she saw the suffering in his eyes.

A silence stretched between them as the words stuck in her throat. But she loved Phillip, and love carries with it responsibilities. Wasn't that what Jude had said? She and Phillip should be married. It was right—she'd made the real choice long ago. She'd done things backward, all wrong. And he needed her. Phillip was dependent on her right now, emotionally, financially. Where would he go if he left? How would he live without a real job? He'd trusted her; she was his family, he'd said.

She loved Phillip. She did . . . she *did*.

"All right." She breathed out the words before she could change her mind.

He stood very still. "Tomorrow."

Amalise stood motionless. "At the courthouse?" A sharp pain struck her in the chest. This wasn't how she'd pictured her wedding through the years. Where were the bridesmaids? The flowers? Her parents? Her lifelong friends?

Jude.

He nodded, and Amalise followed suit with a hard swallow. "But only if you promise one thing. We'll repeat our vows in church as soon as we can. You'll promise that . . . that you'll take instructions . . . and do whatever we have to do to repeat the vows before God."

He grimaced, but after a moment he nodded. "All right." He gave her a steady look. "I'll do that for you, Ama."

"Is that a promise?"

"Yes."

Her heart raced and she took a deep, calming breath. "I'll call my parents now."

"No." His hand shot out to stop her. "They'll want us to wait."

She hesitated. Of course he was right. Mama would insist on a church wedding, and she'd have to refuse, and she would be torn between Mama and Dad and Phillip.

Through the turmoil of her thoughts, this one emerged above all others: Phillip needed her right now. And she couldn't bear to lose him. So if marrying Phillip immediately meant hurting Mama and Dad a little bit, just until they understood that the marriage would be blessed in church later on—a few weeks at most—then that's how things would have to stand.

She looked at Phillip and suddenly knew it wasn't marriage that frightened her most. It was continuing this endless wandering, failing to commit to one decision or the other. She closed her eyes for an instant. *I'm going to make things right, Abba. But what about Jude?*

The question whispered through her, and a hollow, sorrowful feeling swelled inside. She cut off the thought. "Tomorrow. We'll do it."

Phillip's face transformed. He slid his arms around her, pressing her head against his shoulder and caressing her. She breathed in his scent—a musky, smoky, masculine scent—and leaned against him. As minutes passed and still he held her tight, it seemed that his flesh, muscle, bones were melting into hers—as if his blood flowed through her veins and mingled with her own, pumping right into her heart. All thoughts of Mama and Dad, Jude, making the vow before God now instead of later . . . all of those worries faded away. Slowly she felt herself already becoming a part of him.

SHE REARRANGED HER LUNCH plans as soon as she got into the office the next morning, but none of it seemed real, even when Phillip picked her up in front of the building in a Chevrolet. That was a surprise. He'd rented it for the occasion, he said. Cabs were unreliable for such an important event. But by the time she burst from the building at ten minutes past noon, late, and opened the door to slide in beside him, he was irritable. He'd had to circle the block three times waiting for her, he said. A horn blasted behind them, and he accelerated with a screech of the tires. Amalise ducked her head, hoping no one from the firm had seen.

They both sat silent all the way to city hall. It was a solemn occasion, she reflected, a time for quiet. They parked in a crowded lot in the government-building complex. When she opened the door to get out, Amalise was assaulted by the heat shimmering from the pavement, hot dust from a nearby construction site, and a din of noise from the adjoining parking lot—a cement mixer and an unrelenting drill. Phillip locked the car, slung his arm around her shoulders, and they started for the building.

It took no time to obtain the license—happily, the old requirement for blood tests was suspended. License in hand, Phillip smiled at her now for the first time. He'd been as nervous as she, she realized.

He leaned down to peck her cheek. "Are you hungry?"

She nodded, feeling hot and strangely detached, as if she were watching a movie up on the screen of the Regal Theater. She'd seen the movie many times—the joyful young bride, the proud, expectant husband. The first time they'd met, in Porter's Gallery on that rainy day, she'd fantasized their relationship, she recalled. On cue the observer reeled out the memories: *Phillip's studio, the fall chill in the air, the artist's head bent over his easel, the amber light streaming in through the windows high above.*

He rolled the license into a cone and, tapping it in the palm of his hand, gave her an embarrassed look. "Sorry about my temper back there. It's the fool drivers in this city." She nodded, and he grinned down at her and tweaked her nose. "It's not every day a girl gets a marriage license, is it?"

They bought sandwiches and cold drinks and settled at a table in the corner of the cafeteria. The room was cool compared to the heat outside. Phillip sat close so that their thighs pressed together, and his hand under the table rubbed her knee in a distracted, companionable way like she'd seen Dad do with Mama sometimes.

Both were quiet while they ate, and her thoughts settled as her eyes swept over the room, taking in the couples at tables around them, and she thought how natural this really was after all, that she and Phillip should be married. With a sudden spark of excitement, it occurred to her that Mama would be happy about this marriage—once she got over the disappointment of the surprise.

Phillip lit a cigarette when they'd finished eating, and she sat quietly beside him with a growing feeling of companionship. After a moment he ground out the cigarette in his plate and took a deep breath.

"Well? Are we going to do this thing, Amalise?"

"You mean . . . right now?"

He smiled and pulled her close. "Yes. I love you."

"I love you, too." She looked up at him and pursed her lips. "My parents—"

"They'll like the thought that we couldn't wait," he said, laughing. "It's romantic." Fumbling in his pocket, he pulled out a small, black velvet box. She stared at it. "Look inside." He handed her the box.

Opening it she saw, first, the shining ring, gold and studded with a row of tiny, sparkling, square-cut colored gems—miniature cuts of emeralds, rubies, sapphires. Second, she saw the scrolling golden name—Adlers Jewelers—stamped across the satin lining inside. Adlers on Canal Street. She'd gazed into those glittering windows many times. "Oh," she breathed.

"Try it on." Phillip took the box from her. He pulled the ring from the velvet cushion and slipped it onto Amalise's finger. "There!" He held up her left hand. A woman at the table beside them clapped, and Amalise turned to see her beaming face nodding . . . yes . . . yes . . . yes.

"It's beautiful," the woman said.

Amalise spread her fingers and examined the ring glittering in the bright white cafeteria light. It was lovely.

"Shall we do the deed?" Phillip kissed the soft skin under her earlobe.

She smiled. Phillip stood and pulled her up.

They were directed to a small, sunless office where the judge presided. Stale cigarette smoke hung in the air. The judge's desk was piled high with papers and books and bits and pieces of plastic that appeared to belong to a model boat he was building. Her high spirits faded.

Will you bless our marriage now, Abba? Now? She relaxed. Yes. She knew He would. God didn't need the four walls either. And she would show Phillip the way to Him with love and patience.

Phillip strolled into the hallway and encountering a man and woman, pulled them laughing into the room to be the witnesses.

The woman inspected Amalise and grinned. "How lucky you are. Your husband . . . husband to be, that is"—she giggled, looking at Phillip and back at Amalise—"he's in love!"

The ceremony was short. At the end Phillip removed the ring from Amalise's finger and replaced it again, and everyone laughed. "That's what I call prepared." The judge closed the book.

Prepared. The judge's word startled her. The car. The ring. Phillip had thought this through. But the incipient thought slipped from her mind when Phillip stepped forward, kissed her, and called her "Mrs. Sharp." In that instant the strange pull she'd felt toward him from the first time they'd met seemed to deepen.

It's the bond that marriage creates. She'd finally made things right. For better or worse, rich or poor. Forever. The commitment.

Do You see, Abba?

She twisted the ring on her finger, watching as the two witnesses signed the marriage certificate and the judge shook Phillip's hand. And then it was done.

She was, indeed, Mrs. Phillip Sharp.

SHE'D TOLD NO ONE what was happening, so she had to return to work. Phillip said he had to return the car. They were quiet on the drive from the courthouse. Phillip seemed strangely detached. When they arrived in front of the building, he leaned across and dropped a kiss on her cheek. "See you later," was all he said.

Not much of a parting for newlyweds.

She slid out and stood on the curb, deflated, watching while the car disappeared into the traffic. He'd said nothing about celebrating. Walking into the building it struck her that she didn't really feel different, as she'd expected. She looked around—same dark suits strolling through the lobby without noticing that she had changed, the same gray marble walls rose around her, the wide doors to her left still opened to the busy bank with the soaring ceilings and high arched windows, and the same lines ranged in front of the tellers. Nothing seemed to have changed since she'd become Amalise Catoir Sharp.

As she pressed the button for an elevator, Amalise felt an urge to announce her news to a woman waiting beside her. But when it arrived and the doors opened, they stepped in together and ascended in silence.

Josephine didn't look up when Amalise strolled past the row of secretaries' desks toward her own office, holding her left hand aloft to tuck her hair behind her ear, even though the ring was clearly visible. How could Josephine not notice? Once in her office Amalise turned the ring round and round on her finger, trying to revive that earlier excitement and the sense of connection she'd felt with Phillip during the ceremony.

Rebecca stopped in the doorway. "Are you coming?"

Amalise looked up and waved Rebecca into her office. "Coming where?" She held up her hand to display the ring finger.

"Doug wants to see all the summer clerks in the conference room around the corner." Her eyes riveted to the shining gold band. "What's this?"

Amalise told her.

"How romantic!" Rebecca came around the desk to hug Amalise. She lifted Amalise's hand and turned the ring, inspecting it. Smiling, she sat on the corner of the desk. "I take it you solved the problem."

"Yes."

"Sweeping you off your feet like that. What more can a girl ask?"

The phone rang, startling them. It was Josephine, reminding them that they were wanted in the conference room.

Mrs. Sharp, Mrs. Sharp, she repeated to herself all the way down the hall. She'd pay the piper later, though, when she called Mama and Dad.

Maybe she'd let Mama call Jude.

BY THE END OF the afternoon, her married status was news at the firm. Josephine even warmed up a bit on hearing that she was married at lunchtime. Her surprise wedding provided plenty of excuse from the party scheduled for that night, and so at six thirty she hurried home. With a slight sense of relief, she found that Phillip wasn't yet home. He'd walk through that door any minute, she was certain, but she needed time alone to think.

She wandered into the kitchen, considering how to break the news of the marriage to her parents. Glancing at the clock, she realized that right now Mama would be finished with the dishes and sitting with Dad in the living room. The television would be on, but Mama would be sewing, and Dad would be reading, glancing up over his glasses at the screen once in a while. She picked up the telephone but set it down again. Where was the bridegroom on her wedding night? They'd want to speak to him.

Looking down, she touched the ring with the tips of her fingers. Yes, it was real enough. Suddenly shaken, she lowered herself into a chair near the telephone. She was married. How had this happened so fast? Five minutes passed before she picked up the phone, dialed the number, and sat listening to it ring, resting her head in her hands, and pressing her eyelids closed with her thumb and fingers.

But the sound of Mama's voice made her sit up straight.

"Hi Mama." The news was going to jolt them. She studied the wall in front of her and told Mama about her job and the people at the firm and about Jude's new car.

"That Jude," Mama said, and Amalise could hear the smile in her voice.

Dad took the phone. "When do classes start, Amalise?"

"Early September."

"How about that." She heard the excitement in his voice and a new tone of pride. "Well, unless I'm stupid, by the end of the summer, you'll have an offer from Mangen & Morris in your pocket."

Murmuring in the background and the phone shifted to Mama. "When do classes start, Amalise?" Amalise repeated her answer.

"Are you taking that waitress job back? You know we can send a little more if that would help." Amalise said no. They couldn't afford to spend another dime on her right now. The firm paid well, she said. She'd saved some money, and she liked the job at the café just fine, liked the people, the tips.

Mama lowered her voice, as if she sensed that Amalise was keeping secrets. "Is something wrong? If you need something, just say so. Let us know."

"Mama, I'm . . ." *Just say it, Amalise. It's good news! Tell them so they can be happy for you.* "Phillip and I are married, Mama. We got married today at city hall, but we're going to take our vows again in church . . . in just a few weeks or so."

There was a long silence. Murmuring. Dad came on the phone, and the questions came rapid fire: We've only seen him once. What do you know? Have you met his family? Why jump into this?

She answered the questions as they came, one at a time, shoving the words through the gravel in her chest and throat. She could hear the pain in their voices, the attempts to be cheerful, the fake smiles in the tone.

When the call was over, she put down the phone and stared at it. Tears brimmed and spilled. She'd let them down, cut them out of a celebration they'd planned since the day she was born. She crossed the room, grabbed a paper napkin from a basket on the counter, blew her nose, and dried the tears. And then another thought struck.

She'd forgotten to ask them to call Jude.

Without giving herself time to think of what she would say, she picked up the telephone again. She'd try Pilottown first. She wanted to hear his voice.

Catching her breath on a sob, she began to dial the number for the station house down at the end of the world. She wanted to hear his voice.

Chapter Twenty-five

M ama sat in her chair, eyes closed.
I'm trying to hold myself together for William's sake. I will be strong. But our little girl is married. I can hardly form the word in my mind . . . married. She called last night . . . I could barely think, couldn't put what she said together in my thoughts.

Mama pressed her hands to her heated face. *Who is Phillip Sharp? We don't know anything about him, Lord. He only visited us that one time at the beginning of the summer. I think she might have mentioned him once or twice before but nothing that would tickle your ear. Nothing that would stick.*

William hadn't taken to the young man when he visited, but Mama thought he was nice enough. They'd worried a little about the church, but she could understand how a person might want to go to his own church. He said that himself, in fact. That he was going to his own church that night, back in the city.

But still, he'd been their guest.

Amalise. My 'tite fille. My heart. Oh Father, who is Phillip Sharp? How long has she known him? How well does she know him?

And where is Jude?

SHE'D CALLED LAST NIGHT.

Jude grasped the rope ladder as it swung out over the churning

184

Gulf water, away from the boat. Each time it settled, he continued climbing up toward the deck. The twenty-mile buoy was hidden from sight by high, crested waves. Weather was fast moving in. It'd caught everyone by surprise.

A rough gust whipped the ladder off the hull as he was climbing, and he should have stopped right then, should have just held on, but fury drove him, raising shouts from above. The ladder had come partially loose from the fastenings. He knew what could happen if he fell into the water between the ship and the pilot boat, or maybe worse, if he landed on the pilot boat itself. Several pilots had met their end that way.

But he couldn't focus, and he didn't care much right now, anyway. His thoughts spun as he climbed.

Amalise was married.

She'd actually married that reptile, Phillip Sharp. How *could* she?

So he climbed, refusing to ask himself why this news had sparked such rage. If Amalise was determined to ignore his advice, to sweep aside everything he'd told her about this man, everything she believed, then why should he care?

If God allowed this to happen, why should he care? In the instant the wind picked up as if to rebuke him.

"Hold a minute!" This time the shout came from the pilot boat below. "Take your time, Jude. We're not going anywhere yet."

Ignoring the warnings, muscles and tendons stretched and swelling, he hunkered against the wind and went on pulling himself up the lurching rope while the ship heaved and rain began to fall. Her voice on the phone last night had sounded brittle, disconnected, as if she were making a duty call. It hadn't helped that they'd had a bad connection.

Mama and Dad were happy about the marriage, she'd said. He snorted. The judge would have seen through Phillip, just as he'd done. There'd be a party, she'd said. A party . . . or something. He winced at that thought.

Rain came, a salty spray gusted over him. The ropes were wet and his hand slipped. Fire shot through the flesh of his right palm as he flailed, then hung on, gasping for breath. Shouts now from above and below. All his weight on one rope pulled the ladder askew, and it spiraled in the wind. The ship rolled in the waves. Still he held on, scrambling for a solid foothold.

The boatman down below: "Hold tight! Don't move."

The rain hit like a storm of needles. Wind whipped around him, twisting the rope in his hands, searing his flesh. He used all of his strength to cling to the ladder, arms stretched overhead, shoulders straining, aching, his head beginning to throb as he lifted one foot after the next and one name echoed through his mind: Amalise.

From the depths even the wind seemed to echo her name.

When the immediate danger of his situation finally rose to the level of clear understanding, piercing the rage shrouding Jude's inner pain, the full impact of Amalise's marriage hit too, all at once, and he felt that a part of him was dissolving.

Why couldn't she have waited until he returned to the city? So much for the talk they'd had. A fierce urge to be alone gripped him. To sink into himself, to be solitary. If only he were working at the house on State Street right now, pounding with a hammer, smashing something. Physical pain kicked in as the ladder swung, arcing out over the Gulf. His hands were raw, his muscles on fire.

Still he hung on and climbed Jacob's ladder, knotting his fists around the ropes, resolving with each pull to forget he'd ever heard the name Phillip Sharp, absorbing the blows when the ladder slammed back against the hull the way he'd like to slam Phillip; and each time this happened he would inch up, rung by rung, fighting to beat the ladder's swing.

So he forced himself on, focusing now on the pain in his arms and shoulders and thighs, the raw burn of his hands—eyes fixed now on the battered ship beside him, now out to sea, now out over the water to the gray clouds, low and thick, smoldering all the way to the horizon.

"Fool thing to do, Ahab," the captain said, when he made it top deck. "You almost cost me a good ladder."

JUDE WIPED THE PERSPIRATION from his neck as he hiked down Royal Street toward Porter Gallery looking neither right nor left. It had been a long two weeks in Pilottown. Despite his resolution to forget Amalise's stupidity and her new husband, he couldn't quit thinking of the whole mess, as if a force greater than his rage, like that wind on the ladder the other day, urged him on.

He'd just come from the cathedral where he'd prayed, knotted up inside because he couldn't rid himself of the feeling that there was a dark, hidden side to Phillip's nature—that Amalise could be in danger. He was unable to pin down the cause of this presentiment, but he was unable to forget it either. He'd just take one more look at those paintings, maybe find someone at the gallery who knew something about Phillip Sharp.

Bells jangled as Jude opened the door to the gallery. The room was empty at the moment, so he turned to the pictures on display and saw that Phillip's work was gone. He halted in the middle of the room, frowning. This possibility had not occurred to him.

"May I help you?"

He turned to see a woman coming toward him from a door behind a desk in the back corner of the gallery.

"I was looking for some paintings I saw in here last fall, about a year ago I think."

"We don't usually keep work that long."

"Oh." Jude pushed out his bottom lip and shook his head.

She smiled. "Can you describe them or give me a hint? Perhaps I can help you locate the artist."

He turned to her. "His name is Phillip Sharp. The paintings were somewhat unusual, I thought."

Her smile died. She looked at him through half-closed eyes. "I know them. That exhibition was only here for a week or two." She crossed her arms and took a step back. "You'll have to find him yourself. I don't know where he's showing now."

"The pictures weren't very good." Jude watched two red spots appear high on her cheekbones. He would take the chance. "Actually, I didn't come here to buy." She arched an eyebrow, fingered a dangling earring, and waited. "I'm looking for someone who can tell me something about him . . . Phillip Sharp."

Her hand slid down her throat, stopped, and spread over her collarbones. Jude set the duffel bag on the floor by his feet, straightened, and tried to smile. "I'm making a mess of this I know."

"Get out of here." She wheeled and walked away.

Jude dropped his arms. He should have sent that detective to do this work. What did he know about background checks?

As she reached the desk, she turned to face him. "Get out or I'll call someone."

Jude raised his hands and stepped back. "Don't do that. I'm sorry I bothered you. I'm leaving."

She smacked the corner of the desk with her hand and dropped down into a chair. He picked up the duffel bag and started for the door. But the sound of choking sobs stopped him. Hesitating, he turned to see her hunched, face hidden in her hands, shoulders heaving.

"I'm sorry, Miss. I didn't mean to upset you."

She looked up. Swiped at the tears on her face. "Joanna. My name is Joanna. And you should have thought of that before coming here."

Jude studied the pictures displayed on the wall behind the desk. "I'm not good at this." He gave her a thoughtful look. "It's really for a friend. I'm worried about her."

Her eyes shifted from his, and for a fleeting moment he glimpsed something on her face that paralyzed him: a flash of pity.

"Amalise Catoir?"

Jude held his breath and nodded.

She pulled tissue from a box on the desk and dabbed at her eyes, then looked down, snuffling. "He . . . Phillip . . . latched onto her about a year ago." Dropping the tissue, she touched the tips of her fingers together. "There's not much good to say about the man. He . . . he's malevolent."

Jude's spine turned to ice. "Then why exhibit his pictures?"

"Because I was a fool!" The words came out sudden, fierce. "Phillip is a predator, a leech." Her face flushed. "He used me and I fell for it. When a better deal came along—" She averted her eyes. "Your friend, when he found her, he left . . . just like that." She snapped her fingers in the air.

Jude's stomach lurched. *God, Father God, what has Amalise done?*

She shook her head. "But if it hadn't happened with her, he would have found someone else. He got what he wanted from me. I haven't seen him since." She looked up at him. "I'm sorry for your friend."

"Is it money he's after?"

She gave an abrupt laugh. "That's the least of it. Phillip wants your soul, the breath of your life." She clasped her hands, and her eyes bounced around the room from Jude to pictures, to the floor, to her hands, then she went on. "Money . . . yes. Lots of that. He lived off me for over a year. There were others before me. I don't know their names. Didn't know about them until later, after he left." She began tracing zigzagged lines on the top of the desk with a finger.

"I financed his show here. Bought some of his pictures so he'd feel good about himself. Paid his bills. Dealt with his creditors." She glanced at Jude and sucked in her lips. "Believed his lies. Lived by his rules! He begged me not to abandon him, not to leave him—right up to the instant he left." She shook her head and fixed her eyes on the desktop. "What a fool I was. I thought he loved me." She smeared the invisible lines from the desktop with the flat of her hand and looked up.

Unable to speak, Jude roused himself and walked over to the desk. He placed the duffel on the floor by his feet, leaned against the wall beside her, and crossing his arms, gazed mindlessly at a couple on the sidewalk admiring a picture on an easel in the window. "How old would you say he is?"

"Thirty-four," she replied without hesitation. "I'm fifty-three. Isn't that a laugh? He used to call me his old neuter." Her eyes teared up again.

Jude frowned. He could see the touches of gray in the part of the woman's hair. The light exposed her thick makeup, the deep grooves around her mouth and eyes.

He spoke gently. "He's cruel. I've seen him in action." He straightened, stuck his hands in his pockets, and lowered his voice. "Is there anything in his background to make you think—"

"That he's dangerous?" She studied her hands and pressed one down flat on top of the other. "Sure." Her mouth trembled. "If she tries to leave him before he's ready. I can vouch for that." Her chin jutted out as she spoke. "But it's not my problem now. He forgot me the moment he found your friend. For Phillip the past is generally nonexistent."

A bell rang over the door as a couple entered the gallery. Joanna looked toward the customers, her face turning blank. "Ummm . . ."

The sound rose from deep inside her chest as she pushed back the chair. Standing abruptly, she waved Jude off. "That's all I have to say."

He nodded. "Thanks. I'm sorry if I've stirred up bad memories." Jude started for the door.

"Hey, just a minute."

Jude turned and watched as she reached for her purse and began rummaging through it.

"I'll be right with you," she called to the customers. "Here it is." She pulled out a folded card and handed it to Jude. He glanced down and fingered the worn, creased notepaper. She stood behind the desk, leaning forward, fingers splayed over the surface. "Tell your friend if you get the chance that there's no end to it until he leaves. He will take and take and take until he's sucked her dry, and then he'll move on to someone else."

She nodded to the paper she'd given Jude. "Give her this, if you think she should see it." She frowned, then with a nudge of her chin and a quick bright smile, she walked around the desk, heading toward the customers. "I've kept it around to remind me of what he is," she said in an undertone as she passed him. "But I've had it long enough, I think."

IT WAS A LETTER from Phillip's father to Joanna, dated almost a year ago. Jude was sitting on the porch upstairs on State Street as he read it again for the third time. It was handwritten on a cream-colored card, bordered in black. The letter was in response to one Joanna had written right after Phillip exchanged her for Amalise, he supposed. It was short, cool, and to the point.

I can't help you. Regardless of what my son has said and done, you're better off without him. As for money lent—consider it gone. Consider it a lesson learned. If this is any comfort, you're not the first to be taken in by Phillip, and you won't be the last. Narcissistic, you've said. Yes. Pathological liar? That, too. He has no conscience, no regrets, no real self. But so far as we're aware, he's never been in trouble with the law. You sound like a decent person, but we don't know you, and he's our son, so that's all we have to say. Please don't contact us again.

Jude called the detective. Romar answered the phone himself.

"It's Jude," he said.

"I thought you might be back."

"Right. I need more help." He opened the letter Joanna had given him and read it to Romar over the phone.

There was a hissing sound on the line, a long expiration of breath. Romar grunted. "That's from the father, huh?"

"Yes." Jude could picture the PI swinging around, looking through his window into the brown haze.

Romar heaved a sigh. "You got a bad seed that ain't sprouted yet, Jude. Not much we can do right now." He paused and Jude gripped the phone. He knew what was coming. "It's like trying to get a restraining order against one of those nuts that makes threats. You know, we're hamstrung until he crosses a line."

"Look into those seven years you mentioned, the time before he came south. Maybe you could talk to the father."

"I already did that. Phillip was pretty transient then, and Dad's not going to tell us anything. From the letter I'd guess Phillip was living off women during most of that time. Can't prove it though. Mighta stayed at home for a while. Mighta rented for all we know—no records there."

Jude heard a smacking sound, as if Romar were picking his teeth. He waited.

"Sure didn't own any property," the detective muttered after a moment. "Not in New York State. Not in Louisiana either. I checked."

"Well, see if there's anything else." Jude looked through the window, envisioning Amalise rushing between classes uptown, on to the café, walking home alone at midnight while Phillip bought drinks for those women at the Hound & Hare. How had her life spun out of control so quickly? He gazed over his orderly neighborhood, wishing that he could gather her up and bring her here, uptown, where neat sidewalks ran like ribbons between manicured patches of bright green grass and shining cars were parked at the curb where there were still forests of trees and shade. Where she'd be safe. Suddenly it came to him, a realization that hit him like a physical blow . . .

He'd always imagined her in his future. And in that way. A part of his life.

A part of him.

"Check again." His throat tightened, and his voice grew thick as he added: "Look for a divorce, a DWI. Something."

Romar heaved another sigh. "I can do that, Jude. But I hate to take money on low odds. Like I said, there's nothing on record—family court, criminal, civil."

"What about credit reports? Wouldn't that tell us where he worked?"

"Yeah, it might," the detective said in a reluctant tone, drawing out the words. "It'll cost but I can get those."

"I'll pay whatever it takes. Let me know."

"Okay. You got it." A yawn drifted through the phone as he hung up.

Jude returned to the upstairs porch and slumped on the sagging chair, holding the card from Phillip's father. The old tree's thick branches provided shade, and today it was cool out here. Amalise had always loved sitting on this porch. She'd lounge out here like Miss Scarlet. He closed his eyes, remembering

And now here was Phillip.

His eyes popped open. Anger and a current of fear shot through him as he fingered the letter in his hand, shaking his head. So far as Amalise was concerned, nothing would undo the mistakes she'd made. They were married, and he knew Amalise—once she'd committed herself to something, she was a missile honed in on a target. And her upbringing would not permit thoughts of divorce. An old saying around Marianus came to mind, and he shuddered. *L'enfant est nee—*the baby is born; you've got to feed him.

For Maraine and the judge, she would do anything to make this marriage work, just as she'd done to get through law school.

He dropped the letter into his lap. He'd put it away for now. *Lord, please help because it's a sure thing that Amalise won't. She's dealing with evil that she doesn't understand.*

He couldn't interfere, but there was something he could do. He would be there when she needed him.

Chapter Twenty-Six

As her new husband, Phillip accompanied her to every social event planned for the clerks for the rest of the summer. He remembered names, charmed the older ladies with his attention, flirted a bit with the younger wives, though always with a wink at Amalise. He was somewhat cool to Rebecca, she noticed. But Rebecca appeared to sense his dislike and kept her distance. Amazingly he carried his weight in conversations on sports, fishing, hunting—things he'd never shown interest in before.

"How does a New York boy like you manage to dredge up such information on the spur of the moment?"

"Preparation." He shrugged. "Books—I go to the library. Past lives. It's easy to fool most people."

Once she glimpsed him practicing a variety of facial expressions before the mirror in the bathroom. She'd been lying in bed, and from just a certain angle she could see his reflection as he grinned at himself, teeth bared, head full tilt to the side, then quick as a wink turning sober, looking straight into his own eyes with a grave, reflective expression. Quickly she'd shifted her gaze to the courtyard window.

A few days after the wedding, she'd talked to Father Peltier at the cathedral about scheduling their marriage vows in the church. He'd been kind but said he'd have to talk to Phillip first. Phillip had waved the idea off, but she realized he was preoccupied with the upcoming fall semester at the university. He'd keep his end of the bargain soon. So she told herself each time he put her off.

One afternoon on her way home from the office, she saw Mouse, lounging in his chair near the fence at Jackson Square, watching the crowds for a possible sale. She'd been avoiding him, she realized. Their eyes met before she could turn away, and with a flush of pleasure, she realized how much she'd missed him. Waving her over with the paintbrush in his hand, he stood.

She embraced him. "It's been a long time, Mouse. I've missed our talks."

"I've seen you around. Been right here." But he softened the words with a grin. "Sit a while." He pointed the paintbrush to his customer chair.

Glancing over her shoulder at the clock on the cathedral tower, she saw that it was seven o'clock. Phillip would be waiting, but she hadn't seen Mouse in so long. "Only for a minute." She lowered herself into the canvas chair. "I'm working downtown now. For a law firm, Mouse!"

He grinned and sat, moving the easel aside, out of the way. "I knew you could do it. So you've finished? Graduated?"

"No." She explained the system, the summer clerkship, how she hoped it would lead to an offer for the real job after graduation, and Mouse nodded.

"That's good news." He crossed his legs, propping his ankle on his knee. "I've been worried about you some."

She held her breath, watching the paintbrush tap, tapping on the sole of his shoe.

"I was worried about that fellow you'd hooked up with. He's gone?"

After a pause she swallowed and met his eyes, tilting up her chin. "Of course not, Mouse. I thought you knew." She blushed—of course he wouldn't know. How could he? "We're married."

The long silence told her everything. Uncrossing his legs Mouse slowly pushed himself up from the chair. "I thought you had more sense than that, Amalise." Speechless, she just looked at him. He shook his head, moved the easel back into its place, and set a fresh canvas on it. She watched as he sat down behind the easel and picked up the paintbrush.

"You've made a mistake." He shook his head as he spoke.

She stood, pushing back the customer chair. A young couple nearby turned to look, and she lowered her voice. "Take care, Mouse. Phillip is my husband. The mistake was telling you." She was surprised to hear that her voice was steady, free of the tension twisting inside.

He set the paintbrush down and looked up. "Ahhh, Amalise." His hand reached out for hers and she stepped back. He'd insulted Phillip, her husband.

Mouse's hand dropped into his lap. She caught his covert glance at the corner of the Cabildo where he claimed Phillip had waited for her that night. "I didn't like what I saw of him that night, and I can't pretend that I'm happy for you. But if you ever need a friend, I'll be around, for a while at least."

She looked at him and knew that in the years ahead she'd remember this moment. This instant when their friendship had faded into nothing.

"Where are you going?" She picked up her purse.

Reaching for the brush, he dipped it into a swab of color on the tabletop and focused on the canvas as he began to paint. "I've been thinking of Key West lately. It's a good place to paint. Good money from tourists down there." He shrugged. "There's nothing holding me here." He gestured with the paintbrush at the little circle of belongings around him. "Everything I own can be carried."

"Not friendship."

"Hunh!" He stroked color across the canvas with a swipe. "Pity the man who falls and has no one to help him up."

"I'd be there to help you."

"My Amalise." With an abrupt laugh: "Where've you been all my life?" He gave her a sideways look. "Or better yet, where have you been in the past . . . oh . . ."—he scanned the sky and went back to painting—"in the past year or so?"

Loyalty to Phillip held her tongue. A heavy gloom descended as she turned, walking on, past the cathedral, past the park, toward the apartment, wishing that she could somehow swing back through time and undo the damage she had inflicted upon her lost friendship with Mouse. But it was too late.

And all for Phillip.

IN MID-AUGUST, THE FINAL week of the summer program, offers for permanent employment after graduation were given to each summer clerk, including Amalise and Rebecca, the first women ever to receive such an offer from the firm. Joe and Rusty invited the group to lunch at Antoine's. In a mad spurt of exultation, Amalise purchased a gray, well-fitted suit and a pair of three-inch heels at Godchaux's department store on Canal Street.

"You're tricked out this morning," Phillip said when she appeared at breakfast in the new suit.

"It's for lunch today. We're going to Antoine's." She put her hands on her hips and whirled, preening. "Oysters Rockefeller . . . Baked Alaska!"

He looked back down without saying anything. Sitting at the kitchen table, he dug the point of the knife into the wood with sharp little twists, silently flicking shavings onto the floor with each cut. He'd quit going down to the university studio since they'd gotten married.

As she left the apartment, she felt his eyes on her and turned to catch him scrutinizing her from head to toe. She hesitated, waiting to hear a whistle or something, but he ducked his head, carving again, so she closed the door softly behind her.

At two o'clock in the afternoon as Joe and Rusty and the giddy group of summer clerks returning from the long lunch strolled through the marble lobby of the building, she saw Phillip lounging against the wall on the far side, hands jammed into his pockets. She halted and smiled, lifting her hand to wave, when suddenly she realized that he had remained motionless, glowering at her. Lowering her hand and feeling like a rabbit in a trap, she stared back through suspended time. Her stomach churned while people crossed between them, entering and exiting the building, yet still he stood immobile.

Joe stopped beside her. "What's wrong?"

"Nothing." Of course she should walk right over to Phillip, but he looked furious standing there and cold and strange and out of place. Would he cause a scene?

Joe lifted his eyebrows—What? She glanced back across the lobby, but Phillip had disappeared. Slowly she exhaled. "I thought I saw someone I knew."

"Too much champagne?" He put his hand on her shoulder, and she shrugged it off. *Please . . . don't let Phillip still be watching.*

She waited for an hour before calling home, but if he was there, he didn't answer. The remainder of the day was spent with the image of Phillip hovering as she cleaned out her office, dreading the confrontation she knew would come. Struggling not to think, she veiled the creeping fear and made a presentation to Josephine of a bottle of Chanel No. 5.

At five thirty she took one last look at Marshall Eugene Poche's office, silently thanked him, turned off the lights, and strolled down the row of secretary desks carrying the box of her belongings: a sweater she'd kept in the office, some pens with the firm's name imprinted on them, some notebooks, and a heavy copy of *Black's Law Dictionary* that was presented to each law clerk. She told each person good-bye and that she'd see them next summer after graduation, fighting off thoughts of Phillip's angry face in the lobby. Josephine gave her a booklet with internal phone numbers: call us anytime, everyone urged.

Rebecca was in the elevator when she got in, and they rode down to the first floor together. On the sidewalk they said good bye, see you soon in class . . . our last year, can you believe it?

Rebecca headed for the streetcar stop while Amalise turned left, toward the Quarter.

The searing August heat increased her black mood as she worked her way through the evening crowd heading home and crossed Canal Street to the Vieux Carré. Taking the familiar route down Royal Street past Porter Gallery, she rushed along without the lift of spirits the Quarter usually conjured. In the distance thunder rolled. Clouds clustered overhead, smudges of darkness that hid the sinking sun.

She turned onto St. Peter and passed the ice cream shop where the proprietor, Nick, sat behind the counter reading his newspaper. She didn't knock on the window and wave as usual—wasn't in a mood to pretend right now that she was cheerful. Rounding the corner at the Cabildo across from the café, she realized that now the summer clerkship was over, she'd have to get used to being a waitress again, at least until graduation next spring. She and Phillip needed the money. Thunder rumbled, closer this time. Lightning flashed, and she glanced up through the lowering gray haze, now damp, heavy with the scent of coming rain.

Across the street she spotted Mouse packing up his easel and supplies near Jackson Square, his pictures, paints, and folding chairs. She hesitated, shot through with sudden remorse. But remembering his response to her news of the marriage, she turned and hurried on past without calling out to him.

A clap of thunder startled her just as the rain began. She ran the last few blocks to the apartment. Lightning glowed yellow and dimmed as she inserted the key and opened the door. Inside she dropped the box on the couch in the living room and ran her fingers through her wet hair. She slipped off wet shoes and shivered. Rain drenched clothing clung to her skin.

Through the archway she could see Phillip sitting at the kitchen table, bent over a figure he was carving. He was silent, as if he hadn't heard her enter. Was this the same carving he'd been working on when she'd left this morning? She crossed into the bedroom and entered the bathroom. She stripped off the wet clothes, dried herself with a towel, and slipped on her robe.

Heart pumping, she headed for the kitchen. As she entered, he glanced up without speaking and back down at the figure. It was a miniature duck, she saw, as he scraped the wood with small, sharp cuts to form the wings. Watching the lines emerge under the knife, she stood in the middle of the room. "I saw you in the lobby at lunchtime. Why did you disappear?"

"I didn't want to interfere with your social life."

At his ominous tone she watched him, perplexed. He sat very still. Only his hands moved as he carved. The sharp knife seemed to cut into the wood with no effort. He stopped for an instant to brush off debris with his thumb, flicking it onto the table, then he leaned close to blow away the remaining dust before cutting again.

A lump rose in her throat and she choked back the tears that she'd held off all afternoon. "I don't understand."

Still Phillip didn't answer.

Rain now battered the windowpane over the sink. There was a heavy silence in the kitchen, like a physical barrier had risen between them. She struggled against an irrational flicker of fear. This was Phillip, her husband. Taking a deep breath, she walked to the counter and turned to face him, folding her arms over her chest. Shivering, she rubbed her upper arms.

"You knew I had lunch plans, and you knew everyone in the group." Thunder shook the old building. Outside the rain came down in torrents, slapping the pavement in the courtyard. "I wish you had joined us."

The knife stopped moving. She stared as he extended his hand toward the wall before him, uncurled his fingers, and held the carving tool flat on his palm. "I only saw Joe." He inspected the knife. A glint of hard light glanced off the tip of the blade.

A chill traveled up her arms, through her chest. He sounded so different. Looked different. For a moment she had the feeling this wasn't Phillip, the man that she'd married, but some frightening stranger who'd invaded her home.

She hugged herself, but still her heart skipped from beat to beat. "Why were you waiting for me?"

He set the carving and the knife down on the table in front of him, his actions slow, deliberate. "That's a strange thing for a wife to ask her husband." He brushed more dust from the area where he'd been working with wide, exaggerated sweeps. When he looked up, his eyes were hard and cold, though the hint of a smile played at the corners of his lips. "What's wrong, Ama? Feeling a twinge of guilt?"

Her mouth fell open. He was enjoying this!

Pushing back his chair, he rose. She stood without moving, watching him make his way toward her like an actor going through paces on a stage, conscious that his every movement was being studied. When he halted just before her, too close, she took a step back. His shoulders lifted as he frowned, and then he gave her a sharp little shove with the tips of his fingers.

"If something's going on with Joe, you'll regret it."

With a rush of anger, she braced herself, lifted her chin, and glared back at him. "If you touch me like that again, *you'll* regret it. I'll call the police." The words surprised her as she spoke. What was happening?

Three seconds passed before he stepped back from her. "What are you talking about?" He raised his eyebrows and studied her with that almost imperceptible smile. He turned away, and she watched him cross the kitchen, pick up the carving knife, snap it shut, and stick it into his pocket. At the doorway he halted without turning.

His shoulders were still hiked with tension, swallowing his neck. With his back to her, he suddenly drooped, and his arms went limp at his sides. His voice broke and she could barely hear his whisper: "When I saw you there with him . . . with Joe, I thought I'd lost you."

Before she could respond, he switched off the light, leaving her in darkness. His voice came to her, flat. Disembodied. "You're mine, Ama." His tread was heavy as he went into the living room and turned off more lights. In the bedroom he did the same.

Her arms trembled and she dropped them to her sides, standing rigid as she looked into the darkness after Phillip, frightened and filled with despair. With the lights off, the apartment walls that had always comforted now seemed to close around her. Minutes later she heard the creak of the mattress in the bedroom.

Phillip wasn't coming back.

She let out a deep breath and slumped, flooded with a sense of relief that almost brought her to her knees. *Abba, what have I done? Where are You?*

She looked around seeking an anchor for her turbulent emotions. Until Phillip arrived, this apartment was her refuge. Tightening her lips, she crossed the kitchen and switched the lights back on. Light changed everything. Slowly she turned, looking at the pictures of Mama and Dad that she'd placed on the windowpane over the sink—

She frowned. Where was the one of Jude when they were children? It was gone. Her eyes moved on to the little butter jar painted with tiny yellow flowers that was her grandmother's, the plates she'd bought with her first paycheck from the café, books stacked in corners and on the table. All the familiar things.

At last she pulled a chair from under the table and lowered herself into it. She was married to Phillip, and she had to make it work. Marriage was forever, she reminded herself. Images of Mama and Dad rose, that special look she'd caught between them often when she was a girl. She couldn't imagine Mama and Dad without each other—their constant steady bond was her lodestar.

She pursed her lips, rested her arm on the table, and looked at the carving Phillip had left there. Fingering the piece of wood, she tried to place herself in Phillip's shoes, envisioning the scene in the lobby earlier that afternoon, as he would have seen it. There she was wearing a new and expensive suit they could not afford. There was Joe, walking beside her in his tailored suit, always impeccable— Joe, former quarterback for Tulane with his confidence and air of success—and she, laughing with him over something she could not now recall. The large group excluding Phillip as they breezed along as one through the lobby, owning the space around them.

She closed her eyes. Slowly it came to her and she began to understand— saw it all now—the busy lobby, everyone hurrying off to someplace certain, to offices and jobs and meetings and appointments while Phillip watched alone, an outsider, perhaps for the first time conscious of the enormous changes in her life. Perhaps fearing she'd leave him behind.

Responsibility in marriage worked both ways. She would make this marriage work. Phillip had reasons for his sometimes moody behavior. Consciously she struggled to resurrect the image of Phillip she'd stamped in her mind early in their relationship.

The obedient observer emerged, editing the memories: *Phillip in his studio, as always in her imagination, absorbed in his painting, serious, dedicated, enlarged by his milieu.* But, like cracked brown leaves at summer's end in a garden where flowers once bloomed, the glowing image was marred by the face of a small tortured boy—the man-child always alone, always uncertain, waiting for someone to care. Again a wave of pity for that child, and now the man, washed over her.

She sat listening to the rain, turning this over in her mind, and frowned. The flaw in the reasoning was that Jude had a hard childhood too. She remembered the bruises she'd seen on him once when he was twelve—a black eye, a cut on his cheek she hadn't, at the time, understood.

How was it that one child could grow strong and confident despite such experiences, while another seemed unable to fight his way up through the rocky soil to sunlight?

A noise from the bedroom startled her. She froze, waiting as she heard Phillip's heavy footsteps crossing the floor. He was supposed to be asleep. When he appeared in the doorway, disheveled—shirt wrinkled and untucked, hair hanging over his forehead, she pushed back in the chair, stiff-armed against the table, watching him.

He looked at her through narrowed eyes. "What are you doing? Why aren't you in bed?"

"I was just sitting here thinking . . . listening to the rain. I thought you were asleep."

"Well, I'm not." He crossed the kitchen to the sink, turned on the faucet and leaned forward, cupping his hands to splash water over his face. When he'd finished, blindly he reached out for the dish towel. Patting his skin dry, he set down the towel and turned to her. "I've come to a decision about something, Ama."

Her throat seemed to close. He leaned back against the counter, crossing his arms, and gave her a long look. "Forget about that church wedding, or blessing, or whatever you call it that you're always talking about."

She dropped her hands into her lap, wide-eyed. "But you promised!"

He shrugged and pushed himself off from the counter. Twisting to tuck the shirttail into the back of his pants, he said in an offhand manner, "Well, I've thought it over, and I've decided it's not for me. We're legally married, and there's no need to go through all that." He finished with the shirt and looked up. "Besides, I have my beliefs, too. You're not the only one with a philosophy."

"Philosophy?"

"Call it what you want." He headed for the door. "I don't want anything to do with religion, any religion." Hand on the light switch, he glanced at her over his shoulder. "So forget it. I don't want to hear anything more about your church." He smiled and lowered his chin. "I love you, Ama. Don't misunderstand. But I'm not going to change my mind. Now come to bed."

He switched off the light, but Amalise sat in the dark kitchen for several hours after he'd gone. Who was Phillip Sharp?

And what had she done?

A FEW DAYS LATER Amalise sat on an iron bench facing the cathedral across the street. The doors were shut against her. Well, they were closed.

Streetlights glimmered on around her, one after the other, as if they woke one another up. Laughter came from Café Pontalba, just winding up for the evening crowd. She'd started working at the café again, but her shift was over, and she was on her way home. She'd looked for Mouse, wanting to make amends, but he wasn't around.

Now, somehow, without making a conscious decision, she found herself sitting here on this bench in front of the park fence, ignoring the activity around her, eyes fixed on those doors like Tiny Tim on Christmas Eve.

Phillip was waiting, expecting her to arrive home in the exact time it would take to walk those few blocks from the café to the apartment on Dumaine. A bitter taste rose in the back of her throat. She knew he was at home because he had nowhere else to go, having placed himself in a holding pattern all summer, waiting for fall teaching assignments to be announced at the art department. He would be looking at the clock on the wall because every minute she delayed was a minute stolen from him, he would say. But he would say this with a smile.

With a sigh she stared at the cathedral doors, mulling over Phillip's broken promise. She'd misjudged him. She squinted through the twilight at the closed doors, willing them to swing open and invite her in. Or she could walk across the street and open them herself. She could walk through the nave, open the inner doors, enter the sanctuary, fall upon her knees, and cry out, *"Abba, here I am!"*

Oh, how she wanted to do that. To cry out. But it wouldn't be right. She'd gotten into this mess herself, and she had to fix it herself.

She closed her eyes, and when she opened them and gazed again at those doors, she saw better days—herself smiling, walking out into the sunlight with Jude, as they had so many times before, heads together, talking, Jude gesturing. Sometimes they would go to the café for coffee after Sunday morning Mass. Her mouth trembled. How she longed for the old days before she'd met Phillip! But as soon as the thought struck, she thrust it away.

That was a disloyal thought. She was married to Phillip, that was the choice she had made, the commitment. Pushing her hair back on one side, she tucked it behind her ear and rose, eying those doors. She loved Phillip. She loved him! And she would make this marriage work. As the bells of St. Louis tolled the hour, she stood there motionless until they stopped.

With the last reverberation of the bells shimmering through her mind, she straightened her shoulders, adjusted the strap on her purse, and turned, walking slowly in the direction of her apartment, running her fingers along the iron fence.

One step at a time . . . that's how she'd walk home, that's how she'd open those doors across the street, and that's how she'd fix her marriage. Jesus had set the example; she would show Phillip what love really meant. His words would be her compass, and she would lead Phillip, pull him up from the mire, out of the darkness that seemed to encase him.

For the first time since Phillip had broken his promise, she smiled. Stepping lighter, she picked up her pace. She had a plan. And tomorrow she would call Jude. She would confess how much she missed him, how much she missed his friendship. He would understand, and she would ask him for help in taking the first step. With a last glance back at the cathedral doors, she hurried down Chartres toward Dumaine. Jude would help, as he always had, even though the favor she would ask of him was outrageous.

It was outrageous.

But Jude would help. Of that, at least, she had no doubt.

JUDE WALKED INTO THE sanctuary of Holy Name of Jesus Cathedral on St. Charles Avenue, uptown, near the university campus. The dim, cavernous room was cool and quiet on this weekday afternoon. An elderly woman working a rosary knelt in the back pew to his right. Farther down the aisle on the left, he saw a man sitting motionless, staring straight ahead.

It was a moment before he spotted Amalise, about ten pews up, far to the left, in shadows near the glorious stained-glass windows. She was sitting, head bent, waiting for him. She'd called yesterday—from a pay phone in the law school, he thought, judging from the background noise—and asked him to meet her here this afternoon. He suspected she was afraid to call him from home, where Phillip might overhear. And he suspected she'd chosen this place because it was far from Phillip and the apartment on Dumaine Street. Even so, he couldn't imagine what was on her mind.

So here he was. He shifted his shoulders, smoothed the frown from his brow, and walked to where she sat, waiting. She looked up suddenly, as if startled, and with a wry smile shuffled aside to make room for him to sit.

"Thanks, Jude." Her eyes were red, ringed with dark circles as if she'd not been sleeping.

He slid into the pew beside her. A tear slipped down her cheek, and without thinking, he reached out and pulled her to him. Ah, Amalise. How he wanted the power to whisk her away, to take her back to Marianus, like in the old days. She collapsed against him, and with her face buried in his chest, she shivered while he held her tight, stroking her hair and saying nothing because if he opened his mouth he'd say something she'd never forgive: That Phillip's salvation was not in her hands.

When she pushed back, her eyes were dry. She straightened, looked at him, and tucked her hair behind her ears in that old familiar way. "I'm sorry," she whispered, smearing her cheek with the heel of her hand.

"What's going on, Amalise?" Jude leaned back and worked for a casual tone, but a wave of fear pumped up his heart, and he heard the flint in his own voice. There was a rushing sound in his ears, and he clenched his fingers into a tight fist. If Phillip Sharp had hurt her, he would kill him.

Lord, help me do the right thing, here. Last time I messed things up.

Her eyes widened and she shook her head. "It's not like that. Nothing like that." She twisted around and reached for a prayer book in the holder behind the next pew. "I need you with me for this, Jude."

Looking down at the prayer book, she murmured, "You'll think this is crazy, I know. But it's something I have to do." She looked up at him. "I miss you. I love Phillip, of course. But I feel so blue sometimes."

"I'm here now."

"Yes." He watched as she opened the prayer book to a place marked with a thin red satin ribbon, as if she'd placed it there. "Here." She spread the pages for him to see. Her face flushed as she looked at him.

He leaned forward to see what was written on the page, then frowned, and glanced up at Amalise.

"I can't explain." She tried a smile and failed. "This is something I have to do. I can't sleep." She stopped, pressed her lips together. Looked past him, over his shoulder. "Can you just kneel here beside me, Jude, and just listen? Just listen and not ask why."

He puckered his mouth and stared at her. The last thing in the world he wanted to do was support what he thought she was asking. If her bond with Phillip was tensile now, it would be forged to steel after this. The angry, rushing sound returned, but she'd asked his help, and he couldn't refuse even though he'd have no answer to his questions. Not today.

"Will you kneel with me?" She slipped onto the padded wooden kneeler, bracing her arms on the back of the next pew, gripping the prayer book with both hands, and turned her head to look at him. When he didn't move, she whispered, "Please?"

With a heavy heart Jude knelt beside her.

She hesitated and he heard her swallow before she began. "Forgive me, Father, for I have sinned. I know I haven't been around much. But I'm here now."

When she bowed her head and began reading the marriage vows from the prayer book in a hushed tone, Jude saw the trembling in her arms, in her neck and throat. He slipped his arm around her and dipped his head so that it almost touched hers. And then he forced himself to hold silent, to listen as Amalise read alone in a low, halting murmur the words from the marriage ceremony, the commitment she'd made to Phillip Sharp in the courthouse. And now before God.

Masking the mixture of anger, fear, and pity that simmered inside, Jude huddled over her in the shadows. When she came to the end and said "Amen," he did too, knowing that when they walked out of the church and into the sunshine, there was nothing he could do to help Amalise.

Things would go on as they had.

They went for coffee, after, at K&B Drugstore on the corner of Broadway and St. Charles. She was subdued at first. They talked about Pilottown, Amalise's summer job, the wedding party, Rebecca, the judge and Maraine . . . everything except what had just occurred inside the church. True to his word, Jude didn't ask and Amalise gave no explanation. Soon, though, color returned to her cheeks. As they went on talking and he kept his promise, the light returned to her eyes. Once she even laughed at something he said, and Jude, studying her covertly, decided that she was all right for the moment.

It was ironic, he thought, as they rose to go their separate ways. She seemed stronger after reading those vows in church and more at peace. But he couldn't shake a sense that Amalise would soon be faced with a malignant truth: a shadow of evil hung over her marriage with Phillip Sharp, and she would have to make a hard choice.

What was even worse was that Amalise had everything backward. The commitment she believed she'd just made was misconceived. Her instinct was to protect Phillip, as if he were her child, not her husband. A mother's instinct was a powerful force. But, in this case, that instinct warred with her faith, and he was certain Amalise was wrong. He was just going to have to trust her to God's care.

That . . . and be ready.

Chapter Twenty-Seven

Mama knew she should be happy. Amalise and Phillip were in Marianus for the wedding party. And yet all she could think to do was beg God to give her strength and patience because she knew she couldn't do this all alone. Amalise looked so tired, tense, like someone balancing on a tightrope. And William had gone off in his boat by himself this morning.

Mama didn't like that Amalise and Phillip couldn't wait a few weeks to get married in the church. Nor did she like that she didn't know what kind of relationship Phillip had with God. Neither she nor William seemed able to draw the young man out on that. He was all twists and turns when either of them brought it up. Still Amalise said they'd go to church and ask for God's blessing soon.

She says. I know she's asked You already in her heart.

Please help my little girl, Lord. I just don't like this man she's married. There's something about him, but Amalise is so protective, just like she was with that puppy she found when she was five or six. Sally. Sally would tear something up, like Mama's best lap blanket, and Amalise would try to fix it so she wouldn't see, so she wouldn't be angry with the poor little pup. Mama would pretend . . . her daughter cared so much. Put so much effort into hiding her puppy's faults.

I'll say these things right out to You, Lord, but never to William. William and I seem to have reached a silent pact—we will not

*disparage Amalise's new husband. Parents have to get along with
a son-in-law. So we talk about William's day at the courthouse, or
a book I'm reading that I think he might like, or the price of food and
gasoline. Or we'll watch* Gunsmoke *on the television set. But neither
one of us can bring ourselves to actually say out loud what we're
thinking inside: that our little girl's in trouble.*

Amalise had made the choice. It was done. Mama had taught her
growing up that when one makes a choice, there are consequences.
But Amalise had her faith, and that would have to guide her now.
Like sailors used a compass to find their way back home. *Guide her,
Lord, because she's not looking to me for that. All that I can do now
is be here for her when she needs me. I don't know if there's anything
bad about this man. There's something strange about him though—
I sense it. And, well . . . the best I can say is that we don't know
anything much at all about him or his past.*

I wish You could tell me Your thoughts, Lord.

*William and I will . . . we will . . . enjoy Amalise's wedding party.
Please protect her, Father.*

"AMALISE, WHERE ARE YOU, chère?"

Mama was calling through the kitchen window. Phillip jumped
up from the porch swing, grabbed Amalise's hands, and pulled her up.

"Come on, chère." He laughed and tilted his head. "Did I say that
right?"

"Yes. First thing we know, you'll be a down-home Cajun."

It was late August. They walked together through the living
room filled with summer's last blooms—white roses, camellias, and
indigo lilies from the garden, bouquets tied together with trailing
satin ribbons. Amalise lifted her nose, inhaling the fragrance. As they
reached the kitchen door, Phillip grabbed her hand and pulled her into
the kitchen. "I've brought her," he announced, swinging her around to
stand before him—a cat presenting a mouse.

"Thank you, Phillip." Mama wiped her hands on her apron and
patted a stool near the sink as she looked at Amalise. "Without you,
I expect she'd still be out there dreaming."

Phillip laughed.

On the counter in front of the stool was a pile of tarnished silver flatware that Amalise hadn't seen in years. "Are we using these tonight?"

Mama nodded. "If you'll help me polish."

Amalise opened her mouth to object. This was supposed to be a small celebration for Phillip and her, just family and a few friends. Why bring out the silver? But the expression on Mama's face stopped her.

"This is your wedding party," Mama said. Unspoken words whispered an accusation. Amalise averted her eyes. Mama would never understand how difficult Phillip could be.

Amalise sat down on the stool, picked up the damp cleaning cloth, and dipped it into the silver polish. This was the least she could do.

Phillip squeezed the back of her neck, ducked and kissed her cheek. "I'll be down at the pier if you need me."

"You're waiting for Dad?" He'd taken the skiff down the river alone this morning. She'd hoped he would invite Phillip, but Phillip was still sleeping when he left. Needed to get away, Dad had said, wanted to fish awhile. He'd appeared to Amalise somewhat grave and distracted. Just being sentimental, Mama said.

Phillip nodded and looked at his watch. "He'll be back soon. There's a chair down there. I want to see what he's caught."

Mama's eyes followed Phillip from the kitchen. Through the window Amalise could see him wandering down the hill, stopping to look at fish in the pond before heading down the slope of lawn to the bayou.

"No wedding, but you'll keep going to church, Amalise?"

"Sure."

"It's important."

"Yes, Mama." *I will, Abba. As soon as Phillip settles down enough not to think that every minute away from him is theft.* She began rubbing tarnish from the silver spoon. She looked down at the spoon she was cleaning and rubbed harder, but no matter how she scrubbed that spoon, some of the dark spots remained. It hadn't been used in years. She frowned and held the spoon up to the light, still tarnished.

Mama gave her a sideways smile. "I forgot to tell you, chère.

Jude's coming. He didn't think he'd be able to make it at first, and then it worked out after all."

A wave of hope and longing surged. She hadn't heard from Jude since the day they'd met at church and she'd repeated the vows of the wedding ceremony without Phillip. "That's good." She set aside the shining silver spoon with the tarnished rim of black on the pretty scrolling handle and picked up the next one.

"WHEN YOU TALKED ABOUT Marianus, somehow, I didn't picture it like this." Rebecca looked around. "Your home is lovely." The green lawn stretching down to the bayou was velvet in the twilight. Japanese lanterns hung in the trees and around the pier, colored lights glowed inside the paper boxes. The fragrance of night-blooming jasmine and pungent legustrum and fresh-cut grass drifted around them.

"It is pretty, isn't it?" Amalise pointed past the pier to the bayou and the swampland beyond. "That's where Jude taught me to pirogue—how to balance, paddle, navigate. We keep the skiff at the pier, too, for fishing."

"Will Jude be here tonight?" Rebecca's tone ascended the scale as she looked about. "I want to meet him." Amalise gave her a quick look and Rebecca flushed. "You talk about him so often, I feel I already know him."

"Yes. He should be here soon. He's coming from Pilottown."

Rebecca had driven over for the party and, despite Phillip's objections, was to stay the night. He and Amalise had argued. His dislike for her friend was senseless, Amalise told him, extracting a promise that he'd be attentive to Rebecca tonight. She looked around for him now and saw him watching them from the bar set up at the other end of the long, covered gallery. He lifted his hand in a cheerful wave when she caught his eye, and she let out a sigh of relief. A crowd pressed around him at the bar while the gardener, hired for the evening and bullied into wearing a white jacket, made drinks.

"Hi, beautiful!" Phillip's arm slid around Rebecca's shoulders a few minutes later. "I've got a surprise." He held up a glass filled with froth and chunks of pineapple.

Rebecca looked at Amalise, then Phillip. "How'd you know?" She took a sip, and Phillip grinned.

"I make a point of remembering what beautiful ladies drink. Right, Amalise?"

"Right. And I'd like a lemonade."

"One minute, my love, and you'll have it." He saluted and strolled off in the direction of the bar.

Rebecca looked after him, sipping her drink. "He seems happy." Her tone was noncommittal.

Mama's sister, Tante Alyese, interrupted Phillip's return from the bar. He held two glasses while he halted and said something that made the elderly lady laugh. They talked for a few seconds, and Phillip offered her one of the drinks. She shook her head, but he teased, pushing it at her, and finally she took it. Phillip drank from the other while they chatted.

So much for libations. Amalise turned back to Rebecca, but she'd disappeared. So, linking her hands behind her back, she let her eyes roam over the guests who'd arrived so far—an assortment of uncles, aunts, cousins, neighbors, friends from high school, some from college. The men wore linen jackets they'd shed soon or seersucker. The women were a confection of colors in light summer dresses.

Dad had rented a dance floor for the occasion. The raised stage was large, about one foot above the grass, made of hardwood, and placed halfway between the porch where she stood and the bayou. The musicians were arriving now, and she watched as they unpacked and began tuning up their instruments, testing the microphones, strumming chords.

Only a sliver of moon rose, but the night was clear and bright. Fireflies flickered through the dusk. To warm things up, the band began with "Soul Man" from those innocent, happy days of the sixties, before "advisors" in Vietnam morphed to thousands of soldiers and the national lottery draft commenced, before Joey Cain from Marianus High, class of '67, crashed and burned there, before cat-5 Lady Camille lay waste Bay St. Louis and Gulfport and Biloxi, before our flag was planted by Neil Armstrong in the silver dust of the moon, before Janice and the music died, before the oil embargo and the gas shortage and Watergate, and before that Air America plane, full of children, crashed in Saigon. Before the children in Cambodia were shrouded under a black veil of death by the Khmer Rouge.

The band segued to a slow song. Phillip appeared and led her out onto the empty dance floor where they two-stepped alone and everyone packed around to watch. He pulled her close and she led herself into that dreamy state—the way it *should* be—and through half-closed eyes she smiled up at her husband, feeling a flicker of connection again, that magnetic pull. The singer's voice was husky, blue, and Phillip held her close as he swung her around.

When the song finished, Dad claimed her. "Are you happy, chère?"

She decided that, as Mama had said earlier that morning, he was turning sentimental.

Afterward the band picked up the pace. A dance with Emmett Beale from second grade finally sent her slipping away to the porch, where she dropped onto the swing, wanting to be alone for a while. It had been a long day.

"Hey."

At the sound of the familiar voice from behind her, she brightened and turned. Jude. With a smile she moved aside, patting the space beside her. "I'm so glad you could make it." She no longer felt tired.

"Wouldn't miss it for the world." He sat down and dropped his arm over the back of the swing, describing his race from Pilottown to get here. He didn't mention the last time they'd met. A minute passed and, spotting Phillip in the crowd on the dance floor below, she let herself relax, leaning into the curve of Jude's arm, listening to her old friend's voice and feeling that familiar surge of warmth.

The band was playing John Denver's hit song—"Sunshine on My Shoulders"—one of her favorites. "How about a dance with the bride?" Jude stood and pulled her up from the swing.

"Remember when you taught me to dance?" She slipped into his arms right there on the porch. "It was for some party at school, I think."

He wrinkled his forehead, then smiled and nodded. "You were twelve. Danced like a wounded three-legged cat."

"What?"

He laughed, pulling her close. She pinched his arm and tucked her head under his chin while he hummed out of tune with the band. When the music stopped, she dragged him back to the swing. "I haven't seen you in awhile! Stay a few minutes."

So they leaned back, swinging. She didn't want to talk about now, so she reminded him of those summer nights when he'd climb the oak tree, their *thinking place* just outside her bedroom window and whistle; and he . . . interrupting, finishing the story, chuckled and told how she'd crawl through the window and out on the limb to sit with him, legs dangling. And they laughed at how young they were then, excited about new ideas you ponder at night when darkness illuminates the full wonder of creation—planets and stars, the reflected light of the old moon, eternity, the spinning of the earth, the ebb and flow of tides.

Jude grew quiet.

"I've missed you." She leaned against him. "Why don't you call when you're in town?"

"I'll do that." He looked off, his tone vague.

"You might like Phillip if you got to know him."

He didn't answer. She slipped her arm through his, feeling the muscular strength honed from years of working on the river. He patted her hand.

Rebecca wandered up. Amalise shook herself, sat up straight, and introduced them. Jude stood.

"I've seen pictures of you in Amalise's office." She gazed under half-closed lids at Jude.

"Uh-oh. One of those when we were kids?" Jude smiled at Rebecca with those clear blue eyes, and Amalise's breath caught. He'd never looked at *her* that way. The thought was so foreign that she blinked.

"Hardly." Rebecca's eyes shone. "Come dance with me." She pulled him away, laughing in a tinkling glissando that Amalise had not heard from her before. Smiling, Jude threw Amalise a glance that said he'd see her later.

Amalise watched Rebecca take on the musical beat as they walked through the grass. Jude bent his head, listening to something she said, and their laughter drifted back. Rebecca's skirt twirled around her thighs as she stepped up onto the dance floor and spun.

A quicksilver jab jolted Amalise as Jude took Rebecca in his arms. What was that? Envy? But . . .

She shook her head. No, of course not. This was Jude.

As she watched them dance, musing, she fixed her eyes on him and then lifted her gaze to find the bright star, the evening star. She and Jude had spent many hours pondering that star over the years. Despite Jude's appearance tonight, a hole seemed to open up inside, a hollow place where the essence of their friendship used to nest, and now . . . something had changed between them; something was missing. When she looked back at the dance floor, Jude and Rebecca had disappeared into the crowd.

The dancers, the moon over the bayou, the lighted lawn—the whole scene blurred. She was married and committed to make the marriage work, and this was her wedding party. She should be happy here at home in Marianus with Mama and Dad and Jude and her husband.

Step by step, Amalise. Take things step by step to shore up your marriage, to bring order to your life, to keep your eyes on the compass—the right things. She looked again at the dancers—colors spinning on the wooden platform Dad had arranged for the celebration, the moon's reflection shining in the bayou, the little Japanese lanterns dancing in the evening breeze—and reminded herself how lucky she was to have all of this.

With a push that sent the bench swinging, she stood, made a smile, and went to look for Phillip. She would make this marriage work.

She would.

A WEEK LATER JUDE returned to New Orleans from Pilottown. Picking up his car in the parking lot of the bus terminal, he drove to his house on State Street, whistling as he maneuvered through the traffic on Poydras, around Lee Circle, and down St. Charles Avenue, uptown. He would pick up Rebecca tonight at seven, and they'd have dinner someplace nice. She'd pick the place, she'd said.

Mrs. Landry handed him the mail she collected each day while he was out of town. Thanking her, he jumped the divider between the porches and opened the door to his side of the duplex. Shuffling through the mail, he walked into the living room and halted. He'd seen an envelope from Romar in the pile, and now he worked his way back through the stack until he found it. Tossing the rest of the mail on the coffee table, Jude sat down on the couch, slit open the envelope from the PI's office, and read.

When he'd finished, Jude rolled the papers into a cone and tapped it against the palm of his hand, looking off. The report contained nothing new—nothing specifically damning about Phillip, except to emphasize the lack of character that hung around him like a cloud of dirty smoke. Phillip's credit was as low as it could get. He'd been in debt for years. Ten or fifteen possible employers were listed on the report for the time prior to Tulane, but those who remembered Phillip at all were vague, had nothing to say to Romar.

His good mood vanished. Frustrated, Jude retrieved his duffel bag from the car, dropped it on the floor in the living room, and drove down to Romar's office without bothering to call. The secretary was irritable at his unexpected appearance. Romar kept him waiting twenty minutes. But, now, sitting across the desk and facing the detective's hangdog look, he realized that there really was nothing more to tell.

Romar leaned back and clasped his hands behind his head. "Still pretty much the same information, Jude. Phillip Sharp's never been arrested. Doesn't appear to have kept a job for any length of time, except for this part-time work at Tulane." He dropped his hands on the desk. "Wonder how he lives?"

Jude shot him a look of disgust, remembering Joanna's words. "He's a leech."

The detective curled his hands and examined his fingernails. "Probably." He dipped his chin to his chest and lowered his voice. "I know this is tough to handle, Jude. Whoever you're worried about—"

"She's an old friend."

The detective nodded. "Just keep your eyes open. Guys like this one . . ." He gave Jude a hard look and grunted. "It could take years, but when things start falling apart or someone interferes with something he wants, he could explode. You read about it in the newspapers all the time."

Chapter Twenty-Eight

A malise swung off the streetcar and crossed Canal Street. The new term had just begun—her last year of law school— and a job at Mangen & Morris was waiting for her when she graduated. She gave a satisfied look around as she headed down Royal. An old woman sat on the curb with an empty brown slouch hat placed upside down on the street before her. Amalise stopped, dug into her purse, and bent to drop fifty cents into the hat.

"Thank you, dear."

Amalise smiled at her and hurried on. She felt fine, despite a dark cloud on the horizon. Phillip had been assigned only one class to teach this semester, although he'd said not to worry; he was certain that would change next semester. But it left him with time on his hands. So she supposed he'd be waiting for her at the café again, looking at his watch, and he would ask why she was late. She wished he had more to do than clock her. Ten minutes. He would notice that.

But, she chided herself—he was trying. After the wedding party in Marianus, he'd announced that he wanted to handle the money in the family—bills, bank accounts—so she wouldn't have to worry about those things. He'd buffer those intrusions to give her time to study.

So they'd opened a joint bank account two days ago, and she'd just signed wherever he said to sign. To tell the truth, she was relieved. He'd get her life organized, he said. They would have mutual wills prepared. They would go on a budget—he'd work it up. They'd get insurance—health and some small life policies that would be good investments, ten thousand each, just in case. They'd taken medical exams for the policies just yesterday.

She knew this new behavior probably had something to do with Phillip's situation at the university, that he wanted to take control of something. *Well, can you blame him?* the observer broke in. *It may be 1975, but it's hard for a man sometimes when his woman's the big wage earner. This is a new thing. Your success only adds to his insecurity. Phillip is the outsider, the loner.*

She'd have to be more sensitive to that. As she strolled on down Royal, she turned onto St. Peter, shifted the heavy book bag to her other shoulder, wiped perspiration from her neck, and peered through the window of Nick's ice cream shop on her left, wishing she had time to stop for a strawberry cone. A few customers waited inside.

Something placed at the end of the counter made her halt and stare. It was the birdhouse that Phillip built for her, white, trimmed in dark blue with the same pictures of two birds in the squares. Phillip had painted the birds himself. And there it sat, right beside the cash register at the end of Nick's counter.

Confused, she pushed through the door, working her way around the milling customers. There was a sign begging donations for St. Elizabeth's girl's home next to her birdhouse. As she reached out and touched it, she could see that an opening had been cut from the top.

"Do you like it?" Nick glanced over while he scooped peach ice cream into a cone and handed it to a woman digging into her purse for change.

"Yes, but . . ."

"Twenty-five cents," he said to the customer. He dropped the change into the cash register and shuffled over to Amalise.

"I have one just like it," Amalise said in a neutral tone. "Except for this." She touched the edge of the square opening.

With a grunt, Nick took a seat on the stool behind the counter. "It's been crazy in here for the last few days." He rested his arm on the counter. "There's a run on ice cream this week." He looked down at her fingers tracing the opening in the top of the birdhouse. "I cut that out myself. Thought it would be nice for donations, better than a can or a box."

"Where'd you get it?" She didn't want to hear the answer.

"Down near Canal Street. There's a little shop on Chartres, on the right side of the street." He waved his hand in the general direction. "They're not expensive. The guy makes them himself."

"He paints them, too?"

Nick nodded.

So. Here was one more thread in the ever-expanding web of Phillip's lies. Would she mention it to him?

Better not, the observer murmured. *Now isn't the time.*

Amalise pulled a dollar bill from her book bag and tucked it into the opening of the birdhouse, pushing it down with two fingers.

"Can I fix you a cone?" Nick asked. Unable to answer, she shook her head. Nick picked up a newspaper on the counter. Shaking the paper, he nodded, folded it into squares, slipped on his glasses, and began to read.

Phillip was not waiting when she hurried into the café a few doors down and across the street, and she breathed a sigh of relief. Henry looked up from behind the bar. Phillip hadn't been around that he recalled.

She gave him a quick wave and disappeared into the kitchen where she deposited her book bag on a shelf in the corner. Deliberately she banished the birdhouse from her thoughts. She looked around comparing the café kitchen to her office at the firm last summer while she fought with the apron strings, tying them around her waist. This job, all of these problems with Phillip, all of this was temporary.

Things would sort themselves out soon enough.

THANKSGIVING, SEMESTER EXAMS, AND Christmas passed without event as she forced herself to focus on graduation day with single-minded purpose. The new year arrived: 1976. In January again Phillip was assigned only one class to teach. He still had use of the studio, though, and was painting again, he said.

Over time Amalise grew more conscious of that particular hole in her life, the space that Jude had filled. Her awareness of this increased gradually, like she noticed the sound of crickets at night in Marianus only when they were silent. In the back of her mind like a swarm of bees buzzed the recognition that Jude had changed, too. Maybe he'd left her behind. Maybe that had something to do with Rebecca. Since the wedding party they'd been dating.

At the café, as graduation approached, Gina and Henry turned sentimental—don't know how we'll make it without you, Amalise. Mardi Gras rolled through the city, spring break was spent studying, and Miss Germaine Wells, wearing her wide-brimmed hat—gay-nineties style this year—led the Easter parade through the Quarter to Arnaud's Restaurant in a flowered and beribboned horse-drawn buggy.

When final exams were at last conquered and azaleas, crepe myrtle, confederate jasmine, and all the summer flowers bloomed and the sky turned clear and blue, it seemed that in a blink the great day had wheeled around. The future was the present. On a sunny afternoon in May, Amalise found herself wearing the cap and long black gown—emancipated, dedicated, and consecrated to the law at last—grasping a rolled-up diploma and circled by Mama, Dad, Phillip, and Jude, all beaming.

Jude! Rebecca was with her family today, but—Amalise's spirits soared—Jude had chosen to be with her.

The weather was hot and the ceremony long. Afterward they celebrated at Jude's house. Amalise hadn't seen it since he'd changed it so. It looks wonderful, she told him, and Jude grinned. Late in the afternoon Mama pulled her aside, set her hands on Amalise's shoulders, and gave her a long look.

"I knew you could do it, chère," she said in a thick voice. Remembering that day years ago in the laundry shed, Amalise felt a swelling in her own throat as she saw Mama's eyes fill.

Mama blinked back the tears, touched the corner of her eye, and gave a little laugh. "You did it all on your own, and Dad and I . . . we're so proud of you." She shook her head. "You've got your dream, and, Amalise?" She paused for a few beats. "Just so you'll know, you've given me mine too."

Mama's eyes lit on Phillip across the room, and in her gentle smile Amalise glimpsed a hint of sorrow. With a small sigh she pulled

Amalise to her soft breast and whispered, "You're the light in my life, child."

Over Mama's shoulder Amalise looked at Phillip. The thoughts came unbidden: *Ahhh . . . Mama. If only I could tell you some things. If only I didn't have to keep secrets all the time.*

Chapter Twenty-Nine

In the middle of July, the last hurdle to a new lawyer's success was breached. The pinnacle, the ultimate thrill: walking out of the bland cement-and-limestone government building after taking the bar exam—a three-day examination, the ticket to ride—and knowing she'd done well. She could feel it. Despite the two months of cramming after graduation, despite the exhaustion she'd felt this morning, despite the three-year threat of sudden extinction throughout law school that she'd suffered every day at the thought of this test, she'd done it!

Adrenaline raced through her as she bounced down the steps. Laughing out loud, she pumped her fist in the air. Excitement drove her on down the broad flight of stairs unseeing. The results of the examination would be published in a few months, and that would seal the path of her career, but she wasn't worried.

She skipped down a few more steps and looked about, exultant, proud, barely containing the urge to shout. *Thank You, Abba*! Other escapees now burst from the building behind her like, as Jude would say, a rousted covey of quail.

It was a steamy July evening without a hint of breeze. The air was filled with urban smells—hot cement and tar, exhaust fumes from traffic on the street below, body odors, and the massive release of tension in the crowd. She looked up at the sky flushed with pink and gold as the sun streaked toward the horizon. Her watch read seven thirty and, with a thrill of excitement, she picked up her pace. The exams had started an hour late this afternoon. Phillip would be waiting so they could celebrate; they were going to the Blue Room at the Roosevelt Hotel to dance, he'd said. Irma Thomas was singing tonight.

A taxi in front of the building was not to be had. She walked two blocks before finding one. Sliding into the back seat, she relaxed and closed her eyes while they wound through the business district, crossing Canal Street and entering the Quarter. Perhaps she would call Jude when she reached home and share this moment with him. But a shadow crossed her mind as she envisioned the scowl such a call would bring to Phillip's face. And then she thought of Rebecca and Jude . . . and dismissed the idea as quickly as it came.

It was almost dark when the taxi pulled up in front of the apartment. She leaned forward to pay the driver, adding an extra two dollars. "It's a big day. A once-in-a-lifetime day," she said, and, taking the money, he tipped an imaginary hat.

The driver waited while she opened the entrance gate and closed it behind her. Unlocking the door to the apartment, she pushed it open and broke into a smile. As she tossed her purse onto the couch, she tossed off years of classes, studying, examinations, pinching pennies, working at the café.

"I'm home!" The words came out an excited yelp. She was free, free, free! No longer a student. She pirouetted and suddenly stopped, conscious of the silence and darkness in the apartment.

For a moment she stood listening. "Phillip?" In the distance the steamboat calliope played at the river dock, the tinny melody, high and shrill, summoning passengers as it prepared for departure.

Phillip didn't answer and alarm crept though her. She straightened her back and took several careful steps through the living room. To her left she saw that the kitchen was dark as well. "Phillip?" Crossing to the bedroom, she clamped her hand on the open door frame and stared as her heart began to thump.

In the filtered twilight Phillip lay stretched lengthwise on the bed with his head pillowed on cushions, chin dropped forward to his chest. His eyes were fixed on a glass of dark liquid resting on the inverted curve of his chest. Bourbon, she guessed. Both hands cupped the glass loosely, turning it so that ice cubes cracked against the glass. The brittle, menacing sound broke the silence.

"Where've you been?" He didn't look up. His voice was low and harsh, the words slightly slurred. Her hand tightened on the door frame. He frowned and tipped the glass to wet his lips, as if the effort of lifting was too great. In the gloaming she could see a trail of spittle sliding from the corner of his mouth.

"Please"—a sudden, inexplicable fear trembled through her—"Please, Phillip, don't ruin this day."

She felt the blow before she saw him move—a hammering fist on the left side of her head above her ear. A sharp, splitting pain that rocked her.

A searing cloud of terror and confusion engulfed her as Phillip loomed, shoulders hiked, swallowing his neck. She lifted her arms to ward off the blows.

He'll kill me!

This was her last clear thought as strange, hate-filled words battered her, words she'd never heard anyone speak before, each striking like a poisoned dart. And the rapid blur of fists, hammering, hammering . . . and she was sliding, slipping down onto the floor and huddling as he kicked, and she curled into a ball, and then she couldn't move and couldn't think and couldn't rise or run . . .

When she heard the keening, keening, keening . . . somehow she knew the sound was hers.

And then, mercifully, everything went black.

IT WAS DARK WHEN she came to. She could feel the hard surface of the floor beneath her, the wood cold on her bare legs. She lay there for a very long time without moving. Hours passed while she huddled, curled, unable to summon even the will to move, gripped by disbelief, despair, raw fear, and the throbbing pain . . . the swelling pain in her head, her chest, her back, her legs.

Why? What did she do? Where was Phillip? When would he return and—her breath caught, bringing pain stabbing through her— what would happen then?

Abba. Father . . . ! She curled tighter. *Where were You? Why did You let this happen?*

But even through the gauzy haze right now, she knew. We aren't in the garden of Eden anymore. Like Jude had warned. She'd made bad choices. This wasn't Abba's fault. In the blur of pain she lay, waiting in the dark.

And after a time she began whispering her secrets to her Abba.

MORNING LIGHT FILTERED INTO the bedroom.

"Ama."

The disembodied voice was raw, anguished.

She'd fallen asleep. The pain rose, bringing with it memory. Opening her lids just enough to glimpse him, she moaned and closed them again. He was on the floor beside her, and when he saw that she was awake, he whispered her name, gathered her into his arms . . . ahhhh . . . pressing her against his chest. Holding her tight, he rocked back and forth, back and forth, each movement bringing fresh pain. Confined, she struggled to push back away from him, struggled to breathe. To be free.

Let me alone . . . leave me! But the pleading words were silent, trapped inside.

Minutes passed as he whispered over and over and over again, "Ama, Ama, Ama, don't leave me, Ama . . . I love you. You're mine."

At last the familiar words took on a cadence and calmed the terror, settling her. This was the Phillip she knew. Blinking open her eyes, she pushed back against his chest, struggling to hold him at arm's length.

"It was the alcohol!" He pulled her back to him. He looked down, brows drawn together as he held her eyes, and she found she could not look away. "I drank too much and you were late. Where were you, Ama?" His voice was high and shrill, pleading. She watched as a tear slipped over his bottom lashes. He squeezed her arms and shook her, crying. She flinched and closed her eyes.

He frowned, loosening his grip. "How could you do that to me, Ama? I waited . . . like I used to wait at home." His eyes darted past her, to the door, the bed, the chest of drawers. Wildly he shook his head.

"No! This is home. *This*—is—home!" He shot her a challenging look. "And you left me alone, closed . . . in the dark . . . waiting, always waiting. . . . Everything's changing. You're leaving me behind—"

Suddenly he stopped talking. Lines in his face smoothed. The tips of his eyes turned down. Still holding onto her, he drew back, studying her. "I'm sorry, babe." Each word now pronounced in a slow deliberate manner, as if he were scolding a young child. He reached out and touched the tip of her nose with his finger.

She looked at him. *What . . . ?*

"You shouldn't worry me like that, you know?" He cocked his head. "We'd had such plans to celebrate!" His finger brushed across her cheek, traced her jawline.

With a shudder she pulled away.

His hand dropped to his side. His neck bowed. She barely caught the murmured words. "I thought I'd lost you, Ama."

Fury and pity rose together. She fought against the fury for fear of his response. Would he hit her again? Every muscle in her body cringed. She fought against the power of the pity beginning to emerge—nothing he said could justify what he'd done.

Her mind slowly woke from the stupor. She could push him away and walk out of here right now. She could do it, she realized, looking at him beside her on the floor. She could rise, dress, and walk out the door. She could call someone—Jude perhaps, or even the police. She could walk over to the church, fall on her knees, and seek guidance and shelter.

In this one moment she could change everything.

But in the instant his face folded, and he slumped against her, convulsed. "Help me, Ama." The words were whispered, broken.

Her husband was asking for help.

With reluctance she slid her arms around him. Strangely she thought of Sally, the little mutt she'd saved from the chinaberry attack. Phillip looked up. Their eyes met, and for one instant she imagined she saw something in his face that made no sense: a flash of victory. But it disappeared, and when he dropped his head to her shoulder, she held onto him, protecting now, soothing the lost and lonely child inside the man that had cried out for help.

"This will never happen again. I promise. You have my word."

Another promise. But she wanted to believe him. As she held him, slowly she approached the rim of the fault line. "I promise, Ama," he said again. She hesitated, balanced on the edge, and then dropped right in. He needed her, now more than ever.

The fatal words slipped through her lips: "It wasn't your fault. It was the alcohol. And I was late."

This will be temporary, the observer soothed. *We'll get through this minute, and the next, and the next, and on another day we will think things through and find a solution.*

Yes, she thought. A solution. There had to be one and, this time with Abba's help, she'd find it and make things right.

LATER, LYING ON THE bed where he arranged her in the midst of soft pillows and blankets like a precious thing, she looked through the open window. She let her eyes roam over the patio with the fountain sparkling in the sunshine, the tree—shade dappling the spot where she loved to sit. She was fatigued, sluggish, as if she'd come through a storm. But Phillip had turned on the overhead fan, and the breeze revived her. She watched as two brown sparrows landed on the edge of the fountain.

The world was still moving along as it always had. The wind chimes rippled. *Thank you. Everything's still lovely.*

She concentrated on the pretty scene. Right now she just wanted to forget. Last night was an aberration that began to recede, as if it had all happened to someone else, someone unconnected in the morning light to Amalise Catoir and Phillip Sharp. So that in the end, in the sunny room in that bright new morning, she was gradually left with only a blurred memory of the violence and terror she'd endured.

From the nest in the bed, she could hear Phillip moving around in the kitchen, clanging pots and pans, opening and closing the refrigerator door, running tap water from the faucet. A few minutes later he returned to the bedroom holding a tray on top of which were a plate of scrambled eggs, bacon, buttered toast, and a cold glass of orange juice. Seconds passed as she looked at the offering. At last she pushed herself up and fluffed the pillows behind her, and he set the tray down on the bed. There was a single rose beside the plate, a napkin and knife and fork, and two small white aspirin.

"Where'd you get the rose?"

His face grew red and he lowered his eyes. "I bought it for you . . . before I started drinking yesterday." With a wan smile he picked up the rose and held it out to her. "Can you forget?"

Her head hurt. With a slight feeling of nausea, she averted her eyes and took the flower from him. She swallowed the aspirin with the orange juice. While she began to pick through the food, pretending that she was hungry, he pulled a chair over to the side of the bed and watched her intently. A fragrant breeze drifted from the courtyard.

Phillip's eyes followed the fork as she lifted it from the plate to her mouth. He watched her chew the food and swallow. She turned to avoid the intense scrutiny. Over his shoulder and through the window screen, she could see the pair of sparrows fluttering in the fountain.

He lifted his nose in the air and sniffed. "Something reminds me of you. Jasmine, isn't it?"

How had he remembered that? She'd planted the vine in the courtyard herself, and she'd been waiting for it to bloom. She looked at him and was surprised to see the change. He was transformed, smiling, his eyes crinkling around the edges.

In the days that followed, even after the pain disappeared, a shadow of that night loomed in the back of her mind. Strangely there were few bruises, as if Phillip had known just where to hit—highest impact, least visibility. But the implications of that thought caught her off guard and instantly she forced it into the graveyard of the past. Phillip had apologized, he'd changed. She told herself that what had happened on the night of the bar exam would never happen again—Phillip had promised. It was a secret she could bury. No one else would ever know. Not Mama and Dad—it would hurt them too much. Not Jude.

With a few dabs of makeup, she made certain that neither Rebecca nor Gina would notice. And Mouse was not around—he'd moved on. This, too, would be her secret.

Chapter Thirty

She'd only been in the office at Mangen & Morris for a week, but it was her own office this time. She'd put family pictures on the wall, as Marshall Eugene Poche had done. One with Dad, Mama, and herself, one of Phillip in the apartment courtyard, one of Jude in the skiff. And she'd also brought a green plant from the farmer's market. She stood contemplating the picture of Jude for a moment, then shook it off and let her eyes roam over the rest of the office with satisfaction, thinking that it was all lovely and telling herself that this must be a dream; it couldn't be true that someone was actually paying her to come to work here each day.

She'd mentioned that thought to Rebecca yesterday, and Rebecca had grinned at her. "Hush. Don't talk like that around here, Cinderella."

As she leaned back savoring her new place in the universe, an unwanted vision of the wild disorder at home rose in her mind. It was September and university classes were starting, but for some reason Phillip seemed to have emptied his entire studio into the apartment in the last few weeks. Sketchpads, pencils, paints and brushes, several easels, and stacks and stacks of canvases, used and unused, were everywhere in the apartment now, and they seemed to her to be reproducing.

The thought made her press her hand to her forehead. Why hadn't he left these things in the studio where they belonged? She'd asked, but he was moody these days and wouldn't answer. Tucking away the worry, she sidled back behind the desk, sat, pulled a file folder toward her, and opened it. New lawyers were expected to concentrate on billable hours and getting things done, not on personal matters.

A rap on the open door made her look up. A man leaned into her office. "Is that a girl I see in there?" His eyebrows shot up.

Amalise smiled, searching her memory for his name as she scooted back the chair and looked down, inspecting her shoes, her suit skirt. She stretched out her arm, jangled the gold bracelet she wore, a graduation present from Mama and Dad. "I suppose so!"

He grinned and leaned against the door, crossing his arms. They'd met last summer at one of the parties, and he was a mid-level associate, she recalled. His light brown hair was short and brushed to the side. He wore a blue-and-white seersucker suit for the still warm weather, a crisp white cotton shirt, and a dark blue tie.

"I'm Raymond Hardy, if you've forgotten."

Her expression must have given her away.

He spread his hands, smiling. "Hey, there are more of us than you think. Welcome to the firm. How about lunch today? Do you have plans?"

"No plans yet. Thanks, I'd love that."

"Great." He sauntered into her office. "Rebecca's coming, too, and Preston Gray. He's a sixth year. You met him last summer."

She nodded. "I remember you both."

After inspecting the pictures she'd hung, he sat on the corner of her desk, drumming his fingers on the top. "Women have a way with things. The office looks nice. Comfortable."

"Thanks."

He snorted. "It's just as well. You'd better think of this as home." He reached across her desk, slid the file folder she'd just opened toward him, and glanced at the first page. "Looks like we'll be working together soon"—he ran his eyes down the page and turned it back to her. "This is one of Doug Bastion's new deals."

She glanced down at the folder and back to him. This would be her first assignment as a real lawyer. "Great," she said, in a cool tone, concealing her excitement. "What time for lunch?"

"Oh, around noon or so." He stood. "I'll stop by for you." He headed for the door.

When he'd gone, she pulled her purse from the bottom desk drawer and counted the money left in her wallet. Who was supposed to pay the check? She needed a credit card but had never had one. As a summer clerk she'd been coddled, problems like who should pay lunch checks were clear: the firm paid. But now . . . what rules applied for women in business in a man's world? She supposed there was a protocol that everyone else understood, but it wasn't obvious to her.

She picked up the phone and called Rebecca. Rebecca didn't know either. Amalise hung up. She didn't know the rules yet, but she'd figure them out soon enough. She'd tackle this just like everything else that came along, each problem one at a time.

THEY WENT TO BAILEY'S at the Roosevelt Hotel just off Canal Street, a hot spot at noon and after-five for the young downtown business crowd. High ceilings, a constant busy hum, a crowd waiting near the bar for tables. Everyone wore suits, it seemed. The room was brightly lit with sunshine streaming through the long row of windows that looked out on Baronne Street and from colorful Tiffany chandeliers above. Raymond and Preston seemed to know everyone.

In fifteen minutes they were shown to a table near the windows. People rushed past on the sidewalks below, and Amalise caught herself looking for Phillip and then felt foolish. Since the day of the bar exam when he'd confessed his fear that she was leaving him behind, she'd been guarded with him about her work. Phillip seemed to have grown perpetually angry again. It crossed her mind that he might be envious of her new job, but she was certain that was wrong because her success was supposed to be his too, and he clung to her when they were together.

Rebecca, unmarried and unfettered, sat directly across the table from Amalise. She was so at ease. Well, why shouldn't she be? Amalise picked up her napkin. There was no edgy husband waiting at home for Rebecca, watching her every move. Instead, there was Jude . . .

Were Rebecca and Jude in love? The thought brought a sharp pang. Jude hadn't called in months, and in his absence she sometimes caught herself wrapping old memories of him around her like a warm blanket. Stealing a glance at Rebecca from under her lashes, she spread the napkin over her lap. Would Rebecca claim Jude in the years ahead?

Rebecca said something just then and laughed, and Amalise snapped to, turning her attention to the conversation.

"You're telling me that most associates work an average of sixty hours or more a week?" Rebecca cast an incredulous look at Raymond.

Amalise did the calculation and swallowed. Eight to five, six days a week, with an hour for lunch and Sundays off tallied only forty-eight. And that was *six* days a week.

Raymond smiled and nodded. "Not just here. Everywhere. Look at the hours bankers work on Wall Street. If you're on a fast-moving deal, it's more like eighty."

So . . . late nights and no Sundays off?

"But those are just the billable hours, give or take a few. That doesn't include time worked that isn't productive." As Raymond spoke, he unwrapped the silverware from the napkin, set it aside, and placed the napkin on his lap. He seemed to relish giving out this information.

Rebecca stared. "Productive? Give me an example of nonproductive time."

"Floundering. Figuring things out. Can't bill clients for that."

This is bluster, Amalise thought, masking her alarm with a smile. She'd be working seven days a week and late into the evenings to match those hours if he was right.

"The work's competitive." Raymond glanced at Preston, who confirmed with a nod. "You could get away with less if you're not ambitious," he went on, shaking his head. "You can make that choice. But you won't be tapped for the best transactions that way." He shrugged. "It depends on what you want."

Preston interrupted. "Let's order." He scrutinized the menu, then signaled the waiter. "Counting hours is the wrong way to look at things," he said, with a frowning glance at Raymond. "When you're assigned work, you get it done." He paused. "But Raymond's right in one sense. Good billable hours get you assigned to the best deals."

"With rainmakers, like Doug Bastion." Raymond ran his eyes down the menu, set it down on the table, and hunched forward. "If you want to work on Doug's transactions, you'll be drones at first. Long hours on document review, due diligence, proofing agreements." Amalise met Rebecca's eyes. "And you'll stay as long as it takes to get it done," Raymond said.

"I've been a drone for three years in law school," Rebecca said. The waiter appeared and Amalise ordered a salad. So did Rebecca.

When he'd gone, Preston gave Rebecca a look. "Get used to it. That's how you make it when you're starting out." He arched one eyebrow. "Smile. It's gender neutral."

"Think of it as an investment," Raymond said. "It gets easier as you move up the food chain. In a year or two you'll know the ropes; you'll get to work on the interesting stuff."

The waiter arrived with bread and butter and filled their glasses with water. Raymond reached for the basket of sliced French bread in the center of the table, took a piece, and buttered it. "It's a long haul, though. Seven, maybe eight years to the partnership vote." He offered a sly smile. "Maybe ten for girls." Grinning, he leaned back and clutched the edge of the table with both hands. "That's a joke."

Amalise and Rebecca laughed. The fragrance of fresh-baked bread wafted toward Amalise as he began chewing. Crumbs flaked into Raymond's lap. He brushed them away.

Amalise reached for the bread, too, as she listened, not wanting to miss a word. This is what she'd been working for. The plan. Buttering the bread, she bit into it. The butter was salted, the bread soft under the crust.

"Just think of the firm as your life for the next seven years," Preston said with a breezy smile. "Don't even try to have outside friends for awhile."

Rebecca grimaced. "Outside?"

"Outside the firm. Believe me. It's the same everywhere in this business. Friends won't understand." He shrugged. "Get to know the night janitors and security guards."

Rebecca coughed and took a sip of water. "Is that a problem?" Preston glanced from Rebecca to Amalise, and his expression struck her as slightly smug.

"Of course not," Amalise replied.

"That's because you're married," Rebecca said under her breath.

Amalise smiled to herself at the irony of Rebecca's words.

"Atta girl." Raymond smiled at Amalise as the waiter arrived with their food. "That's what it takes."

They split the check four ways.

Chapter Thirty-One

A malise leaned back in the swivel desk chair, her hands clasped behind her head. After a week of sitting on the sidelines during preliminary meetings—and snappy requests from Raymond for answers to questions that required hours of digging through old files—Doug's deal was taking off. Raymond had dropped off the files for her first real assignment, leaving her with a term sheet—the outline of the negotiating points for the transaction—to review.

Six agreements, all governed by the term sheet, were piled up now in front of her, one on top of the other. She smiled. After all the years working toward her goal, she was on track. She couldn't wait to get started.

Phillip's face rose before her, tamping down the flush of anticipation as she remembered the problem he was facing at the university. The light around her dimmed as the scene a week ago again repeated in her mind. She straightened in the chair, propped her elbows on the desk, and dropped her face into her hands.

I'm frightened, Abba. My heart feels worn down and heavy. I don't know Phillip any more . . . and You seem . . . You seem so far away.

Phillip had been asked to leave the university. There was no room in the department budget for him this year. Angry red patches had flushed his face as he told her, and then he'd picked up a tin of oil, tilted it, and dripped three drops onto the whetstone he used, sliding the blade back and forth over the stone, the oily sound creating a slushy counterpoint to the hum of silence in the room.

His mouth tightened as he honed the blade, and tears had filled her eyes. "What are *you* worried about?" He glanced up. "You have what you want, don't you?" His tone was hard, bitter. He looked at her as though, somehow, her success had something to do with his failure. "What now, Amalise? Do I beg?"

That would help. But the look that flashed across his face before he bowed his head and pressed the blade against the whetstone silenced her. In one instant a rush of passions had combined in his expression—love, hate, arrogance, humiliation, and finally, sorrow. She froze, stunned.

Still the vulnerability of the angry child drew her toward him. He needed her.

"This will be their loss." She said it with heat, but he hunched his shoulders, shrugging off her touch, angling the blade across the surface of the stone.

Now, outside her office, typewriters clacked. Desk drawers slammed shut. Voices murmured. Telephones rang. She pressed the heels of her hands hard against her eyeballs. The worst of it was that Phillip moved through the days like an automaton, as if his life had contracted to match those miniature, carved replications. Every minute she was with him, he leaned on her, demanding assurance that she loved him. *You are mine, Ama.* He demanded accountings for her day, for the evenings she worked. Asked for phone numbers for the conference rooms, who she'd seen, whom she'd talked to that day, details of her assignments. She provided everything to him. He needed this affirmation, and these were small things she could do for him.

She'd urged him to look for a job, to no avail. Two days ago she'd finally talked him into applying for a teaching position in the city recreation program. She'd seen it advertised in *The Times Picayune.*

Grudgingly, he called, and the personnel office made an appointment to see him immediately. As a surprise, she'd purchased a navy sport coat for the interview.

"These people know nothing about art," he'd sneered, tossing the jacket onto the floor and pulling on his old paint-streaked jeans and a T-shirt. "It's the city recreation department, Ama. If I don't wear something with paint on it, they won't know I'm the artist." He'd stalked out of the bedroom, waving her off. "They can take me as I am, or not. Who cares." The front door slammed behind him.

He'd said nothing since, and finally, this morning, she'd asked.

"They offered the job right away." She stared and he shrugged. "There was a time clock!" His look was one of contempt. "You're asking me to punch a time clock? I'm an artist, not a clerk."

And that was that.

Rousing herself, Amalise lifted her face from her hands. Not now. She couldn't think of Phillip's problems now. Suddenly the solution came to her. Simple really. Home and work were separate lives. She would hold them in separate compartments in her mind. If she let the worries intermingle, she knew she'd fail at both.

With new resolve Amalise forced her attention back to the files Raymond had left. There was a memorandum on top from Doug instructing her to conform the provisions of the six agreements to the items on the term sheet and circulate the revised drafts to the transaction team by ten o'clock in the morning. She read the memo several times before the gloom of Phillip lifted and she could focus, really concentrate, on the words.

Amalise glanced at the list of people on the transaction team who would need this work from her in the morning. There were four lawyers, other than Doug and herself—a layer of associates in order of seniority with Amalise, the newest one, at the bottom. She checked her watch and called her assigned secretary on the intercom.

"Yeah?" The sigh drifted through the phone.

Amalise smiled at the receiver. "Ashley Elizabeth?" She had announced on the first day that she'd never worked for a woman before.

"Well, yes?" Who else could this possibly be? her tone implied.

"Um . . ." Amalise lifted her chin. "It looks like I'll be working late tonight. Can you possibly—"

"No. Not tonight. I have tennis tonight. Try the typing pool."

Amalise frowned. She didn't have time for this. "Listen, call them for me, will you?" She pictured Ashley Elizabeth rolling her eyes and added in a firm tone. "Let them know that I'll need a typist until at least midnight. Please handle it."

"I'll see what I can do." Ashley Elizabeth hung up.

Amalise hung up too, pulled open the desk drawer, and rummaged for a number two pencil, then picked up the top document and shoved the rest of the pile out of the way. She would mark her comments on each page of the agreement, then send the whole thing to be retyped with the changes. Raymond had showed her how to have changes marked by the proofreaders with red underlines after they were typed.

Proofreaders! She'd forgotten that. Add several hours for proofing the changes, and then copies must be made for the working group. Once again she picked up the phone and dialed Ashley Elizabeth. Someone else picked up—an unfamiliar voice. Amalise left an urgent message: secure proofreaders to help tonight as well and someone to run all of the copies. She hung up and went back to the documents.

Forcing distractions from her mind, she picked up the first agreement in the pile and flipped through it to the back. There were eighty-nine pages. She began to read. When at last she reached the final page, she glanced again at her watch. Her heart raced, and every muscle in her body tensed as she saw the time. She'd used three hours merely trying to understand the basics of the agreement. Floundering, Raymond might say. Unbillable time.

Focus, she told herself, battling rising anxiety. *Fix your attention on the agreement; take it word by word, page by page.* With a deep breath she closed her eyes and folded her hands on top of the closed agreement. *You can do this. This assignment is a problem to be solved, like any other. Prioritize. Concentrate.*

So she began again, and soon she was deep into the provisions of the contract, fascinated. The various sections formed the pieces of a puzzle. This is how the company involved would obtain the money. This is how they'll spend it. This is how they'll have to pay it back.

Sounds outside her bubble of thought faded as she worked— the clacking typewriters, telephones, slamming drawers, the mail carts rolling past, muffled laughter from the row of desks along the hallway, horns honking on the streets below—all disappeared. She parsed convoluted sentences, inverted phrases, flipped back and forth between the sections and paragraphs, and gradually she connected the dots.

Squinting through tired eyes, Amalise finally looked up. With a smile she closed the document and thumped the cover page. . . . She had it!

Not bad.

Invigorated, she reached for the pencil to begin marking each page against deviations from the term sheet when she caught sight of the remaining five agreements piled up beside her for similar review. She'd forgotten those, and she'd forgotten to check back with Ashley Elizabeth. Glancing at her watch, she saw that it was almost five o'clock. Where had the time gone? Holding her breath, Amalise picked up the phone and dialed. The phone rang several times before it was answered.

"Yes?" The tone was abrupt.

"Ashley Elizabeth, I left an urgent message earlier."

"Sorry."

"I'll need someone to stay later tonight than I'd first thought, and I'll need more than one typist, several proofreaders, and people to make copies."

"I'm on my way out. You'll have to talk to Mrs. Jones . . . extension 614, I think."

Amalise stabbed the paper in front of her with the lead of the pencil, creating a straight row of heavy dots. "Is that who you talked to earlier?" She worked to suppress rising anger.

"Hold on."

Amalise could hear muffled bits and scraps of conversation. . . . *She's new. . . . Can she type? . . .* laughter. *. . . You're kidding, right?*

"Okay. Listen, Mrs. Jones is in charge of the night work, but she never rang back. You'd better give her a call."

Amalise gripped the receiver, struggling for control as the documents on her desk seemed to expand and multiply. "You don't understand." She hunched over the phone, dropped the pencil, and propped her forehead on thumb and forefinger. "Look, I'm sorry, but I don't have time for this right now. I need help. Maybe you'll have to stay. Could you just stay?" She closed her eyes against the sight of the pile of work before her.

"No. I'm late." The phone clicked off and Amalise's eyes flew open.

Seconds passed while she listened to the dial tone, then banged down the receiver. For a moment she glared at the telephone, then she picked it up again. The numbers blurred as she dialed the typing pool. This would take all night! Phillip would be furious. Spasms of pain radiated up the back of her neck while the phone rang on the other end.

"This is Amalise Catoir . . . Sharp," she said breathlessly when someone answered. She concentrated on breathing. Inhale. Exhale.

"Hello?"

"Yes, yes. I'm here." Amalise was surprised that her voice was steady. "Is this Mrs. Jones? No? All right. My name is Amalise Sharp. I want to make sure I have time reserved for work tonight. My secretary called earlier. Yes, of course, I'll wait." Amalise drummed her fingers on the desk, waiting. Beads of perspiration formed on her forehead as minutes passed.

Finally, the line clicked on again. "I'm sorry, Miss Sharp. My supervisor says she told Ashley Elizabeth everyone is booked for tonight. I guess she'll have to stay for you after all."

"But she's gone." Amalise fought tears as she envisioned Doug Bastion's fury in the morning when she confessed that she'd failed her first big assignment.

"Um . . . Ah. I'm afraid we just can't help you. We have a list, you see. Partners come first, then associates, according to when they call. Everyone up here is booked for tonight."

Fury swept Amalise as she thought of Ashley Elizabeth on the tennis court right now.

"I'm sorry," the voice added in a helpless tone. "You'll have to leave it with me, and someone will get to it in the morning."

"That won't work." She heard the pleading tone in her voice and cringed. "And I need copies of everything, too, by ten in the morning."

"I'm sorry." Now the voice grew bored. "The copy machines are on our floor, but those people will be gone by midnight if they weren't booked. You can come up and use them yourself if that helps." The phone clicked off before Amalise could say another word.

She slammed down the receiver and dropped her face into her

hands. The changes could not be typed as Doug had instructed. Minutes flew while she thought of possible solutions. At last, lifting her head, she resigned herself to the only option: write her comments on each page by hand inserting margin balloons, like she'd seen before, and then she would copy the drafts herself.

She called Phillip to tell him that she'd be late. He picked up on the first ring.

"Forget it." His tone was matter-of-fact. "You're not working all night. You're my wife. Come home where you belong."

"I can't."

"Who's there with you?"

"I'm alone in my office. Where else—"

"I mean this, Ama. Come home right now." His voice turned strident, bullying. "Just tell them it will take an extra day. Explain."

Amalise took a deep breath. Rationing energy, she told herself to prioritize. Pick the battles.

"No." So saying, she hung up the phone and, with a glimmer of subliminal satisfaction, opened the next agreement

"WHERE HAVE YOU BEEN?"

Phillip glared from the breakfast table as Amalise opened the front door. He lowered the newspaper he'd been reading and gave the clock in the kitchen a pointed look. Amalise didn't need to look at it. She knew that it was nine o'clock in the morning. She'd been up all night and hadn't eaten since lunchtime the day before. But she'd accomplished the job, and copies were on everyone's desk, waiting.

"You know exactly what happened." She tossed her purse and coat on the couch and stalked into the kitchen past him.

"Who were you with all night?"

She halted in the middle of the room and turned.

"Who were you with?" He braced his arms on the table and raked her with cold eyes.

Don't show fear, instinct warned. But a trembling began and her throat closed as she understood the accusation. Memories rose—his fury on the night of the bar exam—but she pushed them aside, recalling his tears, his promises, the rose. She forced herself to look straight back at him but reminded herself that he was under stress, unemployed and lonely and depressed.

Careful, Amalise.

But this was home. She'd resolved to create a sturdy wall between her two lives. At work were friends, challenges she could handle, rewards, feelings of accomplishment and pride. And here . . .

Phillip was sitting in the same place at the same table where he now sat all day, every day, when she was gone. Carving, waiting for her return,

Here her husband needed her. The urgency of keeping these two lives separate struck her again. And this was Phillip's time.

She felt his eyes on her, watching as she walked past him to the refrigerator with a stiff, straight back. "I was alone. Have you eaten breakfast?"

"No."

She pulled a carton of eggs from the refrigerator, along with a bottle of milk. She scrambled the eggs, toasted bread, poured two glasses of the milk. When she set the plates down on the table, with milk for each of them, he put the paper aside with a grateful look that took her by surprise. Sitting down across from him, she felt the tension release and realized that she'd been holding her breath. Still she was guarded while they ate in silence.

"There's a meeting at two this afternoon on the work I did last night." A rush of fatigue swept her. "I have to sleep for a couple of hours before going back to work." Feeling almost dizzy, she drained the glass on the table beside her and stood. "Will you wake me at noon?" As she leaned across the table for his plate, he caught her wrist.

"So soon?" He watched her eyes. "I've been alone all night. I'll come with you."

"To sleep?" she asked with a sinking heart as she picked up the plates.

"No."

She said nothing as he rose, took the dishes from her hand, set them back down on the table, and led her into the bedroom.

Chapter Thirty-Two

One Saturday night Phillip accompanied Amalise to a party at Doug Bastion's house for the newly hired associates. It was a lovely old place on Camp Street in the Garden District with wide galleries upstairs and down, and long windows you could walk through. Phillip had insisted on taking a taxi instead of the streetcar because of the heat. The air was sticky tonight, hot and humid. She slid her hand over his in the backseat of the taxi, and he jerked it away. Amalise tensed. He was probably nervous.

Alice and Doug Bastion greeted them at the door, and a servant dressed in a starched white jacket led them into rooms on the right, where, it seemed to Amalise, over a hundred people milled. Sliding doors between two parlors were drawn back, creating an area the size of a ballroom that was bathed in soft light from matching chandeliers. On the shining old heart-pine floors were rich-colored carpets from Iran and Turkey so intricate she thought they'd be more at home on the walls of a museum. Beyond open French doors at the back, Amalise could see a courtyard lit with lanterns.

The high-ceilinged rooms were resplendent. There were Audubon prints and paintings on the walls, Chinese vases, sofas with delicately carved wooden frames and upholstered in rich brocades on which ladies centuries ago arranged their skirts, stiff-backed chairs, and an ebony grand piano in the corner with sprays of flowers in crystal baskets on top. The sweet scent of the flowers drifted around them as they entered—Amalise detected iris, roses, lilies—flowers Mama grew back home. A pianist wearing a tuxedo was playing crisp Chopin sonatas.

Across the room she saw Rebecca. She waved and Rebecca began threading her way through the glittering crowd.

"Evening folks. I'm so glad you've come. Jude's in Pilottown, I'm by myself tonight, and I can't remember anyone's name." She leaned over and whispered to Amalise, "The whole firm must be here, and their wives. I don't know half of them."

"Why would you want to know them?" Phillip gave her a cool look. He turned, scanned the scene, and raised a finger high. "Waiter. Over here."

The waiter arrived and Phillip asked for bourbon and water. "Just a touch of that water," he added with a grin, pinching his thumb and finger together to indicate the amount. A hand clamped down upon his shoulder and he turned.

"Wilbur Montgomery." The man clasped Phillip's hand. "Call me Will. We're happy to have you with us . . . ah . . ."

"Phillip Sharp," Rebecca said with a sly smile.

Amalise started. She opened her mouth to speak, but Will, shaking hands with Phillip, interrupted. "Of course. Phillip. Good to see you again."

Ignoring Amalise, Will turned back to Rebecca, eyes crinkling. "And Rebecca? I know we've met. I recognize that red hair." A woman standing beside him leaned forward, and he swept his arm around her, pulling her toward them. "My wife, Sara"—he turned and dipped his head toward Sara—"and these are some of our new associates, Phillip Sharp and Rebecca . . ."

"Downer." Rebecca nodded and Sara gave her a half-smile before glancing over at Amalise.

Will ducked his head, tapped two fingers together on his forehead, and inspected Amalise from under his brows with an apologetic frown. "I think we've met as well, but . . . I'm sorry, I don't . . ."

"Amalise Sharp."

"Amalise is the new associate." Rebecca watched him, the hint of a smile hovering. "Phillip is her husband."

Will glanced from Amalise to Phillip, clearly startled. Phillip flushed, glared at Rebecca, and sipped his drink.

"I'm glad to meet you both." Amalise reached across Phillip to shake Will's hand, then Sara's.

With another irate glance at Rebecca, Phillip stood aside, sipping his drink while they chatted. Amalise worked in vain to include him in the conversation. Sara seemed to be scrutinizing all three of them while they talked. When Will and Sara drifted off, Rebecca whispered that Will was a senior associate and that they were new parents. He was a fifth year or sixth year, she thought, and up for partner soon. People were saying he'd make it—he was on track.

Rebecca disappeared and, as time passed and Phillip remained quiet, Amalise began to relax. He'd seemed fragile, particularly high-strung lately. In the next hour she watched, intrigued, as an interesting pattern seemed to evolve among the guests, a perhaps unconscious but choreographed circling of partners and associates and their wives around the new women lawyers. The older wives were like remote and lovely swans when they were introduced, speaking in soft, practiced tones. With intimate, knowing looks they spoke to Amalise of their homes, their gardens, books, husbands and children, volunteer work, the children's schools.

But there was an air of curiosity in the younger women, wives of the associates. These lowered their voices after a few drinks and asked questions about this new thing. How was it to be a woman in the firm? The deadlines, the stress, the long hours . . . how can anyone breathe in those smoke-filled conference rooms?

"Isn't it difficult?"

"Amalise enjoys doing things the hard way," Phillip said.

Waiters soon learned to stop at Phillip's elbow so that he could exchange his empty glass for a full one. Amalise watched him from the corners of her eyes. During one pause in the stream of introductions, an instant when they stood alone together in the center of the humming hive, she heard the click of Phillip's lighter and, turning to him, saw that he'd lit a cigarette. She touched his wrist and glanced around. No one else was smoking. But he lifted the cigarette to his lips, ignored her, and drew on it.

She felt her face muscles stiffen, mask-like. "Please don't smoke in here," she whispered, tugging on his arm. He gave her an unconcerned look. She nodded toward the back, toward the courtyard doors. "Outside. Let's go outside."

He swayed, lurching against her, spilling some of his drink as he grabbed her arm to steady himself. "Why are you whispering?" he demanded in a loud, clear voice.

Like an apparition Alice Bastion appeared at her side. "Are you enjoying yourselves?" She kept her smile bright, spreading her arms around the couple. With a slight squeeze, she pulled Amalise close. For an instant Amalise caught the flash of understanding in her eyes.

"Lovely," Amalise murmured, shrinking as she spotted the almost imperceptible shake of the head that Alice gave to an advancing waiter, causing the man to veer off into another direction, avoiding Phillip.

Alice's lips curled into a wide smile. She turned to Phillip. "I understand from Amalise that you're a talented artist." He brightened and looked at her. Her eyes moved from his, to the cigarette and back again as she slipped her hand under his elbow and turned him toward the courtyard. "Tell me, which gallery shows your work?"

"I have several," he replied cheerfully, watching her.

"Porter on Royal recently showed some of his paintings," Amalise offered.

Alice opened her eyes wide and her smile grew. "How impressive!" She tipped back her head to observe him. A wisp of smoke drifted from the corner of Phillip's mouth as she moved him with her toward the doors. Her voice turned low and confidential. "Come outside and tell me all about your shows. It's stuffy in here."

Phillip nodded. Amalise followed, trailing behind.

"What do you like to paint?" Alice strolled along as if in a park and, with a sultry chuckle, leaned close. "Do you paint pictures that look like real people?"

Phillip bent his head to hers, and she listened as if entranced. Amalise couldn't hear what he said, but when he'd finished speaking, Alice gave him an astonished look. "Good! That's wonderful. Oh, I've always thought it must be so difficult to get the eyes right. The eyes are the important thing." She touched Doug's arm as they passed him by, and he turned, glancing at his wife, then at Phillip.

Amalise halted.

"I dislike pictures without lines," Alice rambled on, having almost reached the double doors. Amalise watched Phillip, head bent toward Alice as he deposited his empty glass on a nearby waiter's tray. Then he linked his arm through Alice's and, just as she opened the door, flung his lit cigarette onto the shining wooden floor, grinding it with the toe of his shoe into the wood in passing.

Behind him, Amalise sucked in her breath, staring at the cigarette and the burn mark on the floor. She glanced around, but no one seemed to have noticed—no one gave her an accusing look, no shrieks ensued. Clasping her hands behind her back, she turned to a small group nearby, giving their conversation all of her attention.

"Don't ever ask me to attend one of those things again," Phillip said when they returned home. He kicked off his shoes as they entered the apartment, unknotted the tie she'd insisted he wear, and flung that off, too. The jacket followed. Electric lights in the kitchen sharpened his brow, his cheekbones, giving him a stark look.

"I'm not your shadow, Ama. And I'm not just your spouse. I'm an artist."

With a small sigh Amalise sank into the nearest chair. "I've worked hard for this opportunity. Rebecca and I are the first women lawyers ever hired by the firm. If you mess things up—"

"Rebecca!" Phillip's brows came together, and his lips twisted into a disbelieving grimace. "Rebecca is not a friend. Don't talk to me about Rebecca." His eyes narrowed. "You've changed, Ama. It seems you're for sale. I'll have to live with that, I suppose. But it doesn't mean I have to be part of your scramble up the ladder."

Amalise sucked in her breath.

He walked to the front door, opened it, halted, and looked about, as if seeing the room for the first time. "I should get something out of this arrangement, too. This apartment is too small. We're moving out of this squalor, Ama. We can afford it now. We're moving away from the Quarter to uptown. It's my turn now."

Before she could answer, he left, slamming the door behind him.

Chapter Thirty-Three

The phone rang and she waited for Phillip to answer it. She was in the kitchen, and he was in the bedroom where he'd installed a new telephone extension. Sometimes, when the call was for her, she was certain he stayed on the line. She could detect a slight change in the background tone when three were on the line. When she wanted to talk to Rebecca, she usually called from the café. Gina didn't mind.

On the third ring she picked up the phone. It was Dad, of course, with that worried undertone in his voice. She knew what he'd say because he said it every time: When were she and Phillip coming to visit? Was she feeling all right?

How could she answer? How could she tell him she wasn't feeling all right. She had a headache, and she was worried about her prospects at the firm. Doug Bastion had given her a strange look in a meeting yesterday, and she was certain it had to do with Phillip's behavior at that party.

Abba, forgive me for what I'm going to do. This is Dad. I don't want him to worry. And Mama . . . she couldn't handle the truth. I'll fix this too, later on. Her hand tightened around the receiver, and she thought of that snowball Jude had described rolling down the hill. But what else could she do?

She forced a smile into her voice. "Hi, Dad."

"Amalise." His tone was hearty, too. "How are you and Phillip doing, chère? We haven't heard from you in a while."

A spasm touched the back of her throat, pitching her voice higher than usual. "I know. I'm sorry, we've just been so . . ." She heard the click in the background on the line, that subtle change in resonance. Phillip had picked up the extension. She continued talking, letting the careful words stream out over the wire . . . so busy lately with work, you know. The hours are long . . . Phillip's preparing for a show. A lie.

"Hello there, Judge!" Phillip's jovial voice broke in on the stilted conversation. "It's about time we heard from you. We've been wondering if you and Mama had forgotten us over here in the big city. Is everything all right?"

Amalise closed her eyes.

Dad hesitated. "Oh. Hello, Phillip. I didn't hear you pick up the phone. No. No, everything's fine here. We're wondering if you and Amalise could get home for a visit, maybe in the next couple of weeks?"

"Only if we can try out that fishing spot of yours. I'm new at it, I know, but when you've grown up in a city like New York, it's a real treat to go fishing with an expert. My father never fished, of course." Phillip's voice modulated to a minor key and trailed off.

"Of course, of course." Concern deepened Dad's voice. "Amalise told us . . . ah . . . about all that. I can teach you what you'll need to know to catch our supper. When do you think you'll be coming?"

"Don't know, sir. You know how it is with Amalise's schedule at that firm. I don't see much of her either these days. How about we get back to you after she checks on that?"

"Amalise? Are you there?" Dad's voice.

"Yes. I'm here." There were things she'd wanted to ask, but suddenly the questions were gone.

"Will you try to do that, chère? Check your schedule at work and see if you can make time to come on down for a weekend sometime soon." He must have smiled to himself—she could hear it in his voice as he added, "Mama wants to pinch you—check you out, make sure you're doing okay."

She squeezed her eyes together. With effort Amalise put a smile in her voice, too. "I'll do that, Dad. I'll call, soon as I . . . we . . . know."

She stood with her hand on the receiver after they'd hung up, looking through the kitchen window at the tree in the courtyard. A small brown bird, a sparrow or maybe a warbler made its way across a branch in a series of short little hops. She watched as the bird pecked at the bark, snapping its head up from time to time to look around as if aware that someone was watching. Just like her. When Phillip entered the room, she jumped.

She dropped her hand to her side. "When do you want to go?"

He shrugged, leaned against the door frame, and examined his fingernails. "You're not dragging me out there again to fish for hours in the hot sun in that ratty boat with your father."

Fury surged. A vision of Dad's face rose, his eyes filled with compassion when she'd told him of Phillip's childhood. She swallowed her rage. "All right." She walked to the living room closet where she kept her briefcase. It was Saturday, but she had work to do at the office. "I'll go by myself. Maybe next weekend."

"Think again."

She froze. A thrumming started in her veins, sounded the warning. Turning, she found him standing close, right before her, so that the toes of his shoes touched hers. Hand to her chest, she took one step back. Phillip reached out, grasped her arm, and his fingers pressed into her flesh as he lowered his head so that their foreheads touched.

His voice was low and flat, a threatening monotone. "I sit home by myself day and night while you play around in that office of yours." He emphasized the words, squeezing her arm.

No. He promised. *Abba, help me.* But there came the beating, rushing sound as she stood rigid, waiting.

"I let you do that because we need the money. But"—he lifted his finger to her lips and pressed them hard against her teeth— "don't think you're free to leave whenever the fancy strikes you. We're married, Ama. Marriage is a commitment. Marriage carries obligations. You owe me."

Ahhh. What have I done? What have I done?

She whipped her head around, twisting away, and he released her. She moved back and rubbed her arm, staring up at him—at the muscles squeezing the corners of his eyes, the deep furrows in his forehead, the lowered brows. In the silence of the room, her heart seemed to pound. When he turned and went back into the kitchen, she swallowed her tears, picked up the briefcase, walked to the front door, opened it, and closed it behind her.

If only she could call Jude. He'd been right all along. And now what? Longing for Jude's solid support, his strength, enveloped her—and then she remembered Rebecca. If she called, would Jude even care? No. Probably not.

For a moment she thought of calling Mama and Dad from her office, of telling them everything. But she banished the idea as soon as it rose. They'd worry so—take the burden on themselves. Besides, she admitted, once they understood the truth of her relationship with Phillip, they'd press her for decisions and changes that she wasn't yet ready to make because in this turmoil she didn't know which way to turn. Phillip was right about one thing—marriage was a commitment. And bitterly she admitted that he still needed her and it was her responsibility to try to make things work.

She turned the corner from Dumaine onto Chartres and walked on. Phillip was changing in terrifying ways. No longer did he soften his temper with smiles and apologies and roses.

The observer spoke up: *Perhaps you've not ever seen Phillip clearly, as he really is.*

Once when Jude was helping her with a biology project, he'd shown her a cicada larvae in the final stages of metamorphosis, *chrysalis.* They'd sat watching the squirming larvae split the hibernation shell for over two hours until at last it emerged as a full-grown cicada, leaving the brown exoskeleton behind as it crawled away—transformed—to begin a new life. The larvae sometimes hid quietly, unmoving underground for as long as seventeen years before this moment came, Jude had said.

The back of her neck prickled. Phillip was morphing into someone she didn't know. Was this his chrysalis? She shuddered and picked up her pace. Jackson Square was straight ahead, and then about eight blocks on she'd cross Canal Street into the business district and head for the office where she could lose these thoughts in her work for a few hours. But as the cathedral came into view, she halted.

Abba. I know You're listening. I know You are. You know what's in my heart. I've gotten things wrong, all wrong. Will You show me?

She hesitated and added: *You know how I am though. . . . I need pretty clear directions.*

But even as she looked at the heavy doors of the cathedral, that comforting certainty she'd always felt as a child that Abba was listening now eluded her.

Free will. It was a blessing and a heavy burden. Slowly she walked on. She'd made her choices. It was her own fault, and she would take responsibility for those choices.

TRUE TO HIS THREAT, Phillip found an apartment uptown on Palmer Avenue near Tulane and Loyola Universities. Amalise had argued a bit, but she didn't really take a stand on staying in the Quarter. Doug Bastion's deal at the firm was rolling along, gaining steam, and this issue was one she had no energy to fight.

So now she stood in the center of her new spacious, bright living room. The movers had just gone. Amalise tilted back her head to examine the intricate molding around the light fixture on the high ceiling. Her eyes scanned the room, the shining wooden floors . . .

Phillip was right, she told herself. The old place on Dumaine had been too small. Turning, she gazed at the new couch and matching chairs, an oriental rug, and the new cherry-wood dining table and six chairs. Phillip had bought them all without mentioning this to her. With a giddy laugh he'd refused to divulge the cost. "I handle the money, remember?"

But still he wasn't working, and despite the enormous salary even new associates earned at Mangen & Morris—which Phillip seemed to have fixed upon—she couldn't help pinching her forehead and closing her eyes. When she opened them again, her look glanced off the large color television set Phillip had purchased to replace the old one he'd put in the bedroom. She winced and turned away.

Phillip insisted on air-conditioning, which in New Orleans was reasonable, she had to admit, but the room was as cold as an icehouse. Goose bumps rose. She rubbed her arms, remembering the pleasant courtyard breezes that had drifted through the old French Quarter apartment in the springtime. Attic fans always cooled the house in

Marianus when she was growing up. She liked the feel of fresh air moving through a room.

Amalise shook herself from the rumination and walked to the row of flat windowpanes stretching across the front of the house. This was home now.

She could hear Phillip humming somewhere in the back, in his studio, she supposed. The room he'd chosen was large, with plenty of space for equipment—his easels, canvases, and paints, and a table for carving, too. He'd bought a black ironwork daybed, a desk and chair, a telephone table, and a new music system for the studio—radio, receiver, turntable with a fully automatic changer and an eight-track cassette player.

Everything was waiting when she arrived—the new furnishings had been delivered directly from the stores, Phillip explained. She'd managed to check her initial anger and fear just in time when he'd grabbed her, whirling her around the room in a tight hug. "I'm so happy here, Ama. This is my first real home."

His first real home. Pity welled. So she had her life at the office, and if Phillip was happy here, she would be too. She stood looking out over a small patch of bright green grass and the quiet shaded street, fighting off a longing for the Quarter. The small square yard and a sidewalk separated the house from the street, and in the yard were two oak trees with bright green leaves, young enough that the knotty branches were just beginning to spread and twist. Everything was so . . . orderly. So neat.

The apartment took up the entire first floor of a two-storied house. The upstairs was empty of tenants right now. There was a carpeted bedroom that she and Phillip would use and a large bathroom with an antique claw-foot tub. The tub was the best thing, she decided, smiling to herself. Someone had painted it with bright colored figures of flowers and animals and birds, and there was a modern glassed-in shower nearby as well.

There was a small kitchen with an electric stove, a dishwasher—Mama had never had one of those—and a new avocado-green refrigerator. And—she couldn't help thinking of this as Phillip's coup de grâce—there was a garage for the car, a second-hand Dodge Charger that, to put it mildly, was a surprise. Hot car—muscle car, good engine, Phillip had said. We need it, Phillip had said.

Another anxious flutter ran through her at the thought of this particular expense. It seemed so over the top. The St. Charles Avenue streetcar was good transportation, only two blocks away. And she could take a car service or cabs home at night. The firm would pay.

"How do you like it?" Phillip's voice made her jump. He encircled her from behind with his arms.

She turned her head and smiled. "I didn't hear you come up."

"I'm good at surprises."

"I know." She swallowed the complaints clamoring for release—the new furniture, the expense. She hadn't wanted to move. "How's the studio?"

He leaned against her, craning his neck, looking over her shoulder and through the window. "It's okay."

Disappointment pierced—she'd thought he'd still be thrilled. She followed his gaze to a young woman peddling a bicycle down the sidewalk. She wore tight white shorts that set off a dark suntan and a sleeveless shirt tied high up around her midriff. Her long hair bounced in a ponytail behind her.

An unwanted recollection of Jude's story about Phillip at the Hound & Hare arose. She didn't believe what he had described, of course. Jude had misunderstood. Nevertheless, Amalise unhooked herself from Phillip's grasp. Without seeming to notice, he continued gazing through the window, riveted. Sidestepping him, she smoothed her own practical short hair, pushing it back behind her ears.

"This apartment is much larger than the old one." Had the girl on the bicycle ever cleaned up behind a husband? "I'll need a maid." Rebecca had a maid.

"No maid." He spun back from the window, walking past her, heading for the studio. "I don't want strangers around. Your office is downtown. The studio is my office, Ama."

But this was her home too. As heat shimmers from a hot surface, a wave of anger rose. "I can't . . . won't . . . handle two full-time jobs at the same time. Take your pick."

Phillip ignored her, snapping his fingers double-time as he ambled down the hallway.

Chapter Thirty-four

Mama hung up the phone, her hand resting on it as she considered the call from Amalise. She and Phillip had moved uptown in the city. She was surprised at first, but now, thinking about it, she was glad. She knew Amalise loved the Vieux Carré, but she'd always worried a little about that part of the city. Walking around at night and all, away from the central areas. Uptown was safer.

It had been so good to hear from her daughter. Amalise didn't phone often, not like she used to before . . . well, before. Her hand moved from the phone to her lap. *Of course, Lord, when you don't hear from them, you worry, but you can't call and tell them that because they're all grown up. Married. I guess that's part of letting go. I keep reminding myself that she has a husband now. And a new house.*

Maybe that would settle Amalise down a bit. Still . . . Mama frowned. She'd heard something in her daughter's voice when she called. Something tight, strained . . .

A mother knows.

William had said today that maybe they'd go to the city, visit them soon, see how they're getting on, look at the new house. Mama smiled. Her husband was a little bit like Amalise, stuffing his feelings way back in a separate part of his mind when something was wrong. All the while going on with life as if everything was fine.

But he senses it too, I know, Father. Because nothing else could make him leave Marianus and go down to that city. He knows, and I do too . . .

Something's wrong.

AMALISE WAS LATE AND Phillip would be angry. This was the first exhibition of his work since Porter's, almost two and one-half years ago. She was elated that he was finally on the verge of being recognized. But a client had called looking for Preston, who was gone for the day, so his secretary had transferred the man over to Amalise. It had taken forty-five minutes to answer his questions.

It was seven o'clock, and she'd called Phillip from the office to say she'd meet him at the gallery. It was a small one on Pine Street, near the university. He was distant on the phone. She'd bought a new silk tie to surprise him and had laid it on the bed along with a cashmere jacket she'd found in his closet that she'd never seen him wear before. But he didn't mention the tie.

She felt a frisson of anxiety as she hurried toward the entrance of the gallery. Phillip had included her portrait in the show. She smiled to herself, thinking of it hanging on the wall just inside and imagining the strangers that would view it, that would stand in front of it looking up and then would glance over at her, recognizing the model. Would they like it? *What if they criticize it, and what if I overhear?* She halted at that.

"Hello, there."

She turned at the cheerful voice calling from inside the open door. A young woman stood in front of her clutching a handful of slick brochures. Loose blonde hair tumbled over her shoulders, and her green eyes slanted up at the outer corners. "I'm Sophie. We're so glad you could make it tonight."

Amalise smiled. Sophie must have recognized her from the portrait on display inside. Instead, the girl shoved a brochure into her hand, looked past her toward the street and waved.

"Here you go. This will acquaint you with Phillip's work."

The new arrivals called out, and Sophie stretched on her toes to see. Duly dismissed, Amalise moved aside.

"Just make yourself at home"—Sophie slipped past Amalise—"the bar's over there if you'd like a drink."

Sophie disappeared and Amalise shifted her gaze to the milling crowd, suddenly aware that the other women wore casual clothes, tight jeans, and lacy blouses, or filmy things that clung and seemed to float around them when they moved. She should have changed, she thought, smoothing the stiff fabric of her own plain suit with the flat of her hands. Unbuttoning the jacket with one hand and clutching the brochure with the other, she surveyed the room once again and, finding no familiar faces, turned in the direction of the bar.

Someone turned up the music; it was smooth jazz, Coltrane, she guessed, edging through the crowd. Phillip liked Coltrane. This week. His taste in music seemed to change, like everything else, according to his mood. She asked the bartender for soda with lime, and when he handed it to her, she adopted a nonchalant expression and turned, leaning against the bar, cradling the glass in her hands. She took an occasional sip, assessing the situation like Doug Bastion would do when he walked into the conference room at the beginning of a deal. He'd just step aside for an instant, alone, and measure the situation before plunging in, hand out, claiming his place.

"He was at Tulane, I believe," a voice beside her said, emerging from the din around them. "Saw some of his work years ago and liked it." A tan, fit older man stood in front of one of Phillip's pictures, which was mounted on an easel. It was the one Phillip called *The Blue Hour*.

Amalise raised the glass to her lips. The woman stepped back, fingering a long strand of pearls as she studied Phillip's painting. Amalise held her breath.

"I like it."

Amalise slowly exhaled.

But the woman beside him frowned and tilted her head to one side. "The color's good." She twisted the pearls around her fingers. "I don't know. There's something about it that's depressing."

The man shook his head and the two wandered off.

Amalise set down her glass and drifted toward the back of the room where several pictures were hung. Perhaps she'd find her own.

Moving to the left, she stood in front of the first one, arms locked behind her back as she studied it.

She'd like to see the expression on Sophie's face when she realized Amalise was Phillip's wife. Moving slowly along the display wall, she tightened her mouth at the thought of that young girl's insolent manner when she'd arrived. She ran her hands down the crease on the lapels of her jacket and, setting Sophie aside, stopped before each picture, feeling herself relax as she examined each one as though they were old friends. Her own portrait was not displayed in this group, but she'd find it soon.

A burst of laughter from across the room drew her attention. Near the door at the front of the gallery, she saw Phillip standing with Sophie and two other women she did not know. Amalise raised her hand to attract his attention, but he was busy talking while his audience listened, transfixed. Amalise dropped her hand to her side and eyed the group, certain that Phillip would sense her presence and signal her to join them.

She stood watching, fascinated by this new gregarious Phillip. Even in the early years of their relationship, he'd never been this relaxed. His expression and movements were lively, animated—brows rising and falling with his words, drink glass waving while he talked. When he smiled, his cheeks plumped and rounded, crinkling the corners of his eyes and transforming his face. She stared, thinking of the sullen mask he usually wore at her business functions . . . when she could get him to attend.

But now, his eyes shone as they darted from one listener to the next, sometimes teasing and rocking toward them, thrusting his face within inches of theirs to make a point, drawing back and laughing when they laughed, sometimes throwing back his head in a raucous manner. Once Sophie's gaze wandered. Her smile was fixed as she stood silent, looking into the distance. Immediately Phillip rested his hand on her shoulder and turned her back into the circle.

Something cold slid through Amalise. Phillip disliked crowds, but here he was so excited. He was charged up, like that car of his. As she stood watching, he grinned at each of the women, and a wave of shock surged through her. He wore an expression she'd seen him practicing at home before the mirror. Everyone laughed at something he said, and for the first time it struck her that Phillip harbored a special talent for fishing out people's hidden interests.

And weaknesses.

She started, realizing she'd been standing at the edge of the crowd for too long. Squaring her shoulders, she pushed her way through the room toward Phillip. When she arrived at his side, his eyes widened, and he slipped his arm around her shoulders.

"My wife," he said, eyeing her suit. "As you can probably tell, she's a lawyer."

Sophie gave her a disinterested smile. "We've met," she said, while her eyes roved over the scene behind them. One of the other women nodded and drifted off, and the third looked at Amalise.

"I'm Amanda." She smiled. "Are you a trial lawyer?" Without waiting for an answer, Amanda turned to Phillip. "Why haven't you told us of your pretty wife? You must be very proud of her." She brushed bangs off her forehead as she spoke and crinkled her eyes at Amalise. "I do love the way you attorneys all rush for the cameras at the end of a trial, standing on the courthouse steps like gladiators."

"She's not a real lawyer," Phillip replied with a snort, releasing Amalise. "She couldn't beat her way out of a courtroom if it was a paper bag." Sophie gave a short laugh.

Amalise looked at Amanda, fighting for composure as she felt her face flush. Conscious that both women were watching, Amalise curled her lips into a playful smile. "I'm a corporate lawyer. It's business law, not trial work."

With a glance at Phillip, Amanda nodded, and her mouth formed a circle. Sophie wore a polite smile. Her pale hair gleamed and swung from side to side when she turned her head. Her luminous skin— tanned and unblemished, with a slight blush on her cheekbones—was as smooth as a baby's. Amalise rubbed the nape of her own neck with her fingertips. Why did such youthful skin seem to radiate light from within?

Suddenly she felt a strong urge to leave the party—and Phillip— and go home to a hot shower and her old, soft bathrobe.

A waiter appeared and Amalise turned with relief at the interruption. She watched as Phillip switched glasses, picking up a full drink. Under her lashes she studied Sophie, resolving not to ruin the evening. This was Phillip's night.

"Well, I don't know anything at all about practicing law," Amanda was saying, "but I'm certain corporate lawyers have as difficult work as those prancing around in the courtroom."

"Of course they do," Sophie interjected in a stern tone. She touched Phillip lightly on his arm.

"Of course they do," Phillip echoed, lowering his voice an octave. "That was just a figure of speech."

Amalise blinked.

Amanda turned to Amalise. "And how did you two meet?"

"At Porter Gallery." Amalise looked from Phillip's arm, where Sophie's hand still rested, to Sophie's flat eyes, then back to Amanda. "And a few days later Phillip asked me to pose." Deliberately she let the observer summon the memories—Phillip working at the easel, the autumn light, the fall chill of the room. Remembering, she almost smiled. "It was very romantic."

"Ama, Ama," Phillip sang. "Always romancing." He chuckled and drew her close for an instant before releasing her.

Amanda rocked back on her heels, eyes shining. "Well, that is romantic, isn't it? It's like a scene in a movie." She turned to Sophie, who gave her a quizzical look.

"And so"—Amanda spread her arms and looked about—"where's the painting? Let's all go take a look." She linked her arm through Sophie's and turned to Phillip. "Where'd you put your portrait of Ama, Phillip?"

Amalise turned, too, waiting for his answer with a strange sense of victory. In the pause before Phillip answered, she heard him whispering in her mind: *Ama, Ama, you are mine.* This was a moment she'd hoped for way back then. "The picture, Phillip?"

Phillip's shoulders rose and his smile was tight, false.

"Where is it?" Amanda pressed, eyes wide and expectant.

He shook his head. "It's not here." He cast an irate look in Amanda's direction. Amalise stood very still.

Phillip turned to her with his hands spread, as if weighing something. From far away she heard him saying that he was sorry . . . that the picture wasn't a good likeness of her anyway, that his work had evolved . . . and through all of this, she must have said something smart or glib that pleased them, got them all off the hook, because Amanda and Sophie and Phillip laughed, and Phillip squeezed her shoulder. After a few minutes Amanda was pulled away, and Amalise was left alone with Phillip and Sophie.

"I have to leave, Phillip," she heard Sophie say. Phillip shot Amalise a covert glance, as if she, his wife, was the cause of this disruption.

The music swirled around them. Modern jazz quartet now, soothing, unreal. She heard Phillip's voice, then Sophie's.

"Don't go yet." Phillip's eyes were fixed on Sophie, and Amalise saw the smile that hovered around the corners of his mouth. He lifted his drink glass and took a sip. "The night is but a pup . . . and all that."

Sophie's look shifted to Amalise, and Phillip tilted back his head, draining the glass. The girl cocked her head and shrugged one shoulder. "I have an early class tomorrow."

So she was a student. Just as Amalise had been when she'd first met Phillip.

Phillip's eyes followed as Sophie turned away, then he smiled at her parting comment.

"The show was a success. We sold some tonight."

"Yes, thanks to you," he called after her. He turned back to Amalise. "Her mother owns the gallery. Sophie planned the whole thing."

Amalise stared at Phillip and he frowned. Slipping his arm around her shoulders and squeezing her, he said out loud to anyone who might be listening, "Ama here's the best part of my life. I couldn't have made it this far without her."

But when he looked down at her, the bold lie was on his face in his eyes, in his smile. She felt it in the weight of his arm on her shoulders. The trembling began on the inside, emerging slowly but steadily through her fingers, up her arm, convulsing her neck and throat, tightening the muscles there, and the muscles in her jaw.

His smile faded and he lifted his arm, releasing her. "I need another drink." His tone was abrupt as he gazed over the room. "Introduce yourself around, will you?"

With a quick wave over his shoulder, he swung away from her in the direction of the bar. Still trembling, she watched the earlier animation return as he pushed through the crowd, stopping for a hug with a woman she didn't know, then on, with a slap on the shoulder for someone else, and a laugh.

Yes. He'd changed. The chrysalis was complete.

Chapter Thirty-five

~~~~~~

Jude sprawled sideways at the corner table, feet up, resting on another chair. The Hound & Hare wasn't crowded yet. It was ten o'clock on a Thursday night. A loner hunched over a drink not far from Jude. He was fixed on something in the depths of the glass right now. He'd been here a while, drinking hard.

The room was cool and lit by a red neon sign over the bar that said *Jax Beer*—that'd be pop art soon, Jude mused, now that the brewery was closed—the dull row of inset lights over the bar, bare bulbs over the restroom entrances, and the flashing colors on the jukebox. Jude lifted his ginger ale and drank, vaguely aware of the warped linoleum floor around him littered with wadded napkins, peanut shells, cigarette stubs, a sock—his eyes paused for a second on that one—and random paper cups. But the jukebox was playing and the music was good.

He'd gotten into town this morning and was alone tonight and glad of it. Rebecca had to work late. He'd spent the day building that porch off the kitchen, hauling more lumber from the front where the delivery truck had dumped it, down the alleyway to the back. He'd sawed, framed, and fitted the wood. Pounded nails. His neck was burned, scorched by the June heat, and his back hurt from bending and lifting all day.

And this is what I do on my days off. He'd come here to cool off and get away from the work for a while. Days like this made him think he'd better start considering air-conditioning, despite what that would cost with the high ceilings and the drafty rooms of the raised duplex. He dropped his chin and gazed out at the room from under heavy, lowered lids.

The Broadway street door opened, and three women came into the bar, followed by a man. The first two were university students, he could tell—they wore wide bell-bottomed, low-cut jeans and short tees and carried canvas bags bulging with books. They peeled off and took a table by themselves. Jude inspected the pretty blonde behind them. She had a cute little figure. The pretty woman and the man chose a table near the bar. Jude sat up straight and gave them another look.

The man . . . was Phillip Sharp.

Jude tensed and watched as Phillip pulled a chair out from under the table and the woman sat. She was facing Jude, and he could see that she was younger than he'd first realized. Not a day over eighteen. If that.

Standing over her, Phillip pulled a pack of cigarettes from his jacket and offered her one. She took it, held it up between her fingers, and waited while he lit it. He lit one for himself, inhaled, blew smoke at the ceiling, and said something that made her smile. Tilting up her chin with the tips of his fingers, he bent and kissed her. Before they pulled apart, she traded a quick kiss on the tip of his nose. He laughed and straightened, cigarette now dangling from the corner of his mouth. She said something. He nodded and sauntered over to the bar.

Jude crossed his arms, gripping his biceps and digging his fingers into muscle as he watched them. Day after day Amalise worked to support this loser, to pay the rent, feed him, buy the clothes on his back.

And he did *this* to her?

Phillip stood at the bar, chatting with the bartender like they were old friends. Jude's chest ached with a dull spreading pain as the dislike he'd struggled to contain for months rose with force once again. As for Amalise . . . he groaned inside. What did she see in this man? *Lord, what will it take to make her understand that Phillip is no good?* He watched as Phillip dug into his pocket, pulled out his wallet, and paid for the drinks. As he turned, Jude drilled him with a look, willing Phillip to glance at him, to make one false move, to give him one excuse.

But Phillip looked past him as he crossed the room and set the drinks down on the table in front of the blonde. Jude watched as Phillip sat, said something to the woman, and moved his chair close to her. Jude picked up his glass. Should he tell Amalise of this? He shook his head. She'd made her choice. Last time he'd tried to warn her, she'd married the guy. The thought was enough to make him lurch forward, forearms splayed around the glass like that loner across the room.

He fought them but images rose. He pictured Amalise dancing down Royal Street just ahead of him on a sunny day almost two years ago, effervescent, turning back again and again, laughing and urging him on toward Porter's Gallery where Phillip's pictures were on display. If only he'd known back then, perhaps . . . He saw her eyes filling with tears when he'd confronted her with the truth about Phillip over a year ago. She'd refused to believe him. He fought a fierce urge to storm over to Phillip Sharp, jerk him out of that chair, and pound him into the filthy floor.

Amalise.

The tenderness that welled up with her name rocked him. As did the sudden urge to hold her in his arms and soothe her. He covered his face with his hands and asked himself the question he'd avoided for so many years: Was he in love with Amalise?

No. It wasn't possible.

And besides, what did it matter now?

He was too late.

A CRUSHED CAN ROSE in a perfect arc over the conference table in the firm offices downtown and landed in the wastebasket. It was one o'clock in the morning. Raymond smirked, clasped his hands behind his head, and leaned back. Rebecca glanced up from the other end of the long table and grunted. "You're lucky, my boy. Because if that one had hit the finished documents and we'd had to send them back to the typing pool, you'd be in pain right now."

They were in the large conference room on the eighteenth floor of the Merchant Bank Building in the offices of Mangen & Morris preparing for a closing in the morning. Clients would arrive at 8:30 a.m. if they kept to the schedule, ready to sign the mountain of documents that had been drafted, negotiated, and shepherded through numerous contentious drafts by the company borrowing funds, the lenders, and all their lawyers for the past six weeks.

Amalise, sitting beside Raymond, flipped another page, made a note on it, and marked the spot with a clip before turning to the next one. This was the workhorse session. Negotiations on the real issues had taken place in meeting after meeting. Clients were now home, sleeping. Partners, too.

She bent over copies of several dense agreements marking errors for the typists to correct. She and Rebecca were the junior associates on this transaction. Again Doug Bastion was the partner in charge. The work she was doing right now wasn't momentous, but she was learning.

"How's that coming?" Raymond didn't even look up. "We've got to get these to the typists right away. This deal has to close on time tomorrow morning."

"It'll close on time," Amalise said.

"It has to," Preston said. "Interest rates are climbing."

Rebecca gave a mock grunt of disgust, lifting the piles of paper stacked around her. "Where's my pen? I need my pen." She slammed the paper and a pencil with a broken lead down on the table, leaned back, and rubbed her eyes.

Amalise glanced at her. Rebecca was in a black mood. Perhaps things weren't going well with Jude. She dismissed the thought with more vehemence than warranted. But she was tired, exhausted. If she'd gotten three hours of sleep on any one night of this deal, she'd count herself lucky.

"Use this one." A man sitting midway down the table tossed Rebecca a pen. Andre something-or-other, Amalise recalled, an attorney for the lead lender. He'd arrived with a younger associate early this morning, wearing, as everyone else, a suit. At this moment however, his wrinkled shirtsleeves were rolled to his elbows, and his tie and coat were hanging in a closet near the door along with all of the other suit jackets. The younger lawyer had been sent downstairs to meet the pizza delivery man.

"Thanks." Rebecca straightened in her chair and went back to work. The room was silent now except for the shuffling of paper. Amalise let her gaze roam over the sparkling city spread out below. Despite the late hour lights still blazed in the Quarter and up and down Canal Street, the bright horizon that separated business from pleasure in this city.

She bent her head again over the piles of documents. There was something wonderful and liberating about working against a deadline in this room high over the city, focusing on work instead of problems. Problems. Automatically she glanced at the telephone on the credenza across the room. Phillip often called when she worked late at night. To check up on her. She shook her head. It was the why of it that she couldn't understand.

"What's left?" Raymond asked Amalise.

"These are the last of my pages."

"Rebecca?"

"Ditto."

"That should give us time. We've got until eight o'clock tomorrow morning to get these changes made, proof them, make execution copies, and check everything against the closing list." Raymond stood and stretched. "I'll take them down to the typists."

"You can take these also." Preston handed a stack of paper to Raymond. He glanced at Andre. "Where's our pizza?"

Andre shrugged.

"Call Doug Bastion. Tell him we need to be fed." Raymond walked around the table to where Rebecca sat and stood over her, hand outstretched. She picked up the changed pages, tapped them on the table to straighten them, and handed them over.

"I'll go see what's happened to the pizza." Amalise stood and eyed the telephone on the credenza across the room, praying that Phillip wouldn't call while she was gone and demand to know where she was.

AMALISE FELT THAT SHE'D simply melted into the chair—she couldn't move. The conference room was quiet now, with occasional sleepy shuffling back and forth to the trays of croissants and juice and hot coffee on the credenza. Amalise watched under heavy lids as

Rebecca poured another cup of coffee, added cream, and sugar. Real sugar, for energy. Next to her elbow was the telephone. Amalise closed her eyes for a second, grateful that Phillip had not called to check on her last night. Just the thought was humiliating.

"Coffee, Amalise?"

Rebecca's voice made her jump. She'd almost fallen asleep. Amalise straightened in the chair. "Yes, thanks. I'll come fix it." She wanted it strong and black to keep her going for the next few hours. Clients and the partners on both sides of the deal would be here soon.

The sun rose, a faint tinge of rosy gold at first, then white as it arced higher in the sky, past eight o'clock, and nine. Preston and Andre moved around the conference table with Amalise's closing list in hand, making one last inspection of the documents. Contracts, loan agreements, government permits and approvals, promissory notes, officer's certificates, certificates from secretaries of state, rating agency confirmations, and other certifications. They checked off each item on the list as they ambled around the table.

The door burst open at nine thirty a.m., and Doug Bastion walked in, fresh from a good night's sleep, wearing his standard neat gray suit, Hermes tie, and starched white shirt. With him were Thomas Runston, chief financial officer of the company the firm was representing, the corporate secretary, and a vice president. Amalise had met them all before, and she stood, fiddling with the papers in front of her as they entered the room. Doug shot her a smile as the group moved to the credenza for coffee.

"I see you've been working all night."

Amalise detected a hint of sarcasm in Thomas's comment to Doug.

Doug turned, scanned the table, and pressed his lapel with the flat of his hand. "You could say that. By proxy." He laughed and Thomas smiled.

Doug took a sip of coffee. "Is everything ready?"

"Yes." Preston gave Raymond a look, and Raymond walked to a chair at the end of the table near the door.

"Why don't you sit there," Doug said to Thomas, nodding in Raymond's direction. "We'll get started while we're waiting for the others to arrive."

Thomas set down the coffee cup. As he walked toward Raymond, he inspected the closing table. "Everything looks fine." He glanced over his shoulder at Amalise, looked her up and down, and nodded. As he took a seat in the indicated chair, Raymond began guiding him through the pages of each document, showing him where his signature was required. Andre's client arrived, and they huddled at the other end of the table, reviewing last night's changes.

By noon the room was crowded and warm. The other bankers in the lending group had arrived with their own lawyers, who deferred to Andre on changes and final approvals. Things were going well. Clients and bankers were now all seated around the table, quietly signing each stack of agreements set in front of them.

Doug sidled up to her. "Good work, Amalise. You and Rebecca. Not a hitch. We'll be closed with time to have the funds wired today."

"Thanks." A thrill ran through her. Fatigue vanished. From across the room Rebecca gave a subtle high sign. She smiled inside. They were on track, she and Rebecca.

But now that the rush to meet a deadline was over, Phillip's face rose, haunting, as often seemed to happen these days, almost as if a direct inverse proportion existed between her happiness and Phillip's misery. He'd sold no more paintings since that show at Sophie's mother's gallery. The smile died as the familiar rush of guilt washed over her. Her work was finished here. She should get on home. Phillip had spent the night alone and was probably miserable.

Reluctant to leave, she watched Rebecca working her way through the clients and lawyers standing and congratulating one another. They were relaxed now, turning jovial. Amalise massaged the back of her neck and shoulders, managing to resurrect a smile by the time Rebecca arrived.

"It's been thirty-one hours since I last slept." Rebecca sighed, leaning back against the credenza beside Amalise. "You think it's worth it?"

"I do." Amalise surveyed the room and forgot Phillip for the moment. "We're getting better work as time goes by."

"Only six years to go."

Amalise smiled at her friend's sardonic tone. "Right. But we're the silver girls, remember? All our dreams will come true."

Rebecca laughed. "You are definitely in a post-closing mode."

THE MORNING AFTER SEEING Phillip at the Hound & Hare, Jude called Amalise at work. He'd had no intention of doing this after the last time, when he'd messed things up. But he'd stopped in at Holy Name Cathedral this morning, just for a moment, and in the dark, empty sanctuary he'd prayed as hard as he'd ever prayed that God would show him how to protect Amalise.

As he'd left, something nudged him to open the door for her, to give her the chance to talk to him if she could.

To trust him.

She wasn't available, the secretary said. He said he'd call back.

Now what? He mulled over it for a while and formed a plan. He would invite her to meet him some place nice for lunch one day soon, and then he would decide whether to tell her about Phillip and the woman he'd been with the other night. Again came that nudge.

Yes. He would do that.

But when he finally reached her late in the afternoon and they ran through the initial catch-up, she'd spiraled off into an excited description of some legal thing she was working on. She'd just wrapped up a transaction—a great deal, is the way she'd put it—and he had to laugh because the next thing she'd said was that she'd gone without sleep for days to get the work done in time. Only Amalise would think that was something to get excited about.

So telling her that her husband was betraying her was one of those things that dropped by sheer weight to the bottom of his list today. He'd hung up the phone and sat on his upstairs front porch, high in the treetop, musing. She had enough to think about right now. A few more days wouldn't make much difference.

Now it was a hot day and he had a pitcher of iced tea beside him and a fan blowing out through the bedroom window onto the porch. He took a drink of the cold tea, and anger rose again as he envisioned Phillip and that woman at the Hound & Hare, wrapped around each other while Amalise was working.

Finally he set down the glass and stood. Enough. There was still some sunlight left. He'd work on the new porch. Maybe he could sand it down before dark and paint it tomorrow. Maybe he'd get to work on digging that garden tomorrow, too.

As for his plan, well time for a new option: Forget about Amalise and Phillip Sharp. They were married. She'd ignored Jude before, what made him think that she'd listen to him now? Opening the back door he sighed. That really wasn't an option.

He was on God's clock right now, not his own.

Chapter Thirty-Six

Two weeks later Amalise stood in the large conference room on the managing partners' floor, watching the moving crowd. She pressed the edge of the glass against her bottom lip, listening to Rebecca argue some esoteric point of law with Raymond. She'd become fond of Raymond, Preston, and Rebecca. Raymond called this bonding. And this morning Preston asked her to work on a new deal with him.

She smiled to herself, detecting something around her like a change in weather, an acknowledgment of sorts by people at the firm. It was evident in the work she was assigned, by the way the secretaries responded to her now, by how quickly copies were run or time was found for her work after last-minute calls to the typing pool. Rebecca said Doug had spread the word: the women are going to be all right. Almost as good as the men!

They'd both laughed at that.

The conference room had been cleared for the party, but still it was noisy and smoke filled, jammed with too many people—partners and associates. She and Rebecca were the only females present, and a headache was crawling up the back of her neck. Her eyes roved over the group, and she realized that in spite of the headache and worrying about Phillip's volatile moods, she was comfortable here. She knew almost everyone's name now, had worked with most of them at one time or another. She was beginning to understand the tribal language, the inside jokes, what inspired and drove the other lawyers.

She belonged.

She turned, gazing at reflections in the window mirrored by the darkness outside. Watery images of people in the room washed the glass dream-like over lights of the city below. But, as always, the happy feeling faded as Phillip intruded. Phillip and she had argued again this morning. She'd planned to skip this party tonight because of that, but Rebecca fixed her with a look and said she had no choice. Not if she wanted to make partner. She had to attend. Besides, Rebecca didn't want to be left alone, the sole X with all these Ys.

Now she looked about, agitated. No one was paying attention—she could slip out. Raymond and Rebecca beside her were still arguing. They stood facing each other in a standoff, gesturing to make their points. Amalise set her glass down on the table behind them.

Instantly Raymond turned and grasped her arm. "We're all going to dinner. Come with us, Amalise. We'll drive you back here afterward to pick up your car."

"I can't." She shook her head. Raymond gave her a strange look but lifted his hand. Were people starting to realize? "I have to get home early tonight."

"Doug's motioning to us"—Rebecca looked across the room— "I think he wants us to ride with him. You can't leave yet."

She couldn't go with them—Phillip would be furious. Work was one thing, social occasions were another. And his moods were more volatile lately—there was an undercurrent of suspicion and hostility in his manner that kept her off-balance these days. Every muscle in her body seemed to tense at the thought. She no longer knew him. It was past time to make decisions, and yet marriage was such a serious vow. *Abba, Abba. Tell me what to do. Let me know what I should do.*

Rebecca leaned close and hissed, "It's Doug Bastion! You should come."

With a stiff smile, Amalise shook her head. Rebecca could never understand her quandary. "I wish I could," she said in a tone that sounded false, even to her, "but Phillip and I are meeting with a gallery owner tonight." The lie slid from her lips as she shifted the strap of her purse onto her shoulder.

"Oh don't be a sap. Come with us, Amalise," Rebecca insisted in an exasperated tone. "Just this once. Forget about Phillip. He won't mind."

Amalise gave her a sharp look. What did Rebecca know? As she gazed at Rebecca, a cold shock pierced her. The wall she'd built to separate her two lives was crumbling.

Holding onto her smile, she raked her fingers through her hair, brushing it back from her face, and looked directly into Rebecca's eyes. "He's expecting me. Don't push."

Rebecca's expression turned inscrutable, and after a moment she shrugged and turned away. Raymond narrowed his eyes, watching her.

From across the room Preston was calling. Rebecca was already heading for the group.

"You're sure you won't come with us?" Raymond asked.

"No. Thanks. Have fun." She spoke carefully and walked away from Raymond, conscious each second of his scrutiny.

PULLING OUT OF THE parking lot, she fought off the sight of Rebecca's expression before she'd turned away. *"Don't push,"* Amalise had said.

Gloom descended as she drove and imagined Rebecca sitting in the restaurant with Doug and Preston and Raymond while she was rushing home to Phillip like a trained puppy begging for a treat. The depression sank through her like a damp, gray fog. The apartment would be dark when she got home. Turning off the lights was Phillip's favorite trick, a warning sign—taking away the light.

She gripped the steering wheel. Pins pricked up her spine, and she began to shiver even though it was a steamy night in June. Reaching down to adjust the air-conditioning, she looked up just in time to catch the red light at Lee Circle. She slammed her foot down on the brake, and when the car swerved and stopped just at the turn, she dropped her head onto the steering wheel.

The area was dark and deserted. Breathing hard, feeling the cool smooth plastic steering wheel against her forehead, she thought again of Phillip waiting in the dark. She never knew what he would do in the dark. It was the unknown, the uncertainty of what she would find in Phillip each day that kept her always dancing lightly, lightly over shattered glass.

Guide me, Abba. Lead me. Show me.

When the light changed, she sat upright and gripped the wheel, driving on around the traffic circle and down St. Charles Avenue, toward uptown and the apartment.

Turning onto Palmer Avenue, from even a block away she could see lights blazing in the house. Surprise and relief rushed through her. She pulled into the driveway and parked the car, watching the windows in front for signs of Phillip.

The apartment when she entered was bright and cheerful. She heard music coming from the studio, took a deep breath, and exhaled. As usual there was mail on the table by the door, and she picked it up, sorting it as she walked through the living room and into the kitchen. In the kitchen she could smell the flavors of cooked food and was grateful after all that she'd decided against the restaurant.

Phillip had actually cooked a meal. He was apologizing for the argument this morning, she realized, scanning the mess on the counter—a mustard jar sans top, a knife slathered with mayonnaise and lying beside it, shreds of tomatoes and lettuce and onions. *Thank you.* He was trying, at least. Perhaps Abba had answered her prayers at last. Perhaps now things would change.

Setting the briefcase down on a chair and tossing the mail onto the kitchen table, she walked down the hall to the studio, heels clicking on the wooden floor, tap-tapping: one-two, one-two, one-two. Smiling as she drew closer, she could hear him laughing, high, manic bursts over the music. He was working on something he liked. She turned the doorknob, and at the instant the door swung open, Amalise realized that the uninhibited laughter wasn't Phillip's.

Her smile faded. She halted just inside the door, looking in. Phillip was bending over a mass of blonde hair. Bare suntanned arms and legs stretched lengthwise down the daybed. One of the lithe tan legs lifted and crooked around Phillip's just as the door hit the wall behind her with a clunk. At the sound the leg dropped to the daybed, and in one smooth motion Phillip straightened, turned, and smiled toward Amalise, lifting his hand in salute.

"Hello, Ama," he said, as if he'd been waiting for her. The music blared. She looked past him at Sophie, reclining. Phillip emitted a strange, abrupt sound that made Sophie laugh, and with a glance over his shoulder, he walked to the easel standing in the center of the room. "I'm working on a new picture." He picked up a paintbrush, looking at Sophie over the top of the easel.

Just as he'd watched Amalise, years ago.

"Come on in and help me position this silly child," he went on in a jovial tone when Amalise stood, motionless. "Sophie's agreed to pose for me." As if an afterthought, he added: "Where've you been?"

Staring at Sophie, she couldn't speak. Jude's warnings came back to her. She envisioned Sophie's hand resting on Phillip's arm at the art show. She recalled Joanna's scorn at the café. Phillip's late hours in the university studio. All of his lies flew through her mind in an instant. How could she have been so blind? How many Sophies had there been?

Phillip didn't seem to notice her struggle. He dipped the brush into some paint and streaked it across the empty canvas. She could see now that Sophie was partially covered with a loose paisley shawl, which Amalise recognized as one of her own. She lay sprawled on one hip and elbow, chin braced upon her knuckles, watching Phillip and ignoring Amalise. The shawl fell in soft folds over her hips. Amalise reached out for the door frame with a sense that gravity had disappeared.

Just then the music stopped.

Sophie tugged at the shawl with a self-conscious giggle. "Hi." She barely glanced at Amalise. "Phillip, put that record on again."

Phillip gave the girl a puckish look, set down the paintbrush he'd just picked up, and strolled past Amalise to the record player. Throwing up his hands, he said to Amalise, laughing, "Can you believe what I have to go through to get work done?" He glanced back at Sophie as she giggled and shook his head. "I've had to cook, wine and dine her, play music, talk her into sitting still."

"He cooked hamburgers," Sophie said, rearranging the scarf. "I was starved."

Amalise stood rooted near the door. "Come on in." Phillip made a winding gesture with his hand as he bent to sort through a pile of records stacked on the floor. "Maybe you can calm her down so I can get some paint on that canvas."

The blonde head fell back against the daybed with a loud sigh.

Instinct cooled Amalise's thoughts. Holding on to the door frame, she pretended to yawn as she stared into the room. "I can't. I'm tired." She hesitated. "How long have you been . . . working?"

"A few hours." Phillip set the new seventy-eight down on the turntable, lifted the arm, and placed the needle carefully on the edge of the vinyl disk.

"Seems more like a month," Sophie complained. The raw voice of Doctor John filled the room, joined by a bass and pounding drums.

As Amalise closed the door behind her, Sophie's giggles were submerged by the music. *Breathe. Don't try to think, not just yet. Inhale.* She stood motionless, thoughts whirling. *Now exhale.* Slowly she walked back down the hallway to the kitchen, scanning this time with heightened clarity the two plates covered with crumpled napkins, and the empty bottle of red wine, uncorked. No wineglasses visible.

Phillip's voice and Sophie's high notes burst from the studio. A piano riff from the record player followed peals of laughter. Her sudden appearance had no effect on them at all.

Whirling, Amalise grabbed her briefcase, turned off the light, and went into the bedroom. She yanked a suitcase from the closet, threw the bag onto the bed and began to pack, struggling not to hear the music and laughter drifting down the hall from the studio.

SHE WAS IN THE car. . . . She'd taken the car; at least she'd have that. His voice whispered in her mind, warning . . . demanding: *Don't leave, Ama. Don't ever try to leave.* He'd told her many times that she could never leave. Fear and pity warred with rage. Images of small-boy Phillip . . . waiting, waiting, waiting for his parents to return . . . juxtaposed against the scene that she'd just witnessed. Sophie and Phillip. Tonight the fear and pity were at last consumed by rage.

But she slowed the car at the corner of Palmer and St. Charles Avenue. Where to go? There was no one to call. Not Dad and Mama. She couldn't face that yet. She'd seen the quick, sideways looks they'd exchanged at the wedding party. She heard it in their voices on the phone—the worry, the little hesitations. She'd talk to them later, after she'd made some decisions.

And she couldn't call Rebecca. Humiliating judgments ripped through her mind—things that Rebecca would think but never say: Amalise is smart, successful, earns a large salary—and yet she can't handle her marriage. If Rebecca knew what Phillip was really like, ever after she would view Amalise in the degrading light of her submission to this broken man. Besides, she told herself, right at this moment, Rebecca was in that restaurant downtown with everyone else, where Amalise should be.

And Mouse was gone. He was probably painting sunsets in Key West. But even if he were here, it would be hard to admit to Mouse after all this time that she'd been wrong.

That left Jude. She had no other real friends, friends she could confide in, friends she could trust. Without thinking she turned left on St. Charles Avenue in the direction of Jude's street, replaying in her mind all that he had told her about Phillip before they'd married.

Jude was right all along.

The image of Jude rose before her as she drove—good, weathered, and steady, the outer corners of his eyes sprayed with fine lines from looking into the sun and the glare off the river and the Gulf. She could feel his rough hands covering hers on the paddles of the skiff when she was small. She felt his muscular arms around her shoulders all those times when things would go wrong when they were growing up, when she was frightened or needed advice or help.

The car slowed. She ached to see Jude, and yet she hesitated. She'd let him down, too, just as she'd done to Mama and Dad . . . and Abba. She'd buried secrets, lied about her marriage, abandoned the principals she'd learned as a child. Did Jude still care? If he was in love with Rebecca, was she now only a nuisance to him?

At the corner of State and St. Charles she coasted on trust, the bond of old friendships, and turned. She would take the chance. Jude knew her weakness and he knew her strengths. He was her closest, dearest friend. So she squared her shoulders and drove on, and seven blocks down she pulled up in front of Jude's house and turned off the engine.

Her spirits lifted, but as she opened the car door, she saw that the house was dark; and for the first time it occurred to her that Jude might not be around. Hesitating, she stood, heart racing. The urge to talk to Jude was overwhelming.

She slammed the car door behind her, and, straining to see a light inside, she pushed open the small black iron gate that led to Jude's half of the duplex, hurrying up the steps to the front door. Ringing the bell, banging on the door, calling out his name brought only silence. She cupped her hands around her eyes and peered in through the window but could see no light. At last she gave up and sat on the top step of Jude's porch.

She drew up her legs, wrapped her arms around them, and rested her chin on her knees. State Street was quiet this hour of night. Cicadas buzzed. A small animal scampered across a telephone wire linked to the light pole on the other side of the street. Pooled light from the street lamp over there only deepened the darkness around her. Tears rose and she blinked them back as she sat alone, waiting, musing on the years she'd spent with Phillip. No cars passed. Windows in houses across the way were blackened with curtains and shades, closed to the outside world. The wooden step she sat on grew hard, and her lower back began to ache.

The sound of a door opening on the other side of the partitioned porch caught her off guard. She straightened, turned, and pushed her hair behind one ear as an elderly gray head emerged. Jude's tenant, Mrs. Landry.

"Are you waiting for Jude, dear?"

Amalise looked up, sudden hope sparking. "Yes, ma'am. Is he in town?"

Mrs. Landry paused, looked around. "No . . . No. He's not." Amalise's heart sank. "It's late, you know," Mrs. Landry added in the tone you'd use to shoo a cat. "You can't sit out here." She shook her head, frowning. "It's too late."

"Yes. I'll go." As hope fled, a desolate, lonely shadow descended, and she had to force herself to rise from the step and stand. "Will you tell Jude that I stopped by?"

Mrs. Landry gave her a blank look. She raised her voice. "Amalise. Tell him that Amalise was here."

Mrs. Landry cupped her ear. "Lisa?" Turning back into the house, she waved Amalise off, nodding. "I'll tell him, dear. You go on home. It's late." The door closed behind her.

Amalise stood, listless and frightened, feeling lost as she looked at Mrs. Landry's closed door. The elderly lady brought Mama to mind, and this thought ushered along such a stream of recrimination for all the hurt she'd caused—to Mama and Dad, to Jude, that she began to cry.

Turning, she wiped away the tears as she started down the steps. In the car she turned the key. and as the engine started, she sat motionless while minutes passed and she stared straight ahead at the lamp-lit street. A sob choked in the back of her throat, and she dropped her face into her hands. Suddenly it came to her, and she almost smiled through her tears.

Well, I asked You to show me, and You did.

You never know what answer you'll get when you pray.

It was a little harsh, Abba. But effective.

Chapter Thirty-Seven

Sitting at her desk at work the next afternoon, the cloud of depression that had enveloped her at the drab hotel where she'd stayed the night lifted. Problems at home receded, submerged by events in her alternate life as she hung up the telephone with a spark of excitement.

"We're leaving right away," Preston had said.

She picked up the phone again and asked Ashley Elizabeth to make the travel arrangements Preston had specified while she prepared for the trip. New York, the city she'd seen in so many films but had visited only in her imagination. She'd never been included on an out-of-town transaction team before.

Scanning the office, she did a quick inventory of what she'd need to take with her. She rounded up the current transaction files from the file cabinet and from orderly stacks on top of her desk—notebooks, draft agreements marked with her comments, tablets to write on, pens, pencils—and stuffed them all into her briefcase. Without thinking she reached for the phone to call Phillip, then stopped.

She hadn't heard from him all day. Her hand hovered over the receiver for seconds while a storm of emotion swept her. Confusion. Sorrow, as the future she'd envisioned with Phillip slowly dissolved. It had been nothing more than an illusion. Fury at Phillip's infidelity, his lies, the violence. And pity for the reasons, for all Phillip had endured—his childhood horrors, his lack of self. Those were real.

But even as these emotions rose and fell like the tides, she knew that for the first time in years she was seeing things as they really were. And now she was free . . . if she chose. She thought of life before she'd met Phillip Sharp, how happy she'd been. Slowly she dropped her hand and stood, gazing around her office.

There wasn't time to examine her emotions or to make final decisions right now. She'd grabbed a few clothes last night when she'd fled—a couple of blouses, a pair of pants, some underwear, a nightgown and toothbrush. They wouldn't do for this first business trip. Dread rose through her as she accepted that she'd have to go home to pack. Lifting her shoulders, she grabbed some business cards and stuffed them into her purse. She could do this. She picked up the briefcase and walked out to Ashley Elizabeth's desk.

"I'm off." She'd just have to face it. If Phillip was home, she'd be noncommittal, and they could talk when she returned.

Ashley Elizabeth glanced up over the typewriter and nodded without removing her hands from the keys. "Tickets are at the counter when you check in. And I've got you all confirmed at the Helmsley Palace Hotel, East 50th and Madison. Three rooms, nonsmoking." She smiled. "You're on the side with that view of the cathedral everyone likes."

"Thanks," Amalise said, smiling back. She and Ashley Elizabeth had come to terms over the past year. At last they were a team.

"Preston said they'll meet you at the gate. He's with the client . . ."

"George Tillman."

"Right. Mr. Tillman. The flight leaves at five." Ashley Elizabeth's eyes returned to the page in the typewriter.

"I'll check in for messages tomorrow morning." Amalise gave the typewriter a nervous double tap and shouldered her briefcase and purse before turning to go. She had an extra hour to go home for clothes and handle Phillip.

"Have a safe trip," Ashley Elizabeth called after her.

She drove too fast on the way home, skimming through yellow lights as she rehearsed what she would say to Phillip. It's not the time to talk, not right now, she would say. And maybe never, she told herself as she recalled that scene with Sophie. Maybe never. But she wouldn't tell him that. Not right now. She would focus only on work.

Her muscles tensed as she neared Palmer Avenue. When she

turned into the driveway and parked, she left her purse and briefcase on the front seat, just in case, and climbed the stairs with a sense of growing dread.

Ama. Don't ever leave me, Ama.

How would Phillip deal with this?

Unexpected silence greeted her when she opened the door. The living room was dark and cool. Out of habit she picked up the mail he'd left on the table and closed the door quietly behind her, suddenly hopeful. Perhaps she'd had a reprieve; perhaps Phillip wasn't here. She stood listening, but the house was quiet. Walking softly into the bedroom, she was flooded with relief to see the empty bed.

"Phillip?" She toured the house, starting with his studio, but every room was empty. Finally she hurried back into the bedroom, switched on the light, tossed the mail onto a chair, and grabbed a shoulder garment bag. Clients don't like waiting for checked luggage, Preston had warned. Rummaging in the closet, she picked out the clothes she'd need in New York—two skirted suits, one black, one tan, an extra jacket, some blouses, more stockings and underwear—and shoved all of it into the suitcase. She could wear the plain black pumps she had on with everything she'd packed. Turning, she stopped and looked about, taking measure, trying to recall if there was anything she'd missed.

Adrenaline raced through her. What should she do—leave a note? Picking up a pen from the night table, she glanced around and grabbed a large envelope from the mail she'd thrown on the chair. As she began to scribble a message on the back of the envelope, her eyes lit on the disheveled bed once again. An image of Sophie with Phillip rose. She stared, taking in the twisted sheets, the blanket tossed over a post, and the flattened pillows askew. Betrayal.

Forget the note.

A car on Palmer Avenue clattered by, startling her. A glance at her watch told her she was late. The plane would leave in just over an hour. Suddenly alert to the risk of an encounter with Phillip, she tossed the pen and scribbled envelope into the suitcase along with the clothes, slammed it shut, and, with a last glance around, tore out of the apartment. The thought of Phillip's arrival ignited the familiar trembling that gripped her jaw, tightening the muscles in her neck and shoulders as she raced to the car.

AT THE AIRPORT IT took longer to park than she'd expected. She finally found a place on level four. There were only a few minutes to spare before the plane began boarding. She shouldered her purse and briefcase, retrieved the suitcase from the trunk of the car, and took off, with the high-heeled shoes pinching her toes. Feeling like a packhorse, she checked in and dashed down the concourse to the gate where Preston and the client waited.

When the plane taxied down the runway, she looked out of the window, conscious that she'd done it. Divorce or not, she would never go back to Phillip. Pity threatened, creeping around the edges of her mind like a dark, moldering fungus.

Remember. Poor Phillip. The boy left behind.

With a fierce effort she fought back the invasion, struggling against the silent pleas, the lies, the clawing need.

Ama, Ama, Ama, you are mine.

Those were his weapons, yes. But she realized now that there was nothing she could do to change his past or how he dealt with it now. Unlike Jude, Phillip had learned to use his sad childhood as a lure and, at long last she saw that pity was the trap. She'd thought she could change him, but by confusing his needs with love, she'd sanctioned his behavior every step of the way.

Abba, forgive me. And Phillip. Help me.

The hum of the engine and vibration of the plane lulled her. Outside the sky turned dark. Preston and George were seated in another row. She didn't have to talk or pretend. Her lids grew heavy. Twenty minutes out of New Orleans she fell into a deep, cleansing sleep.

IT WAS ELEVEN O'CLOCK Eastern time when she checked into the hotel in Manhattan. There was a long night ahead in a conference room in the bank's offices on Wall Street, but now she sat in her room on the edge of the double bed, procrastinating and gazing out at the illuminated spire of St. Patrick's Cathedral. A cellophane-covered basket of ancient-looking fruit waited on the desk near the window, reminding her of Mrs. Haversham's cobwebbed wedding dress. A handwritten greeting from the hotel's owner, Miss Leona Helmsley, was attached to the ribbon. She almost smiled. How many times had that same unopened basket of fruit been left in rooms to welcome a guest?

She stiffened her spine so as not to slump, so as not to submit to a wave of fatigue. Preston and George Tillman had said they'd meet her downstairs in the hotel grill. She should unpack. She should take a quick shower. She should change clothes.

When the phone rang, she looked at it and knew.

He'd found her.

On the fourth ring, she answered, squeezing her eyes shut, knowing that Preston and George were probably already waiting. She hadn't eaten on the plane, and Preston said one couldn't count on bankers to provide food late at night. Lawyers, yes, George had agreed. But bankers? No. They were oblivious.

"Ama, what's going on?"

Phillip's voice. Angry. Hurt. In the background she heard loud music and guessed that he was in the studio.

Her hand trembled. "How'd you find me?"

"From Ashley Elizabeth, of course." His voice rose an octave. "She said you were going to the airport?" She didn't answer, letting the silence drag on until he added, "I tried to call you earlier." There was a touch of panic in the words as they rushed out. "I've been here all day, waiting for you to come home. What are you doing? Is this because of Sophie?"

He didn't realize she'd been home. "No."

"Oh." He groaned. "I knew this was about Sophie. Look. Her mother owns the gallery." He lowered his voice so that it was difficult to hear him over the music. "Don't you understand? There's nothing between us." He paused. "Her mother wanted Sophie's portrait done, and now it's finished."

This was the voice of a stranger. It was as though Phillip and his explanation and the reasons for his words didn't touch her. Didn't involve her. She'd expected pain, anger, fear, bitterness, and yes . . . sorrow when they first spoke. But here she was, two thousand miles away from him, safe, untouchable. She felt nothing as she listened to his lies. Nothing.

At last, he paused. She spoke up. "We'll talk later . . . when there's time." But the marriage was over.

"Don't be a fool." His voice was strained. "It's called figure modeling. Remember?"

Oh, how well she remembered.

"I think you've been working too hard. We should take a vacation. Would you like that? A vacation?"

"No."

"We have to talk, Ama. You're not making sense."

"We'll talk when I return."

She gazed at the shining cathedral spire just outside her window. Beyond, the lights of Manhattan stretched over blazing miles. Downstairs Preston and George waited. Her voice was steady as she told him she was hanging up. "They're waiting for me now. We're working all night."

"Who's waiting?" His voice was lost in a blast of music in the studio. The volume decreased as he went on. "When will you be home?"

She wouldn't tell him now. Not like this. "I don't know."

"Ah." The music cut off in the middle of a song. His voice changed. He was casual now, matter-of-fact. "All right. Call me when you know, will you, babe?"

She envisioned him standing at the telephone table near the daybed. The image split in two, and she saw the record player across the room, far from the telephone. Sophie was there.

"Sure." A fire truck raced by on the street below, echoing alarms that slid up the walls of the hotel and mingled with the tinkling sound of a woman's distant voice in the background, drifting through the wire.

"You're overwrought, Ama. I think you need a rest."

Slowly, deliberately, she set the receiver down in its cradle. The phone was ringing again when she left the room.

JUDE STOOD DRUMMING HIS fingers on his duffel bag as he waited for the bus to pull into the station in New Orleans. He blew out his cheeks. He'd been on watch for the past two weeks and spent the entire time worrying about Amalise. A distraction he couldn't afford, considering the work he did. But Amalise was in trouble.

He'd called her office again from Pilottown a few days ago, but she was out of town, so he'd left a message, resolved to find her as soon as she returned to see how she was getting along. Perhaps then he'd tell her about Phillip and that woman. He flicked the canvas bag again and looked out the window. He hadn't decided on that part yet. Had been praying over that decision. But if he didn't tell her the truth about her husband, who would?

It was the middle of the day on Thursday, so he stopped for lunch at a sandwich shop near the bus station, ate, and looked for a telephone. A booth in the corner would do. He dug out his wallet and searched through the scraps of paper inside for her number at work. Slipped a dime into the slot, and dialed.

"Mizz Sharp's office."

"Amalise Sharp, please." Jude hated the sound of Phillip's name.

"She's not here. May I take a message?"

Jude puckered his mouth. Looked off. "I left a message two days ago. This is Jude Perret. I'm an old—"

"Oh yes. Mr. Perret. She's talked about you." The woman's voice changed, gained a lilt. "I'm Ashley Elizabeth, her secretary. She's been in New York, but her flight gets in this afternoon. We're expecting her back in the office around four thirty or five."

Relief washed over him. He wouldn't have to tell her today. "That's all right. Just ask her to call me when she gets in. She knows the number."

"Will do."

AMALISE SLID INTO THE shining black town car on East 50th, followed by George and Preston. Preston handed the driver a voucher and sat in the passenger seat beside him. Traffic was heavy for a Thursday morning in Manhattan.

The leather seats were slick and cool, and tinted windows distanced the frenzied scenes rolling past outside. She breathed in the smell of the new and expensive leather in the car.

"What time's your flight?" the driver asked.

They told him. Ashley Elizabeth had confirmed reservations back to New Orleans for Amalise and George, but Preston was going on to Chicago an hour later.

"It'll be tight," the driver said, speeding up.

"Mine's okay, but you'll have to run," Preston said to the backseat.

"No problem, we'll make it." Amalise leaned her head back against the cushions.

"This is a switch." Preston glanced over his shoulder. "You're usually the one to worry."

She smiled and closed her eyes, tired but satisfied, thinking of the easy camaraderie that developed as everyone had worked together in the conference room over the last few days. She hadn't had to worry once about the telephone ringing and Phillip being on the other end. Preston had let her sit in on the negotiations this time. Even asked her questions about points in the documents that he couldn't recall.

Tempers flared once in a while, but the thing about business law was that generally it wasn't a zero sum game and things were friendly. Most of the time everyone wanted what everyone else wanted, so you'd slip in a piece of the puzzle here, and someone would slide a piece in over there, someone else pushed them around, and pretty soon the picture was clear and everyone had won.

She let her thoughts roam as the car raced toward the airport. The conference room they'd used in the new World Trade Center Tower looked out over the bay where there were ships and tour boats in the harbor and the Statue of Liberty shining in the sun, and all of it bathed in light at night. She yawned. They'd worked until three this morning, and she, George, and Preston, giddy with fatigue, had stopped for breakfast before turning in.

When the driver dropped them off and sped away with Preston, Amalise and George checked in and ran for the concourse, shoulder bags flying behind them. An old man moved aside and yelled out to George: "Hey Buddy! Help the little lady with her luggage, why don'cha!"

"That's no lady," George called back. "That's my lawyer."

Amalise let out a laugh.

Chapter Thirty-Eight

Amalise narrowed her eyes, looking at Phillip. George had taken the shuttle to the off-site parking lot a few blocks away. She'd had to park in the airport garage with its higher fees because she'd been late. She'd just dropped her bag onto the floor to rearrange her purse and briefcase for the walk, when an arm snaked around her from behind and picked up the bag. She turned, and there was Phillip.

He grinned. "I've missed you, Ama." Picking up the bag, he leaned forward and kissed her cheek.

"What are you doing here?" Phillip was the last person she wanted to see right now. The elation she'd felt leaving New York had dissipated during the long flight back. She still had to find a place to stay. She still had to face giving the news to Mama and Dad and Jude. She still mourned her failed marriage, and she was tired and hungry. There'd been no time for lunch before the flight, and the food on the plane was inedible.

"Ashley Elizabeth said you were coming back today. I called the hotel and you'd checked out, so I've been waiting." Phillip put his hand on her shoulder and turned her in the direction of the exit door. "Come with me. I have a surprise."

"No." She pulled back, but his hand slid to her upper arm, and he propelled her forward.

There were people around so she lowered her voice. "Let *go* of me," she hissed, twisting her arm. He tightened his grip, still smiling, but his fingers dug into her flesh.

"Don't be stupid, Ama." His voice rose and she flinched, glancing around, hoping that no one she knew was watching. Phillip would not hesitate to create an embarrassing scene.

He halted and pulled her close. "I have something to show you," he said in a querulous tone. "It'll only take a minute, and then if you still want to leave without me, you can leave."

Without waiting for an answer, he proceeded to guide her through the exit door and across the street to the parking garage. As the crowds dispersed and they drew close to the elevator just inside the garage, she pulled back and he loosened his grip. She would take her luggage from him, locate her car, and find a hotel in the Quarter. There was nothing she could say to Phillip now. She craved time alone to think, to reflect.

But as they rounded the corner, she saw that a man and woman were standing in front of the elevator, waiting. As Amalise and Phillip approached, the elevator door opened. The woman stepped in and the man stood aside, holding it. "You first," he said in a pleasant tone, gesturing to Amalise. Phillip nudged her forward, hefting her bag onto his shoulder, and entered.

"Just home from vacation?" The stranger pushed the button for the fourth floor.

Phillip reached across and touched two. "Business," he said, cheerfully. When the door opened on the second level, Phillip, still guarding the suitcase, steered her out before him.

The elevator door closed and she pulled away. "I'm tired." She eyed her suitcase. She'd parked on four, she recalled, looking around. The garage was empty of people. "Right now, all I want to do is sleep."

Small muscles flexed around the corners of Phillip's eyes, but he grinned again—his lips tight against his teeth. "This will only take a moment." He jerked his head in the direction of the parked cars. She shook her head, but he pulled her over to a sporty looking car, dark blue and slung low to the ground, parked at the end of the row nearest them. "How do you like it? It's a Mustang." His tone was light, almost giddy.

She stared down at the car, trying to calculate the cost. "Did you buy this?"

Laughing, in one swoop he reached down, opened the trunk, and tossed her luggage inside. "Nope. It's rented."

Eyes wide, she started forward, reaching for her bag as he slammed shut the trunk. "Wait!" She spun to face him, but he caught her upper arms and murmuring, soothing, he backed her toward the passenger door. "You can't leave me, Ama. This was the only way I could get you to listen, talk some sense into you. Don't leave me, Ama. You have to listen."

"What are you doing?" He reached around her and opened the passenger door, and she struggled against his grip. "Help!" Her voice echoed through the empty garage.

His hand clamped over her mouth. "Don't be an idiot!" He trapped her between his body and the door. With a violent shove, he thrust her inside, pushed down the lock, and slammed the door behind her. She fought with the handle, which wouldn't budge, so she bent, searching in the dim light for the lock.

The door on the driver's side swung open. "No tricks, Ama." Phillip slid into his seat and started the engine.

"You can't do this!" She twisted around to reach for the key. Playfully, he batted her hand away, shifted into reverse, and began backing out of the parking spot. She swiveled, frantic, looking in vain for someone to help.

"Calm down." Phillip turned his head to look at her as he drove toward the exit sign. "Just calm down a minute, babe. I've got a surprise for you." He smiled, his eyebrows shot up, and his eyes gleamed. "We're taking a vacation."

The trembling began, gripping her as the car entered the exit ramp. She stared at the cement walls spiraling around them. "This trip is something special. Just the two of us."

She sat rigid beside him, hands clasped in her lap, face set toward the walls spinning past. When he stopped at the ticket booth, she would get help.

He reached across and patted her knee as the car wheeled on down . . . first floor . . . ground level. "I've rented a place across the lake that you will love."

"What?" She looked at him and he nodded.

"Rented it the minute I saw it." Excitement pitched his voice high. The car bumped off the ramp onto the pavement. With a mischievous smile, he drove toward the row of ticket booths. "You'll never guess where it is. Guess where!"

"I don't care what you've arranged, or where you think we're going." She had to get out. Now. "Let me out!"

As the car rolled up to the booth, she pushed again on the door handle, and when again it wouldn't budge, she realized Phillip had one of those new master controls for the power locks on his side of the car. Lurching forward, she grabbed Phillip's shoulder to catch the attention of the woman taking the ticket and opened her mouth to scream, but Phillip elbowed her back, knocking the breath from her as he turned to fill the window, blocking her view.

Pain shot through her. Amalise flattened her hands on her chest and doubled as Phillip put the ticket and a dollar bill into the attendant's outstretched hand. "Afternoon," he said to the woman in a cheerful tone. Amalise gasped for breath, reaching up, raking his back with her fingers. He hunched his shoulders and shrugged her off as he rolled up his window again. Twisting away from Phillip, she beat the window with her fists. As she began to scream, the barrier lifted and the car moved forward.

Fury turned to fear as Phillip stepped on the gas and the lights of the parking area and the airport receded. Wildly she looked about. How had this happened? She was alone in the car with Phillip.

As he drove, he kept up a one-sided stream of conversation. "What are you so upset about?" He tilted his head toward her and frowned. "I've been waiting for you all afternoon, babe. I've spent money and time planning this surprise. Humor me, just this once, will you?"

He gripped the steering wheel and leaned forward, peering at the road as she fought for breath. His voice was strained. "Maybe you could give me some credit for planning this trip. Quit thinking of yourself all of the time, Ama." The car merged into the traffic headed for Interstate 10, going east, and then he seemed to relax.

Amalise pressed her lips together and gazed through the window to her right, thoughts roiling, saying nothing. Her stomach plummeted as they exited at Causeway Boulevard, north toward Lake Pontchartrain. They were leaving the city.

Please, Abba! Please. Help me.

He switched on the radio, found a rock-and-roll station, and hummed along.

"The judge found this place for us." He cut his eyes at her.

She gave him a quick look. Dad had sanctioned this? "Dad?" was all she managed to say.

His eyes shone and he nodded. "I told him you need a rest, babe."

She stared at this man she hardly knew. "You told him . . . ?" What else had he told Dad? She took a deep breath. *Stay calm, Amalise.*

"Yes. We found a cottage in the woods, on a lake. He showed it to me. It belongs to a friend of his. It's private. Quiet." He tilted his head and smiled. "We'll have time alone. Time to talk things out."

Dad and Phillip had planned this together! She gathered her thoughts, which had scattered like frightened sparrows. What about work? What could Dad have been thinking? Dad didn't know Phillip— but then, how could he? She'd kept so many secrets.

With effort she focused her attention on the road. They stopped briefly at the causeway tollbooth entrance. As they approached the bridge, she looked down the ribbon of cement stretching across the lake for twenty-three miles. She felt his eyes on her and leaned back in the seat.

His voice turned grave. It seemed to come from far away. "You've misunderstood everything, Ama. Sophie means nothing to me."

Sucking on her lower lip, she looked out over the water. To the right sailboats clustered near the Southern Yacht Club at West End. Fishing boats were anchored farther out. She gazed at them with longing, yearning to be anywhere but here, sitting next to Phillip in this car. Could she jump from the car when they slowed at the end of the causeway? No. The Mustang's locks still held her captive.

"You're exhausted from that job of yours." A sigh. "The demanding hours. The competition. The stress."

She closed her eyes. The rhythmic rocking of the car tires over the joints of the causeway helped calm her. Steady her. "I can't leave work on a whim."

"That's taken care of."

Her eyes flew open and she looked at him. "What does that mean?"

"It means just what I said." She frowned and his expression turned sullen. "Don't worry about your friends downtown. They'll survive without you for a few days." He jutted out his chin, looking at the road. "I told your secretary that we'll be back early next week, on Tuesday. I told her to take care of things."

She slid her hands under her thighs to hide the trembling as she imagined Doug Bastion's face when he learned from Ashley Elizabeth that his junior associate was missing in the middle of a transaction, departed for an unexpected, unsanctioned, incomprehensible vacation. A crossover between the two spans of the causeway came into sight. "Turn around." She pointed. "There's a place where we can turn around, right up there."

"No." His voice was flat, cold.

Careful, Amalise.

As they drove, on she stared at the straight road ahead, running through the options in her mind. When they reached the cottage, she would call Doug—assure him that she'd return tomorrow, that she'd make up the missing time and pray that he would understand. And she'd call Dad if Phillip refused to drive her back. She would call Ashley Elizabeth and help her locate files the transaction team would need.

Phillip launched into a description of the cottage and the lake and the swamp on the other side. He met her eyes, smiling. Once he'd seen the cottage, he realized that he'd been wrong about country life, he said.

She planned her escape as Phillip went on.

"Standing on that pier over the water, I realized something. I saw the lake shining in the sun, smelled the clean air of the pine forest, and understood what I've been missing. I want to paint out there. I've been wasting my talent on malcontents, painting masks and mannequins like Sophie instead of something powerful, like nature. I understand that now." He glanced at her.

Amalise paused. Cold fear struck as she heard the subtle change in Phillip's tone, saw it too in his manner, as he went on describing the cottage and the lake, using gestures that reminded her of Dad. She sat very still, listening, watching him from the corner of her eye. How did he do that? It was the same voice, the same facial expressions Dad might have used if he were sitting there beside her.

Phillip was mimicking Dad, as if by slipping into Dad's skin he could capture some of the love she felt for her father. Fascinated and frightened, she listened to him and gazed at the water, at the mile markers flying by, at the seagulls and pelicans cruising past. When he stopped talking at last, the tension between them was heavy.

Careful Amalise. Play along. "Is there a boat?"

"There's one of those funny canoes you like." He gave her a sideways look, his smile false.

"A pirogue?"

He nodded.

Exiting the causeway, she sat upright, turned to him, set her expression, and demanded in the calmest tone she could manage that he turn the car around and drive her back to the city. She needed time to make arrangements for a trip like this, she told him in that careful voice. She needed to call people and make arrangements and pack the right clothes, and then they could come back.

But he merely laughed and drove on, heading east through the small town of old Mandeville on a winding two-lane road and then on inland at Lacombe through miles of piney woods.

A million tiny pricks of fear rose on her flesh. She was silent the rest of the way.

Chapter Thirty-Nine

It was eleven o'clock on Friday morning. Amalise should be in the office now, and he'd left two messages already. He'd been reluctant to call again so soon, but he'd felt that nudge again, that sense that something was wrong, that Amalise needed him. There was a slight pause before Ashley Elizabeth answered his question. "She's not come in yet, Mr. Perret."

"Jude."

"Umm . . . thanks, Jude."

"When do you expect her? I've left a couple of messages."

She hesitated. "Ummm, yes. It's hard to say." Her tone grew flustered. "That is, we were expecting her to come in late yesterday afternoon."

Jude frowned at the thin branches of the azalea bushes. June already, and the flowers were gone. Azaleas were nice for a few weeks in spring, but the rest of the time . . .

His attempt to divert himself from a presentiment of bad news didn't work. The strange feeling that something might be wrong kicked in, again. Stronger than before. He didn't want to overreact. "So, she'll be back . . . when?"

Ashley Elizabeth lowered her voice. He could visualize her, leaning forward, cupping her hand over the phone. "Actually, Jude, we don't know."

His heart seemed to stop while he waited for her to go on.

"Actually, everyone's wondering where she is. She was supposed to be on the flight yesterday with the client, and Mr. Bastion was looking for her because he needed some files, but she didn't show up. And she missed a meeting with Mr. Bastion and the group this morning at eight thirty."

"Have you talked to Phillip?"

"Yes. I finally got in touch with him at their house a few minutes ago. He said she'd not come home and he didn't know her schedule." Her tone turned sarcastic. "Said I'd know where she was before he would. I called the hotel in New York, and she checked out yesterday, and now I can't find Phillip again, and the client, Mr. Tillman—he's in meetings—and Mr. Bastion's still looking for her, too."

A burning sensation seared the back of Jude's throat. He swallowed. "Are you saying . . . she's missing?"

There was a long pause. "Well, I don't know if I'd put it like that." He could see her drawing back, sitting upright, realizing what she'd just said. "I mean, she's not really missing or anything. It's just that . . ."

Jude drummed his fingers on the telephone table and frowned. "She'll show up soon, if I know Amalise." He hung up and studied the old black telephone on the table before picking up the receiver again. He really should get a new phone. One of those modern colored ones.

With a heaving sigh, he pulled over a notebook and skimmed the pages until he found Amalise's number. He dialed the number slowly, wanting her to answer so he'd know she was all right, yet not wanting her to answer because when she did he'd have to arrange to meet her someplace alone and decide whether to have that talk.

He let the phone ring eight times. Phillip could be there. He could be sitting right by the phone and not answering. Finally he hung up. Amalise could be there too, but it wasn't like her not to answer. He rose, walked into the kitchen, poured a glass of iced tea, and went back to work on the porch, focusing all of his attention on each nail, each slam of the hammer, the position of each board.

He'd hear from her this afternoon. She would return his call, and she'd have a reasonable explanation, and everything would return to normal.

And this burning anxiety would finally go away.

IT HAD BEEN AN endless day. She stood alone at the end of the cottage pier, hugging herself, and looked out over the small lake. There were eight cypress trees growing out there in the middle, and in the dusk their fluted trunks seemed to lengthen, merging with their reflections in the water. The glazed water, the trees, the Spanish moss, all turned pewter in the waning light. On the far shore evening fog was rising, and a cluster of gum and tupelo and more cypress marked the beginning of a swampy forest.

They'd arrived at the cottage late last night, too late to call anyone, and she'd fallen asleep, exhausted. She'd woken early, thinking of the list of phone calls to be made, but Phillip had woken too. She'd struggled to hide her relief when he said he needed to drive into the city for the day.

"Great. I'll go with you. I can pick up some things at the house. Stop by the office for a few minutes."

He stuck his right hand in his pocket and jangled the car keys as he walked through the living room, with her trailing behind. "I've got a new show scheduled, Ama! The gallery owner wants to see all my work. She's going to hang twelve pieces so I've got to get them to her this morning and steer her in the right direction. It's a real nuisance, an inconvenience, and I told her that." His left hand clenched into a fist, opening and closing while he stalked through the kitchen toward the back door. "I told her about our plans, told her that . . ."

She was right behind him. "Phillip. It's all right. I want to go into town with you."

Rolling his shoulders, hiking them around his neck, he seemed not to hear. She reached out. She had to stop him.

At the back door he shook her off, grabbed the doorknob, and opened the door. "The whole point of this surprise was to spend time together. Just the two of us."

"Wait!"

He stopped and turned. His eyebrows drew together, his mouth curled down at the corners. "Ama, I just want peace and quiet. I want to sit out on the pier and paint."

"Phillip." Her voice quavered and instinct told her to control it—even animals know not to show their fear.

He studied her in silence.

She clasped her hands behind her back, knotting them. "I . . . I want to go into town with you. You can drop me off at the office while you go to the gallery. I'll wait for you there."

"No." She saw the anger rising—that mottled patch of redness rising in his neck, in his cheeks. "I'll be back this afternoon. We'll talk." He shrugged. "If you still want to leave after that . . ."

She moved close to him, struggling for composure. If she could keep him talking, maybe she could change his mind. "The show. Is this . . . ah . . . Sophie's mother's gallery again?"

"No. It's nothing to do with Sophie." He shook his head and held her eyes. "This is a new gallery. I haven't seen Sophie since you left for New York." Smiling now, he reached out for her and, without thinking, she drew back.

If he wouldn't let her go with him, she would call Dad as soon as Phillip left.

As if he'd read her mind, he dropped his hand. "There's no phone out here, Ama." She'd stared, speechless, as he turned to leave. "It's just us. No phones."

Standing on the pier and thinking of it now, the realization that she was truly isolated sent icy shivers up her spine, despite the evening heat. She looked around. Behind her the cottage, facing the lake, was surrounded on either side by a dense pine forest, solid with undergrowth. Across the lake the meandering cut of gauzy trees melted into the fog.

After leaving the causeway and the town of Mandeville behind yesterday, they'd driven for an hour on deserted roads before reaching the entrance to this place. From the route she knew, they were somewhere near the Honey Island Swamp. It had been dark, difficult to see. Phillip slowed the car to steer around deep ruts in the narrow dirt trail that was the driveway, but still the car had jolted along between the tall trees for several miles before arriving at the cottage. In the headlights she could see the bordering thicket forming a solid barrier on either side of the road. She'd had to hold onto the dashboard as they bumped along.

And now, standing on the cottage pier and waiting for Phillip, she looked out over the little lake and told herself that she'd talk to him when he returned and then they'd leave. A flash of white startled her as a large snowy egret she'd seen earlier burst from a thicket of green rushes at the far shore. It was fishing when she'd come out in the morning.

The bird caught a drift and soared up, circling the cypress and the lake before it disappeared over the rushes into the mist. Something moved just beneath the surface of the water near the copse of cypress. A shadow, not a ripple. Long and dark. An alligator perhaps. She watched the shadow glide until it too disappeared, sinking deeper under the reflection of the surface. An ominous melancholy seized her. What was Rebecca doing this moment? Or Preston, or Raymond. *She* should be downtown in her office, working.

Still hugging herself, she turned back toward the cottage. Where was Phillip? Thank heaven Dad knew where she was at least.

Abba. Are You here with me? She felt His presence. At least she thought she did.

JUDE STOOPED, SITTING ON his heels, and nailed the last board into place, swiping the perspiration from his forehead with the back of his hand. When he'd finished, he stood back, admiring his work. Brushing his hands together to rid them of dirt, he started up the stairs. It was time for a break.

The phone rang as he opened the back door and walked into the kitchen. Glancing at his watch—it was six o'clock in the evening—he hurried through the house to the living room. Amalise perhaps? It was about time. He picked up the phone on the fourth ring.

"Jude." He recognized the judge's voice at once.

"Yes, sir?" A flash of disappointment. A flutter of worry.

"Son, I've been trying to get hold of Amalise. Have you talked to her today?"

"No." There was a hairline crack in the wall in front of him, right at eye level. A small defect, but he'd have someone out to check the foundation. He examined the crack, focusing his thoughts on the infinite variations of problems that it could represent, problems that he could solve.

"I called the office and that secretary of hers . . ."

"Ashley Elizabeth."

"Yes. Ashley. She said Amalise hasn't called or come in to the office at all. No one knows where she is. It's clear she was on the plane yesterday. And she got off in New Orleans with someone—a client, I think. But they split up, and she didn't come in to work, and Ashley says Phillip's been no help." There was a pause. "That's not like her, Jude."

His hand tightened on the phone. "I know."

"I called the house, too. Several times. No answer. Phillip's not home now either, I guess." The judge's voice faltered. "Amalise said she'd call when she got in. She knows Mama worries."

"I wouldn't get too concerned, Judge." Jude forced a smile into his voice. "There's been some misunderstanding. I'll call again. Maybe she's taking a little time off."

The judge heaved a sigh. "Likely you're right, son." A cough, muffled quickly. His voice turned hearty, bright, and brittle. "Well, how's P-town treating you, Jude? Caught any good fish lately? I haven't, eh, been out in the boat yet this summer myself. Too hot."

"Yes, it's hot all right. I've got the flatboard down there. Fish in the marsh over by Empire once in a while. Caught a few specs and reds."

"Sounds fine." The judge paused. "Let me know if you hear from our girl, will you? And you come around sometime soon, Jude."

"I'll do that. And please call me, too, if you hear from her."

Jude's stomach tightened as he hung up the phone. He couldn't think of one reason Amalise hadn't called the judge or Maraine when she'd said she would. He swallowed hard, then dialed her number at home again, letting the phone ring for a long time. He dialed Rebecca's number—perhaps she'd know something. But there was no answer at Rebecca's home or at her office.

At last he flipped on the television and sank onto the couch in front of it, unseeing. It would be a long night, but what else could he do? He'd call again in the morning. And she'd be there. And he . . .

He'd feel the perfect fool for having worried.

Chapter Forty

Climbing down from the pier, Amalise started up the pathway to the cottage through a clearing. On each side of the clearing, the forest and thicket extended to the lake. An owl hooted somewhere in the distance, a hollow, haunting sound that echoed through the trees. She shivered and listened with half a mind for the sound of Phillip's rented Mustang, while telling herself to concentrate on something else. So she counted the trees in the shadows of the clearing as she passed them.

There were live oak, water oak, pin oak, pine, red maple, and a clump of chinaberry trees near the long porch that stretched across the back of the house. There were drake elm and crepe myrtles—she went on counting trees instead of minutes. There were magnolias with their waxy dark green leaves, hanging onto the lemon-scented blooms. There were seventeen trees in the clearing, and in the bramble at the edge of the forest were blackberry bushes.

Reaching the cottage, she braced one hand on a railing and pulled herself up the wooden steps to the porch, still listening for the car. A glance through the screened door halted her. The cottage with its small dark rooms and dank smell gave her a caged feeling. Backing up, she spotted a sagging wicker chair on the porch and dragged it over to the railing by the steps, as far as she could get from the cottage door.

There she sat with her feet propped up on the railing, tense, straining to hear the sounds of Phillip's car coming up the drive. What mood would he be in when he returned? She shuddered and looked around.

Cicadas began their summer song. Gradually darkness cloaked the clearing and the lake and the swamp forest on the other side. Still she sat outside, not wanting to be trapped in the little house when Phillip arrived . . . just in case. Slowly the moon rose, high and full, glazing the lake and trees in the dim glow.

Abba, are You here with me?

She looked up, thinking how delicate the ancient moon looked hanging in the sky, and she traced the patterns of the stars and planets and probed with her mind the dark spaces in between, and thought how perfectly the universe balanced even in continual motion. The psalmist's words: *The heavens declare the glory of God and the sky proclaims the work of his hands. . . . There is no speech; there are no words.*

No words were necessary. Her life might be chaos right now, but the order of the universe and God's love were constant.

She sat on the porch for a long time. When at last the unrelenting mosquitoes arrived, Amalise went inside, turning on every light as she walked through the rooms, lamps as well as ceiling lights, listening for the tires grinding up the driveway from the road.

The cottage inside was spare, almost stark. The floors were rough wooden planks, uncovered except for a dull rag rug in the center of the living room. The ceilings were low, and the windows were square and uncovered, but at least they were screened from the insects.

There were two overstuffed chairs in the living room, each with a table and a lamp beside it for reading, and two bookcases, one on each side of a fireplace. Several framed prints were on the walls—faded landscapes, a variety of birds, a hunting scene. There was the table where they'd had breakfast, a small round table with four wooden chairs in the corner near a window overlooking the porch. In the bedroom, there was an iron-framed double bed covered with a beige spread crocheted from stiff, knotted material, and a wooden chest of drawers, and one chair.

Calmed by a strange sense of peace, she dropped into one of the living room chairs, sank back against the cushions, and drew her feet up under her. It was late, long past time for dinner. Phillip had brought some things with him yesterday—some ham and bread and cheese for sandwiches, and some other things he'd stuck in the refrigerator, but the idea of eating right now made her stomach churn. He'd brought along a pair of shorts, a T-shirt, and some sandals for her as well. She was wearing those.

Her limbs were heavy, and despite the open windows and a slight breeze, the room was still warm from the heat of day. Gazing at the empty fireplace nearby, she noticed the gray ashes and remnants of wood left there from last winter. Her lids drooped as, from across the room, she examined paperback books stuffed in a haphazard way on the shelves of the bookcases. Still listening with a part of her mind for Phillip, she thought that maybe she would pull herself up out of the chair and find a book to read, but instead her muscles went slack and refused to budge. After a while her eyes closed, and soon she was asleep.

A CAR DOOR SLAMMED outside, waking her. She glanced up and looked about. Moments later the kitchen door opened, slammed shut, and Phillip rushed into the living room where she sat. He stopped behind her. "I'm sorry about this, Ama."

She tilted her head back to look at him, and he walked around so that he stood next to her, raking his fingers through his hair with a sheepish grin. "It's a longer drive than I realized."

She rubbed her eyes. "What time is it?"

When she looked up, he was gone, but she heard his footsteps in the kitchen, heard the back door slam, the car door slam. When he returned, his arms were full of paints, brushes, canvases, sketchbooks, and the brown leather bag for his carving tools. "What time is it?" she asked again, stifling a yawn.

"Ten." He dropped his armload on the table in the corner. He stacked the canvases together in the middle of the table and set the paints, brushes, and sketchbooks beside them. Opening the bag, he took out his tools—two carving knives, the whetstone and tin of honing oil, a half figure carved from unfinished wood, and an instrument that he'd once explained was a gouge, but resembled a small screwdriver.

She watched him arrange these things. "I want to leave tomorrow morning." For a second he stood motionless, suspended over the table, arms stretched across to the leather bag. He seemed to catch himself then—straightened, folded the bag, placed it on the table, and turned to her. His brows were flat, his mouth drawn down at the corners.

"We just got here. I'm sorry about today."

Careful, Amalise. "It's not just that." She gained courage from the fact that he looked hurt rather than angry. "I have to get back to work."

He walked over to the chair across from hers, sat down, bent his head and rubbed his forehead with his thumbs. "Is it Sophie, again? You're jealous, aren't you? Is that why you want to leave?" His tone held a note of warning.

"No."

He looked up and clasped his hands between splayed knees. "Because an artist has to have someone to paint, Ama. You understand that . . . right?" He scrutinized her, nodded, and she nodded, too. "Right. Models come with the territory when you're married to an artist." He leaned forward. His voice deepened into a guttural tone she'd not heard before. "Artists need that personal connection, like actors. Like musicians need applause."

She nodded, but his eyes glinted back at her. *He knows I'm leaving him . . .*

"I can't lose you, Amalise." He watched her. "I won't ever lose you. If we go home before we straighten things out, you'll leave."

Instinct kept her quiet. Somehow she'd convince him to leave in the morning, even if she had to lie, even if she had to say she loved him, that she was his.

He looked down, twisted his hands palm up and studied them. Outside the cicada chorus seemed to rise in a wave of sound directly proportionate to the silence in the room. His mouth trembled, and at last he heaved a sigh, wiping the corner of his eye as he straightened, giving her a piteous look, a plea for compassion. "Will you stay a day or two—give it a chance?"

The observer nudged, and she nodded. "Of course." Until tomorrow morning.

Instantly he was on his feet, smiling. "I've brought fried chicken. I'm not hungry, but I thought that you might be."

"Thanks." She stood and he reached for her, pulling her to him. She stiffened, then forced herself to slide her arms around his waist as he kissed the hollow between her shoulder and neck, nuzzling. When he released her, she bit her lip, following him into the kitchen. A brown bag, shiny and slick with greasy spots, was on the counter. Avoiding his eyes, she took a plate from the cabinet overhead and opened the bag to pull out a piece of the chicken.

"It's spicy." He gave a forced chuckle, opened the refrigerator, leaned in, and pulled out a bottle of beer. "Come on outside with me, babe." He opened the beer and wandered toward the living room. "We'll watch the moon on the lake."

"I'll be right there." She found a Tab in the refrigerator and carried it and the plate with chicken out to the porch. He was lounging in the wicker chair where she'd sat earlier, feet up on the railing. The moon was still bright.

"This is the life." He gestured toward the lake. "Look at that trail of light on the water. It looks like the man in the moon threw down a bucket of yellow paint. I should paint that."

She looked at it and back at him. "That's very poetic." She took a seat in the other chair.

"Well, I do like poetry sometimes. Sophie read some when I was painting her portrait." He shrugged the thought away. "The only poem I know is the one about the cow jumped over the moon, and the little dog laughed. I guess I learned it when I was four or five. One of those nannies taught that to me, I remember."

Amalise picked up the chicken and said nothing.

"Sophie thinks that's funny." He glanced at Amalise. "Now don't get all worked up again."

She'd wasn't hungry, but she ate the chicken so he wouldn't sense that her nerves were raw. She licked the ends of her fingers as if it were delicious and looked up at the milky way streaked across the sky.

Don't think right now, Amalise.

So she concentrated on the stars, seeking that earlier comfort. There was the Little Dipper and the big one, there was the bear, and Venus, the evening star. She shifted her gaze to the clearing, the pier, the lake. In the lake the cypress trees were shadows now. In the moon and starlight the live oak trees in the clearing gleamed like white bones.

Phillip broke the silence with a sharp little laugh. He bent forward and planted his hand on her knee. "Listen, babe. I didn't mean to mention Sophie again. We're getting older. Don't get upset over a young thing like Sophie. You and me, we're both past our warranties."

What . . . ? She glanced up and caught him scanning her, head to foot.

"Age is a leech." He sat back, looking away, gulping the beer. "It sucks out all the color."

She raised her hand to her cheek, testing her skin. She wasn't old! Dropping her hands, she held onto the plate and started to rise.

"Sit back down."

She obeyed, balancing the plate carefully in the middle of her lap.

He nudged her with his elbow and pointed the neck of the bottle in the direction of the lake. "I love that moon." His voice told her not to move right now—to sit very still.

A breeze rustled through the chinaberry trees at the corner of the porch. Despite the warmth of the night, that trembling gripped her again. She tucked her hands up under her legs, alert, looking out over the clearing. She wished Jude knew she was here. The sharp scent of pine drifted on a breeze. Cicadas buzzed, frogs sang—soprano from the tree frogs, bass from the bulls.

Suddenly she was exhausted. Phillip met her at the airport the day before yesterday, but it seemed like years ago. She longed for nothing more right now than sleep.

She would sleep and talk to Phillip in the morning.

And they would leave.

Chapter Forty-One

He'd tricked her. Her feet dangled from the end of the pier the next morning as she watched the white egret fishing for breakfast. The bird stood poised in the shallows near the far bank, elongated, its slender body stretched, neck arched out over a ripple in the water.

She'd slept badly last night, and when she woke, Phillip was gone. He'd left a note: *Just a few hours this time. Back this afternoon.*

Her head ached this morning and her stomach churned. She'd been manipulated. She sat on the end of the pier in her nightgown. A sudden urge to escape the confines of the dark little house had driven her outside, almost running, without breakfast or even a cup of coffee.

Was anyone even looking for her now?

A thought gradually took hold: she must get out of here on her own, without depending on Phillip. She flipped her toe into the water. Sunlight sprayed through the droplets.

In the reeds across the lake the egret tensed, white neck stretched long. A swift dart into the water brought up a fish clamped in the strong beak. The smaller fish put up a fight as the egret threw back its head and gulped. She could see the victim struggling slowly down the elastic throat. Satisfied, the victor stood inspecting the water and strutted farther out into the hunting ground, neck once again lifted and curved, searching. The graceful bird with the sensuous neck must be female, she mused, and she would call it Iris.

The breakfast battle reminded Amalise of coffee and food. Her stomach growled. She stood, shaking a few leaves from the folds of her nightgown, and walked back to the cottage. In the kitchen she made coffee and scrambled an egg, toasted a slice of wheat bread and buttered it, poured out a cold glass of orange juice, and carried all of this to the table in the corner of the living room by the windows.

Moving aside Phillip's two carving knives and the chisel, she set down the plate. The pocket carver was open. She picked it up, turned it, slid her thumb along the smooth curved rosewood handle and then over the steel blade, a fraction of an inch from the sharp beveled edge. Setting the knife down at the exact angle she'd found it, she gazed out over the yard and pier and lake with a growing sense of alarm over Phillip's strange behavior.

She looked off, trying to recall the last sign of civilization she'd seen on the drive to the cottage day before yesterday, after they'd left the town of Lacombe.

There was a rundown wooden shack just a few miles out of town, she recalled, and after that, only forest. She remembered seeing broken furniture on the front porch of that house—trashed-out old armoires, chairs piled up one on top of the other, and a table or two, she thought, and there were tires and rusted wheel rims piled up in a ditch beside the road. But that was thirty or forty miles from where she now sat, judging by the time it had taken them to reach the driveway to the cottage.

Her eyes touched on the pirogue in the water. Chewing the toast and keeping an eye out for Iris, she scanned the lake—inspecting the rushes at the edge of the swamp, following the bank around to the right, back to the pier. Maybe she could find a water outlet from the lake, a bayou or stream that cut through the swamp. There were bound to be some fishing camps in the area. She set down her fork, then brought the dishes and glass back into the kitchen and hurried into the bedroom to dress.

At the pier Amalise untied the pirogue and dragged it toward the shallows near the grassy bank of the clearing. She took off her sandals and held them as she waded into the water where the pirogue rocked and then dropped the shoes into the boat. She would need them if she found a way out. Bracing her hands on each side of the narrow hull to steady the boat, she stepped in and lowered herself onto the middle of a low wooden seat, distributing her weight for balance.

The paddle rested on the bottom of the hull, and she picked it up, hoisting it with both hands as she jabbed it into the silt and pushed, propelling into deeper water. Once the boat steadied and began to glide, she slipped into the rhythm of the old routine, dipping the paddle into the water on alternate sides with a smooth rolling motion until she found the rhythm of the stroke Jude taught.

It felt good to be doing something. As she reached the middle of the lake, she spotted Iris, roosting high atop a cypress tree. Sunshine illuminated the egret's feathers, and she lifted the paddle from the water for an instant, struck by the stark contrast between the shining white bird and the tall green sentinel rising from the water. She paddled close and stopped, letting the pirogue drift while she looked up. The egret flicked her wings as she drew near. Amalise waited, motionless, and after a moment the bird settled, sinking into herself on the branch, tucking under her wings. *Is she watching me as well?*

But when Amalise dipped the paddle into the water again, the movement startled the egret. She lifted from the branch, white wings spread wide and flat as she dropped with a swoop, gliding once around the lake before disappearing into the trees at the edge of the swamp. *That's where she lives.* Following, Amalise paddled with the slow current. Perhaps there was deeper water there—a way out.

Near the rushes at the edge of the swamp, Amalise's heart jumped when she spotted a narrow culvert cutting through the weeds and silky cattails just ahead. As she paddled closer, she could see that on either side of the culvert was a rise of solid ground. A small, natural levee banking the lake, separating it from the encroaching swamp.

Pushing the pirogue closer into the thick clump of rushes, she peered through the culvert opening. Heat shimmered there, even in the shadows. A familiar odor rose, the smell of wet leaves and warm mud, of moss and algae, of submerged logs and water-soaked cypress and tupelo, of beech and oak smothered by tangles of kudzu, seducing as the glossy vine stole the light. Here at the edge of the watery forest, pale filtered sunlight veiled this world in a dim glow. But her heart sank when she saw that the still water on the other side of the levee was too shallow for a boat, even for the little pirogue.

Amalise sat listless in the sweltering heat remembering old tales of egrets guiding wanderers through the swamp. Old Tom at the bait shop in Marianus swore to this. She shook herself from the lethargy. Maybe so. She'd trust Iris over Phillip right now. Jamming the paddle into the muddy bottom of the lake, she struggled to push the boat farther into the rushes for a better look, but it refused to budge.

The sun burned the bare skin on the back of her neck as she bent, straining to see into the swamp, looking for deep water. She spotted a flock of blue heron hunkered down on the branches of a hackberry tree about forty yards away. There had to be twenty birds on that one tree. She lowered her eyes to scan the twisted delicate underbrush growing in murky pools, some bearing tiny flowers—yellow, white, orange. Small colorful birds moved like shadows through the green haze, darting between the trees. Something rustled in a tangle of vine and brush near the culvert, and Amalise watched without moving as a dead branch became a water moccasin and slithered into the water, gliding away into the dank forest.

A harsh sound—*craggh, craggh*—from the interior of the swampy area caught her attention. Looking up, she saw Iris flash through the trees. The great egret landed on a low cypress branch close by, not far from the culvert. From the pirogue Amalise spotted a natural opening below Iris in the swirling trunk of the tree, big enough for a nesting bird, a cave-like crevice near water level where the trunk had hollowed and split years ago. She sat holding her breath, watching as Iris, sensing her presence, balanced on the branch, torso stretched, poised to flee. A shaft of sunlight caught her feathers through the trees. A minute passed and Amalise did not move. At last Iris hunched her wings and tucked into a brilliant ball of white.

If only she could know such peace.

JUDE STRETCHED AND YAWNED, kicking the sheet aside as he rolled from the bed. For a second he stood still, orienting himself by the sight of the long porch windows and the tree beyond. It was Saturday morning. Right. He was in New Orleans this morning, not Pilottown. Right. He needed coffee. Toast. Newspaper.

Ahhh. Amalise. It came back all at once. Downstairs he put the coffeepot on, filled it with water, and went to the telephone. The book was still open to her number. He dialed, glancing at his watch. Already 9:30. He'd meant to get up early—catch her before she left for the office. Saturday was a working day for Amalise, like any other day. Still he'd call her home first.

Again there was no answer, but someone at the office picked up on the first ring. An unfamiliar voice, someone other than Ashley Elizabeth. Ashley Elizabeth played tennis on Saturday, he recalled. The woman said that last week Mrs. Sharp had booked her for this weekend and she was waiting. No, sir. Mrs. Sharp had not phoned.

Jude sank into a chair beside the telephone table with a sigh of exasperation. "Do you know how I can get in touch with Phillip, her husband?"

There was a pause. "I'm sorry, sir. But you'd have to talk to Mrs. Sharp about that. I'll ask her to call when she gets in if you'd like."

"Yes. Do that." Jude gave her his name and phone number, working to conceal his irritation. The unfamiliar voice turned smooth, soothing, before they hung up. Amalise was probably running late, sleeping in on a Saturday morning.

But that was not like Amalise.

He wandered into the kitchen, fixed a bowl of cereal, polished it off, drank the coffee, and went back upstairs to dress. He pulled on the jeans he'd worn last night and a fresh shirt. Patting the jean pockets for his keys, he slipped his bare feet into loafers and went out to the car.

Nearing her house, he could see that the driveway was empty. He pulled up, yanked out the car keys, and walked to the door. Peering into the windows, he saw no signs of life. No lights. No noise. He rang the doorbell twice. Banged on the door for a while, then left.

The phone was ringing as he reached home. Racing through the living room, he picked up the receiver. "Amalise?"

"Jude?" It was the judge.

Jude braced himself at the sound of the strained voice. *Something's happened to Amalise.* His heart raced as he gripped the phone, waiting for the next words.

"Son, I hate to bother you, but we haven't heard from her yet. From Amalise. We can't find Phillip either. There's no answer at the apartment." Jude exhaled. Heard whispering in the background—Maraine's voice. All right, all right, the judge said aside to his wife. "Jude, you there?"

"Yes, sir." He might as well tell him. "I've been calling, too. Drove over there a while ago. Just got back. No one's home."

"Something's wrong." Jude heard Maraine's voice rising to a hiss. Hold it, Mama. Let me talk. "This isn't like Amalise." The judge's clipped tone said more than the words.

"No, sir." Jude swallowed into the dead air on the wire.

"Was the car in their driveway?"

"No. No car. No lights in the house. No answer when I knocked."

"That office of hers is no help either. Now here's what we do." The judge's voice was tight, strained, but firm. "I'll keep on calling the house."

"Yes, sir."

"So here's what you do. Can you go on out to the airport and look for her car?"

Jude nodded, picturing the immense parking garage and the off-site parking lots. "Sure. Do you have the license number?" No. He did not. But Jude listened as the judge gave him a detailed description of the car.

"Maybe she didn't even take it to the airport. Phillip uses the car too. Maybe she took a taxi. But I don't know what else to do right now." The judge's voice cracked, and he held the phone away, coughing. "Sorry. Just an old man worrying. But we have to do something."

"I'm leaving right now, Judge. If the car's there, I'll find it."

"All right."

"Try not to worry. I'll swing by the house again first, just in case. I'll find Phillip, too. He'll know where she is."

"Good."

"Give Maraine a hug. I'll call you."

"Right. You call me, Jude. Soon as you can."

Hanging up the phone, he grabbed the car keys, stuffed his wallet into his pocket, and headed for the door. Closing it behind him, he locked it and had started down the stairs when Mrs. Landry's door opened wide. "Jude? Is that you?"

Jude halted, looked at the sky, sighed, and turned. "I'm in a hurry today, Mrs. Landry."

She stood at the door, peering out at him. "Did that young lady find you the other night?"

Jude's heart shuddered to a halt and he sucked in his breath. "Who's that?"

Mrs. Landry gave him a vacant look, touched the tip of her ear, and pursed her lips. "She was a small one. Short hair. Dark hair, I think."

Watching her carefully, Jude walked to the partition between the two porches. "When did you see her, Mrs. Landry?" His voice was gentle, coaxing.

She frowned, looked off, then back at him. "It was five or six days ago, I'd say. It was late. I was on my way to bed. Came to turn on the porch light. Heard a noise . . . saw her sitting there." She pointed to the steps. "Right there, waiting."

She braced her hand on the door and shook her head. "You should warn her. It's not safe sitting out here alone at night. I told her that, you know. Turned on the porch light."

Amalise—here late at night? "Did you see a car?"

Mrs. Landry frowned and stared at the curbside as if she saw a vision. Jude shifted his feet, waiting. Something must have happened before Amalise left for New York.

"Did she come here in a car?"

Seconds passed. At last she nodded her head. "Yes, she did." She gave Jude a helpless look. "All I can remember is that it was white. A big, white car. Parked right there." She pointed to Jude's car.

"Thanks." Leaving Mrs. Landry standing in the doorway, he leapt from the porch to the ground, racing for his own car. Something was wrong, he felt it in his bones.

Amalise was missing, and everyone seemed to be concerned but Phillip, if his dismissive response to Ashley Elizabeth's inquiry yesterday morning was any measure. And no one had seen or heard from him since. *Lord. Please let her be safe. Please let her be safe.*

WHILE THE SUN ROSE to its zenith, Amalise picked up the paddle and turned the pirogue, moving along the western shoreline of the lake. The earlier headache and nausea were gone. She liked the feel of the pirogue slipping through the water with barely a ripple as she looked for openings in the underbrush and trees. It felt good to be moving, searching for a solution to a problem, working. The pirogue rolled once and she steadied it.

She completed the half circuit of the lake this way, shading her eyes and squinting through the water's glare as she glided along the shore and back to the clearing and the pier without luck. The forest formed a solid wall on that side of the lake. Underbrush caused the problem, the tangle of thorny bushes entwined and matted among the trees. When she reached the pier, she lifted the paddle and drifted, inspecting the cottage for signs of Phillip's return. Relief flooded her—no signs of life. She still had time to search the other side.

As the pirogue glided around the eastern shoreline of the lake toward the culvert where she'd begun, she spotted a narrow strip of sand running along the edge of the water. It began not far from the cottage clearing. Rushes had hidden it before. Adrenaline shot through her.

Following the strip of sand, she saw that it widened near the culvert where a small beach extended back behind the weeds to the rise of ground containing the swamp. She hadn't noticed that before. Twisting, she looked back at the pier but couldn't see the cottage from this vantage. Her eyes returned to the little beach. If she could get to the beach, she could get a good view of the swamp interior.

Pushing on, she cut through the rushes guarding the small beach and pulled the pirogue up onto the sand. As a precaution, she put on the sandals. A sheen of perspiration rose, and she pushed wet strands of hair from her face. The damp shirt stuck to her skin. The sun was high and hot and the glare from sand and water burned her eyes.

She turned and took stock of the beach area. It was lovely, with a shade tree nestled near the back. There the ground rose to the levee that guarded the swamp. Just beyond the rise she could almost see the white bird's cave. But something hovered in her memory as she looked at the pretty place, causing her to shiver despite the sun. She shook off the sense of foreboding. At any other time she'd bring a picnic blanket and a book out here. She started toward the levee, praying there was navigable water on the other side of the culvert.

Eyes on the levee, Amalise took one step forward and froze as the ground sank beneath her right foot. With a stab of fear, she held herself very still and turned her eyes down, studying the deceptive mixture of sand and mud beneath her. Slowly releasing her breath, she eased her foot from the sandal, leaving the shoe in the grip of the quicksand as she stepped back.

Don't fight . . . Jude's warning from all those days ago. *Stay calm. Move slow, and you'll get out. Never fight quicksand, Amalise. The struggle creates a vacuum underneath, a suction that makes things worse.*

She watched in horror as the mud sucked and swirled and the sandal disappeared. Memories hit with force . . . that day with Jude and the wild hog . . . those almost human screams.

She squatted on her heels, fascinated, as the mud settled again, as if the shoe had never existed. Lifting her eyes and scanning the beach, she could see where the quicksand ended near the tree and the perimeter of solid ground beyond. Standing, she took off the useless remaining sandal, and flung it into the shallow water and rushes behind her. She edged around the quicksand to solid ground on the other side and up onto the rise behind the tree, stepping lightly, shoeless and on guard for thorns, snakes, and any sign of alligators.

At last, standing on the rise, she looked out over the watery forest—and hope faded. The pirogue wouldn't help. Still shallow water pooled in mud as far as she could see. Disappointment, frustration, and fear mingled, spreading through her like that algae feeding on the damp at the realization that this way was a dead end. She'd have to find another way out.

Turning, she glimpsed Iris still hunched in the shadows on her perch. She stared at the elegant bird for a moment before turning away. Bending down, she scooped up a small dead branch and flung it into the quicksand, watching it sink. Disappear.

As completely as any hope of escape this way. Minutes passed as she stood without moving, looking out over the lake surrounded by swampland.

No way out . . . except to walk.

Chapter Forty-Two

⚜

J ude slowed as he drove past Amalise's house. Nothing had changed—no car, no lights, no activity. He stepped on the gas and drove on. As he approached the airport, he turned left into an off site parking lot. Heat rose from the vast expanse of cement, penetrating the automobile even with the air conditioner on. Thirty minutes of winding through the maze of parked cars convinced him to check the cooler interior garage at the airport before he tackled the other outdoor lots.

He entered short-term parking, took a card from the machine, and proceeded into the interior of the garage. A space was available not far from the elevators. He pulled into the parking space, turned the key, and opened the door. Reaching for the black coat hanger he'd brought along, he got out, locked the door and stood looking around, running his hand back and forth over the wire in an absent manner.

As he recalled, long-term parking was on the higher levels. He headed for the elevator, holding the hanger down against the side of his leg. There was a woman in the elevator when the door opened, and he pressed the hanger behind his leg, hoping she wouldn't notice. He couldn't think of any legitimate reason for carrying the thing around the parking garage.

The woman got off on two, and Jude proceeded to three. A man and woman with a small boy were headed his way when he stepped out of the elevator. The man carried a large square brown suitcase, and the woman following at his heels held onto a small, neat travel case. The child hopped along behind them, bouncing up and down. The man nodded to Jude as their paths crossed.

Jude headed down the first row of parked cars looking for the white Dodge Charger the judge had described. Almost new, he'd said, a 1974 model with those fake wire wheel rims. Jude scrutinized the lines of cars to his right and left as he walked. Strange that he had never seen the car. He supposed Phillip usually had it. That would be like him. Leave Amalise to streetcars and taxis.

At the end of the first row, Jude turned and headed back in the direction of the elevators, looking for the tailfins of the Charger. It was a nice-looking automobile in general. Good speed. He'd almost bought one himself. As he completed the circuit and wheeled to the next line of cars he began to think this might take a long time. There were two more floors to check. And odds were, she'd taken a taxi to the airport.

He continued down the line, slapping the hanger against his thigh. *She's always counted on you, Jude.* A ripple of fear ran through him, and he prayed that he wouldn't find the car here at the airport. As much as he hated Phillip, he closed his eyes for an instant with a fervent prayer.

Take care of her, Lord. Let her be safe, let her be somewhere with Phillip having fun, laughing—maybe on a vacation, just the two of them, to patch things up?

Even that was preferable to the thoughts creeping into his mind right now.

AS AMALISE PADDLED THE pirogue back toward the cottage, the sun, now partially hidden behind a cloud, was on the downward march. By the time she reached the pier, she realized that she had to hurry to get to the main road before Phillip arrived. Otherwise she'd be vulnerable on the long driveway, where there was no place to hide.

Crossing the clearing, a thistle pricked her bare foot. She stopped, yanked it out, and straightened, suddenly conscious that she could not walk thirty or forty miles in high-heeled shoes or bare feet, and the sandals were gone. What had she been thinking? She grimaced at the thought of attempting any distance in those tight pumps in her suitcase.

Trudging up the cottage stairs, Amalise faced the cold fact that she was stuck here until Phillip returned. She'd have to make the best of the situation. Her heart skipped a beat, and she told herself to stay calm, that she was overreacting. She would have to play along with Phillip when he returned and see what opportunities developed. Instinct told her to look her best when he arrived. She would shower and change clothes, wash her hair, add a touch of lipstick.

Thunder rolled in the distance. Reaching the door, she turned to see iron-gray clouds sliding in over the swamp. The wind picked up. When it came again, the thunder was louder, closer. A flash of lightening bolted to the earth. She went inside, letting the screen door slam behind her.

In the bedroom the window was open. The air was cool now, heavy with the scent of pine and earth and coming rain. She walked into the bathroom and stood before the mirror brushing her teeth, keeping an eye on the reflected space in the bedroom behind her. Would she hear the car in here?

Remembering Phillip's words last night, she set down the toothbrush, rinsed out her mouth, moved close to the mirror, and touched her limp straight hair, trying to retrieve a memory. Some painting of Phillip's nagged at the back of her mind, something that reminded her of this moment.

She leaned closer, examining fine lines at the outer edges of her eyes, ridges near the corners of her mouth. Those were new. She smoothed them with the tips of her fingers, and it came to her. *The Blue Hour,* the bleak painting of Joanna.

She moved back from her reflection, recalling the bitter woman who'd confronted her at the café. She turned away.

She must find a way to leave this desolate place.

HE FOUND THE CAR on the fourth level of the garage. It matched the judge's description exactly. Without giving himself time to think, Jude began unwinding the curved part of the hanger, twisting and untwisting until it was one long straight wire with a flat hook on the end. He bent the wire at an angle about six inches from the hook. He'd done this many times when he'd lost his keys. Or when Amalise had lost her keys. A tense smile crossed his face at this last thought. That was a common occurrence for her in high school.

No one was around. Jude worked the angled edge of the wire between the rubber rim above the driver's side window and the glass. When the hooked wire slipped through, he twisted it, pressing it against the interior of the door and lowering it slowly until he could see the hook had reached the level of the lock. Angling the wire, he caught the lock with the hook, encircled it, and yanked. The lock snapped up.

Jude opened the car door, retrieved the wire, and bent, sweeping the interior with a glance. There was nothing in plain view that marked this as Amalise's car. Leaning in, he released the lock for the passenger door, and backed out of the car.

On the passenger side he slid into the seat and looked at the closed glove compartment with a feeling of dread. He did not want this to be her car, not without an explanation for her absence. At last he pulled the compartment open and reached in.

Fumbling, he found the packet of papers that many good citizens store in the glove box: insurance, registration, assorted receipts, a manual. He sorted through them all, disbelieving as he saw the name. Phillip Sharp again and again. Even at this moment he registered the fact that the title was held solely in Phillip's name. A weight dropped through his stomach as he was faced with the truth.

Amalise really was missing.

Jude fell back, staring through the windshield unseeing and brushed a hand over his eyes. Phillip's face rose before him—brow bone jutting, shadowing his eyes. Would he hurt Amalise? Romar's words haunted him—

Yes, Phillip would hurt her, if he wanted something and she was in his way.

Shoving the papers back into the glove compartment, Jude slid from the car, slammed the door shut, and folded the wire coat hanger in two. Slapping it against the palm of his hand hard enough to sting, he hurried to the elevator. On the first level he located his own car, got in, and turned the key. The engine started and he backed out. The judge was right.

Amalise had disappeared.

Not Amalise. Not Amalise! Set an angel with her. Keep angels near her.

He forced himself to exit the parking garage at a normal speed. Handing the ticket and a dollar to the toll taker at the booth, he sped off without waiting for change. Should he call the judge first, or should he look for Phillip? He argued the point until he turned from Carrolton onto St. Charles Avenue, left on Palmer, and skidded to a stop in front of Amalise's house. His chest was tight as he exploded from the car, raced up the steps, and pounded his fists on the front door.

AMALISE DRIED HER HAIR, her arms and legs and torso, and wrapped the towel around her. She stared at herself in the mirror seeing an ordinary face in the reflection, oval shaped, dark eyes and brows, plain features—fine enough but not striking like Sophie. Still rebuking herself for not waking up in time to catch Phillip this morning, and stung by the memory of his words last night, she brushed her hair and put on some red lipstick, then went into the bedroom to dress. She dragged the suitcase she'd brought back from New York out of the closet and spread it open on the floor, searching for clean clothes.

A good breeze had worked up with the coming storm, and a fine mist blew through the window screen. She pulled the window down a bit, just enough to stop the rain from blowing in. A crack of nearby thunder came—lightning glowed, followed by another flash, close and harsh and bright. When the rain began, it came hard, all at once, making a racket as it beat down palm leaves and banana plants just beneath the window. The room turned dark. She crossed to the door and switched on the overhead lights. Then she walked into the living room and turned on the lights in there, and into the kitchen where she did the same before returning to the suitcase.

Light would help.

Telling herself that she was worrying for nothing, that Phillip would arrive soon, they'd have a talk and drive back into the city, she hunkered down on her heels and rooted through the suitcase, pulling out suit jackets and skirts, blouses, the pair of pumps, stockings. Rummaging, she ran her hand across the bottom and found only a few pieces of clean underwear and the envelope she'd tossed into the suitcase at the last minute.

She stood, tossed the towel onto the dresser, pulled on the clothes she'd worn that morning, then sank back onto the floor beside the suitcase, weighed down by the realization that she was stuck out here with Phillip. So she watched rain slide down the windowpanes for a few minutes, gazed at the walls, at the worthless clothes and shoes in the suitcase. The large envelope with her unfinished scribbled note to Phillip lay on top of the jumbled clothes and caught her eye. Idly she picked it up, slit it open, and pulled out the contents. Inside was a letter and two slim booklets bound at the left margin.

Glancing at the letter, she recognized the embossed letterhead of an insurance company. The policies were enclosed as requested, the letter said. Tossing it aside, she picked up the first booklet. The name of the insured on the first page was Amalise Sharp. Phillip Sharp was the beneficiary. These would be the term-life policies Phillip had arranged, back when she'd had such hope for their marriage. The coverage was ten thousand dollars.

Wind rattled the panes as the rain came down in torrents. Pursing her lips, she skimmed down through the legalese of the policy, flipping to the next page and the next. On the third page of the policy, in the second paragraph, in bold black letters rising from the paper to meet her eyes she saw it—the coverage on her life that Phillip had purchased.

She had to read the number twice.

Raising her eyes, she studied the iron frame of the bed in front of her and the worn, knotted coverlet. Beyond the bed was the painted plank wall, and to the left was the window with leaves pressed against it, the glass still slick from the rain. Farther on was the perimeter of the forest, the tall straight pine and pin oak trees standing like sentries, barriers to escape. At last the number she'd just read rose to the surface of conscious thought. Again her heart began to race.

One hundred thousand dollars. Not ten thousand, as they'd agreed.

Almost four times what she made in a year at the firm, and associates at Mangen & Morris were well paid. She gripped the edges of the policy. *This number cannot be right. This is a mistake.*

Minutes passed while she sat with the policy opened to page 3. The rain slowed, and she heard first the *harrumph* of the frogs, and after a few more minutes she could hear birds calling in the forest and out over the lake. She closed the booklet, opened it again, and stared at the number. But the enormous sum still gleamed from the page unchanged—numerically and spelled out as well. Outside a blackbird cawed, calling high up in a tree that the storm was gone, that the air was cool, that insurance companies did not make such mistakes.

What a *fool* she'd been!

That's why they'd had to take physical examinations—because of the enormous coverage amount. She stuffed the letter and the two booklets back into the envelope and flung the whole thing into the suitcase.

Sitting on the floor, she drew her knees to her chest and huddled as danger signaled alarms throughout her body in clear, sharp bursts. She could feel her heart drumming, hammering, and the quick blood rush in her ears. Beads of perspiration formed as the truth sank in. She was isolated in this cottage in the middle of the woods, with no telephone, no transportation, and no means of escape. And she was worth one hundred thousand dollars to Phillip Sharp.

Dead.

She hugged her knees as an icy chill ran through her and then she burrowed her head.

Abba, You are my Shepherd. Please calm my burning thoughts. Lead me beside still waters. Lead me to understanding. Restore my soul and guide me along Your path. The oldest prayer she knew— the one Mama had said with her every night before tucking her into bed.

Because I'm filled with terror of the unknown. I fear the evil. I fear it. She choked back a sob. *I fear it, and the fear rushes through my veins even though You're with me. Comfort me, Abba. Give me strength because I am so afraid!*

Raising her eyes, she stared at the wall. No one knew she was here. Not Ashley Elizabeth, or anyone else at the office. Not Dad nor

Mama. Not Jude. She began to tremble. Phillip had planned this every step of the way.

He was going to kill her.

Chapter Forty-Three

Jude bashed his fist against the door one last time and took two steps back, waiting. Seconds passed, and he backed down the stairs, studying the front windows of Amalise's house for any sign of movement. After a moment he turned to the right and walked around to the side of the house. There a narrow three-foot stretch of ground ran between the house and the fence. The grass here was high.

He tried each window as he walked down the alley, pushing up to see if it could be opened. At the back of the house, he came to the last room. There were two windows here. The first one didn't budge. The second did.

Bracing the heels of his hands against the bottom of the window frame, Jude shoved upward. One side of the window jolted, opened half an inch. The window was unlocked but stuck. He pushed on the other side, and on the second attempt it gave, too. Sliding his hands between the windowsill and the bottom frame, he pushed up with all his strength, straining his forearms, his biceps. Slowly the window rose.

With a deep breath Jude pressed his hands flat on the sill and hiked himself up and over the ledge, hooking one knee inside before swinging around through the window and into the room. He landed with a thud. For a moment he stood, looking about as he rubbed his stinging palms on his jeans.

The door to the hallway was open, but the house was silent. A shaft of sunlight from the windows behind him illuminated a picture standing on an easel in the middle of the room. Jude recognized her at once—the woman Phillip had been with at the Hound & Hare. She was stretched across a couch. It was the same blonde—she wasn't easy to forget. Looking past the easel, he saw the daybed in the picture and set his jaw. Phillip had brought her here, into Amalise's house.

The woman in the painting looked back at him with a sly smile. Her hair was in disarray. Propped on the couch were three other paintings of this woman, and six or seven canvases in various states of completion were strewn over the floor around the easel. Jude walked over and picked them up.

The same woman posed in every one. The pictures weren't art—they were lewd. He tossed them down and scooped up a sketchbook. Flipping through the pages, he found numerous sketches of the same model drawn with dark, almost vicious strokes. Understanding struck.

Phillip was obsessed. His mind was in a dark place. Perhaps, as Romar had warned, the bad seed had finally sprouted. As Jude examined the pictures, one thought came clear: Amalise was now an obstacle.

She was in Phillip's way, which meant one thing: she was in danger.

Jude dropped the notebook onto the floor and walked through the studio into the hallway, where he stood for a second, listening. Heading down the hall, he entered the bedroom. Blankets and pillows, even the sheets, were entwined, twisting from the bare mattress onto the floor. A glass of brown liquid sat in a ring of water on the table near the bed. A wine glass clotted with old red wine was beside it, and a splotch of red wine stained the mattress. Clothing was scattered over the floor, over the bed, tossed onto a chair in the corner, on top of the dresser. A soggy towel lay on the floor in the bathroom doorway. Red rage welled, filling him.

Amalise hadn't been here for a while, he realized.

A foul odor in the kitchen—which he found strewn with beer bottles, glasses, dirty plates, mold-covered food—drove him back through the house. The rage was gradually swamped by rising terror for Amalise. One thought clawed its way to conscious level: Phillip was insane.

In the studio he took a seat before a desk and yanked out drawers, riffling through them, looking for anything that could give him a clue where to look for Amalise or Phillip. If he could find Phillip, he was certain he'd find Amalise. But how much time did he have left? She'd been missing for almost forty-eight hours.

His heart pumped double-time at that last thought. Bills, receipts—he tore everything from the drawers, examining each piece of paper for something to guide him, something that would hint at her whereabouts.

At last he sank back. He'd found nothing that would help.

Jude stood, raking his fingers through his hair, and stalked around the room, shoving aside canvases, boxes, records, books, as if following the slime trail of a slug. He ran his hands down between the cushions on the daybed, searched through stacks of old newspapers in one corner. At last he halted in the middle of the room looking at the telephone. Glancing at his watch, he realized he'd have to call the judge. It was time: five after two, already!

So. He would call the judge. And then he'd find Phillip. And when he did, Jude would get the answers he needed.

Chapter Forty-Four

He heard anguish in the judge's voice. Jude had confessed that he'd found the car at the airport. Standing in the studio surrounded by twenty, maybe thirty, paintings and sketches of the woman he'd seen with Phillip, he gripped the phone and listened while Maraine began to cry in the background. He couldn't bring himself to tell them of this room.

"I'm going to . . . I'm going to make some calls from here," the judge said. There was a pause, coughing. "You there, son?"

"Yes sir, I'm here."

"All right. I'm going to make some calls, talk to some people I know up at the DA's office in the city. Maybe . . . see what they think about filing a missing person report. Get an investigation started. Get them to watch the car. See if anyone shows up."

"Good idea."

"And I'm coming into town. I'll catch up with you later."

"Get them started looking for Phillip too," Jude said in a careful tone. "Check airlines. They might be together, you know. It could turn out they went on a vacation . . . or something." Jude lifted his voice. "Maybe he met her at the airport and they went off . . ."

"Right. That's possible, too."

"I'll leave a key under the mat at my place. You and Maraine can stay with me."

Jude's mouth pressed into a thin, tight line as he hung up the telephone, picturing Maraine taking off her eyeglasses and rubbing her eyes, tucking her hair back behind her ears, like she did when things went wrong, like Amalise did. The judge moving about the room quickly, searching for his seersucker jacket, his keys. Both of them silent, not speaking the words aloud.

Amalise was missing.

He started toward the door to the hallway and halted. The cops would cover the car at the airport. But if Phillip came home, he'd be here waiting . . . as long as it took. He didn't know what else to do, where else to look.

But he wouldn't wait inside. Jude turned, walked back to the window, swung his legs over the sill, and dropped onto the ground. Reaching up, he pulled the window closed and walked back down the side of the house. When he reached the front, he hesitated, scanning the area, then went to his car, started the engine, and pulled out of the driveway.

First, he'd go home and leave the key under the mat for the judge. And then . . .

Then he'd come back.

For Phillip.

AT HOME JUDE LOCATED his extra house key in the desk drawer and took it out to the porch, locking the front door behind him. Slipping it under the doormat, he hurried down the steps and returned to Palmer Avenue.

Nothing seemed to have changed. Jude knocked on the door again, checked the windows, walked along the side of the house, peering in. Returning to his car, he pulled to the other side of the street, two houses down. Odds were that Phillip would return home sooner or later, and if Amalise wasn't with him, Jude was ready for anything. Phillip would not recognize this car, Jude was certain.

He slid back into the seat and reclined, keeping his eyes on the rearview mirror. The sun blazed overhead, heating up the interior. Perspiring, he rolled down the windows. The clock on the dashboard read ten minutes to three, and he struggled not to think of Amalise.

Drumming his fingers on the steering wheel, he watched a child wheeling a tricycle down the walkway on Amalise's side of the street. The mother trailed behind. He focused on the child. He would not think of Amalise in danger while he waited. Not yet.

When an hour had passed, he began to wonder if he'd made a mistake. Rubbing his eyes, he hitched up straight and stared down the street. *What makes you think he'll come?*

Because this was where Phillip lived. Slugs return to their nesting sites. His studio was here, and this was where Ashley Elizabeth reached him on the phone yesterday morning, after Amalise was missing. And he had nothing else to go on, no place else to look.

The obsessive pictures he'd seen in Phillip's studio hovered in his mind. A gray-and-white cat stalked past the car, and Jude watched it, giving it all of his attention until it disappeared under an automobile parked farther down the street. Then he shifted his gaze to the sidewalks that lined the street, the small square yards, trim bushes, stately trees . . . waiting, unwilling to think about what might be happening right now to Amalise.

The heat was almost unbearable. His eyelids grew heavy, but each time he caught himself and blinked them open again. He stretched his arms, his legs. When he knew he'd fall asleep if he didn't move, he opened the car door and strolled around the hood to the sidewalk where he stood in the shade, flexing his knees. He ambled to the end of the block and back, cracking his knuckles. When at last he returned to his place behind the steering wheel, he was alert again. Ready. Watching and waiting.

A half hour later he saw it in the rearview mirror, an unfamiliar car approaching from St. Charles Avenue that began to slow as it neared her house. Angling the mirror, Jude slid down in the seat and watched as a blue Mustang pulled into Amalise's driveway. He recognized the blonde from the pictures first. She sat in the front passenger seat, nearest him. The driver was Phillip.

Jude sat motionless as Phillip said something to the woman, opened the car door, and went inside. She pulled down the visor, inspected herself in the small mirror, and ducked. Returning to the mirror, she swiped a tube of lipstick around her lips, practiced a smile, then pushed back the visor, closed the lipstick, and reclined, feet up and braced against the dashboard. Jude tensed, fighting off an urge to confront the two of them. Instead, eyes riveted on the rearview mirror, he waited. In a few minutes Phillip returned.

Leaning forward, Jude ducked his head and adjusted knobs on the dashboard as Phillip drove past. Starting the engine, Jude pulled out behind them, keeping a distance between the cars. Phillip's car wound through the narrow one-way streets of the university area. Acid simmered in Jude's chest as he drove, surging up into the back of his throat. He grimaced, swallowed, and straightened his shoulders, never taking his eyes from the Mustang.

"Five minutes alone in a room with you . . . When this is done, that's all I want, buddy. Just five minutes."

The Mustang stopped in front of a small store on Pine Street. Jude pulled over in the block behind them and peered through the windshield. No, he'd been wrong. The small building was something else, a shop, or perhaps an art gallery. The Mustang passenger door swung open, and the woman emerged, bare legs first. As she stood, street side, Phillip came around the front of the car, arms wide, and lifted her off the ground. She laughed, and when he released her, they stood toe to toe, whispering. Phillip bent, nuzzling, planting kisses on the nape of her neck.

Jude pressed the steering wheel with the heel of his hand, squeezed his eyes together, and opened them wide. Emotion was a luxury he couldn't afford right now.

He tensed. The woman was leaving, going into the gallery. Phillip watched her for a moment before returning to the driver's side of the car and getting in. As the engine started, Jude's heart skipped a beat. He waited until Phillip had turned the corner one block ahead before following, swerving onto Broadway, keeping well behind the Mustang.

Claiborne to Carrolton and up the ramp onto I-10, traveling west toward Baton Rouge. Here we go, Jude thought with a stab of fear. Phillip pulled over into the right lane. Jude did so, too. Exiting onto Causeway Boulevard without a signal, the Mustang entered the stream of traffic heading toward Lake Pontchartrain. Jude gripped the wheel, eyes riveted on Phillip ten lengths ahead, muttering over and over, . . . *please, not Amalise!* . . . and struggling not to think of what might come.

Holding the wheel with both hands, he concentrated on matching Phillip's speed. He'd been right to wait. Now take this one step at a time, he told himself, and almost smiled at the thought. That's something Amalise would have said.

It was five o'clock when they hit the causeway. The air was bright and clear, the clouds high and white. Out on the lake there were sailboats, motorboats, seagulls, a fishing boat dropping nets in water near the bridge. Jude ignored it all, eyes fixed on the car ahead. Weekend traffic was light. Phillip cruised along at sixty, seeming in no hurry as others passed him on the left. Behind him, Jude watched as Phillip moved in close behind another, slower car, tailgating until the driver whipped into the left lane. Phillip drove on, and the irate driver wheeled back into the slow lane, keeping his distance now.

Exiting the causeway, Phillip took a right and continued through the town of Mandeville, then Lacombe, and north onto a two-lane highway through a stretch of dense pine woods. Jude glanced at the clock on the dashboard. It was six thirty but still light as the last houses of Lacombe receded in the rearview mirror. He reached over his shoulder, massaging the taut muscles at the back of his neck. Realizing he was hunched forward and gripping the wheel, Jude shifted in the seat, telling himself to relax as the road narrowed. Trees blocked remnants of the fading light.

Jude slowed, letting his car fall farther behind the Mustang as traffic diminished. Hot bile rose again, fear burning the back of his throat. Where was Phillip going and where was Amalise? The sun disappeared behind the trees. Above the clouds were gray now, streaked and low. In the distance thunder rolled. Raindrops splattered the windshield. The Mustang's lights blinked on ahead. Jude kept his own lights off, afraid that Phillip would spot him.

That's when the sky erupted. The windshield wipers did their work, but ahead the Mustang's lights were dim. Peering through the rain, Jude realized that Phillip was losing him. He pressed down on the accelerator and switched on the headlights, but the relentless rain was blinding, and the country road was narrow and unfamiliar. Wind gusted through the trees, bowing the trunks of smaller ones.

A small animal darted from the trees and Jude swerved. As if the road had turned to glass, he could feel the tires sliding, rear end gliding forward as the steering wheel jolted from his hands. Jude fought for control, easing into the skid as the car spun off the raised asphalt onto a soft shoulder. Instinctively he lifted his foot from the accelerator, but still the car floated, dreamlike alongside the road, through a muddy slough, wet grass, bumping over fallen branches . . . had he seen a ditch?

At last the car slowed. Gradually Jude forced it back onto the road without coming to a stop and leaned forward again, straining to see lights ahead. Lightning flashed.

In the utter darkness that followed, Phillip's car was no longer visible.

A SHARP RUSTLING JUST outside the cottage window startled her. Amalise turned her head toward the sound and saw a small gray squirrel scampering across the ledge. It leapt onto the branch of a nearby tree. Holding still, she followed it until it disappeared.

She shook herself from the trance, unscrambled her arms and legs, and rose from the floor. A glance at her watch set her mind spinning—it was already early evening. Was there still time to get to the main road? In her mind she glimpsed the long narrow drive from the cottage to the road, miles of thick bramble and trees encroaching at the edges. If Phillip came along, . . . she began to tremble at the thought. There would be no escape.

Leave now! Run!

Looking down at her bare feet, she brushed away tears, bent, and pushed aside clothes in the suitcase until she located the high-heeled shoes. Slamming the suitcase shut, she whirled and stumbled into the bathroom, tossed one shoe onto the floor, and began pounding the heel of the other against the edge of the bathtub. Pounding. Pounding. The sound seemed to ricochet through the cottage. If she could break off the heels, perhaps she could wear the shoes, and then she could run. Perhaps she could make it to the main road where there were places to hide.

If Phillip didn't get here first.

JUDE ACCELERATED, PEERING THROUGH the rain for a turn, a road or driveway that Phillip might have taken. After a few miles the rain slackened, turning to drizzle, then to mist. For twenty minutes more Jude drove, searching. When at last he reached the tree line of the forest, which opened to miles of flat marsh, and there was still no sign of Phillip, he pulled over to the side of the road.

Braking, he looked back. Just over the trees a glimmer of twilight seeped through wisps of cloud as the summer storm moved on. Terror struck him at the realization that Amalise must be with Phillip now, and he cried out then, in that desolate place—*Lord, let this fire burn. Don't extinguish the flame! Work through me, work through me*!

With a surge of despair, he leaned forward, resting his forehead on the wheel. At last he drew a deep breath, shuddered, and straightened. He would go back. Somewhere back there he'd missed a turnoff. He'd search all night if he had to.

Please, God. . . . Let me find her in time.

Chapter Forty-Five

She pounded the shoe against the edge of the bathtub with every ounce of strength she possessed. Once. Twice. She could feel the heel weakening. Twice more, and the heel flew off, landing in the bottom of the tub with a clatter. Amalise looked down at the portion of the shoe left in her hand with a thrill of exhilaration. But as she turned to pick up the second one, she heard it—a faint drone in the distance. She rose, holding the shoes, and stood listening.

Motionless she waited. Through the drip, drip of water from the roof over the window and the whisper of wind still rustling the pine, she heard the unmistakable hum of an automobile coming slowly up the drive. She heard car tires crushing shells near the cottage. The engine died. And then the absence of sound left her suspended.

Phillip was here.

The slam of the heavy car door turned her cold. *Play along,* she commanded herself, gripping the shoes, one in each hand. *That's all that's left.* She breathed in, shallow breaths. *Just feel your way along.* But still she stood paralyzed by images of his fists that other time, the hard dark eyes, and she knew this would be worse.

Much, much worse.

Whirling, she ran for the suitcase, squatted, lifted the lid, and threw in the shoes. If he found her with those, he'd know what she'd been planning.

Call for help.

There is no phone.

Run!

There is no time.

"Ama?" His voice reedy, high pitched, came from the direction of the kitchen. She turned her head to the door. She was trapped. "In here."

Suddenly she remembered the broken heel still in the bathtub. If he spotted it, . . . nausea rose. With a frantic push up from the suitcase, she dashed into the bathroom to retrieve the heel of the shoe, lying exposed. But as her stomach erupted, she fell onto her knees instead, driving her bones into the floor as she gripped the cool porcelain toilet bowl with both hands, leaned over, and retched.

"Ama!"

She heard his footsteps coming toward her. The heel. She had to get the heel before he saw it. Tears spilled down her cheeks. Trembling, she struggled to rise, retched again, and slipped back down. His footsteps slowed as he crossed the wooden bedroom floor.

"Ama?" His voice came close behind her, brisk, clipped. Each creak of his shoes on the floorboards made her flinch. He halted just inside the bathroom door. With heightened senses she could smell the sour odor of his body and the smoke in his clothing. As she knelt, his cold fingers touched the flesh of her bowed, heaving neck. Leaning over the toilet bowl, she squeezed her eyes together, waiting, sobbing, . . . praying.

When his fingers lifted from her, she did not move and could not breathe. Water ran in the sink. A cool wet cloth touched her skin. "Babe, what's wrong?" He leaned down, his voice soft, thick with compassion.

"It's something I ate." *Perhaps this part is real,* the observer whispered, *and the rest . . . only your imagination.*

The cloth moved slowly over the knotted muscles of her neck, her throat, cooling her hot skin. The broken heel—he would see the broken heel. The words clanged in her mind as she knelt, motionless, waiting, and the cloth slid around her neck and under her chin. He would see the heel and he would know.

"Poor thing," he breathed into her ear, wiping the cloth gently around her mouth. "Would a glass of water help?"

She shook her head, unable to speak. Suddenly the cool cloth disappeared. Seconds passed. She twisted around, looked up, and saw him gazing down at her with two deep lines grooving his forehead.

Wiping tears from her face, she braced herself and stood, facing him, too close, so that he could not see beyond her into the bathtub. He said nothing, and after a beat he moved aside to let her pass, following her into the bedroom.

He hadn't seen it.

But behind her he halted. "Were you packing?"

She turned, looked from him to the suitcase, still in the middle of the floor where she'd left it, and back to him. He raised his brows.

Hopelessness swept her. The suitcase had been in the closet when he'd left this morning. She'd forgotten that.

The words rushed out. "I want to go home, Phillip. I was packing so you could take me home. Back into town. I have to get to work." His eyes narrowed at her words "You don't understand. I cannot leave work like this." She moved toward him, reaching out, pleading, but he stepped back.

"Just you and me," she said. Then softer: "Please. Let's go home."

"I'm here now, Ama." He shook his head as his eyes strayed to the window. "It's stopped raining. We'll go out to the pier and see if there's a sunset." She saw the fleeting look of distaste that crossed his face as he turned and scrutinized her.

She could not move.

"Come," he said impatiently, lifting his arm and curling his fingers, commanding. "I'll get some wine. We'll talk." With a cool look he inspected her. "Brush your hair and clean up." He fixed his eyes on her, nodded his head slowly, and she did too.

"That's my girl." He turned on his heels.

Staring at her reflection in the bathroom mirror, she heard him in the kitchen opening the wine, searching for glasses. Quickly she splashed her face, brushed her teeth, and ran a comb through her hair. Perhaps if she could find the rental car keys.

Where would he have put the car keys?

"Ama?"

"I'll be right there." She heard the screened door slam and his footsteps on the porch. Struggling for control, she hurried through the bedroom, the living room, and into the kitchen, scanning the counters for keys.

"What are you doing?"

She wheeled around, startled. He stood in the doorway behind her, holding a glass of wine in each hand.

Beside her on the counter was the open wine bottle. She picked it up and pushed in the loose cork with the heel of her hand. "I knew you couldn't carry this as well." It was a miracle that her voice was steady. He looked down at the bottle, up into her eyes, and smiled.

He will drink too much, and then I'll find the keys. Following him, with a desperate glance at the corner table, she swept her eyes over Phillip's canvasses and paints and carving tools, searching in vain for the car keys. He pushed the door open with his knee and stood against it while she brushed past him, cradling the wine bottle in her arm.

The screen door slammed, and he followed her down the steps and into the clearing as they walked toward the pier. "I'm ready to relax," he said, holding the glasses and looking around. "It's nice out here."

"Yes." *Though I walk through the valley of the shadow of death . . .*

"Look at the silver in those clouds."

She looked up.

He will drink too much and he will fall asleep. But the keys . . . and the thought of what would happen if she guessed wrong, brought nausea again. She choked it back, thoughts reeling, half listening as he admired the scene—the lake and the cypress rising from the water—all of it seeming so remote, so unreal as they walked along like two normal people toward the end of the pier. Fear engulfed her, but she fought it.

Abba, help me keep my thoughts clear, my mind sharp. If I have to run, let Phillip have left the keys in the car.

When they came to the end of the pier, he motioned for her to sit. She set the bottle down and lowered herself so that her feet dangled over the water. Phillip put the two filled wine glasses next to the bottle and sat down beside her, drawing his knees up and encircling them with his arms.

I shall fear no evil.

Amalise lifted her eyes to see Iris roosting in the top of a cypress tree. She fixed her eyes on the bird while the number reeled through her mind—one hundred thousand dollars. *Until I have the keys, I'll pretend.* The thought brought a bitter taste. She'd become good at that—pretending.

Phillip picked up his glass and sipped from it. He glanced at her and arched his brows. "You're not drinking your wine."

Amalise lifted her glass from the pier.

Iris rose from the tree, spreading her wings. *For Thou art with me.*

"She's a beauty," Phillip said.

Eyes anchored on Iris, Amalise sat poised, ready to grasp any opportunity. Phillip stirred beside her, set down his glass, and stretched out his right leg so that he could reach into the hip pocket of his jeans. Her mind went blank as keys rattled. As in a dream she watched as he pulled out first the car keys, next the partially carved wooden figure she'd seen on the table this morning, and last, his pocket carving knife. Her fingers tightened on the stem of the glass.

He jammed the keys back into his pocket and, holding the carver in the palm of one hand and the wooden figure in the other, he sat back on his haunches, spread his thighs and hunched, bracing his elbows on his knees as he began scrapping tiny cuts in the wood with the tip of the knife.

Abba . . . Abba . . .

The keys were in his pocket and she couldn't breathe, sitting tensed beside him, unable to think now of anything except the quick, sharp movements of the knife as he carved. The egret circled the cypress and flew into the swampy area on the other side of the lake.

"She's showing off for me," Phillip said without looking up.

Amalise pressed the glass against her lips and said nothing. The sky was darkening—lingering clouds hid the last light of day. The storm had stirred things up; the lake water ruffled in the damp breeze. She shivered.

Phillip's hands grew still as he turned to her. "That suitcase." He paused. "You're planning to leave me, aren't you?"

Thy rod and Thy staff shall comfort me.

She set the glass down and met his eyes. The child's eyes looked back at her, suspicious, drawn, fixed on her. Pressing her hands down flat on the wooden boards of the pier, she struggled to keep from looking at the knife. Fought for a casual tone, for the semblance of a smile.

"No." She widened her eyes, gave a slight lift of one shoulder. "I was looking for clean clothes to wear." But the trembling began, running into her shoulders and neck, gripping her jaw, and she heard the shudder in her voice even as she tensed, willing the violent shaking to stop . . . . *Willing* it to stop. "If you want to stay out here in the country, we will. You can paint the bird—"

"Don't tell me what to paint." He lowered his chin onto his chest and watched her.

She looked into his eyes, those black reflecting pools.

In that instant his hand flexed, tightening on the knife, and the carving dropped to the pier. Clawing her fingers into the deck below, heart racing, pumping, she felt the sound before she heard it, a rumbling moan from his chest, a primeval snarl rising to a howl in the back of his throat, harsh and raw as his face transformed, contorting with his hatred even as tears spilled from the boy's eyes.

A flash of razored light on the beveled blade as his fist rose . . . staccato hammering fury as the knife arced . . . *Ama* . . . *Ama* . . . steel tip slashing toward her as she sprang, pushing off the pier with pulsing desperation, launching through the air, flying. Viscous water closed around her in the split-second she heard the knife smash into the planks above.

Cool dark water. She let it carry her a short distance before rising to the surface, spewing, rubbing her eyes, turning, searching.

He was on the pier above, planted on one knee, hands braced on the knife as he fought to pull it free from the wood. She dove deep, deeper down into the water, driven by sheer terror as she kicked and pulled, swimming away from the pier toward the sandy bank where the clearing ended at the forest edge.

But when she reached the shallows, a down stroke jammed her hand into the mud bottom of the lake. Jolted, struggling to her knees, blinded by water, she rose, and with her pulse surging wildly in her ears, she turned and ran.

Muffled shouts came, and then his footsteps pounding, pounding down the pier behind her.

JUDE GLANCED AT HIS watch and wheeled the car around, heading back, searching the lines of trees for an opening to explain Phillip's disappearance—a driveway, a cutoff, a clearing. Headlights caught a raccoon. Automatically he slowed and it skittered off into the shadows.

It was twenty minutes before he saw it. The sun was gone, the road dark. He'd almost missed the entrance, a small dirt drive to his left. Slamming on the brakes, he backed up and turned in. Immediately the car swerved into parallel ruts and he guessed he'd found a driveway. Lowering the window, he listened for the sound of another car, for sounds of life. An owl hooted somewhere in the forest. He could hear a small animal mewling in the distance, a fox perhaps. Ahead he heard the craggy shriek of an egret. He breathed in the familiar dank smell of algae and wet wood, sodden plants and animals—the sounds and odors that permeate inland water—swamps, small ponds, rivers, and lakes.

No light escaped the canopy above; the road was dark, rough, and endless in the headlights. Minutes passed with no change as he drove on, winding through the trees. His hands tightened on the wheel, tendons straining.

Let me find her, God. Please. Let me find her before Phillip hurts her.

A sharp curve of the road to the right, immediately followed by a turn to the left, surprised him. Headlights streamed into the forest as he straightened the car and peered through the beam of light. Jude leaned forward, tensing. Was that something in the road ahead . . . a shadow or a deer?

A scream in the distance curdled his blood. Despite the rutted, curving road, he stepped on the gas.

Amalise!

Chapter Forty-Six

L ast light was gone, hidden by the clouds. She ran, shoeless and weighed down by wet clothes. Splashing through the shallows, she could hear him running, too, coming after her. Glancing back, even through the dim light, she saw the rage on his face, fists pumping as he came.

"Ama!" he shouted, and then she heard him splashing through the water. Branches broke beneath her feet as she ran. She could hear him cursing as he drew closer, infusing new energy, propelling her onto the strip of sand that she'd explored this morning.

Breathe, breathe—

The word ricocheted through her mind, pushing her on. Gasping, she raced toward the edge of the swamp. Burning pain knifed up her leg as something sliced the bottom of her foot, but she ran on through the water, flailing now through reeds, gaining speed on the hard-packed sand, stumbling, slapping aside branches . . . running . . . running . . . running, with his ragged breath too close behind.

Don't think—just run. Her chest radiated pain. *Don't think of that, or of Phillip, or of anything. Just run. Breathe and run.*

Phillip's voice behind her came—Ama, Ama stop!—and she concentrated on the breathing. With each breath she would think that this one was the last, and with the next she'd explode. But each time she slowed, he'd curse, shout, splash, and drive her on.

When at last she reached the pretty beach—saw the tree beyond the bog, saw the edge of the swamp and the rise of earth, the levee—she dragged in one last breath and skirted the edge of the quicksand around to the other side, halting under the tree, dazed and fighting to fill her lungs with air.

This was how he found her—sobbing, bent double, gasping for breath, hands splayed on knees, head bowed and praying, because she knew he would kill her now.

She looked up and there he was—on the other side of the bog, twenty-five feet from her. The moon hung low over the lake, dreamlike after the rain. Fog from the warm surface of the water behind him gave everything an eerie look. He stood completely still, a silhouette in the mist, watching her in silence as he held his chest and caught his breath. After a moment he took two steps forward, and she could see the flat, grotesque smile on his face, the practiced look of sorrow in his eyes, pulled down now at the outer corners.

"I didn't want to hurt you, Ama. It could have been easier." He reached into his pocket and slid out the knife, opened it, and held it at his waist, blade pointed at her.

"You can have a divorce." She pushed the words through clenched, chattering teeth. Across the bog, in the murky light, she saw his face twist.

Then he shook his head.

"You've carried things too far, as you always do." His features tightened. "It's too late for that." He smiled and she saw it in his eyes, the confidence, the certainty that she was trapped. His eyes locked on hers, and he came toward her with slow, careful steps. "You're mine, Ama. I choose when and how . . . and *if* you live."

And there was the money.

She stood watching, paralyzed as he moved toward her, the knife in his hand. When she took a sudden step back, he cursed and flew at her. Her instinctive warning shout came the instant he entered the quicksand, his forward motion propelled by rage, slowing only when he'd reached the middle, where the mud caught and held him in its grip.

With a quizzical look his eyes followed hers to the water pooling around his ankles.

Never struggle, Amalise.

Impatiently Phillip shifted his weight, fighting to free his legs from the mud, first one, then the other, and they both heard the sucking sound as he sank deeper into the vacuum and liquid pooled underneath.

Just as Jude had said would happen

She opened her mouth to warn him, to tell him not to struggle, and heard the whisper from inside: *He will kill you.*

Memories—terrors—flooded her as she looked at him. His fists pounding, pounding on the day of the bar exam. Sophie, laughing in the studio. Phillip watching, always testing, the little lies and big ones, the cruelties, the insurance policy. And now—

Could she just leave him here to die? Could she?

She turned away, just for time to think, and listened to the music of the swamp instead, the cicadas and frogs and birds, the rustle of wind high in the pine. Only for one moment . . . just long enough to calm her spinning thoughts.

A shrill, terrified scream forced her gaze back to him. The quicksand held him firmly. It sucked at his calves, his knees. Frantically he braced his hands under each thigh, sinking as he tugged on one, then the other, ever creating the deadly vacuum.

"Don't fight! Don't move!"

"Ama! Help me. Please! Pull me out." He twisted toward her, flailing, his voice raw with fear. "Please!"

She pressed herself back against the trunk of the tree, battered by the lies . . . love you, Ama, Ama . . . love, love, love . . .

"Help me, Amalise!"

And then she started. *What* was she doing? She couldn't let him die! *Abba, forgive me!* Her gaze raked the area, stopping on a long branch of water oak, probably brought down in the storm. It looked strong enough to hold Phillip's weight. She could pull. She could pull him out.

Still, she hesitated. The knife . . .

He saw her hesitation. Dropping the knife into the sand, he lowered his voice. "Please. I won't hurt you. Pick the branch up." His voice broke. "Please, babe."

She hurried to the branch, bent, and grasped it. When she rose, her leg muscles bore some of the heavy weight. A glance back at Phillip shook her as she saw the sand had reached his hips.

"Hurry!" Phillip shouted in a new, sharp tone.

"Don't move!" Dragging the branch through the sand, she wondered how she'd ever lift the weight and hold it out. Not much time was left.

"Good girl."

She knelt under the tree beside the bog. Tilting her head to the sky, she closed her eyes for an instant. *Abba, give me strength.* Then, with a deep breath, almost as with the help of some invisible force, she lifted the branch and began pushing the shaking limb out toward Phillip, inching it toward him over the bog.

"Come on, Ama, come on, come on."

But the farther the limb extended, the harder it was to hold. Amalise's arms, shoulders, neck muscles all trembled, straining from the effort.

When the end of the branch was close, Phillip flailed out for it and missed.

Heart pounding, Amalise leaned forward, thrusting it further, sliding her hands back on the branch bit by bit until she reached the thick broken end. Spiked bark cut through the flesh of her palms, her muscles burned, and the heavy wood wobbled.

Once more he flailed. Angry. Cursing. Again and again.

Amalise fought to hold on. *Inhale.*

And then at last he caught and held the branch.

Exhale! She threw her head back. *Thank you.*

"Finally!" Phillip shouted.

She readied herself for the pull, but Phillip, heaving, dropped his head onto the branch, forehead resting on the wood. Amalise waited and tightened her grip as the thought struck.

Abba, what will happen when he is free?

Her own strength was sapped from the struggle to save him. He didn't need a knife to kill.

Thrusting the thought away, she firmed her grip and steadied her stance, waiting. Only seconds had passed, but it seemed like an eternity before Phillip lifted his head from the branch, drew a deep breath, and riveted her with a look. "All right now. Get me out of here." A sudden tug on the branch almost caused her to lose her grip. "Pull, Ama!"

Abba, help me!

Bracing herself with feet wide apart, one foot behind the other, knees bent and splayed, she dug her heels deep into the solid sand at the edge of the bog and pulled against his weight, ignoring the cuts on her hands from the ravaging bark and the burning muscles in her shoulders and arms. Phillip, grunting, hands crabbing up the branch, firming his grip as she pulled . . . and—

They felt it together. An almost imperceptible release of the quicksand.

With a jubilant cry, he yanked hard on the limb and her foot slid. Off balance, she struggled to hold on as the branch began slipping through her hands, the knots and bark tearing her flesh.

Phillip lurched back from the sudden release, hanging onto his end, screaming. "You *idiot!* I'll tear you apart if you drop it!"

She caught it just before it fell.

Thrashing, he shoved the branch. "Hold on, you fool!"

Tears slipped down her cheeks anticipating his fury when he was released. But she could not let him die. Ducking her head, she held on and began again to pull.

Yea, though I walk through the valley of the shadow of death, I shall fear no evil.

"Who are you calling on, Ama? The God of justice?" His voice was strange, savage. "The God of *mercy?*"

She looked up, stunned. She hadn't said the words out loud, she was certain.

He laughed, a harsh, bitter sound. "Ask *me* about his mercy." He'd stopped pulling himself forward on the branch. She stared. The quicksand was rising against him, but his brows lowered, and his eyes turned to slits, and he studied her as though he'd just seen her for the first time.

"You want to *save* me." The statement was a revelation, not a question. He shook his head. "You're the one who can fix everything, the angel of mercy who'll save poor Phillip from his death." As he stared, seconds passed. "Hunh. That will earn you some marks upstairs."

"Phillip! Quit wasting time."

He smiled and nodded as if time no longer mattered, as if he were invincible. "Guess I don't have to work quite so hard. You want the points, then you do the work. Pull, Ama." His mocking tested her remaining strength. And her will. But she tightened her grip on the branch and dug her heels deeper into the sand.

He threw back his head and laughed. "What irony! Pull as hard as you can because if you fail, baby, you'll live with this moment the rest of your life. You'll be chained to me forever if that happens."

He jerked on the branch. "Go ahead, *pull* Saint Ama! It's your obligation. Your *mission*."

Shuddering as his cold stream of hatred pierced her, Amalise wrapped her hands around the branch and pulled against Phillip's dead weight with every ounce of strength she possessed.

It wasn't enough.

"Phillip, help me!" She heard the tremor in her voice. "We're wasting time."

In a sudden fury Phillip cursed, stretching his arms forward, as if to crawl up over the branch to Amalise. But the sand heaved and swirled as he twisted, fighting to reach her.

"Phillip, don't! Don't fight the sand!" He was mad. Utterly, truly mad.

Yea, though I walk through the shadow of death, I will fear no evil. I shall fear no evil. I shall fear no evil.

But the sand was roused from his thrashing. Once again it turned hungry, a heaving, sucking, living thing. Still his weight bore down the branch as he fought to get to her, and she struggled to hold on. And he, fought like a fury against her and against the sand.

Tears streamed down her cheeks, blinding. "Stay still, Phillip. Just hold on and inch your hands forward."

But rage consumed him. Suddenly the vortex swirled, the violent whirlpool opening around him. He seemed to sense the change. Seconds passed as he looked at her, eyes round, wild. Then, arching his back, releasing a warlike howl, he flung out one arm, hand reaching up, up for the sky, holding onto the branch with his other. Amalise moaned as he slipped sideways into the turbulent spin, and the sand, like a living thing, swallowed the free arm, then his shoulder.

O God, Abba, Creator, help us!

"Hold on, hold on, hold on, hold on!" Her heart raced as she watched, helpless, still holding tight to the now useless wood. With one arm in the sand, he was trapped.

And she hadn't the strength to do it alone.

Tears coursed down her cheeks as she held on to the branch, watching Phillip fight the futile battle. She could have pulled him out. She *knew* she could have done it if he'd listened.

It's the fight that will kill him.

Phillip understood. Still clutching the branch, he twisted, facing her, and in that moment she saw the full fury, the hatred and contempt. Saw it consuming everything. Even, at last, his instinct for survival.

His mask had slipped.

"You lose." His mouth stretched as he spoke, his smile a rictus.

High and full, the scream ripped from her core, filling the night. *"Abba!"*

His eyes widened, and in the instant she saw in his face the final understanding of human mortality, the certain knowledge that death loomed. Lifting high, arching up, up over the whirlpool, he screamed as the bog slowly claimed its prize, swirling over him, pulling him down with powerful fingers of sand. Until at last all that was visible of Phillip Sharp was his hand . . . still holding onto the branch.

One still, lifeless hand.

Amalise stood immobile. No . . . *No!* Tears washed her cheeks, and in the sudden silence she fell to her knees on the solid sand, sobbing. *Abba. Abba!* And slowly she bent until her head touched the ground.

There was nothing more she could do.

Minutes passed, and at last, lifting, straightening, she sat back on her heels and carefully rested her end of the branch on the sand. Not a sound pierced the deathly silence as she stared over the bog, conscious that the image of Phillip's hand still clutching the branch would be stamped in her mind forever, that it would become a part of who she was in the years ahead, wherever she went, whatever she did— this image, this last legacy of Phillip Sharp—would haunt her until death.

We pay a price for our bad choices, Jude had said. Perhaps this was part of her price.

A flash of white rose from the swamp, just ahead, among the trees. She lifted her eyes as the great egret, Iris, soared out over the lake.

You're alive, Amalise. Let go . . . breathe.

Eyes riveted on the white bird, conscious thought dissolved, and she fixed instead on Iris as her heart and mind separated Phillip Sharp from Amalise Catoir . . . until at last everything but Iris disappeared. She could almost feel the soft feathery shape lifting her, the air current beneath her, the power in the wings as they swooped together, rising, soaring into the dark sky with silver stars shooting toward them, and the wind in her hair and the ribbon of yellow moonlight sliding down, down into the lake.

With a shuddering sigh, reality slipped back in, pulling her from the dream as Iris flew away. Amalise turned and edged around the bog to the sandy strip by the water and the rushes—and then she ran, ran, ran . . . praying for Phillip's soul, and her own, stumbling down the sandy strip . . . running, running, running. Away from the evil Phillip had become.

Run. Just run.

The car lights caught her first, stumbling, running, like an apparition from the darkness around a curve in the road. At first he thought it was a deer. Slamming on the brakes, Jude glimpsed her face in the beam and heard the sickening scream while the car skidded forward, slamming into her just before the engine died. In slow motion she sank through the light and disappeared. For a split second he sat immobile, horrified, staring over the rain-slicked hood of the car into the space where Amalise had just appeared before him.

Then he was out of the car, bending over her inert body on the muddy road . . . please, please, please . . . he stooped and touched her . . . forehead, arms, legs . . . praying, praying for a sign of life. *Please, Lord, let her live.*

A groan, a small movement, and hope rushed through him. Ignoring everything he'd ever learned about such injuries, gently he slid his hands beneath her and felt along her spine, feeling for . . . he knew not what, an obvious break? But they couldn't stay out here, so he worked his left arm under the small of her back, bracing her there, and slipped his right arm under the crook behind her knees.

Closing his eyes for one second, he said another prayer, lifted her into his arms, and stood. Jude cradled Amalise against his chest as he carried her to the driver's side of the car where the door was open as he'd left it. He pushed the front seat forward with his knee, and arms trembling, lowered her carefully onto the rear seat.

It wasn't until, bending over Amalise as she lay stretched out on the seat and unconscious, he noticed the gash along the side of her head, near the right temple, where the blood, thick and bright, streamed into her hair, down her face. Stepping back and straightening, he saw the crimson smears on his arms and down the front of his shirt.

There was no space on the narrow road to turn the car around. He was forced to drive all the way down to the cottage. The Mustang was there, but Phillip was nowhere in sight. Time seemed to stop as he maneuvered the car and headed back down the rough driveway, retracing the pathways formed by the ruts, turning left at the road leading to Lacombe and Mandeville, right toward Covington and the emergency room at St. Tammany Parish hospital, about fifty miles or so, he calculated. He raced through the tunnels of trees without letting himself think of what might be, focusing only on the road, the car lights, the steering wheel in his hand; refusing to let himself dwell on the pain she must feel from the jolting car or how badly she was hurt. Or worse—whether she was even still alive.

Chapter Forty-Seven

They've pushed us out of the room, me and William. We're her parents, what can they be thinking? Hands splayed, Mama pressed against the cold glass window that separated her from her daughter, pressing, pressing against the glass to find her child's life spirit. *My girl, ma 'tite fille . . . ahhh . . . she's so still, Lord, and they won't let me come to her now, won't let me hold her here with me . . .* Leaning forward, she touched her forehead to the glass, too, eyes riveted to the bits and pieces she could see of Amalise lying on that bed surrounded by doctors, nurses, technicians. Watching, she held her breath . . . tears washed her cheeks. *If I could just hold her . . .*

And then . . . slowly, as if in a trance, she took one step back from the window, pulled in a long deep breath, closed her eyes, and arched her hands so that only the smooth tips of her fingers remained on the glass, touching it lightly as one would piano keys, and after a moment she felt it, the uncertainty, the shimmering stir of her daughter's earthly life ebbing and flowing in the ether, like the vibration of music not yet heard, as a musician feels in that split second just before touching the keys.

She sighed. *I can touch you, Amalise, even from this distance. I feel your terror, your pain, your goodness, and your love. Mama's with you. Mama's here. God is with you.* White noise filled the world as she streamed mother-love to her daughter through the window.

Hold on 'tite fille. Stay with us. Stay, please stay. Please don't call her yet, Lord, my only child. Please, please, please, I beg, please . . . not yet. Take me instead. Not my baby girl.

Suddenly her eyes flew open. *No no no no.* . . . She slapped her hands against the glass, flat, frantic, pushing, pushing against the glass, longing to reach through it for her child. Whipping around she looked *blindly* from side to side, then back to Amalise.

She's leaving, Father. Grant a mother's prayer! Father, Lord, Jehovah, Jesus Christ. Let her live. Take me instead. Let her stay! If . . . if you will leave her with me for just a little longer, I will build for You a garden of glory where the dry yard used to be back behind the laundry shed. Do you remember when she was little? Amalise would play back there for hours, and she would pick bouquets of sweet peas for You, for her Abba, from the trellis? Ahhhh . . . I can feel those soft little hands in mine, like silk, cupping bunches of those sweet peas.

William slipped his arms around her, and she turned, sinking against him, head buried in his chest, sobbing. *Remember? Do You remember?*

Please please please. . . . *Isn't that memory worth a little more time?*

AMALISE.

She drifted unfettered in the light. No gravity. No pain. It was a warm and loving, living light, each particle glittering, like snow, but the whole, a white of purest peace and love sinking through her, embracing her.

Phillip.

Comprehension slowly filled her. Sorrow rose from each atom, molecule, particle that was Amalise—from her heart, her soul. Something was wrong with Phillip. She longed to help him but couldn't.

Weeping. Weeping. Invisible tears from an infinite well.

Help me. Help. . . . She spun in her tears, in the light. *Do You know me, Abba? I am the lost one.*

The light cradled her. A voice came.

I am the Shepherd.

The words unspoken, like the vibration of perfectly tuned bells in a gentle breeze or the tumbling of shallow water over stones in a clear mountain brook. There was more, and she listened . . . listened . . . while calm and peace and every musical word embraced her . . . her life . . . purpose . . . she must live this love, absorb and learn.

When a rim of black framed the white light, she reached out, longing to hold on, to remain, but the black slowly ate away the light . . . the warm and loving light, the luminous comforting light dissolving . . . until just slivers of light remained, glittering points of light, and then, at last, at last, only the stars . . . the stars, the stars, or shattered glass, and distant voices . . .

Voices . . . and the stars winked off one by one, and then she was alone.

But the voices crawled up through the dark now, clawing, reaching for her. She longed to shut them out. She longed for the white light, but Mama cried from far away. Oh, oh her heart ached for Mama's cry, and there: Dad called her name, and Mama cried again—Oh poor chère, my baby! Think of life, silver girl—bursting through the void.

But one voice rose above them all, insistent, urging, "Amalise! Amalise!"

Eyes opened. She blinked.

"Amalise," Jude said again, and then another time, and louder. Jude. Dear Jude.

"Yes," she whispered, smiling. And then she fell into a deep and restful sleep.

WHERE WAS SHE?

Far away doors slammed, occasionally a voice called out, a bell rang, shoes pattered past. Otherwise silence was broken only by chirping machines attached by translucent lines to her arms and chest—humming, blinking, streaming information through coils and chips and graphs and charts, creating numbers and lines on a pale blue screen mounted overhead. The hospital room was dark. Amalise was sleeping.

Sleeping?

Perhaps. When she opened her eyes, the room whirled. She wasn't ready yet. And every time she opened her eyes, they asked questions— what day is this, what is your name?

Phillip is dead, they said. She struggled to remember.

Something . . . something. What did they mean—found him? Was he lost? The thought drifted off.

When she woke again, eyes still closed, she heard voices speaking nearby in the room. The doctor . . . she recognized the milky voice. ". . . retrograde amnesia," he murmured. ". . . traumatic brain injury . . . hematoma." They thought she was asleep.

"Retrograde amnesia?" Mama's voice, pitched high.

"Loss of memory. Not unusual for the twenty minutes or so prior to trauma, before Jude's car hit. I spent some time with her this morning." There was a brief pause, as if the doctor was collecting his thoughts. "She's beginning to remember . . . selectively. She recalls sitting on a pier with her husband, watching a white bird fly over the lake. There was a rainstorm earlier, and the sun was going down about the time her memory folds."

"That's what Jude said, too. Rain, then dusk as he began driving down that road." Mama's voice caught—grew thick. "The road to the cottage. He heard a scream in the distance. "

"That's all she remembers?" Dad's voice, brisk. Confused.

"Yes," the doctor said.

"Will she ever remember?"

"Probably not. Not that last twenty minutes or so. She'll remember everything else."

"Retrograde amnesia." Mama's cool hand stroked Amalise's forehead.

"It may be for the best, Mama." Dad—soothing. "There's no telling what happened out there."

Weeping. Someone weeping.

"Yes," Mama's tone grew resolute. "And it's God's grace she can't remember. Knowing . . . well . . ." Her words choked off.

"I hope she never remembers," is the last thing Amalise heard as she drifted back to sleep.

SHE WAS FULLY AWAKE. Mama held her hand, studying her every movement.

The overhead lights were off, in favor of soft lighting from a lamp near the bed. The floor was carpeted in a neutral color, the walls were beige, not gray as in the other room—all meant to soothe, she supposed. On the walls were pictures in soft colors; a large one at the foot of the bed showed a woman with yellow hair running down the beach. She carried a straw hat with ribbons blowing in the wind. Yellow hair, like Sophie. Her eyes stopped on that one for a second.

She turned her eyes to Mama and formed a smile, then to Dad, standing beside her, and then . . . across the room, to Jude watching. Ah, Jude.

Careful, Amalise. She squeezed her eyes shut, pressing her hand to her forehead as watery memories, pregnant with danger and secrets rose again . . .

Phillip . . . a white bird.

With a shudder she suddenly remembered the suitcase in the bedroom of the cottage, the insurance policy.

"Amalise, do you remember the cottage?" Dad's voice came from far away.

Yes. She remembered. She remembered watching the sunset with Phillip, and they were sitting on the end of the pier. But after that . . . nothing. Her eyes closed and once again she slept.

THE FEELING OF COLD steel woke her. He was all in white, the familiar doctor, bending over her, taking the measure of her heart. As he straightened and hung the stethoscope around his neck, he saw that she was awake. "Hello, Amalise."

She smiled as his face came clear. Doctor Gilbert, from Marianus, smiled too. "You're doing fine, chère." He sat down on a chair beside the bed. She bent her left wrist back, lifting the limp hand just above the softness for an instant. He took that hand, bandage and all, in both of his, hands that had held hers since she was a baby.

"Your Mama and Dad are just outside."

"I know." She looked past him. "They've explained. I have a concussion and some sort of amnesia."

He looked down at the bandages on her hands. "Yes. And you really tore up your hands, but they're healing well. Just be careful until the bandages come off."

She nodded.

"I've spent time with the doctors here. For a while we thought we'd lost you. We were worried, Amalise." He gave her a hard look. "But now you're doing just fine."

She frowned, closed her eyes and opened them again, squinting at the ceiling. "Well, it bothers me a little, not remembering. They say I've lost about twenty minutes. I've tried. I've tried, but I can't remember what happened out there . . . at the end." She scrutinized the old man's face, certain she'd find truth there.

The wrinkles folding over his forehead, at the corners of his eyes, around his mouth, all deepened. "The head injury's knocked that out of you."

"It frightens me some."

When he settled back in the chair, it creaked from his weight. He said nothing for a few minutes, just clasped his hands over his round stomach like she'd seen him do when he was lost in thought. She gave him time. Resting his head on the back of the chair, he leaned his neck back a little and became engrossed by a point in the ceiling where two walls intersected near the door to the hallway.

He sighed and his eyes turned to her. "It's nothing to be frightened about. Maybe you should think of this forgetfulness as a kind of gift, chère."

"You've been talking to Mama."

He nodded. "Yes. Well, perhaps she's on to something. I've seen plenty of patients over the years who've endured terrible pain, emotional and physical . . . an accident or a trauma." His fingers polished the stethoscope hanging around his neck, sliding up and down the shining steel. "And occasionally when they wake up with this kind of amnesia, like you, I've thought, Well maybe it's a good thing not to remember. What good to remember that pain?"

Amalise said nothing.

He chuckled, as if to himself, and took off the stethoscope. Folded it and put it in his shirt pocket. "I've even wondered if amnesia might be the answer to some big questions when we get to the pearly gates."

"What do you mean?"

He blew out his lips, pondering. "Maybe we just don't carry memories of pain in this life with us when we pass on. Maybe it's as if those things never happened at all. Ever think of that?"

"Not in my wildest dreams." Amalise smiled.

He laughed. Shook his head. Pushed up from the chair. "I'm an old man. But that'll give you something to think about when you're bored." He looked at her, and his eyes clouded for an instant. Then he leaned down and planted a kiss on her forehead. "You almost died, child. There's a reason you're here with us today. A purpose. Never forget that."

"I won't." Suddenly she remembered the brilliant light, the warm, living light. As the door closed behind him, she turned her head on the pillow and closed her eyes.

The words came to her from some distant place—remembered wisdom: *Though I fall, I will rise. Though I dwell in darkness, You are my light.*

And in the instant she understood. As clear as the sound of those distant bells, she knew that new purpose had entered her life, and for whatever occurred at the end at the cottage with Phillip, for her separation from Abba, her family, and Jude, she was forgiven.

She'd been given a second chance.

Chapter Forty-Eight

Later, when she tried to recall the funeral that Mama and Dad arranged, the images floated through her mind in dreaming bits and pieces, taunting, like a reel of film with crucial scenes missing. Her skull fracture was on the mend, they said. Her foot was badly cut, nineteen stitches there. Her hands were still bandaged.

She'd sat in a wheelchair in the church and at the graveside. She remembered a constant hum of white noise in the church, as if a projector was spinning out of control, and none of it seemed real.

When the film faltered and started up again, she was in her old bedroom, at home in Marianus. She looked at the bouquets of flowers Mama arranged around the room, a large one from the firm, smaller ones from Rebecca, Ashley Elizabeth, a dozen roses from Preston and Raymond, more from Doug and Alice Bastion. The cards that Mama had read out loud for her—*we're thinking of you, come back soon.*

One from Henry and Gina made her smile.

A few days later Dad sat by her side, studying her. She turned to meet his eyes.

"The police want to know what happened out there . . . at the cottage on the lake, Amalise."

As she absorbed his words, the room grew cold. Something. Something dangerous . . . frightening . . . fluttered around the edge of memory. Trembling, she pulled the blanket up around her neck.

A cloud crossed Dad's face. "Do you think knowing how Phillip died . . . would help you remember?"

She didn't know, but she nodded. Waiting.

He told her then of the quicksand, his voice catching on that word—*quicksand*—out near the cottage. That's where Phillip died, he said.

Quicksand.

A vague memory rose to the surface as he said the word. She closed her eyes, remembering—sitting in the pirogue in the lake behind the cottage in the afternoon sun, high and hot. Then exploring the small pretty beach. Picturing the shade tree just behind the quicksand bog. Again, something pricked at the edge of conscious thought.

"I wish I could spare you this pain, chère." Dad turned his eyes to the windows. She followed his gaze, watched the oak tree's leaves flutter and shine like spangles in the sun. "But Phillip's gone. And the police . . . have a right to ask questions." He looked back at her. "I'd rather talk to you about it first. Better me than them."

After a moment she blinked, shaking her head. It was all so unreal. And she couldn't remember. But minutes passed and still Dad waited.

So she began at the beginning. "He . . . he picked me up at the airport and took me out to the cottage." *Careful, Amalise. Not the terrors, not your secrets. Those burdens aren't for Dad and Mama's ears or hearts.* "I remember going out in the pirogue. I was alone that day, Phillip had gone into the city."

"That's a long drive."

"Yes." She felt his eyes on her, probing, waiting. "I remember a white egret that lives on the lake . . . so pretty, that bird . . . soaring up around the cypress trees." *Thank You, Abba, for the comfort of Iris.*

"There's a swamp, and a small levee—a rise of land—and a culvert. In the afternoon I found a strip of sand, a little beach, on the bank beside the culvert . . . and . . . ."

A sudden chill dampened the room, and she shuddered, thinking of Dad's words, stunned at the realization that this was where Phillip died!

"Go on."

"I remember . . . near the culvert I beached the boat in the shallows, in the rushes, to look at the beach. But there was quicksand."

"You recognized the quicksand?"

"Not at first. I walked toward the tree and stepped into it, right at the edge." Dad said nothing. "Lost a shoe."

"That was in the afternoon, before Phillip returned?"

She nodded.

"And then what?"

"I went back to the cottage" She passed her hand over her eyes, shaking her head. "Nothing's clear. It comes in bits and pieces."

Silence.

"And later I . . . I . . . remember Phillip arriving."

"What time?"

"I don't know, Dad." She leaned back her head, closing her eyes. If only she could rest. "Six or seven o'clock. I'm not sure. It rained earlier. I wasn't feeling well . . . and—"

Flashes of memory. Emotions flooded her. Fear . . . the insurance policies. Shock . . . an ugly realization. He was going to kill her.

She turned her head to watch Dad's expression. "I was frightened. I knew I was in danger." She caught the pain on his face, but he waited for her to tell him more. Guarded, she told him some things, things that she thought he and Mama could bear. Enough to confirm what he'd already figured out, that Phillip was not the man he'd seemed, not the person he'd shown to Dad. To Mama.

When she finished, she wanted only to sleep. "I cannot think of this anymore. Not right now." She looked again at the tree, at the fluttering leaves. "I've told you all I can remember after that."

"The police want to talk to you, Amalise. The district attorney—"

"I cannot remember anything else. Not yet."

Dad said nothing.

When she remained silent, too, staring straight ahead because if she looked at him she knew that she'd break down, he called out. "Jude."

The door opened and Jude came in. He looked from Amalise to Dad and nodded. "I'll talk to her."

Dad rose. "You tell Jude as much as you can remember, chère."

He patted Jude's shoulder as he passed him. "You two have a talk. I'll be in the other room."

Jude took the chair beside her bed. He reached for her hand and held it between his own. "They know about Sophie, Amalise."

She assumed a neutral expression and waited.

"They found the insurance policies, too. Big numbers, so they have questions. They're trying to piece together what happened." His fingers tightened around hers. "Amalise, what happened?"

"I thought . . ." She turned her head to face him, and as she did, she knew that Jude would understand. He'd always understood. He'd always been there when she needed him. Jude would help.

"You were right about him all along." She blinked back the tears as the words rushed out. "When we walked out to the pier, I thought he was going to kill me, Jude." She looked down at his hand, covering hers, then back into his eyes.

"I'd found the policies. " She gave him a fierce look. "I was afraid. And that's the last thing I remember . . . that terrible fear."

"I know, chère." His face contorted.

She would tell him all. Jude was strong enough to listen.

So she started from the beginning, when she first met Phillip Sharp, slowly revealing the secrets, one at a time, eyes intent upon his face, watching his expression, continuing when he nodded his understanding. When she'd finished, she blinked back the tears. She stole a look at Jude, saw no condemnation. Only understanding. Through the open window she heard sounds that had comforted her in this room in her youth—wind rustling the tree just outside, a skiff motoring up the bayou, probably on the way to Old Tom's place, a lawn mower humming in the distance.

She took a deep breath. "How long was I unconscious, Jude?"

"Thirty-six hours, and some." He smiled and released her hands, placing them gently down on the blanket. Amalise let out her breath as he stroked her cheek with the tip of his fingers and leaned back in the chair. "You're safe now."

WHEN JUDE HAD GONE, Amalise lay in the bed staring at the ceiling. Quicksand. Phillip died in quicksand on that little beach, Dad said, and where was she when that happened? The thought of Phillip's death made her feel sick. Dizzy. Twenty minutes of her life had disappeared, and what had happened during that time?

She closed her eyes and struggled to understand, calling up the old images of Phillip that used to make her feel better when times were bad—Phillip standing behind the easel in his studio, or images that explained him, that might explain her attraction to him in the first place—Phillip, the lonely child, waiting, waiting in the darkened room.

Minutes passed as she waited for the illusion to unfold. She waited but the observer did not appear with the silken shining veil through which she could view the world as she seemed to have seen it with Phillip, perhaps the way she had at some point trained herself to see romance, like a story from a book that she would tell to herself or a movie at the Regal Theater; idealized, as a child idealizes—even a perfect child—perhaps, despite what Doctor Freud might say, perhaps *especially* a perfect child with a perfect childhood.

Such a child would want the safety and perfection to go on and on, want to make good things happen, and when events spun out of control or somehow become unbalanced, the child would think she could find the solutions, put the pieces back together on her own.

But a person like Phillip lived on illusion and pity that distorted truth, and when you're the one pulled into that trap, you give and give until at last you find yourself stripped bare—directing your best energy and effort toward survival and making the relationship work. And then, after a while you're no longer able to pluck the gold from the dross, and soon you're skimming past hard truths, looking the other way. Until at last when you look into the mirror, you don't recognize yourself because the glass is splintered with infinite and near invisible hairline cracks.

For an instant the room blurred, and she glimpsed Phillip's eyes— she should have caught it in his eyes. They were hard and slick, like glass with darkness just behind them, mirroring her reflection. That's all there ever was with Phillip. She knew that now. He was empty. She had filled him. Phillip was a chameleon, fragmented, playing roles, mimicking what he pried from others, whittling the wooden people around him, like his miniatures. Like her. Sucking the oxygen from the air so she almost couldn't breathe.

But she was different now.

She turned her head and looked at the strong trunk of the oak tree outside her bedroom window growing to the sunlight, bending, curving, beautiful but always growing up, up into the light. She would be like that tree from now on. Strong. Solid at the core, sap flowing to help her live in truth.

God, Abba, formed her seed before time, before the stars, sun, and moon were formed, before planets were formed, before winds moved and waters flowed.

Before Phillip. Long before Phillip entered her life.

What would she do with this new strength? A breeze rustled the leaves of the oak tree and she smiled. She didn't know, not yet. But she would learn from her mistakes, she vowed, and she would guard this strength, and when the time came, she would know.

Twenty minutes of lost time. A gift, Dr. Gilbert said. God's grace, Mama had said. Unearned grace. A breeze rustled the leaves of the oak tree and she smiled. She was not alone.

Chapter Forty-Nine

ill the police leave her alone now?"

W Jude watched the judge, who'd just spent two hours closeted in his study with the district attorney. The DA had arrived this afternoon from Baton Rouge. He'd just now left, and Amalise's father was fatigued, Jude could tell.

He sat with the judge, struggling to contain his anger, working to steady his voice. After all she'd been through, Amalise should be left alone right now.

The room was dark except for a circle of yellow light from a lamp on the judge's desk. The judge had aged in the past few days, Jude thought. Shadows played on the old man's face as he moved, leaning back in the chair behind his desk and folding his hands together.

The judge looked at Jude and nodded. "They're satisfied. I've given them the short version. I don't think they ever had much doubt that she's blameless, given the circumstances." A flicker of pain crossed his face, and he dropped his eyes. "When they found Phillip . . ." He cleared his throat and looked down at his hands. His thumbs began slowly to rotate around one another. "When they found him in the quicksand, only one hand was visible."

He screwed up his eyes, glanced at Jude, and his mouth tightened. "He was holding onto a branch, still gripping it. Looks like she was trying to pull him out. That explains her hands, the cuts and tears."

Jude groaned. Slipped one hand over his eyes.

The lines in the judge's forehead deepened as he squinted into the light. "They've put the picture together from her footprints and a mark in the sand where the branch was dragged to the side of the bog. She was obviously holding onto the other end at some point. They'll get fingerprints, too, but they'll leave her alone now."

Jude dropped his hand and straightened in the chair. His mouth tightened and he lowered his voice. "She was afraid. He'd have killed her if he could."

The judge closed his eyes for a split second. "I've worried it was something like that."

Jude was silent.

"But that's Amalise."

The judge shifted in the chair, slapping the palms of his hands on the desk in front of him, and leaned back. "Like Mama says, let's just hope she never remembers all of what happened that night."

Jude looked out the window. "Speaking of Maraine, what's she doing out there?"

The judge followed his eyes. Across the lawn, out near the old wash shed, Mama was on her knees, trowel in hand, digging. He shook his head. "She's been out there all afternoon. Had the Valmont boy come over and dig her a new garden against that old shed. Had him put up a trellis." He looked at Jude and smiled a crooked smile. "For sweet peas, she said." He touched the corners of his eyes and looked away.

Jude watched Amalise's mother for a moment, remembering the garden of sweet peas she used to have out there years ago, when he and Amalise were children. Amalise had always loved those little flowers. The judge clucked his tongue and shook his head. "Flowers! You never can tell what goes through a woman's mind when she's upset."

Chapter Fifty

I t was eight o'clock at night, and Jude and Amalise sat together on the back porch swing looking out over the lawn and bayou. She gazed up at the dark and light spots on the moon. Which one was the place called the Sea of Tranquility? Why was it given that name? She imagined what it must have been like for the *Apollo 11* astronaut eight years ago, standing back and viewing the earth from up there. Seeing the oceans and continents spread out before him—such a small globe suspended in God's majestic universe. Seeing earth for the first time as a whole instead of piece by piece as on a map—country by country, town by town, road by road. When he turned his eyes beyond the earth, had he been humbled by the knowledge that there was so much more that he couldn't see or comprehend?

That limitation was what she'd begun to understand. She'd talked it over with Jude. "Use the brain God gave you," Jude said of the choices she'd made. He'd handed her his old Bible. "The law of the Spirit frees you. You're a lawyer. Read it for yourself. You don't need anyone else to interpret."

She leaned her head back against the swing. Life was complex, but each human being had purpose. Without a compass though, no one would ever find a way through the maze. Abba had shown her the way during the years growing up, had shown her His truth. God's truth. Yet when Phillip came along she'd struck out on her own, seeing things by thirds and halves instead of the whole.

That, she was beginning to understand, was the difficult side of faith. Each person must *sanctify* right and wrong and then make choices based on those principles rather than on emotion. The truth was simple: stick with what you believe and trust because when you leave the compass behind you're lost.

She breathed in the night air, feeling a deep sense of peace. Of tranquility . . . *Ah. That's it.*

She smiled to herself.

Beside her, Jude sat, hands crossed behind his head, elbows winged as he too looked up at the sky. Or was he sleeping? She gave him a sideways look.

Earlier she heard Jude talking in the kitchen with Mama and Dad, attempting to explain Phillip in as few words as possible. But she hadn't wanted to listen. A wall, like glass, rose around her then, separating her from the part of her life that was behind her. So she'd come out here to wait for him, and when at last he strolled out and sat down on the swing beside her, he gave her a look that said he'd left them with only a bare sketch of their daughter's complicated relationship with her husband.

Jude yawned and closed his eyes. Minutes passed. She gazed out into the night in silence as the swing moved gently back and forth, fusing with the rhythm of his slow, even breath.

"Jude, are you awake?"

"No."

A warm breeze rippled. She listened to the songs of the cicadas and frogs on the banks of the bayou and breathed in the fragrance of dew-damp grass, conscious that something was different tonight. This was the same night music, the same sultry breeze, the same air she'd breathed in all her life, but suddenly everything seemed new, fresh, and pungent.

"Jude?"

"Hmmm."

"I can't wait to get back to work." She felt a sudden sensation of power and strength, a remnant of the light, the musical voice, memories that hovered now just at the boundaries of conscious thought. Excitement shot through her, like the way she imagined Neil Armstrong must have felt just before he set foot on the moon.

New beginnings. She straightened, pressing her spine against the back of the swing. "There's something I have to do."

"What?"

"I don't know yet. But . . . I'll recognize when it happens."

"I imagine the doctors will have something to say about that. What's the hurry? Rest up a bit. This isn't the Indy 500."

"I've been out of things for too long."

"Why do I think I hear someone calling 'Gentlemen, start your engines'?"

Fireflies hovered nearby, twinkling, as if the stars were dancing among them. She hoped one would come close and touch her; sometimes, if you held very still, they would do that. But instead they flew away, and she watched them shimmer off into the night. Once, when she was little, she'd tried to capture their light in a glass jar she put by her bed.

But Abba is with me. Abba is my light.

She had her own light.

"Jude?"

"I'm asleep."

"Thank you."

"You're welcome."

Jude shifted, reached his arm around her, and pulled her close, folding her against him. She sank back, head resting on Jude's shoulder as she looked back up at the moon. The scent of sweet olive drifted around them. Night birds called from the swamp across the bayou. A breeze stirred.

For the first time since she'd met Phillip Sharp, Amalise felt free. And safe.

Author Note

Reader, *Dancing on Glass* is fiction, but the problem is real. The bond that held Amalise to Phillip was an illusion created through manipulation. Manipulation is usually hidden at first by charm. In personal relationships a man or woman like Phillip consciously or unconsciously seeks someone with strength and compassion to fill a wounding void inside. Understanding and knowledge are the keys. If you are interested in exploring further, a nonfiction book titled *I Hate You—Don't Leave Me* by Jerold Kreisman and Hal Straus is worth reading. Not all such relationships reach the level of violent abuse, but they create prisons just the same.

If you are in such a situation, I urge you to tell someone. To seek help. For starters, the National Domestic Violence Hotline—800-799-SAFE (7233)—is anonymous and confidential.

Most important, as Amalise found, know that you are not alone.

On the historical side, Jude's Pilottown, at the mouth of the Mississippi River, sprang from a small French village fortress in the 1700s called La Balize, meaning *beacon* or *mark*. Over the years under French and Spanish governance, and—after the Louisiana Purchase from Napoleon at a price of four cents an acre—under protection of the United States, the watery island town built itself up on piers. It was accessible for centuries only by boat, making it a natural home for river pilots guiding ships from the Gulf of Mexico over delta sandbars into and up the river. From 1700 pilots have guarded the river and New Orleans from pirates, warships, storms. During WWII ships in the Gulf waiting for pilots became sitting ducks for wolf packs of German submarines hunting them down. Bar pilots saved the day using fast picket boats, moving at speed with lights out, boarding ships underway in the Gulf—a dangerous maneuver.

Today the Associated Branch Pilots (bar pilots), chartered in 1879, and Crescent River Port Pilots (river pilots) formed in 1908, boast members who are descendents of those first brave men. Some of them became my friends while I researched this book. For sharing their stories of life on the river and at the mouth of the river, first, I want to thank bar pilot, Captain Jacques Michell, member of the Associated Branch Pilots since 1966, and his wife Wendy Michell. Captain Jacques comes from generations of bar pilots, and from 1984 to 1991, he served as president of the association. His wife, Wendy Michell, is truly one strong lady—she lived in Pilottown and taught in the one-room schoolhouse for four years in the 1970s. I want also to thank Captain Charles Crawford, member of the Crescent River Port Pilots Association since 1978, and his wonderful wife, Sherry Crawford. Captain Charlie's father was a merchant seaman, sailing the Banana Fruit Company's White Fleet in the Caribbean, who passed on his love of ships and seaman's skills to his son.

If there are mistakes in my descriptions of the pilots' work, or Pilotttown, or the river, I apologize in advance, as they are my own. My thanks also go to Ms. Abbie Adams of Madisonville, Louisiana, for her fascinating book, *Crossing the Bar,* containing an invaluable store of history, stories, maps, news clippings, and pictures of La Balize and Pilottown and the people who lived there over the centuries. And thanks to my brother, Michael Binnings, a U.S. Navy production engineer, for answering my numerous maritime questions.

Thanks also go to my friends Barbara Ray, Camille Cline, and Leanne Truehart, M.D., psychiatry, for their insight and comments on various drafts of this story. And I would also like to thank Anna Marie Catoir, poet, artist, and friend, for allowing Amalise to use her beautiful last name! Anna Marie passed away on Christmas night, 2001, but her smile, that happy laugh, and her shimmering spirit all live on.

Reader, this book would not be in your hands without the hard work, talent, and commitment of everyone at B&H Publishing Group. To my B&H family, you are all wonderful! To Julie Gwinn, special thanks for your support and friendship and good cheer. Diana Lawrence, you have created a beautiful cover that strikes just the right chord! Thanks to Kim Stanford, Managing Editor, for adding her special polish and shine. To the sales force, you rock! And to Karen Ball, I'm lucky to have you as an editor—to paraphrase the psalmist: You separate the dross from the silver and out comes a vessel for the smith. Thank you for your patience.

To Steve Laube, my wonderful agent, thanks for your advice, guidance, and talent, and for keeping me gently grounded.

And last, but most important, I thank my husband, Jimmy, for his support, strength, and understanding, and for recognizing and pulling me back into the sunshine with his love each time the story turned a little dark.

PAMELA
BINNINGS EWEN

THE MOON IN THE MANGO TREE

PAMELA B[INNINGS EWEN]

PAMELA BINNINGS EWEN

SECRET
OF THE
SHROUD

a novel

The Moon in the Mango Tree, was a 2009 Christy Award finalist.

"Ewen is a talented writer, and this is a strong addition to Christian fiction."
—*Publisher's Weekly*

B&H
FICTION

Pure Enjoyment™

www.PureEnjoyment.com